# *Also By*
# HEATHER BARTLESON

## *Coming Soon*

Blue Blood
Blue Moon

Ethereal Mutation Productions, LLC

# Carolina Blue

## HEATHER BARTLESON

Ethereal Mutation Productions, LLC

ISBN 979-8-9898335-0-4 (ebook)
ISBN 979-8-9898335-1-1 (paperback)
ISBN 979-8-9898335-2-8 (hardcover)
IBSN 979-8-9898335-3-5 (hardcover)



Book Cover by Ethereal Mutation Productions, LLC
Graphic Artist: Heather Bartleson

Published by Ethereal Mutation Productions, LLC
etherealmutationprd@gmail.com

First edition 2024

To Derek,
For loving me and my characters with a passion that couldn't be matched by anyone else... I still Love You More.

# Chapter One

I was having one of those moments again. The one where the world just seemed to stop, and the everyday noises disappeared. Where the colors of life faded, and people seemed to slow until they weren't moving at all. It wasn't something I could explain or even understand.

It just...happened.

I often wondered if there was a glitch in my brain. Or if maybe the movie writers had it right, and we were all just hardwired into some huge computer program.

"Earth to Blue. Come in, Blue... Sometimes, I wonder where she goes off to all the time..."

My friend's southern drawl broke through the silence, and I flinched. Sound suddenly came flooding back, and time snapped into motion. As I closed my eyes against the abrupt assault, I took in several deep breaths trying to re-center myself. After a few moments, colors started dancing behind my closed lids, moving to the rhythm and cadence of the energy that flowed around me. I followed the hues as they spiraled and mixed until they touched something deep inside, where they exploded into hundreds of fireworks that sent warmth from within, spreading slowly outward until my skin tingled.

I held my breath as the heat gradually dissipated before letting it out and opening my eyes. Cautiously, I watched people pass by me again, once more at a normal speed as they laughed and embraced the excitement that seemed to permeate the very air around them. As I watched, they continued to move in and out of the many booths that lined the sides of the closed-off street, enjoying food, drink, and spectacles of daring and delight performed by a multitude of street performers, unaware that, for a moment, they had all just…stopped.

I finally turned around to see my three best friends staring at me, looking a bit concerned. Uh-oh…busted. I smiled at them, pretending like I didn't just have a psychotic episode straight out of the twilight zone.

Caitlin tentatively laid a hand on my shoulder. "Blue, honey. Are you okay?"

"Pfft. Of course. You know how I am when in large crowds. No worries." I waved her off and returned my gaze to the gathering of people as though nothing had happened.

Out of the corner of my eye, I saw my friends exchange glances before they finally resumed their conversation. I sighed in relief. They didn't know why I tuned out like that. I had just made up an excuse about feeling closed in. I couldn't share the real reason with anyone, not even my best friends. I'd learned that lesson a long time ago—the hard way.

Shaking off those uncomfortable thoughts, I moved my gaze back to the girls as they continued to talk. It was hard to believe we'd been best friends since high school. While they were all part of the popular crowd growing up, I had been the odd man out…well, *woman* in this case. I'd flown under the radar in school—not popular, not picked on, just…invisible. I preferred watching people to having people watch me. That was probably why, though we often worked together, I had chosen to be behind the camera's lens while my friends decided to be in front of it.

They were models—supermodels, at that—and while my friends were all intensely beautiful, I tended to blend in. Which, considering what I did professionally, was probably a good thing. I had nondescript brown hair that curled and waved in the oddest ways, a straight, boring nose, lips that leaned toward a perpetual pout due to their fullness, and large hazel eyes—one of my only redeeming features in my opinion. I had an average figure with a small waist and a mostly athletic build, other than a...well, a *slightly* overlarge chest. Okay. So I had enough cleavage to pass out to all three of my besties and still have ample left over for myself. Sometimes, I considered my boobs the bane of my existence. Men, in particular, tended to speak to them rather than me. I'd actually gotten to the point where I'd named them just so I could be a part of the conversation when I introduced myself.

*"Hello. Have you met the twins, Pinky and the Brain? And, oh, by the way, I'm Blue."* Most men stared at me like I was from another planet, stammered an excuse, and walked off.

It was amusing, to say the least.

Suddenly, I realized that my friends were all looking expectantly at me. Obviously, I'd missed something. Again. Jessica sighed and shook her head. "Never mind, it wasn't important anyway."

I simply shrugged in the way of apology as they went back to talking.

My three best friends and I were currently waiting to get into downtown Charleston's newly renovated Dock Street Theatre. After undergoing a nineteen-million-dollar face-lift, the theater owners were holding a black-tie affair tonight to celebrate its grand reopening. And, of course, my friends just happened to get four tickets to the event.

Go figure.

So, instead of enjoying the street fair with the rest of the locals, I was one of the *elite few* getting to view the renovated theater first.

Insert dramatic eye roll.

While I loved the theater, my idea of going to see a show included a pair of comfortable shorts, a nice shirt, and most definitely my Converse sneakers. Instead, I was dressed in strappy, four-inch silver heels and a floor-length gown made of...I didn't know what. I just knew that it sparkled and shimmered every time I moved.

Honestly, if I wasn't stuck here, I might have admired the woman in my place. I might have noted how her dress reflected the night sky filled with stars to perfection or hugged her curves in all the right places. I may have even wanted to be that woman. However, as I *was* that woman, suffice it to say those were definitely not the thoughts at the forefront of my mind.

Instead, I silently apologized to my poor feet while praying that Pinky and the Brain didn't decide to make a *grand* appearance of their own. The sheer mechanics of a strapless dress were mind-boggling. I probably had enough tape loaded into my cleavage to hold up the Chrysler Building, and that didn't even take into account the ridiculous bra they'd made me put on. That, in and of itself, should be considered a modern-day torture device. I shifted it away from where it poked me in the side yet again and wondered if I could find a way to ditch it.

I paused in my adjustments when I saw Caitlin eyeing me in amusement, her lips pressed together as if trying to hide a smile. "You look great, Blue. Stop fidgeting."

Caitlin. Ah, Caitlin. Ever the voice of reason—unless a pair of Jimmy Choos was on sale. But I guess everyone had their Achilles heel, right? I snickered at my mental pun, which caused Brianna to turn around and glare at me. She probably thought I was insulting her handiwork with tonight's ensemble since she had practically held me down and forced me into it earlier. I decided to ignore her for the time being.

It was easier that way.

"Sorry, Cait. You know I'm not used to all...this." I gestured down at myself to emphasize the point. "I mean, you guys even made me put on pantyhose. Have I ever told you how much I despise pantyhose?" I tugged at the offending garment. Yet another great American torture device, and in this case, they came complete with waist restraints and leg shackles.

Brianna rolled her eyes at me. "They're not pantyhose. They're thigh highs."

I gave her a deadpan look. "Same difference."

She pursed her lips, surely wanting to argue with me but clearly thinking better of it. "Come on, Blue. You couldn't very well come to a black-tie affair in shorts and sneakers."

I narrowed my eyes and gave her a measured look. "I mean, I could have. You paid for the tickets, right? Who's to say my idea of black tie isn't just something entirely different than theirs?"

Brianna didn't look the least bit convinced. As a matter of fact, she looked a little annoyed, though I couldn't imagine why. "Blue, how many times do we have to go over this? If you don't dress up and go out to events like this, how are you ever going to meet the right kind of man?"

Ugh, not this conversation again. It was always about men with her. I threw up my hands and turned away dramatically, hoping to put her off, but it didn't appear to be working. Instead, she gave me one of her looks. The kind that said she was thoroughly annoyed with me, even though she loved me dearly, and I was about to get the patented, this-is-for-your-own-good speech.

Hoping to distract her, I quickly interjected. "So, uh…when do we get to meet this Fabio you've been telling us about?" Fabio was Brianna's current fling. Though his name wasn't really Fabio. At least, I didn't think it was. Yet another hot male model Brianna had worked with recently and decided to bring home with her to show off as arm candy. At least, that's how I liked to think of them: kept men, merely there for the purpose of display and perhaps a snack now and then. I giggled a bit.

"Blue…" I quickly closed my mouth and smiled innocently at her. For some reason, that only seemed to annoy her further.

As Brianna opened her mouth to no doubt give me another scolding, Caitlin stepped between us. "Brie, leave her alone about it tonight, okay? Let's all just enjoy each other's company and have a good time. It's been too long since we've had a girls' night out."

Brianna narrowed her eyes playfully at me. "Okay, but don't think this is the last you've heard of it." She smiled. "And Christophe is just fine. You'll finally get to meet him tomorrow night when we go to the Market Street Saloon."

Whew, that was close. I knew I could count on Caitlin to be the voice of reason. And to step up and diffuse a possible Brianna speech.

Just then, the large clock on the nearby church struck seven. Almost simultaneously, the doors to the theater opened, and I saw the silhouette of a tall gentleman in full evening dress, outlined by the glowing lights from within.

"Welcome, honored guests. The time is finally upon us for the crowning event of the evening." Several bouts of applause broke out from the surrounding crowd, and the gentleman took his top hat in hand and bowed to them. Placing the hat back upon his head, he again addressed the gathering, his melodic voice flowing smoothly over our heads.

"Ladies and gentlemen, for those of you privileged enough to be joining us this evening, prepare yourselves for the extraordinary grandeur of the spectacle you are about to witness. Never before has such a show been seen by human eyes."

*Human eyes?* That was an odd way of putting it. As the gentleman continued to wax poetic about the coming show, I found my attention wandering—as usual. Poor thing. I hoped it didn't get too lost. I would need it later.

Looking around, I suddenly realized everything appeared to have come to a halt again, though not quite like before. The music playing quietly in the background was gone, as was the thrum of voices, but sound as a whole was still there. It seemed everyone had stopped to stare at the man before them as if in thrall. Their eyes were glued to him, and they all seemed to lean forward as if hanging on his every word. It was hard to find one pair of eyes that wasn't focused on him.

I turned back and looked again, trying to figure out what held their undivided attention. He wasn't bad to look at...okay, so he was gorgeous in an almost unnatural way. He had high cheekbones, a strong jaw, and a full, sensual mouth. A mop of unruly dark hair was under his top hat, the kind that made you itch to run your fingers through it. It was a bit long, curling around his ears at the ends, but it suited him. He was pretty tall—at least six feet—with a well-built body. Not heavily muscled, but enough to get a girl's attention. And he really did have a beautiful voice. It had a deep timbre and an old-world sound, almost like he was from a different century.

Suddenly, our eyes met, and I found myself staring into the deepest sapphire-blue eyes I had ever seen. I couldn't move or breathe. It was like the wind had been knocked right out of me. I felt all the energy from the crowd earlier start swirling around inside me again, causing my body to heat up. This time, instead of a tingling sensation on my skin, a delicious warmth pooled deep in my abdomen, where it continued to build and pulse.

I inhaled sharply as something akin to an electric current shot down my spine, seeming to expand with the energy building in my center and pushing it through my entire body.

He, too, seemed to feel something as his speech faltered. We stared at each other for what felt like minutes but was probably only a matter of seconds before he seemed to shake himself and continue. Once he broke eye contact, my breath left me in a whoosh, and the energy that had built dissipated abruptly, leaving me feeling a bit disoriented.

"Wow, that was intense."

Jess turned in my direction, looking at me questioningly. "What was intense?"

"Ahh..." I hadn't realized I'd said that out loud.

She smiled, shook her head, and looped her arm with mine. "Come on. I can see that brain of yours starting to veer off in all directions. It's time to go into the theater."

I looked around and, sure enough, everyone was making their way through the three sets of double doors that led into the building. They had all been opened wide, and ushers dressed to the nines in tuxes held them, welcoming all who entered.

I looked around for the mystery announcer, but he seemed to have vanished, which was probably just as well since I was still catching my breath and trying to slow my heart rate from our earlier eye contact. Who knew what would happen if I met him up close and personal?

"You okay, Blue? You look a little more out of sorts than usual."

I looked over at Jess, who still had her arm looped through mine, and smiled. "I'm fine. You know me when my brain goes off on a tangent. It's sometimes hard to get centered again."

Jess shook her head in amusement but didn't say anything further as she continued to move us forward.

As we entered what was considered the grand foyer of the theater, I looked around and noted all the changes. Some were so small the average person wouldn't notice, like the color of a painting frame here or a new doorknob there. Others were startling in their beauty, like the red-and-gold carpet that had been laid, and the shiny new banister on the stairs that led to the private boxes on the second floor. Everything had been returned to its former glory as it would have been in the nineteen thirties, yet it still held true to the original character of the building.

Back in the eighteen hundreds, before it became the theater it was today, the building had once been the home of the famous Planter Hotel. The proof was still evident in the high, open ceilings that extended above what would have been the main reception area, and the sweeping staircases leading to the second floor, giving one a bird's eye view of the goings-on below. While the design had done well for the hotel, it was superb for the renovated theater.

Before I could comment on the changes, Jess whisked me over to the stairs, where Brianna and Caitlin waited by one of the ushers. He was dressed in an evening ensemble you would expect to find on the movie screen: black tails, a starched white tux shirt, a low white vest, and a white bow tie.

She presented our tickets to him. "We're in box five."

This statement, of course, brought forth visions of the *Phantom of the Opera—Box five is to be left empty.* I giggled a bit to myself.

"Ah, yes, mademoiselle. Please, follow me. I will be happy to personally escort you to your seats." His voice had a charming French lilt, further deepening the illusion my brain was creating that we were in the Opera Populaire. I absently wondered if his accent was real or fake.

I took the time as we ascended the stairs to scope out the people around us. As I did, my gaze collided with a memorable pair of blue eyes. He stood on the outside ring of the crowd below.

Almost missing a step, I stuttered to a halt and leaned against the banister lest I fall over and make a fool of myself—well, more so than I already had. He was watching me, and his lips twitched until they finally tipped up at the corners. Almost imperceptibly, he tilted his head toward me in acknowledgment. I returned the gesture, blushing slightly in embarrassment as I again started up the stairs, wondering about the strange man. He seemed like an ordinary guy, albeit better-looking than most, yet something about him was different. Something I couldn't quite figure out.

As I reached the top of the landing, I glanced down again to see him still following me with his eyes. There was an overwhelming curiosity in them that seemed to match my interest. Shaking off his gaze before it drew me back down the stairs, I turned and followed my friends into our designated box.

As I sat, I glanced down at the playbill the usher had handed me. It seemed tonight's play was, *A Midsummer Night's Dream* by William Shakespeare. I tried to remember exactly what it was about, but the only thing that came to mind was fairies. As a bunch of people dressed in Elizabethan-era clothes moved onto the stage for the first act, talking in old Shakespearian, I groaned. This would be a long night. I side-eyed the girls and wondered if I could take a nap without them noticing.

⁓ℓℓ⁓

As the actors took their final bows to the thundering applause of the audience, I yawned and settled into my chair to wait. There was no reason to rush into the crush of the crowd that was sure to be outside in the hallway, making their way to the foyer and out of the theater. It seemed my friends had other ideas, however.

"Come on, Blue! We want to get to the foyer before Claude does."

I looked at them in confusion. "Who's Claude?"

I received a collective round of annoyed groans from my friends. "The actor who played King Oberon. The really hot, buff one. Weren't you listening to anything we said earlier?"

I shrugged, not admitting I'd slept through most of the play and had no idea what they were talking about. "Why is he going to be in the foyer?"

"The actors always meet and greet the guests after their performances. And if we're lucky, he'll still be shirtless."

I shook my head in amusement. "You guys go ahead. I'll catch up in a few once the people clear out." They seemed about to argue with me, so

I waved them toward the door. "You'd better hurry if you want to beat the crowd."

They looked torn, but with my promise to find them in a few minutes, they scooted out the door. I sighed in relief. I had no interest in meeting this Claude or competing with a bunch of other adoring fans who, no doubt at this moment, were crowding into the foyer, hoping to get his attention.

I sat in the quiet created by the absence of my friends and let my thoughts drift to a certain pair of compelling blue eyes. Who was he? And why had I reacted the way I had to him? It had been a long time since a man had captured my interest with a mere look, and never had I felt that kind of strange energy bond.

Suddenly, I felt the air around me start to prickle in awareness as it sometimes did, signaling that someone was nearby. Looking up and expecting it to be one of the ushers, I felt the greeting stick in my throat when I realized the person standing at the box's entrance was none other than the man of my thoughts.

"How did...?" I trailed off and stared at him, unable to complete my sentence.

"Good evening. I hope I'm not intruding."

His voice felt like a smooth caress over my skin, and I shivered.

"Uh... Hi. N-no. You're not intruding."

*Smooth, Blue, real smooth.*

"I couldn't help but notice you earlier this evening."

"O-oh?" Great, I'd been reduced to a stuttering half-wit who could only seem to get out one syllable at a time. What was it about this guy? I rarely got choked up around men, even ones as good-looking as this. I mean, really. Between photographing them, and my best friends ever-changing love lives, I'd seen every male model on the runway and off. In every state of dress and lack thereof. And not one of them had affected me like this.

*Come on, girl, wake up!*

I took in a deep breath and then let it out slowly. "I'm sorry. I'm not usually so inarticulate. Let's start again. Hi, I'm Blue." I stood and reached out my hand. Instead of shaking it as I thought he would, he stepped forward, turned my hand over, and brushed his lips across my knuckles. I felt the blood rush to my cheeks.

"Such an unusual name." His voice was a soft murmur against my skin.

"Th-thanks my full name is actually Carolina Blue, but my friends just call me Blue." I had to stop myself from rambling on nervously.

He inclined his head in acknowledgment. "Blue it is, then. It's indeed a pleasure to make your acquaintance." He still hadn't released my hand and remained staring deeply into my eyes. I felt as if he could see into my soul through them. It was a bit disconcerting, and I had to check my natural inclination to squirm where I stood.

That lovely mouth of his quirked up into a half smile as if he were reading my thoughts—which, thankfully, was impossible.

"Allow me to introduce myself. My name is Tristan Montague."

"I'm glad to meet you, Tristan."

As we stood there staring silently at each other, an odd tension began building around us. I found myself trembling slightly in anticipation, not knowing what it meant. I jumped when his soft voice broke the silence.

"I felt compelled to come see you, drawn by some strange power..." His voice was barely above a whisper, almost as if he were merely talking to himself. I nervously tugged on my lower lip with my teeth, causing his gaze to lower to my mouth. I immediately released my grip, my lips parting on a soft intake of breath.

His gaze slowly rose to meet mine again as he pulled me closer, our hands still clasped between our bodies. My heart rate spiked as his free hand rose to my face, and his fingertips lightly traced along my jawline. A buzzing started in the back of my brain, seeming to shut out the rest of the world as his face slowly lowered toward mine.

Suddenly, he stopped, his body going rigid. His eyes widened, and something flickered in their depths before he pulled back. The world came crashing back in around us, and I winced.

He dropped my hand while clearing his throat and took another step back. "It would seem that your friends have left without you."

"Um, yeah." I laughed shakily, not sure what had just happened. "They went to meet...ah, the actors."

Tristan laughed lightly, his eyes meeting mine. "No doubt to see if they could get close to the indomitable Claude."

I smiled, some of the tension ebbing. "Yes, I believe that was who they were looking for."

"May I escort you to join them? I would be more than happy to make the introductions if they have not already managed it."

"That would be wonderful."

He held out his forearm. After a moment's hesitation, I took it gently, placing my hand on his sleeve. When none of the earlier feelings arose, I let out a small sigh. I could do this.

Tristan guided me out of the box and down the main staircase. As we descended, I looked out over the crowd and noted more than a few heads turned in our direction. It seemed we were some of the last to leave the upstairs boxes. Deciding to ignore the stares, I searched for my friends but didn't see them.

"I believe Claude is holding court outside in front of the fountain."

Tristan guided me through the box office area and out into the spacious courtyard, where an entire gaggle of women twittered and fawned over a shirtless gentleman who seemed to be eating up the attention.

I felt Tristan sigh beside me. "Always has to be the center of attention, that one does." People seemed to melt out of our way as we moved across the courtyard, something for which I was glad. Elegant and poised, I was not. It took all my concentration to remain upright in my godforsaken heels. Why, oh why, had I let my friends talk me into them? I felt Tristan chuckle next to me and wondered about it but didn't think I could maintain a conversation and my balance long enough to ask.

Soon enough, we were standing in front of a man who had to be the so-called indomitable Claude. He still wore his costume from the play—no shirt, but a leafy sash that lay diagonally across his heavily muscled chest. He had on legging-style pants nearly bursting at the seams and a pair of soft leather calf-high boots. The fawning crowd fell back to let us pass, but they were still there, eagerly pressing in around us.

Claude's intelligent gray eyes moved to us. He bowed his head in Tristan's direction while pressing his fist against the left side of his chest before addressing him. "Ah, Tristan, there you are. I was wondering when you would show up. And who is this delectable creature you have with you?"

I felt Tristan stiffen at the question. He looked between us before turning slightly in my direction. "Claude, this is my lovely guest, Blue. Blue, this is Claude, one of the more...longstanding actors in our troupe."

Claude took my hand and, like Tristan, lifted it to his mouth for a kiss. Unlike with Tristan, though, I felt no connection. Instead, it felt like something dark and oily crawled up my arm. Yuck. I heard several women in the surrounding crowd sigh, some of whom I was sure were my friends.

I gritted my teeth and smiled, even though all I wanted to do was yank my hand back and wipe it off on my dress. "It's a pleasure to meet you, sir."

"Oh, the pleasure is definitely all mine." He stared at me in a way that made me feel decidedly uncomfortable. Suddenly, an elbow nudged me in the side, and I turned to find my friends standing next to me.

I quickly tugged my hand from Claude's grasp and turned toward them. "Please allow me to introduce my friends: Brianna, Caitlin, and Jessica." I stepped out of the way so he could coo and slobber over them instead of me, which he immediately did. I sighed in relief. Thank goodness for gorgeous friends.

Tristan chuckled, amusement showing on his face. "Not your type, huh?"

I started, having forgotten he was standing there. A slight grimace crossed my lips. "No, a little too...oily for me."

Tristan's grin widened. "Oily, huh?"

I shrugged evasively. I couldn't very well explain to him that's how Claude's energy felt to me, but it was the best description I had.

Tristan tilted his head as if considering what I'd said. "I think it's a fitting description." He smiled and held out his arm. "While your friends are otherwise engaged, why don't I introduce you to some of the other less oily cast members?"

I smiled in relief at his acceptance. "That sounds much more pleasant."

As we made our way around the courtyard to the remaining cast, I began noticing how they all treated Tristan like some type of celebrity or figurehead, bowing and curtsying as he approached. I wasn't sure if it was part of the act they put on or not, but it was decidedly odd. Before I could ask Tristan about it, my friends came running over and tugged on my arm to get my attention.

"Oh my god, Blue, you're never going to guess what just happened."

I turned and shook my head, not sure I wanted to know. "I can't even begin to imagine."

"Claude invited us to go with him to the afterparty tonight!"

"Indeed?" This came from a curious Tristan.

Not realizing he was standing there with me, my friends started in surprise. "Who are you?" They looked between us, noting my hand wrapped securely around Tristan's arm.

I smothered a laugh while Tristan bowed slightly to all three of them. "My name is Tristan. I'm the master of ceremonies, for lack of a better title, here at the theater. You must be Blue's friends. She has been telling me all about you lovely ladies."

He seemed to have confounded them, which I found highly entertaining. They weren't often left speechless. "Uh...yeah, we're ah, Blue's friends."

He nodded at each of them. "It's a pleasure to meet you officially. So, Claude has invited you all to the afterparty tonight? How gracious of him." Though he sounded pleasant, I got the feeling he was less than pleased.

"Yes, it was. Blue, you don't mind, do you? You can take the car home, and we'll catch a cab." She started rummaging around in her clutch.

Claude came up behind my friends then, taking two of their arms. "Are you beautiful ladies ready?" While he talked to them, he leered in my direction. I had to stop myself from raising my hand to cover my chest.

"Sure thing, Claude. We were just giving the keys to our friend so she can get home."

"What? Nonsense. She can't go home now. She must come with us." He let go of Brianna and moved as if to touch me. I recoiled and slid closer to Tristan, tightening my hold on his arm.

Tristan glanced down at me before looking back toward the group in front of us. "Why don't you ladies go ahead with Claude? I will be more than happy to escort Blue."

I saw that Claude was not happy with this scenario. He smiled at Tristan without any humor. "Entirely unnecessary, Tristan. I'm sure you have more important things to see to. I wouldn't want to put you out. After all, I'm more than capable of handling all these beautiful women on my own."

"Be that as it may, I will take care of Blue as she is my guest for this evening."

The two men stared at each other, seemingly in a test of wills, before Claude finally looked away. He bowed his head in Tristan's direction before turning to my friends. "As you wish. Ladies?"

My friends eagerly went with him, though they did throw a few glances back at me to see if I was all right. I waved them on, relieved not to be in Claude's presence any longer. That man gave me the heebie-jeebies.

After they left, I turned to Tristan, who stared after the group with an annoyed look. "You don't need to feel obligated to take me. I can head on home. They won't even notice I'm gone."

Tristan looked down at me, all annoyance gone. "Nonsense. I was actually going to ask you to come with me tonight." I cocked an eyebrow in disbelief, causing him to laugh. "Really, I was. I was moments from the question when your friends interrupted."

I shook my head, still not believing him. "You seemed annoyed that Claude asked."

"I was. But only because he beat me to it." He gave me such a boyish grin, my misgivings faded, and I smiled back. "Shall we?" He excused us from the actress who had quietly stood by during the entire interaction. As we walked away, I noted she continued to watch us with a look of astonishment mixed with a bit of curiosity.

Instead of following the path Claude and the girls had taken, Tristan led me to a door situated behind the outdoor bar that almost seemed to blend in with its surroundings. He stopped before it and did the oddest thing. Instead of reaching out and turning the knob, he first placed his palm on the shiny wooden surface with his fingers splayed. Then, pulling away so just his fingertips touched the wood, he moved them as if drawing small clockwise circles, followed by what appeared to be random swirling patterns that he sketched with his pointer finger. Finally, he reached down and turned the knob, indicating that I should precede him through the door. He had done all of that in a matter of seconds, and I almost thought I'd imagined it.

I let go of his arm and stepped across the threshold. The silence on the other side was almost deafening after all the chatter in the courtyard. I looked back through the opening but couldn't hear any of the noise we had just passed through. Shaking my head at the strangeness of it, I decided to ignore the anomaly, chalking it up to soundproof walls. Instead, I looked curiously to my left and right and saw we had stepped into a long hallway with several doors all painted in different colors. I was surprised, as I had expected that particular entrance to lead us back into the theater's box office.

After he shut the door we'd come in through, Tristan again offered me his arm, and we walked down the hallway to another door painted a deep blue with an ornate handle fitted with an odd-looking lock.

"So, where exactly are we going?"

"To the theater's private quarters. Most of the performers and crew live below."

"Really? I didn't know that."

Tristan smiled down at me, his eyes locking with mine. "Most people don't. It's not something we advertise. I would appreciate your utmost discretion in this matter." He gazed at me with those deep blue eyes, seeming to draw me into them. I felt like if I just tipped forward a bit, I would fall off the edge and drown in their blue depths.

I had to mentally shake myself from his gaze before I could answer. "But of course." My mind was spinning. That was the oddest feeling I'd ever had. The best way to describe it was that it felt as if he had tried to project his will onto me. I silently laughed at myself. I'd obviously been reading too many paranormal novels lately.

Tristan looked at me oddly before shaking his head. Pulling a key from his pocket, he slipped it into the intricate lock on the door. It was a large, old key, like one you would expect to find in an ancient castle. His lips quirked when he saw me looking at it. "We have to keep everything locked in case curious persons should make it through the first door. We wouldn't want anyone wandering in unannounced."

I nodded before indicating the key. "That's a bit of a unique key, isn't it?"

He held it up, and it seemed to sparkle in the air between us. "Yes, it's one of the few originals from when this building was first erected. We have a gentleman on hand who has a way with these old locks, and he keeps them in working order."

After Tristan pushed the door open, I again preceded him through and came face-to-face with an elevator. At least, I assumed it was an elevator. There was an opening not much larger than a standard door with a sliding gold gate on the front. Tristan guided me forward and quickly shut the gate with a series of clicks before moving to what I assumed was the control panel, though it had no numbers or letters I could discern. First, pressing his palm against it much like he had the door, he again drew the clockwise circles with his fingertips, before sketching another series of random motions with his pointer finger. When he was done, a glow encompassed the entire panel, and it suddenly lit up with strange golden symbols.

I glanced in astonishment at Tristan. He merely smiled and punched several symbols, almost like he was entering a passcode. Suddenly, the elevator began sinking downward. I must have jumped when it started as he took my elbow to keep me steady. I smiled my thanks over my shoulder and turned back to the front. In the brief glimpses I had as we drifted downward, I saw the underworkings of the theater: staging rooms, dressing rooms, mechanical machinery for the many moving parts of the stage. Finally, we stopped at a small vestibule that had a set of intricately carved doors at one end.

Tristan opened the gate and stepped out of the elevator, descending the two marble steps in front of us while offering me his hand. I took it, and he guided me carefully down the steps.

"Come, it's time to mingle. I wouldn't want you to miss a minute of it."

Moving my hand once again to his arm, he led me to the double doors. They opened before we got to them, almost as if by magic. As I stepped through, I found myself looking into the largest, most opulent ballroom I had ever seen. It rendered me speechless.

The room below us had to be larger than a football field and was surrounded by tall, marble columns with inlaid gold filigree. Overhead, the high, rounded ceiling was filled with intricate paintings, and huge chandeliers made of crystal glittered and winked from above the many guests. A large sweeping staircase that could put most old Southern mansions to shame sat in front of us. It all reminded me of the Grand Ballroom at the Plaza Hotel in New York City that I'd once seen when I was a little girl.

After taking in the room, my eyes were drawn to the crowd within. There had to be hundreds of people spread from one end of the room to the other. I had no idea that it took so many to run a theater, though I was sure many were guests of the cast and crew. It all looked like something from an old Victorian movie—the most anticipated ball of the season.

Most men sported black tuxes with different-colored vests, starched white shirts, and bow ties—much like the ushers from the theater above. The women formed a sea of whirling color in many-layered dresses lavishly trimmed with every type of frill, flounce, fringe, and ribbon imaginable. It was quite something to take in. I was sure my friends were down there somewhere, too, but I didn't immediately see them.

Tristan started down the grand staircase in front of us, and as we descended, I felt silence begin to overtake the room. It seemed every eye had turned in our direction. I felt decidedly self-conscious by the time we were halfway down, thinking there must be something wrong with my appearance. Tristan, noting my hesitation, leaned over and whispered in my ear. "You are by far the most beautiful woman in this room, Blue. Don't allow anyone to make you feel otherwise." With that statement, he came to a stop and raised his hand. The room fell silent except for the shuffling of feet and clothes swishing. It was strangely eerie.

Tristan spoke once he seemed assured he had everyone's undivided attention. His deep, melodious voice flowed over the crowd below, bouncing off the walls and seeming to blanket everything in a warm embrace. "I want to thank each and every one of you. Tonight was a resounding success, and it would not have been possible without your help and cooperation. From the ushers welcoming everyone into the theater to the performers and stagehands, you have made tonight a magical experience for all who entered. Everything that happened was like a smoothly oiled machine worthy of the praise received. I'm so proud to have every single one of you here, and I foresee a very successful future for this clan."

The silence rang with his words for a few seconds before applause and thunderous cheers erupted from below us.

I looked at him curiously. "You say you are only a master of ceremonies, yet you address the people here as if they are your subjects."

Tristan merely gave me a mysterious smile and took my hand. He placed it back on his arm and led me down the rest of the stairs without a word.

As we made our way across the room, dozens of people stopped us, wanting to get Tristan's opinion or approval on things, which further made me wonder about him. Before I could ask him any questions, though, a young boy came running over and tugged on his sleeve. I watched as Tristan leaned down so the boy could whisper in his ear. I caught something about unexpected visitors. Standing, Tristan turned to me. "Blue, will you excuse me for a moment? Something urgent has come up that requires my immediate attention."

I instantly felt the curious gazes of those around us turn our way as I nodded. "Of course. I'll go find my friends and see what they are doing." He bowed to me before following the young messenger out of the room. I watched him for a second before looking for a place to escape the crowd. I had no intention of going anywhere near my friends while they were still with the indomitable Claude. Finally spotting a corner where I wouldn't be seen but could watch the comings and goings, I politely excused myself from the group we had been talking to and made my way over to it.

After watching the party for a while with no sign of Tristan, I began to feel forgotten. I was about to go in search of someone who could tell me how to get out of this place when a group of women ambled by and stopped not too far from my hiding spot.

"Can you believe he brought her here tonight?" A beautiful woman with shining blond hair pursed her painted red lips as she asked the question. She wore a sumptuous, one-shouldered, pale pink silk Mermaid gown that hugged every curve of her body, leaving little to the imagination. I didn't think she had on any undergarments at all. "Tonight, of all nights. He was supposed to narrow his selection tonight. And I wore my best dress, too." She stuck out her lip in an exaggerated pout. "Now, we'll have to wait...what, another week?"

"What was he thinking?" This came from a woman with a rather large set of breasts and a tiny waist. She was decked out in an off-the-shoulder, canary-yellow gown with black ruffles that did little to hide her overflowing assets. Considering she was barely five feet tall, they were quite something to take in. "It isn't like he can take an outsider. That would be cause for war within the clans."

There was that word again. *Clan.* I wondered why they kept referring to the theater group as a clan. Even Tristan had addressed them that way. It was such an odd term to use.

Standing next to the other two, a young woman in a pale blue confection inhaled sharply and covered her mouth. "You don't suppose he means to actually court her, do you?"

The woman in yellow huffed and rolled her eyes. "Not a chance. He wouldn't dare go outside. No one would accept her."

"I don't know. There must be something special about her for him to bring her here tonight."

"You know as well as I do that the males like to bring trinkets, but they don't remember a minute of it afterward. She will be the same, I'm sure."

"Yeah, I guess so, but Tristan has never brought anyone before."

"You're right…" The woman in pink seemed to consider that. "No reason to take chances. Let's try to find out exactly who or what she is to him. We can't have a stranger muscling in. Too much is at stake here." The group moved off, leaving me wondering what I'd gotten myself into.

"Catty bunch, aren't they?" I started, not realizing anyone else was nearby. I turned to find a gentleman standing not far from where I hid. He was a tall, lanky fellow with blond hair that was so light it was almost white. Bright emerald-green eyes peeked out from under tousled bangs, giving him a rakish air. He had removed his jacket, and his green bow tie hung loosely around his neck.

"Oh. I'm so sorry. I didn't realize anyone else was here."

He smiled, showing exceptionally long, white teeth. "S'okay. I've been hiding out here, too, lest I get caught by some unattached female such as those."

I laughed, enjoying his casual attitude. I stuck my hand out toward him. "I'm Blue, by the way."

He took my hand in his grasp and shook it lightly before letting go and leaning back against the wall. "Cedric."

We stood in companionable silence for a while, watching as a band set up, and people took to the dance floor. I was amazed. Instead of the usual bump and grind, they were actually waltzing. Who did that? Next thing you knew, they'd be doing a quadrille or something. I shook my head. It was a while before I noticed Cedric eyeing me curiously.

"What's the matter?"

"Nothing. I was just trying to figure you out."

I raised an eyebrow. "Figure me out?"

He shook his head in dismissal. "It's nothing."

Suddenly, a figure blocked our view. "Cedric. There you are. I've been searching all over for you, you naughty boy." I heard Cedric groan as I took in the vision before us. She was one of the three women from the group I'd overheard earlier, the blond-haired one in the pale pink. Up close, she looked like a doll. She had large, cornflower-blue eyes framed by long, curling lashes and sharp, defined brows. Her blond hair was piled artfully on her head, with strategic ringlets falling softly around her oval face to accent her high cheekbones. She was short and petite with a slim waist and enviable, small, perky breasts. That was probably how she could wear that dress with no bra—something I could never hope to accomplish. Standing next to her, I actually felt like an Amazon. Come to think of it, most of the women I'd seen here tonight were much shorter than my five-foot-five.

"Hi, Celeste." I could hear the exasperation in Cedric's voice and had to smother an amused grin.

Celeste pretended to pout, completely ignoring me. "Cedric, I've been waiting for you to ask me…"

He interrupted her by leaning forward and putting his hand on my shoulder. "Celeste, have you had a chance to meet Blue yet?"

She turned partially toward me, though her eyes never left Cedric. "Pleasure." I could practically feel the animosity radiating off her, directed at me. "Now, Cedric, about that…"

I smiled widely at her and grabbed Cedric by the hand, cutting her off mid-sentence. "It's indeed a pleasure to make your acquaintance, Celeste. I'm sorry to greet and run, but Cedric and I were about to dance. I'd love to talk with you further, though. At some later time."

I continued toward the dance floor with Cedric in tow and prayed I wouldn't make a fool of myself. It had been a long time since I'd waltzed, and the last time had only been in a class my mother made me take when I was a teenager in order to broaden my cultural horizons or something of that nature.

Who knew the skill would ever come in handy?

Once we were whirling around the floor, and I was certain I wouldn't trip over my feet or his, I looked up and glanced back to see Celeste still standing in the same spot we'd left her in with her fists clenched at her sides. If her expression was anything to go by, I was in for a world of hurt later if she got ahold of me.

*Great, Blue. Way to make new friends.*

I could feel Cedric starting to laugh, and I turned my head to look at him. I wasn't sure how he would react to what I had done and hoped this was a good sign.

"That was quick thinking." Cedric's eyes shone with suppressed amusement, and I felt myself grinning back at him. "I will forever be in your debt for saving me from her clutches."

That caused me to laugh outright. "You're welcome, but she can't be all that bad." I was, of course, trying to give her the benefit of the doubt for Cedric's sake, just in case he was interested in her.

"Oh, you have no idea."

"She's an extremely attractive woman—"

"And knows it. Don't let her looks deceive you. She is most definitely a Wolf in sheep's clothing. Trust me, I'm mighty glad for your interference."

"Hmm. Then, you are most welcome. And for as long as I'm here, you can count on me to act as a buffer or to save you from certain death in her clutches if you would like."

It was Cedric's turn to laugh. "You are an unusual woman, Blue. No matter what anyone else says, I'm glad Tristan brought you here tonight. Regardless of the complications it might bring."

I tilted my head to the side and looked at him. "Complications?"

He stared back at me a bit uneasily. "Please don't ask me to explain. It isn't my place."

I shook my head and smiled. "No questions. Far be it from me to alienate the only friend I seem to have made here."

"You consider me a friend?"

"Anyone up for a game of misdirection will forever be a friend in my book."

He smiled at me playfully. "Hopefully, not just a friend forever. I was hoping there might be a bit more."

I smiled back but didn't make any promises.

We whirled around the floor once more to check and make sure Celeste wasn't watching us before we left from a different spot than where we had entered. We quickly found another nook that hid us from the rest of the room, hoping to avoid any further confrontation.

After watching the floor for a few minutes, I turned to Cedric. "Can I ask you a favor?"

"Anything, if I can grant it."

"If need be, will you show me the way out of here so I can catch a cab? I don't know where Tristan disappeared to, and it would be extremely embarrassing to get lost trying to leave."

"I'll do you one better. I'll give you a ride myself. Though I seriously doubt you'll have to worry about it. Tristan wouldn't leave you to fend for yourself all night. Even if something kept him away, he would make arrangements to get you home." I nodded, though I wasn't as confident. Tristan had felt obligated to bring me here, after all. Contrary to what he had said, I still didn't believe he planned to ask me before Claude forced the issue.

Before I could say anything more, the sound of a gong rose through the room, causing me to start in surprise. I looked questioningly at Cedric.

"That would be the dinner gong."

Amusement bubbled to the surface, causing me to giggle. "And here I thought that just happened in movies."

Cedric smirked. "No. Around here, it's the real deal. Come on. I'll escort you to supper. Tristan will find us there, I'm sure."

"Are you sure there isn't someone else you'd rather take in? I don't want to be in the way of any special young ladies you hoped to escort."

Cedric winked and gave me a conspiratorial smile. "There definitely aren't any special young ladies I hoped to escort, but there are several I most certainly want to avoid." We both laughed as Cedric offered me his arm, which I took happily.

After we'd finished our meal, we stayed at the table talking and getting to know each other.

"So, Blue, what do you do for a living?"

"I'm a photographer."

"Like family portraits?"

I shook my head with a half-smile. "No, I work mostly in the fashion industry, traveling around for magazine photoshoots and designer spreads. Though I do have a small studio in my house where I do special boudoir shoots when I'm not under contract."

"Boudoir? Like naked ladies wrapped in sheets on a big bed, boudoir?"

I snorted. "Something like that."

"Can I come over?"

He looked so hopeful I burst out laughing. "I'll see what I can do."

"What about your parents? Are they famous photographers, too?"

The look on my face must have said it all as Cedric put up his hands in mock defense. "Note to self, don't mention the parents."

I grimaced before smiling wanly. "Sorry, not a subject I'm ready or willing to discuss."

"Gotcha, it's cool. Me? My mom is dead, and my dad is just a deadbeat, so I get it."

"I'm sorry to hear that."

He shrugged as if it didn't bother him. "I don't remember my mom. She died giving birth to me, and my dad decided he wanted nothing to do with me before I was even born. Instead, I was brought here to the theater and raised by the community."

"That had to be interesting."

"I wouldn't have it any other way. It's like having tons of brothers and sisters around all the time, so I don't usually have to worry about being alone. Although, sometimes, that can backfire, too." We both laughed.

Suddenly, I felt a familiar energy wash over me. "I hope I'm not interrupting anything." Looking up, I saw Tristan standing next to my chair, exuding a seemingly possessive aura.

Cedric stood and bowed when Tristan entered, almost as if he felt it was required—which was weird. "Evening, Tristan."

Tristan nodded to him. "Cedric. Thank you so much for keeping Blue occupied while I was away."

"Hey, no problem. Blue has been a wonderful companion all evening."

Tristan turned to me. "Are you done eating?" At my nod, he turned back to Cedric. "Will you excuse us?"

Cedric walked around the table. Taking my hand, he helped me to my feet, bowed, and kissed my knuckles. With a mischievous twinkle in his eyes, he glanced at Tristan before winking at me. "I'll get in touch with you soon."

"Thanks again for everything. I enjoyed our time together tonight." I smiled at him. As an afterthought, I rose to my toes and kissed his cheek. He strutted away with a huge smile on his face.

Turning back to Tristan, I smiled a bit nervously. It was weird how I felt so at ease with Cedric, but now that Tristan was here, I was all nerves again. It wasn't like I knew one man better than the other. "So, did you get everything taken care of?"

Tristan, who had been staring after Cedric, looking slightly annoyed, wiped his expression clean and smiled at me. "Yes, I'm truly sorry for that. I feel I've let you down this evening."

"It's okay. Cedric was a fine companion. I'm glad I got to know him, which I wouldn't have done had you not been called away. He seems to be a kindred spirit."

A frown creased Tristan's brow. "Indeed."

Taking my hand, he placed it on his arm and guided me away from the dining area as every eye seemed to once again turn our way. We walked to the edge of the dance floor, where Tristan turned and rested his hand on my waist. Without thought, I put my left hand on his arm below his shoulder, feeling the muscles flex. As I slipped my right hand into his, he whisked me onto the dance floor in a fast, whirling waltz. I was glad I had danced with Cedric earlier as it gave me the confidence to move smoothly through the steps now, though dancing with Tristan was on a whole new level. He moved with such an easy fluidity. I felt like I was practically floating, my feet barely touching the floor. I didn't have to think about the dance at all. He just seemed to carry me along in his wake.

As we danced, I felt Tristan's hand burning against my waist where it rested, and I shivered from the contact. I swore wherever he touched me, it was like an electric current running from the spot. Looking up, I saw him staring down at me with such intensity I had to blink. Without missing a step, his head slowly lowered to mine, our gazes never breaking apart.

When his lips finally touched mine, my eyes fluttered closed, and a small sigh escaped me. His arm tightened around my waist, and the world around us seemed to melt away until all I could feel was the touch of his lips. I heard a moan, but I wasn't sure whose it was. The hand that had been holding mine was suddenly buried in my hair, scattering the many pins that held it in place. Tristan's mouth slanted heatedly against mine, and I quickly lost myself to the sensations arcing between us.

When I felt him probe against my lips, seeking entrance, I eagerly opened to him. As our tongues met and dueled, fire streaked across my skin, diving to build almost unbearably at my core. It was like outside the theater earlier, but much hotter and faster, and it was all I could do not to push Tristan up against a wall to feel the heat of his body pressed against mine.

Suddenly, I realized we weren't dancing anymore, and it was I who was pressed against the wall. Tristan's mouth left mine and started kissing its way down my throat, distracting me once again. I felt his knee move to fit snuggly between my legs, pressing intimately against the apex of my thighs. A gasp escaped my lips as the ensuing sensations vibrated through my body. At the sound, Tristan brought his mouth back to mine and kissed me deeply, cupping and framing my face between his large hands. I gripped his wrists reflexively, certain I would go up in flames at any moment.

Unexpectedly, I heard an exclamation from behind us, causing my eyes to pop open.

"Oh! Excuse me. I didn't realize there was anyone back here."

It was like a bucket of ice water had been splashed over me. What was I doing? Shaking my head, I looked down at the floor and tried to control my raging emotions.

"Leave, now." Tristan's voice came out as a low growl. I saw a flash of pale pink in my peripheral vision and knew our interruption hadn't been accidental, though I was glad for it nonetheless. Had we not been interrupted, who knew what would have happened?

Tristan's hands reached up and gently tilted my face toward his. I looked into his eyes and saw the same turmoil I felt reflected there. "Blue…"

"I'm sorry. I don't know what came over me."

Tristan's lips quirked involuntarily. "You're apologizing to me?"

That brought a hesitant smile to my face. "Um, yes?"

"Blue…" He rested his forehead against mine and closed his eyes with a sigh. "You have nothing to apologize for. If anyone should say they're sorry, it's me, but I'm not going to, and neither should you."

"I shouldn't?"

He shook his head slightly before opening his eyes again, the blue depths gazing deeply into mine. He hesitated as if struggling with something. "Blue, I want to see you again."

"You do?"

"Yes, but I think I should send you home for now."

"Oh, right." I lowered my gaze in confusion, feeling slightly rejected.

"Blue…" I looked at him again. "I'm only sending you home because I don't trust myself with you. If you stay here, I might do something we'll both regret."

After straightening my clothes and doing the best I could with my hair, we left the alcove we had hidden in. I tried not to look at any of the people we passed, a bit embarrassed at what they might have seen. As we were about to walk up the main staircase, I saw Celeste out of the corner of my eye. She was smirking at me. I imagine thinking she had done something to upset my evening plans. Before I could second-guess myself, I slipped away from Tristan and went to stand before her. Taking both her hands in mine, I looked at her shocked face.

"Celeste, thank you so much. If it hadn't been for you, my evening would have been a lot less... eventful."

"Uh, I, ah..." She glanced almost fearfully at Tristan, who looked at her with his brows drawn together in suspicion. Before she could come up with an answer, I smiled at her and swept up the staircase and out the double doors we had entered through. As I did, I swore I heard Cedric's laughter following me out.

# Chapter Two

As I slowly came to consciousness, I glanced groggily around to see what had awoken me. Not seeing anything, I plumped the pillow under my chest and prepared to go back to sleep. It was Saturday, and I had planned on sleeping in until at least late afternoon.

The pounding on my door made me shoot up onto my elbows, my hair tangling around my face. Grumbling, I glanced at the clock and gave a small cry of outrage. It was only six o'clock in the morning, for heaven's sake. Who would voluntarily be up at this hour? Flopping back down, I threw the pillow over my head. Maybe if I ignored them, they would go away. A few minutes later, I heard a voice carrying through the front door.

"Blue, I know you're in there, so open up."

I groaned. It was Brianna. Something told me that no matter how long I ignored her, she wouldn't give up and go away. Pulling myself out of bed, I snatched up my robe and put it on.

*Save me from early risers.*

"I'm coming, I'm coming." Though I knew she couldn't hear me, I continued to grumble as I crossed the room. I really needed to get keys made for my friends so they could let themselves in. I'd just been so busy lately, I had forgotten that none of them had a set to the new place.

I'd moved into the cottage about a month ago, and since I had been out of the country until recently for work, I hadn't given it a second thought.

When I opened the door, Brianna stood on the other side dressed in her running gear. "Oh, no. It's Saturday. I get to sleep in today. No exercise."

Brianna laughed and pushed her way into the house. "Come on, lazy bones. Saturday or no, you're coming running with me."

I stuck my tongue out at her back and shuffled back into my bedroom. Flopping face-first onto the bed, I proceeded to ignore her as she poked around my new digs. Maybe if I stayed really quiet, she would forget I was even there and go away.

"This place is so cute. I wish I'd found it before you."

I harrumphed into my pillow, forgetting that I was supposed to be pretending to be nonexistent.

"Oh, and the view. Blue, this is to die for. No wonder you didn't tell us about this cottage until after you bought it."

My house wasn't really a *cottage*. That was just a term the locals on Folly Beach gave homes that were all on one floor. My *cottage* was a two-thousand-square-foot, single-story abode with three bedrooms, two bathrooms, my portrait studio, and an open-style living room, dining room, and kitchen. The kitchen featured granite countertops, a large island, and a big, built-in pantry—very un-cottage-like. The house had hardwood floors throughout, and a massive porch that wrapped around from the front to the back before opening onto the beach, giving me my own private entrance.

What had made me fall in love with the place, though, was the view. The entire back of the living area was nothing but glass from the doors to the walls, so you got a panoramic view of the ocean from all sides. Even my bedroom, which faced the water, had the same glass wall. The house had been owned by an architect and his wife prior to me buying it, and he had designed the whole thing. Lucky for me—unluckily for them—they were getting a divorce and had decided to sell this beauty. Since I had a friend in real estate, I snagged it before it even went on the market.

"Blue. Oh, wow, even your bedroom has a gorgeous view. Are you sure you don't want a roommate?" I gave another muffled snort into my pillow. "Hey, it's time to get up." Brianna, never one for modesty, reached down and yanked my robe from me. As I slept in the nude, she was getting quite an eyeful of my backside, but at the moment, I really didn't care. "Really, Blue? Can you not afford some pajamas or at least some sexy underwear? You have to be the only woman I know who sleeps naked, even when she doesn't have a man over. Unless I just missed him..."

I turned my head to look at her grumpily. "You're the one who took my robe off. If you didn't want to see all this awesomeness, then you should've left well enough alone. And no, there isn't and wasn't a man here."

Brianna laughed, used to my morning grumpiness and sarcasm. "Come on. Time to get up and get dressed. Those muscles won't exercise themselves."

I let out an exaggerated groan and put the pillow over my head. I hadn't gotten to sleep until after one this morning, and I didn't deal well with lack of sleep. I was an eight-hour minimum kind of girl. But knowing Brianna, she wouldn't leave me alone until I went out running with her, no matter how much I put her off or complained. I lifted the pillow a bit and gave her the side-eye, which she ignored. "You know, you could've called first... So I could have told you to stay home."

"Mmm. I tried that. But someone didn't answer their phone."

I frowned and looked at my cell on the bedside table. I had forgotten I'd turned it off before bed. Damn her and her logical ways.

"Did it ever occur to you that maybe the someone you called didn't answer their phone because they wanted to sleep in after a late night? Besides, didn't you have a late night yourself? Why are *you* up this early?" I added as much indignation as I could into the question, though I didn't think she bought it. I really needed to work on my acting skills.

Brianna rooted around in my dresser until she found a pair of underwear and a heavy-duty sports bra—the normal kind couldn't stand up to Pinky and the Brain. They tended to break within the first few bounces. So, I had to get the Arnold Schwarzenegger of bras—*the ever impressive...*

Tossing me my undergarments, Brianna quickly started rooting around in my walk-in closet, likely looking for my exercise gear, all the while keeping up a running dialogue and chastising me.

"Oh. Look at how big this closet is. Did you ever think maybe it was because of your late night that I'd want to talk to you? Wow. You even have an organizer unit in here, I am so jealous." I heard more shuffling. "Didn't you think I'd be worried about you when you didn't answer your phone? Geez, look at all these new designer clothes. I am sooo borrowing stuff from your closet later." She came out holding a pair of running shorts and a matching tank top. I shook my head at her disjointed conversation, knowing she really didn't expect answers to any of her questions.

After a glaring contest—which I quickly lost—I begrudgingly got up and dressed before changing tactics. "I did text you that I got home safely last night." I smiled cajolingly. "Couldn't this wait until a normal time? You know, like noon?"

Brianna raised her eyebrows and crossed her arms over her chest. "Do you really think I could wait that long? You're just lucky Jess and Cait aren't into exercising this early in the morning or they'd have been parked on your doorstep, too." She marched out of my room toward the back door, leaving me no choice but to follow her.

Grumbling that *I* wasn't into early-morning exercise either, I grabbed my sneakers and followed her out onto the back porch to put them on. Obviously, there was no use trying to talk her out of this. She was here and raring to go. I might as well resign myself to the inevitable. After tying my shoes, I glanced at Brianna. She stood at the railing with the breeze moving through her hair, enjoying the view of the ocean rolling onto the beach. How she looked so elegant and poised in running gear at six o'clock in the freakin' morning was beyond me. It just wasn't fair.

Standing, I flipped my hair into a messy ponytail. It would take about a gallon of detangler to get it back to normal after last night's updo, so it would have to do. "Okay, let's get this over with."

Over a five-mile circuit along the beach, I listened as Brianna told me all about her exciting evening at the theater—what she could remember of it anyway. A lot of the details were fuzzy, as were *most* of the exciting evenings she and my friends had. Then she started in with the questions. *What happened with the man I had been with? Where did I meet him? Why didn't I take him home with me and have my way with him?* The usual. When we got back to my porch, I was dripping with sweat and ready to crawl back into bed—after a cold shower, of course. Unfortunately for me, Jess and Cait were sitting in the loungers on the back deck. I groaned, thinking I might as well give up on getting any more sleep.

As I stepped onto the porch, Jess handed me a bottle of water. "I thought Brie would have you up early and out running, so we decided to join the party."

"Ugh. I just wanted to skip one day of exercise, is that too much to ask?"

She shook her head at me. "Oh, stop. It's good for you, Blue."

I glared at her through narrowed eyes. "I notice you managed to show up *after* we left."

She snorted, somehow making it sound ladylike, though it was anything but. "I may be blond, but I'm not dumb."

I grumbled as they laughed and followed me into the house. I saw a freshly brewed pot of coffee with four cups next to it, waiting to be filled. Caffeine. The elixir that would keep me sane through the next couple of hours as I entertained every question and observation my three besties had about the night before. I poured a cup like it was my lifeline and closed my eyes in pleasure as I swallowed, cradling the cup to my chest. "How do I love thee? Let me count the ways..."

"Don't be so dramatic, Blue."

Opening my eyes, I looked at Jess. "Oh, you haven't *heard* dramatic yet."

My friends stayed for more than two hours, going over and over everything from last evening, at least what they could remember of it. Surprisingly, they couldn't recall the ballroom itself, or much about the people, or even Claude—other than the fact that he had been hot.

Remembering what Tristan had said about the theater group's privacy, I decided not to fill in the gaps.

I finally kicked them out, telling them I needed some *me* time to shower and maybe catch a nap. They laughed and said they would be back around four to pick me up for our date at the Market Street Saloon, and to make sure I was dressed in something other than shorts and a T-shirt for the evening.

Like that would ever happen.

Waving them off, I went back inside and started the shower in my bathroom. Walking into the bedroom, I stripped off my running clothes, threw them in the hamper, and stretched my arms high above my head, then bent over to touch my toes. As I did, a shiver found its way up my spine as if someone had walked over my grave. I looked around, feeling like I was being watched. I didn't see anything suspicious but closed the sliding curtain panels I used to cover the wall of glass the rest of the way anyway, just in case.

Steam wafted from the bathroom door, so I went and jumped into the shower. The jets of hot water sprayed my body, easing the muscles and relaxing my brain. I loved my three best friends, but they were enough to give anyone a migraine after a while. Lathering up the soap on a loofa, I washed myself from head to toe while thinking about last night, and more specifically, about Tristan. I still couldn't believe my reactions to him. I'd never felt that strange energy bond with anyone before, and it was kind of scary. I almost wished my mom were here so I could talk to her about it...almost. Her betrayal and abandonment still hurt, even after all these years.

My mother just disappeared one day my junior year in high school. A strange man claiming to be my solicitor contacted me, though at the time I had no idea what that even was. He informed me that my mother was gone and would not be returning. When I fearfully asked if she was dead, he only laughed and told me no, she just wasn't coming back. He then proceeded to outline the plan she had set up to take care of everything: who would manage the estate, access to money, a cook, a maid, a housekeeper, even a chauffeur service to take me wherever I needed to go.

I had been dumbfounded. She was gone, just like that. No, *Goodbye, sorry I have to disappear because I'm an international spy and my cover has been blown.* Nothing. First, my dad left us before I was even born, then she up and disappeared when I was sixteen. If it hadn't been for my friends and their families stepping up and taking her place, I never would've known what a real family was. It was a hell of a way to grow up, stuck in a house with just servants who cared more about their paycheck than me.

It gave me a certain level of satisfaction when I sold that ostentatious house with all the furnishings my mother had loved so much. And again when I let all her uncaring servants go when I was old enough to take care of everything myself. I liked to think it gave her heart palpitations to see me not only move into an apartment but also move in with three roommates—something she never would have approved of. Even the house I ultimately bought would have been way below her lofty expectations.

I pushed those disturbing thoughts back into their lockbox in my mind where they belonged. There was no use dredging up old hurts that would never heal. I finished my shower, and considered what I wanted to do until my friends came to get me. Should I get dressed and go do errands, or lie down and take a nap?

Was there really even a question there?

Laughing at myself, I grabbed my laptop from the dresser, and lay down on the bed to check my email. It had been a few days since I'd gone through it, and I was sure there was a ton. Email was worse than regular junk mail, and if you didn't keep cleaning it out, it could easily overwhelm you. After spending a half an hour sorting through and answering multiple messages, I shut the lid on my laptop. Yawning, I lay my head on my pillow, thinking I would just close my eyes for a little bit before I went out to run errands.

Without warning, I found myself standing in a strange room. Turning in a circle, I looked around. How on Earth had I gotten here? It looked like an old library, one you'd see in older movies with floor-to-ceiling bookcases filled with leather-bound volumes, maps, and scrolls. A large table took up one corner of the room, and it, too, was covered in papers and books. Realizing that I must be dreaming, I reached out to touch one of the volumes sitting open on the table.

"What are you doing here?" I spun around at the gruff question. It had come from a shadowy corner of the room, where a fire burned in a large hearth.

"Ah... Actually, I have no idea."

A figure stood and slowly moved out of the shadows. I backed up a step or two, not quite sure how to take this new development. In some dreams, the creature that would start chasing you came from the most innocent of beginnings. The figure here turned out to be an older gentleman, probably in his late fifties, with peppered gray hair and hazel eyes. He didn't appear angry or upset, merely curious.

"Indeed. Who are you?"

"Um, my name is Carolina Blue. And you would be?"

"Now that is an interesting question. But we will start with my name. I am Kieran. Kieran Grayson."

That was weird. This guy had the same last name as my mom's estranged family. Maybe I was just projecting it onto him because this was my dream.

"Where am I?"

"Well, Carolina..."

"Blue."

"Pardon?"

"My name. I usually just go by Blue."

He nodded in concession. "Well, *Blue*, this is my library. And it would appear you are here as a dream."

"As a dream? Don't you mean as part of a dream?"

"No. You are here as a dream, whilst I am here quite awake."

"What do you mean? How is that even possible?"

"Oh, a lot of things are possible. The real question is not how, but why."

He set the book he was holding on the table and moved to a shelf off to the left. Muttering under his breath, he searched the spines until he found what he must have been looking for. Sliding the volume off the shelf, he set it on the table with a bang. It was huge, easily thicker than two encyclopedias put together, and bound in dark blue leather with gold-embossed letters on the front cover and spine. Moving closer, I looked to see the title. *Dream Walking.*

I snorted in amusement, not sure if this guy was serious or not. "Really?"

Kieran smiled patiently in my direction. "Yes, really. Some things are best left to the experts."

"Experts?"

"Mm-hmm. This book was written by some of the Fae Ancients centuries ago. For those of us in the present, it provides knowledge we would otherwise never have access to."

"Fae Ancients? What are those?"

Kieran peered closer at me. "Do you not know what you are?"

"What I...? Uh, last time I checked, I was just a normal person like you."

"I think I understand now. No need for this book. Come with me."

I hesitantly followed him over to the fireplace and a grouping of couches and chairs. He indicated that I should sit, then sat across from me.

"I am not sure why your parents did not explain any of this to you already, but it seems our ancestors have left it to me to bring you into the loop, as it were. Why they waited this long is beyond me. Most Fae children learn of their heritage when they hit puberty, if not before."

I grumbled in annoyance, resisting the urge to roll my eyes. "I guess that would be because I never knew my dad, and my mom disappeared when I was sixteen."

"Good heavens, girl. Who was your mother?"

"Alannah Grayson-Blue."

"No, that cannot be right. Alannah does not have any children."

I looked at him strangely. "You know my mother?"

"Yes, of course. She is my daughter."

"Your daughter?" I stared at him in shock. This had to be the strangest dream I'd ever had. No more coffee before naps for me.

Kieran smiled, shaking his head in amusement. "This dream has nothing to do with drinking too much coffee, my dear, and everything to do with your heritage."

Now I was really weirded out. Had he just read my mind?

"Of course, I can read your mind. I already told you I was Fae... Oh, right, you do not know what that entails yet." He let out a frustrated sigh. "We really must get this sorted out. I will need to do some digging to find out the exact details of your parentage, but until then, let me give you some basic background knowledge."

I sat with my hands clasped on my knees and tried not to think anything. I didn't need this guy rooting around in my head and pulling stuff out. Lord only knew what he'd already seen.

Kieran chuckled but didn't comment on my attempt to block his mind reading. "We, my dear, are Fae. I know you are likely wondering just what exactly that is. To boil it down, the Fae are a group of otherworldly beings with a myriad of mystical abilities."

I thought about the folklore I was familiar with, recognizing the term, *Fae*. "Fae? As in Fairies?"

He laughed lightly and gave a slight shake of his head. "Not exactly. Fae is more of a general term. Unlike humans, there are many different subspecies of Fae, Fairies being one of them. Most Fae are human in appearance and, as such, are able to blend in and live among the general population. You probably see the Fae every day and just do not realize it, at least on a conscious level. Subconsciously, as a Fae, your body of course recognizes what those individuals are and gives you signals."

I sat forward in my chair. I couldn't believe I was actually entertaining the idea that this was all real. Most people would either just laugh it off or run screaming from the room. However, this was a dream of sorts, and I couldn't help but remember all the strange things that had happened to me since puberty. The energy waves and the feelings of euphoria when I was around large sources of it, my reactions to Tristan last night... Oh. Tristan. Was he Fae? Could that be why I'd had such an intense reaction to him?

Kieran smiled at me, reading my thoughts before I even had a chance to voice them. "Yes, he most certainly is. That could be why the Ancients have taken it upon themselves to finally educate you. Did you experience anything different with him than you do with other people?"

"Yes, actually. I've never felt any of the sensations I did with him before."

"He is a very powerful Fae."

I considered everything he had said. "So, if Fae pretend to be human, how do say, Fairies, hide their wings and ears? That is if they really do have those characteristics."

"They do. There are some among the Fae that need to have their appearances magically altered so they can live normal lives."

"Are there Fae who don't look human and can't live among us...er, them?"

"Yes. Those types have to live in the shadows, away from prying eyes, and are what tend to start human legends and myths."

"You mean like Big Foot?"

As Kieran nodded, I slumped back in my chair. Great. Now I had to apologize to Jessica's cousin, Marvin. He had been telling the truth when he said Big Foot was really out there.

Kieran seemed amused by my random thoughts, and I looked at him helplessly. This was a lot to take in, and I still wasn't sure I believed it. It could, after all, just be a strange dream. "How do I know this is real?"

"Search your feelings, Blue. What do you truly believe deep down?"

I giggled to myself. That had almost sounded like a line from *Star Wars*. Deciding to leave the believability factor out of the equation for the time being, I moved forward. "I guess the big question here is, what exactly am I?"

"That, my dear, I cannot tell as yet. It will require me figuring out who your parents are or were."

"But I told you, my mother..."

"I do not believe Alannah was actually your mother, not in the birth sense anyway."

"What do you mean?"

"I believe Alannah was taking care of you for someone else. However, who exactly, remains a mystery. You being here tells me it was one of our family, but it does not reveal much else."

"Alannah isn't my real mother?" I was having a hard time getting past that fact.

"No, I am afraid she cannot be. You see, Alannah isn't Fae. It takes two Fae parents to have a Fae child."

"Isn't Fae? But you said she was your daughter…"

"Her mother wasn't Fae. Alannah is illegitimate."

I choked back a laugh. "Illegitimate? You say that like it's the eighteenth century when children born out of wedlock were considered bastards."

Kieran smiled patiently. "You will learn that we Fae tend to see time differently. As for my choice of words, when I say *illegitimate*, I mean Alannah was born to a woman other than my Fae wife."

"Oh. So, you had an affair?"

"Yes." He said it matter-of-factly, as if it were the most normal thing in the world. Which, if you looked at today's society, I supposed it was.

"So, ah, was your Fae wife pretty ticked about the affair?"

Kieran shook his head at my frankness. "No. It is actually common practice for Fae couples to seek pleasure outside the marriage every century or so to keep things fresh. Though we are usually careful not to sire any children with our human counterparts. In this case, something happened, causing the resulting child."

"Something *happened*?" I laughed sarcastically. "Hate to break this to you, but a child is usually the result of not using protection. That's what the research says, at least."

Kieran smiled tolerantly, ignoring my sarcasm. "Yes, but unlike humans, Fae use a magical type of contraception. As we have no fear of contracting any human diseases, we do not have need of the usual trappings."

"Uh-huh. So, something went wrong with your…spell?"

"It is possible. Or it is also possible the human with whom I had relations knew what I was and did some sort of counterspell. I really do not know, as she never even admitted to having Alannah. I found out quite by chance."

"Does Alannah know what you are?"

"Yes, of course. I explained it all to her. Once I realized she was mine, I was quick to claim her so nothing bad could befall her. Though I do not think she was too happy to learn she had a supernatural parent."

"Hmm. That might actually explain why she left me like she did. I told her about some of the sensations I was starting to experience and the things I was seeing. I remember her looking at me in shock, then almost revulsion. Not long after, she left without a word."

"Interesting. She has never mentioned you in all these years. Perhaps it is time I seek her out and find out what is going on."

I sucked in a breath and held it for a second before letting it out slowly. The thought of seeing her again after all this time was almost like a knife to the stomach. And now to find out that she might not even be my real mother...? But that was a subject for another time. Right now, my mind was on full overload. I didn't think I could handle adding her to the mix.

I grappled with my thoughts, trying to sort through them. "So, earlier, you said *every century or so*. Just how long do Fae live?"

"It depends. I, myself, am over six hundred years old, give or take. One tends to stop counting after a while."

"Six hundred...wow. If I'm one of these Fae, you're saying I might live to be that old?"

Kieran laughed lightly at my thunderstruck expression. "Yes, that is exactly what I am saying."

"How does the aging thing work, then? I didn't age any differently growing up than any of the other kids."

"It actually depends on your Fae powers. Once you come into all of them and your body learns to handle them, that is when the magic slows your aging."

"How about the mind reading? You said you could read my mind since you're Fae. Can all Fae do that?"

"In some form or another. Everyone's abilities differ. Some can read exact thoughts, while others only read emotions. Eventually, you will need to learn how to block your thoughts."

"You're saying I could read someone's mind? I've never done that before."

"You may not have come into all your abilities yet. Some of them have to be honed. And as you did not even know what you were, most of them are probably dormant at the moment."

"And every type of Fae has different abilities, depending on their species?"

"Yes."

"Such as…?"

"For instance, the Vaimpír have the ability to take over a human's will. They can make them do whatever they want. They also have extreme strength and healing capabilities."

"Wait, Vaimpír? As in…vampires?"

"I guess most humans would refer to them as such."

"As in suck human blood?"

"Yes. The Vaimpír live off human blood. But unlike the movies, they do not kill them for it. They actually need the host alive, as it is their life force they siphon out of the blood."

"Oookay." I decided to leave that line of questioning alone for now. Visions of sharp fangs and bloody necks flitted through my mind, and I shook my head to clear it. "What else should I know?"

Now, it was Kieran's turn to sit forward in his chair. "The number one rule of the Fae is that we need to keep ourselves secret from the human population. Do not get me wrong, some humans know of our existence and work with us to keep our secrets. But they have to be chosen very carefully."

"Why do Fae need to remain secret?"

"As a rule, humans do not accept others who are different from them. If they were to realize we exist, and get confirmation that all their legends and myths are real, how do you think the public would react?"

I thought about it. "With fear."

Kieran nodded his head sadly.

"What about my three best friends? Will I be able to tell them?"

"I would prefer if you did not."

"But how on Earth am I supposed to keep this a secret from them?"

"The easiest way is to stop seeing them."

"They're like sisters to me. I'm not going to give them up. They're the only real family I have."

"We can try to come up with a plausible story to explain things, but that can get messy when trying to keep it straight."

"They'll know if I start lying to them."

At my defeated expression, he relented. "Look, we can try telling them, but most human minds are not really open to the possibility of our kind. And you would have to get them to swear secrecy in Rún blood that they won't reveal us."

"Rún blood?"

"Yes, the Rún is a Fae who has the ability to root out any secrets you have, no matter how deep. If your friends sign an agreement in its blood, it will bind them. And if they do attempt to reveal us, we will know immediately."

"What would happen if they revealed the Fae?"

"Depending on the magnitude of the fallout, it could be something as simple as a mind erase, or as severe as death."

I visibly started. "Death? Are you serious?"

"I told you, the Fae take this very seriously." At my horrified expression, he mumbled to himself before looking back at me. "Look, I am good friends with an Eanchainn. I am sure if I asked, he would be willing to help us out."

"What is an Eanchainn?"

"A Fae with the ability to alter human minds."

"What do you mean by *alter*?"

"It doesn't hurt them. The Eanchainn merely manipulates their memories so they do not believe something or remember it the way it really is. He does not erase anything like a Scriosán does. That can leave lasting scarring on the mind. They would merely think it was an illusion of some sort, or something they dreamed about."

"Wow, that's a pretty nifty talent to have."

"It does come in handy in our world. Though the Ancients prefer a mind erase to anything."

"If keeping the Fae a secret is the number-one rule, are there others?"

Kieran took a breath, then hesitated. "You have to understand, Blue, the Fae have a world unto themselves, separate from the humans." At my questioning look, he continued. "We have our own form of government, our own police and cleanup crews…"

"Wait, cleanup crews? Like maids and housekeepers?"

Kieran smiled and shook his head. "No, for occurrences like accidental deaths and things of the sort."

"Accidental deaths? What do you mean by *accidental deaths*?"

"Most Fae feed off humans in some form or another, whether it be chi, other energy, blood, or even flesh."

At my disgusted look, Kieran laughed. "Do not worry, it is already dead flesh. It is against our laws to purposefully kill a human in order to eat them. But back to the cleanup crews. Sometimes, when a Fae is feeding, things go too far, and there can be accidental deaths. Usually, it only happens when Fae are very young and learning to control their gifts. Or when a Fae has gone rogue, in which case, we need someone who can go in and take care of the problem to keep us hidden from the humans."

"Wait a minute. Some Fae feed off energy?"

"Yes, why?"

I thought about all the times I had felt that euphoric feeling around large crowds and wondered if that had been *feeding*.

Kieran looked at me consideringly, of course reading my thoughts before I could voice them aloud. "You could be right. Though have you ever felt hungry for it? Like an empty feeling inside that cannot be satiated by normal human food?"

"No, not that I'm aware."

"Hmm, a clue perhaps, but not an exact explanation. If you do not need it to survive, then you do not feed off it. Fae who feed off human energy will die if they do not have it. But you *do* have the ability to manipulate it, then. Interesting."

"You said there's a government. Is it a monarchy or a democracy?"

"It is a little of both, actually. A group of Elders is elected from each of the clans and they get together to make decisions over things that will affect the Fae as a whole. Laws for instance. They are the ones who decided we must remain concealed from humans. But each clan also has a King and Queen who make decisions for them. To clear up disputes and keep order among their own kind. When a problem arises that they cannot solve or is something that would affect the Fae as a whole, it is then taken to the Elders to resolve."

"So, groups of Fae are called, *clans*?"

"Yes."

"Is the theater group a clan?"

He nodded. "They are the Moon Tree Clan."

"I see." I yawned behind my hand.

Kieran smiled softly at my sleepy expression. "It would seem our time is just about at an end for today. We must meet again soon when I have more information regarding your parentage. I think it would behoove both of us to meet in the mortal realm."

I blinked at him owlishly. "Why do I feel so tired all of a sudden? I'm in a dream, shouldn't I be getting sleep?"

"The feeling of sleepiness in a dream indicates you are about to wake up in the real world. Why don't you give me your phone number? I will give you a call when I have more information. I will text you my number so you can contact me directly if you have any questions in the interim."

I nodded and quickly wrote down my number as another yawn overtook me.

"Goodbye, Blue. It has been a pleasure meeting you."

I was so tired I couldn't keep my eyes open. Closing them, I started to slip off into sleep. As my dream-self hit slumber town, I awoke back in my bedroom. Sitting up in bed, I looked around. Everything was exactly as it had been when I lay down earlier, except the sun had moved farther in the sky. Wow, that had been the most surreal dream I'd ever had, and I'd had some doozies in the past.

Just when I had about convinced myself it hadn't been real, my phone sang out that it had a text message. Looking at the face, I saw a number I didn't recognize.

*It was so good meeting you today, Blue. I really look forward to getting to know you better. Remember, if any questions come up, please do not hesitate to contact me directly. And, above all, please keep our secret. I would hate for any undue action to be taken against you. Yours, Kieran.*

I stared at the phone in astonishment. It was real. I hadn't been dreaming. I sat in stunned silence. What did I do now? Shifting around to grab my laptop, I popped it open and brought up Google. As I opened site after site, I was amazed at all the myths and beliefs associated with the Fae. It seemed like everyone around the world had an opinion or theory. After about an hour, I shut the lid, concluding that I would get no real definitive answers from the net. Which I really shouldn't have been surprised about, considering how secretive Kieran had said the Fae were. Did I really think there would be a *Fae for Dummies* website out there? I laughed at myself. Looking at the clock, I saw that it was almost ten and decided I had better get up and get dressed so I could get some things accomplished before going out with my friends later. I had some definite soul-searching to do so I could come to grips with what Kieran had told me, including the fact that my mother wasn't who I thought she was.

# Chapter Three

After taking care of the normal, everyday essentials, I decided to drive over to downtown Charleston to walk along King Street's boutiques and eclectic shops. It had been a while since I had taken time out for myself, and with everything I had to consider today, it seemed like a good day to do it.

The sun shone down on me through the branch-covered sky, and as I perused the shop windows, a soft breeze countered what would otherwise be considered a hot day. As I caught my reflection in the window glass of one of the shops, I stopped and looked at myself critically. I had on a simple pair of white shorts, a turquoise-colored V-neck t-shirt, and, of course, my Converse sneakers. I had my long, dark hair pulled up into a messy ponytail, and aside from some mascara, I had forgone any other makeup. Still just average, I didn't look any different for knowing I supposedly wasn't human. Shaking my head, I leaned over to look at an exceptionally pretty shell and turquoise necklace in the window. As I did, a shadow fell over me, momentarily blocking the sun. Looking up without concern, my hazel eyes came into contact with a pair of cool blue ones.

"Well, well, well. If it isn't the infamous Blue."

"Oh, ah…hi, Celeste." I could see by the look in her eyes that she hadn't forgotten our last encounter. Refusing to cower before her, I stood and straightened my shoulders.

*Of all the gin joints, in all the towns, in all the world, she walks into mine.*

I decided to play it cool—no reason to panic just yet. "Out shopping?"

She looked around contemptuously. "Not here. I prefer the shops in…just other shops."

"I see." I didn't really, but I wasn't about to encourage further conversation with her.

She looked me up and down before her eyes landed on my necklace. It was a beautiful piece made up of a small, white abalone shell with a smaller teardrop-shaped blue-green agate pendant. A small silver Fairy holding a complicated Celtic knot connected the two pieces, which hung on a corded, turquoise rope. Considering what had transpired in my dream, I felt it was appropriate to wear. Shock shone in Celeste's eyes as she stared at the piece. Looking at me sharply, she narrowed her eyes and pointed to the necklace. "Where did you get that?"

I put my hand over it protectively. "It was my mother's." Suddenly, whether by her reaction or my intuition, I knew this had been my biological mother's, not Alannah's.

"Liar! It's not possible." Celeste slowly backed up. "Who is your mother?" Her tone was demanding as she stopped a few feet away.

"I'm afraid that isn't something I'm willing to discuss with you."

As I watched, something lit in the backs of her eyes, transforming their cornflower-blue color into a strange mixture of different grays. Looking closer, I realized a storm was actually raging there. Not a figurative one, but a literal one. I could see the lightning and clouds swirling around, seeming to converge at her pupils.

"Oh, you will tell me what I want to know."

I figured now might be a good time to retreat. Who knew what Celeste had in store for me? Backing up two steps, I suddenly bumped into a solid chest. As strong hands reached up and took my arms, I tensed, thinking Celeste had brought some goon along to help hold me captive.

"There you are, Blue. I've been looking all over for you."

I sagged in relief at the sound of the male voice. Talk about good timing. Turning, I looked up gratefully to see the familiar face of none other than Cedric. "Hiya, Cedric."

Cedric smiled down at me before looking back at Celeste. "Celeste, what are you doing in this neck of the woods? I thought you hated the shops here?"

Celeste's eyes had returned to their normal blue, and she smiled innocently at Cedric. "Oh, I just wanted to get out and walk a bit before the performance this evening. You never know what you might come across here."

"Uh-huh."

Looking between them, I realized why Celeste was here. She must have been following Cedric again, hoping to get him alone. Since he had just saved my neck, I figured I owed him the same. Looping my arm through his, I smiled as casually as I could at the woman. In turn, she glared at me before looking beseechingly at Cedric.

"Cedric, do you think you could walk me back to the theater? I'm really not feeling well all of a sudden."

"Oh, here. I'll get you a ride." Without looking at her for consent, he stepped to the curb, waved his hand, and whistled shrilly. Almost immediately, a bike rickshaw pulled up.

Cedric stepped forward and offered his hand to Celeste. "There you go." He smiled cheerfully at her.

As she passed me, her eyes once again changed to that raging storm gray, and she whispered, "This isn't over between us, not by a long shot. There won't always be someone around to protect you."

I could almost imagine her skin turning green as she brandished a broom at me. *I'll get you, my pretty...and your little dog, too.*

With that, Celeste smiled sweetly at Cedric and stepped into the rickshaw. As it pulled away, she waved and blew him a kiss. After she was out of sight, Cedric turned to me with a huge grin.

I smiled back in amusement. "It would seem *you* saved *me* from her clutches today." We shared a laugh and, by unspoken agreement, started walking side by side.

"In this case, I think it went both ways. I've been trying to lose her for the past hour. I guess she overheard my plans this morning at the theater. She's been dogging my steps ever since, trying to catch me alone."

"Oh, you poor dear. She won't give up on you, will she? Maybe she thinks you're playing hard to get."

"Oh, she thinks something, that's for sure."

I looked around to make sure we were alone on the street, then glanced sideways at him. "So, ah, what exactly is her talent?"

He looked at me cautiously. "I'm not sure what you mean by that."

"You know, the storm raging in her eyes and all. She said something about making me talk, whether I wanted to or not." Cedric still didn't look as if he would say anything, and I sighed. "It's okay, I know what you guys are."

"What we are?"

I guessed I would have to say it out loud. They really did take the whole secret thing seriously. Though if Celeste's little slip with the eyes was any indication, they could be pushed into revealing themselves. "You're Fae."

He looked at me for a minute, seeming to weigh something before nodding. "Thought you might have an idea. It isn't like Tristan to bring just any human to our home."

"To tell you the truth, I'm not exactly sure I *am* human."

"Could've fooled me. I'm not getting any of the normal signals I usually do when I meet another of our kind."

"I can't explain it, but I had...well, a waking dream this morning. Some guy told me I was Fae."

"What guy?"

"He said his name was Kieran Grayson." I wasn't sure if I should be telling anyone this, but I needed someone to talk to about it, and I trusted Cedric. Besides, what other person did I know for sure was Fae?

Cedric let out a low whistle. "Kieran, huh?"

"Yeah. Why, is that bad?"

"No, he's just kind of a legend with our clan. Been around a long time."

I let out the breath I had been holding. For a minute there, I'd thought Cedric might tell me that Kieran was some evil being in the Fae world and was trying to recruit me to the dark side or something.

Shaking my head at myself, I gave a half laugh. "He said he was over six hundred years old."

"That would be about right. He's one of the Elders."

"He didn't mention that fact." I thought back to what Kieran had said about the Elders.

"You're telling me you didn't know you were Fae until today?" Cedric didn't look quite convinced.

Though I could hardly blame him. Had it been me…well, I guessed it *was* me, and I still wasn't sure I believed it. "Trust me, this all blindsided me, too. If I weren't so open-minded, I might have to question my sanity. When I talked to Kieran, he said something about our ancestors deciding it was time I knew. Only heaven knows why now."

"I know I'm not supposed to mention them, but your parents never told you anything?"

"Honestly, Cedric, I never knew my dad, and my mom took off when I was sixteen. Now, come to find out, she might not have even been my birth mother. It's all so confusing." I kicked a rock across the sidewalk and watched as it skittered away.

"Wow, even though I didn't have my parents growing up, I at least always knew who and what I was."

"Yeah, it's all pretty overwhelming."

"Who does Kieran think your parents are, then?"

I shrugged with a slight shake of my head. "He doesn't know. He said he was going to look into it and get back to me. I might have a clue for him now, though."

"Yeah?"

"From Celeste. She freaked out today when she saw my necklace and demanded to know where I had gotten it from and who my mother was."

"Really?" Cedric stopped and looked at the necklace in question. "May I?" He indicated that he'd like to touch it, and I nodded.

Lifting the pendant into his hands, he closed his eyes. I felt a spark of something shiver through me, though I wasn't sure exactly what it was. When he opened his eyes again, they were glowing.

"Whoa…"

He laughed softly, the glow slowly leaving his eyes until they were green once again.

"What was that all about?"

"Detection. One of my gifts. I can usually tell by touch what something is and what it's made of, whether it be natural or spell-made."

"Cool. Hey, I wonder if it would work if you touched me?"

"I already did. That's why I'm so surprised to hear you say you're Fae. There was no indication that you're anything but human. I still don't feel anything. It's strange."

"Huh. I'll have to ask Kieran about that. There has to be a reason why. He seemed to be able to tell I was Fae easily enough."

"Perhaps because you were more yourself in the dream realm than you are here." I didn't respond as Cedric carefully laid my necklace on my chest. "Either way, this is definitely Fairy-made. Partially anyway. The other half seems to be Nereid."

"A Sea Nymph?"

"Know your mythology, I see."

"Of course, it's always fascinated me."

"As to your necklace, it's loaded with a huge protection spell."

"Protection against what?"

"Anything bad, I guess. I can only tell the basics without delving further into the spell itself."

I slowly grinned, a mischievous glint entering my eyes. "I wonder why it didn't keep Celeste away."

Cedric laughed, merriment dancing in his gaze. "Probably because she hasn't tried to harm you yet. My guess is, had she tried to delve into your mind and take over your will, it would've reacted and done something."

"Take over my will? I thought Vaimpír did that. Is she a Vaimpír, then?"

"Celeste's dad is a Vaimpír, but her mother is a Fairy. See, when Fae of two different species get together, the offspring, while born as one or the other species, tend to display a little of both parents' abilities. So, while Celeste is a Fairy like her mom, she can take over a person's will like her father."

"What kind of Fairy is Celeste's mom?"

"An elemental Fairy. Air is her specialty."

"Hence the stormy eyes."

"You got it."

We started walking again, periodically stopping to look into shop windows but not going into any of the stores. By unspoken agreement, we headed toward the historic Charleston City Market. As we walked, Cedric explained how life was growing up in a Fae clan—at least the Moon Tree Clan. He couldn't say much for others, as each was a bit different.

He explained how Fae children were raised much like humans until they reached puberty or showed signs of having a specific ability. They went to school, had friends they played with every day, enjoyed sports, etcetera. However, it was all done within the Fae community.

Once a Fae realized their powers, usually around puberty, though sometimes later in life, and they learned how to control themselves, they were sent to school with the mortals to learn how to cope within human society. They also had to attend special classes within the Fae community to continue learning about their people.

He explained that after they graduated from college, a few moved out into the world, but most went to work for the theater as performers, in operation roles, or worked the places under the theater itself—whatever that meant. With the slow-aging thing, it was amazing to think that some of the actors had been up on the Dock Street Theatre stage since its creation.

"It's hard to believe an entire clan lives under the theater. I mean, the ballroom I saw was pretty amazing, but to think a whole society not only lives but flourishes there...wow."

"You haven't seen even half of it. The ballroom is only a very small part of where we live. We have stores, movie theaters, bowling alleys, racetracks. You name it. That's where those who don't work at the theater are. Some own their own businesses. Others work for each other. We pretty much have our own commerce system there."

"Are you serious? What does it stretch miles underground?"

Cedric nodded with a smile. "Across and down."

"How do you guys get around the water tables? I would think it would flood if you dug down."

"Magic, of course. How else would you do it?" He furrowed his brows in mock confusion.

"Of course. Magic. How silly of me." Cedric laughed as I rolled my eyes. "What about the types of Fae? Are clans usually all one species?"

"Mostly. The majority of our clan at the theater is some type of Fairy, whether pure or mixed blood, and have generations of family living there. There are a few outsiders—orphans brought in when they lost their parents. There are even a few who were kicked out of other clans that we've accepted into ours."

I glanced at him in astonishment. "That's incredible. Your King must be a compassionate man. I'd love to meet him someday." Cedric looked at me strangely. Thinking I'd touched on something I wasn't supposed to, I asked another question. "What kind of Fairy are you?"

"I'm one of those orphans. They believe my mother was a Fairy, but my father was a Wolf."

"As in a *Werewolf*?"

"No, not quite."

"Not quite?"

"No."

"What exactly are Fae Wolves, then?"

"Same as most Wolves, I guess."

"Seriously?" I looked at him in annoyance. "Do you like...change at the full moon?"

"No."

"Eat people?"

"No."

I gave a long-suffering sigh. He wasn't being very forthcoming with information. "How did you become a Wolf? Did you like get scratched or bitten by another Wolf?"

Cedric shook his head. "I told you, we aren't Werewolves." At my disgruntled look, he just laughed. "Fae Wolves can change anytime, not just on a full moon. They definitely don't eat people, nor can they change other people into Wolves—it's something you have to be born into. We're just big, fuzzy animals with a highly developed sense of smell and some other unique traits."

"Was that so hard?" He just grinned at my sarcasm. "I guess that explains your talent earlier, then, huh? Detection?"

"Yup. I can tell what items are by touch, probably a byproduct of my mom likely being an earth Fairy. And I can smell anything within a couple of miles."

"Whew. Betcha that can get overwhelming."

"Yeah, it can at times, but one learns to block out what they don't want to smell. Speaking of, I like the perfume you're wearing—natural without all the added chemicals you usually find in commercial perfumes."

"Uh, thanks. But I'm not wearing any perfume."

"There's no way that's your natural smell..."

"Maybe it's the soap or shampoo I use."

He leaned over and smelled my hair. "Nope." Then he picked up my arm and brought it to his nose. "Nope. Only one place left."

I squeaked when he put his face into the curve of my neck and inhaled deeply. "Yup. Wow, I can't believe that is your natural smell. I've never come across anyone who smelled like that, though I've heard stories..." He shook his head, not finishing his sentence but seeming to consider something.

Shivering a bit from his breath on my neck, I laughed. "I guess that could be another clue."

He straightened. "I can't figure you out. You are such a mixture of contradictions."

"A woman likes to keep a little mystery about herself."

Cedric laughed as we crossed the street. "You certainly have that in spades."

Picking up my hand, Cedric set it companionably on his arm as we walked to the start of the market. The entrance to the Market Hall looked as though it had been erected in honor of some Greek god or goddess with its tall, rounded columns and square arches. In reality, it had originally been a glorified meat market. Even so, I loved it. No matter how many times I came here, the talent that surrounded Charleston always amazed me.

There were painters, basket weavers, sculptors, jewelry makers, bakers, carpenters, you name it. You could probably find all of it here among these people. As we wove our way through the crowd, Cedric started to subtly point out the Fae. I was amazed at how many there were. Now that Cedric was separating them from the normal populace, it explained the strange prickling energy I had always associated with certain people.

Before long, we came up to one of my favorite sculptors, a gentleman by the name of Brody. He spotted us long before we did him. "What an unexpected surprise. Not one, but two people who I adore. And not only are they here, but they're here together. Wonderful, just wonderful. Cedric, my old friend, I haven't seen you in forever. Still hiding out at Dock Street?"

"Yes, indeed. Can't seem to tear myself away." Cedric laughed as the two men clasped each other's forearm. It was almost like a modified handshake, and I wondered about it but decided not to mention it—probably just a guy thing.

Brody took my outstretched hands in his, bringing them to his lips. "I'm so glad to see you, *ma chérie*. I have a couple of special pieces I saved, for when you stopped by."

"You don't have to save me anything, Brody. What if I don't like it and you miss your chance to sell it?"

"Trust me, that will never happen. I know you. You will love these." Letting go of one of my hands, he turned and led me toward a curtained-off section in the back of his vending area. "Tell me, Blue, how do you know this rascal Cedric here?"

Cedric, who had been following sedately behind us and looking at Brody's sculptures along the way, looked up at his name and smiled. "We actually just met last night. Tristan brought Blue to the afterparty."

Brody's eyes widened. "Indeed. That's an unusual development, is it not?"

"It most definitely was. And it proved to be a very interesting night."

Brody looked at me with new eyes, seeming to consider me. After another quick glance at Cedric, who nodded, he turned to face me. "Blue, would you mind if I touched your face?"

"No, of course not. What's the matter? Do I have something on it?"

"No..." As his fingers came into contact with my skin, I felt a smooth wave wash over me. It almost felt like water, but I was definitely still dry. Glancing at Brody's face, I saw he had closed his eyes.

"How very odd." He reopened them to look at me, then turned to Cedric. "Were you able to get anything?"

"Not a hint."

I raised an eyebrow at Brody. "Are you telling me you're Fae, too?"

He turned to me and smiled widely. "But, of course. Aren't the most talented usually?"

I laughed at his arrogance, not a bit put off by it. "Can I ask what you are? Or is that against some Fae code?"

Brody laughed. "Some might take offense, but I don't think there are any codes or laws against it. I, my dear, am an Ealaín."

"I don't think I'm familiar with that one."

"Not too many are. It is a Fae of the arts. Not only do we appreciate fine art, we also protect it."

"Protect it?"

"Yes. Some are involved in art security, where the  will protect the given art with their very lives. Others, like me, continue to produce it, spreading the word and art for people to appreciate and enjoy. I also work closely with programs that save artistic pursuits, such as those in schools."

"Oh, you mean like Artists for the Arts."

"Exactly."

"What about that probing wave of...whatever earlier?"

Brody chuckled at my description. "Most Fae accomplished in magic can do that. It's just a spell that takes down a person's barriers to expose their inner self."

"Their inner self? So, like, if I was a Fairy, I would suddenly sprout wings?"

"In my mind, yes. It doesn't reveal your true self to humans, just to other Fae. Though there are counterspells to it, as well. For instance, someone must have done something to you to hide your true self. To portray you as strictly human, no matter what. Even to you."

"Even to me? You mean I could have wings, a tail, or something hiding somewhere I didn't know I had?"

"It's entirely possible." He laughed at what had to be a horror-struck look on my face and shook his head. "Don't worry, there are ways to hide those features."

"Great. Just great." Knowing my luck, I had a tail and horns.

"You are not a Demon, though most don't look like you think they do."

I forgot that most Fae could read minds.

Brody grinned and winked at me. "I'll try not to look without your permission, though I would suggest learning how to block."

"It's on my to-do list." I rolled my eyes but smiled good-naturedly as he took my arm and continued forward.

"Don't worry, we'll figure out what is keeping your true nature locked up. It could be as simple as a spell or as complicated as an enchantment."

"It's nothing I did. I can assure you of that."

"No, this had to be done by an extremely old or powerful Fae. Possibly even..." He paused but then shook his head. "Let's just say it's not something the average Fae can accomplish."

As we entered the curtained-off area of Brody's booth where he worked on new projects, he let go of my arm and moved to the far corner. I looked around curiously. I had never been in his back area before. There were tools and materials spread haphazardly throughout the room, along with several unfinished projects. What caught my eye, though, was a tall pedestal in the center of the space with a sculpture covered by a white silk sheet. I wasn't sure what was under there, but I knew I wanted to see. Something about it drew me. I found myself moving closer and closer to the shrouded piece. As I did, a slight buzzing started in my ears, and everything else in the room seemed to fade away. I reached out a hand, hardly daring to breathe as anticipation shivered through my stomach.

"First, I have this…"

I started and blinked several times as Brody's voice penetrated the cloud seeming to surround me. I had to force myself to lower my hand and look away from the sheet-draped sculpture. I wasn't sure what had just happened, but I had a feeling it was significant somehow. Concentrating, I moved my focus from the white sheet to the small sculpture Brody held up for me. It was a delicate Fairy about six inches in height, one of Brody's favorite things to sculpt. I now realized that had more to do with what he was than just a natural fascination with the mythological. It looked so lifelike you could almost believe it was a real Fairy. She was a lithe, beautiful woman with gossamer fabric wings. Her long, wavy blond hair flowed over her shoulders and was topped by a head wreath made of pearls and flowers. You could just make out her small, pointed ears poking through her hair. She wore what looked like a bikini made of vines and moss with one strand creeping from her bottoms diagonally across her stomach to her top—a small flower blooming in the middle. She sat on a thimble and had the sweetest expression on her face—one of pure innocence. I fell in love with her immediately.

"Oh, Brody. This is absolutely beautiful. I've never seen anything so lifelike!"

"I knew you'd like it. Her name is Iridia. She was based on a fearsome warrior Queen, though this is her in her youth."

I held out my hand for her. As Brody set her gently on my palm, I felt warmth permeate my skin. It was almost like the sculpture was a living, breathing thing. I felt an immediate connection to it.

"I'll take it."

As I looked up, I noted Brody looking at me strangely. "When you touched her, did you feel something?"

I nodded, suddenly feeling uncertain, like I'd revealed something that should've remained secret. "A...a warming sensation and a connection. Why, is that strange?"

"It's something Ealaín feel when they come into contact with art. I haven't noted any other Fae who experience that feeling. Perhaps you have some Ealaín in your blood."

I nodded slowly, looking thoughtful. Another small piece of the ever-growing puzzle, I supposed. "I guess I could."

"Have you ever felt an overwhelming urge to protect a piece of art? Like when someone picks up a piece you bought and doesn't seem to show it the respect you do?"

I thought about it but then shook my head. "No, I don't think so. But I have felt this connection for other pieces. I've always just considered it an intuition of some sort."

"Hmm. You're definitely not full-blooded Ealaín, then. This is a most intriguing puzzle."

I gently set Iridia down on her display shelf. "Okay, what else do you have for me?"

He picked up another small Fairy. This one was just as lifelike as the first. She was in a seated position with her long legs stretched out in front of her and her toes pointed. Purple fabric wings, slightly tattered in places, spread out behind her, adding to her allure. Softly pooling purple fabric wrapped around her, starting where she held it to her left shoulder to cover her breasts and lap, leaving the rest of her pearlescent skin to shine. Her long, red hair was braided and wrapped twice around her head, sitting just below a five-point silver crown topped with shining purple stones. Bright green eyes that seemed filled with a world of knowledge stared up at me.

"Her name is Riona. I modeled her after one of our Fairy Queens."

"Oh, wow. She's just as beautiful as Iridia, but where Iridia has a look of innocence, Riona appears worldly."

"You understand my art to an uncanny degree, Blue. Shall we see if you have the same reaction to her as you did to Iridia?"

I nodded, excited to finally unlock something about myself, even if I didn't understand what it meant yet. To have a connection like this with another person, someone who understood what I felt was beyond anything I could have hoped for. With a shaking hand, I reached out for the statue. As soon as Brody set Riona on my open palm, I had that same warm feeling of rightness.

"Amazing."

I smiled up into his wondrous expression. "I'll take her, too. You seem to have a theme going. Did you have Fairies on the brain recently?"

"You could say that." Some of the wonder dropped from Brody's expression, leaving a slightly haunted look on his face, one I couldn't quite interpret.

"Oookay. I think I'll leave that one alone for now."

Brody shook himself and slanted a smile my way. "Sorry." He moved over to the shrouded sculpture that had drawn me since I walked into the room. I felt the same shiver of anticipation I had experienced earlier slither through my stomach. I just knew something about the sculpture was exceptionally special.

"This is something I've been working on for some time now. She has been coming to me in visions for weeks, and I've been working to get her just right. I don't know who she is yet, so I don't have a name for her."

I held my breath. As he whipped the shroud off, I stared at the piece before me and sucked in a breath. It was another Fairy more stunning than the past two. She had an ethereal beauty that seemed to draw the eye. Fifteen inches in height, she was poised as if in the middle of a dance with her right leg fully extended, and her left leg bent up behind her, toes pointed. Her right arm was thrown out to the side, holding the corner of her filmy white dress, while multi-layered, iridescent purple and white wings shimmered and glinted between her shoulder blades. She had her head dipped back with layers of wavy brown hair cascading down behind her. As my eyes finally made their way to her face, I started in surprise. It wasn't the expression there that captivated my attention but the fact that...she looked just like me.

I looked up at Brody in surprise. He seemed to make the connection at the same time I did.

"It's you..." The look he gave me was equal parts surprise and horror.

Cedric walked into the room. "Whoa. Is that Blue?" He stared in amazement at the sculpture before us, while Brody nodded shakily.

My eyebrows drew together in confusion. "What on earth is going on? First, I find out I'm part of a previously unknown race, and now you're unknowingly sculpting me into a Fairy?"

Brody shook his head in confusion. "I don't know, Blue. This has never happened before. But there's something else you should know about me."

I looked at him nervously. This sounded like something I wasn't necessarily going like.

"I see glimpses of the future. My sculpting helps me deal with some of the things I see."

I looked at Cedric, who nodded in affirmation.

"I did Iridia right before she changed from the innocent Fairy she was to the hardened warrior she became so her innocence could be forever captured. She didn't become the warrior she was because of her gifts. She became that way because of something that happened to her."

"And Riona?"

Cedric answered for Brody. "She was our most recent Queen, Tristan's wife." I started at the mention of Tristan. I didn't know he was their King, much less married. "She was taken captive by a rival clan during a rather fierce battle that had been waged over territories. We don't know if she was trying to escape them or it happened completely by accident, but she was killed."

Brody nodded. "I sculpted her before her death as a gift to Tristan to remember her by, but after it happened, he was so devastated he had all likenesses of her removed from Dock Street. I was afraid he would want it destroyed if I gave it to him. I couldn't take that chance."

I looked at the sculpture of Riona. "Then why did you decide to sell her to me?"

"I don't know, to tell you the truth. It just felt right. You know how you were saying you used your intuition to decide on art pieces to buy?

I do the same regarding who to sell them to. If it doesn't feel right, I talk the client into something that does."

"Let me guess…with a little persuasion of the human mind."

The corner of his mouth lifted and he winked. "I never use it to make them buy anything, only when influencing their choice."

I sighed and looked back at the Fairy before me. "So, ah, do you want to talk about your vision that went along with this?"

Brody looked nervous. "I…well…"

"Do I die?" I figured it was best to get it out in the open if I did.

Brody shook his head. "Not that I've seen. This was the most unusual set of premonitions I've ever had. Usually, it's only one vision. These have been ongoing for weeks."

"Is it always the same?"

"No. I see this woman—you—in different places, different time periods. Usually dancing, but doing other things, too. Skilled magic, painting, fighting…it doesn't make sense. There doesn't seem to be any connection between the visions."

"Am I the only one in them?"

"No, there are several other females."

"Always the same ones?"

"Yes."

"Perhaps your premonitions are about one of them?"

"No, you always take center stage. Just like before with Iridia and Riona."

Cedric broke in, looking thoughtful. "You said something felt right about selling these particular sculptures to Blue, right?"

"Yes, and she felt the connection, too."

"I wonder if this has anything to do with the upcoming crowning?"

"Crowning?"

Cedric turned to me. "Yes. It's time for Tristan to take a new bride—overdue, actually."

"What does this have to do with me? I'm definitely not looking for marriage, and I just met Tristan last night."

"The things Brody described seeing sound like the Trials."

Brody interjected sharply, his eyes widening. "But, Cedric, we haven't had the Trials in centuries. The King has always been able to make a choice."

"Yes, but if he were to, say, bring in someone from the outside, and the clan contested that choice…"

Brody looked horror-struck. "But she would never survive. She wasn't raised as a Fae. She doesn't even know what her capabilities are, let alone how to use any of them."

"You said yourself you haven't seen her die, right?"

"I never see an end to whatever I see her doing. She doesn't ever finish the dance…I don't know if my visions are even in order."

I interrupted, my eyebrows drawing together. "Whoa, whoa. Wait. What do you guys mean by the Trials? What are they?"

Turning to me, Cedric answered. "It is written into Fae law that should the crowned ruler of a clan not be wed prior to his or her crowning, they must choose a partner, as no King or Queen can rule without their counterpart. There must always be one male and one female on the throne to maintain balance. If their partner dies at any point during their rule, they are to be given time to grieve their loved one before they must choose another or step down."

"Okay. Makes sense." As much as any of it did. I mean, who could comprehend a society that, up until now, had been thought to be fictional? I felt like my brain was slowly becoming a pile of mush, thinking about all of this in real terms. Up to this point, I'd been putting it in the still-possibly-a-dream category.

"Trust me, Blue, this is real life." I shook my head, hating that they could read my thoughts so easily. Cedric ignored me and continued. "Usually, as has happened for the past millennium, either the crowned ruler was married at the time of their crowning, or their choice was met with the clan's approval."

"Okay, so what happens if their choice *doesn't* meet with the approval of the clan?"

"If a large number of people protest, and the crowned ruler cannot come up with an acceptable solution, then the Elders are called in. They will hear both sides of things. If they cannot see a satisfactory solution, the Trials are called for. Usually, the protestors must have significant support within the clan before the Elders call for the Trials. It's not something they do lightly, as they can end in a lot of death and misery. Not to mention, tear a clan apart."

"Great, death and misery, two things you always want to hear might be a part of your future. So, how do they decide who participates?"

"Anyone who wishes to participate in the Trials is welcome to, including anyone from outside clans. It's another reason the Trials are rarely called for. It opens up a whole new opportunity for rival clans to put one of their own in a place of power to undermine the other clan from the inside."

"This practice sounds very archaic, like something you'd hear about from the medieval times."

"Definitely. Fae law was written a very long time ago, and it's rare for them to change it."

"So, anyone can participate? Even humans?"

"No, you have to be Fae."

"I still don't see what this has to do with me. It's not like I would enter something like that by choice."

"True, unless you were in love with Tristan."

I laughed and shook my head. "I don't even know him. I spent a total of a half an hour in his company, I think—definitely not enough to want to marry him."

Cedric shrugged, looking strangely relieved. "I don't know. It was just a thought."

I turned to Brody. "Have your premonitions ever been wrong?"

"No."

I shivered a little at the certainty in his voice. "Maybe they just mean something else." He shrugged, looking ill at ease. I went over and hugged him. "Regardless, I will take all three pieces, Brody."

I may have sounded confident to Brody and Cedric, but on the inside, I was trembling. I was getting a bad feeling about all of this. Maybe the reason the Ancients suddenly decided on my education had nothing to do with a mere chance meeting.

# Chapter Four

The Market Street Saloon was packed. Of course, it was a Saturday night, and one of the extremely popular local country-rock bands who hadn't been in the public eye for a while was playing instead of the originally slotted band. I had dressed as per my friends' request in something other than a T-shirt and shorts—well, sort of. I still had on a scoop-neck T-shirt—which ironically sported the logo of the band playing—but I had obligingly changed into a pair of dark blue jeans and put on my favorite pair of western boots. I had even attempted to tame the unruly curls in my hair. Though, I doubted it would remain submissive for long with the crowd starting to heat things up. Looking around the bar, I saw that most of the usual patrons had come tonight, and I was glad since that meant a lot of dance partners. As was their claim to fame, the Market Street Saloon girls circulated or stood on the bar, selling body shots.

I glanced toward the stage and saw Keane, the lead singer and guitarist of Ethereal Mutation, adjusting his amps and getting ready for the show. He was tall, well over six feet, with a nice build that sported a wide, muscular chest and corded arms that strained against his plain black T-shirt. Did I mention he was a favorite among the ladies?

Upon closer inspection, I detected the slight sense of different energy I had come to associate with the Fae today. It was amazing how many were out there. I didn't know if it was just the area, or if all places were like this. Perhaps Charleston was like a Fae magnet or something. I laughed.

As if sensing my scrutiny, Keane looked up, and our eyes connected over the heads of the crowd. His turquoise-blue gaze trailed lazily over me before he winked and gave me a roguish grin, showing a hint of what appeared to be fangs. After my initial shock, I slowly smiled back and nodded to him, raising my drink in acknowledgement. I thought I had just seen my first Vaimpír.

"What was that all about?"

I turned to find Brianna at my elbow with her arms draped around a gorgeous guy I assumed was the infamous Christophe. I shrugged in answer to her question and held out my hand to him. "Hi, I'm Blue."

"Christophe."

I looked at him as he shook my hand. Bleached blond hair paired with blue eyes and chiseled features. He had his body poured into a skintight T-shirt and a pair of jeans that hugged every muscled line. He was yet another golden Adonis, tanned from head to toe—and I'd venture to say everywhere in between. It was no wonder Brianna had brought him home. He was everything she loved in a guy.

"Where are Jess and Cait? I thought you rode over with them."

Raising my eyes from Christophe's Italian leather shoes, I noted he indulged in his own perusal of my person and got stuck where Pinky and the Brain nudged the top edge of my shirt. Shaking my head, I turned my attention to Brianna. "I did. They went to drool over the band." We both laughed. Jess and Cait absolutely loved the drummer and bass guitarist from Ethereal Mutation. They constantly dragged us to performances, though tonight was a huge surprise, catching them unaware and thus unprepared. Hence the unprecedented drooling.

"I'll see if I can find them." Brianna wandered off toward the stage, leaving me alone with Christophe.

Leaning back against the bar, I took a sip of my beer and turned toward him. His eyes had finally made their way back to my face. "How did you and Brianna meet?"

"A photoshoot, of course. She was modeling a beautiful diamond necklace, and I was her modesty."

"Her modesty?"

He cupped his hands over his chest.

I laughed and shook my head. "Ah, so you were a hand bra."

He nodded, laughing, too. "Though, if you don't mind me saying, I would have much rather played the bra to you." His gaze had once again slipped to my chest.

"Uh, thanks. I think." Feeling uncomfortable, I turned back toward the band. They had started playing, and it was one of my favorites. I found my booted foot moving in rhythm to the song and itched to get out on the dance floor. I started scanning the room, looking for a possible partner.

"Judging by your western footwear, I assume you know how to properly dance to this music?"

I turned toward Christophe. "Of course. Do you?"

Though he shook his head sadly, there was a gleam in his eyes. "Unfortunately, no, but I'd be willing to learn." He was gazing at my chest again, and I was suddenly loath to the idea of having to dance closely with him. Normally, I didn't mind Pinky and the Brain getting so much attention, but this was my best friend's guy. I didn't like those who tried to play both sides of the fence. As he reached an arm around my waist and pulled me closer with a smile, I looked around wildly for Brianna, but she was nowhere in sight.

"Sorry, buddy, this dance was promised to me." I turned in surprise at the deep-timbred voice I hadn't expected to hear again so soon.

"Tristan." He was dressed for the occasion in low-slung jeans, a dark blue T-shirt, and a pair of well-worn western boots. He looked like every cowgirl's dream.

"Blue." His smile caused my stomach to flip-flop in reaction and doubled my heart rate. He nodded toward Christophe. "If you'll excuse us?" He took my hand and turned toward the dance floor, not even waiting for an answer. Christophe nodded in response, though he didn't look too happy about it. I'd have to remember to warn Brianna that he had a wandering eye.

Guiding me to the edge of the dance floor, Tristan turned me toward him and slipped his arm around my waist. We were off before I could even ask if he knew how to shuffle. He executed a complicated series of turns as we hit the corner, twirling me along. By the time we made our way around, I was out of breath and laughing. "Wow, I was going to ask if you knew how to shuffle, but I guess that answered that question."

He chuckled low and pulled me closer to his body. "I've done it a time or two." We circled the floor, not talking, just dancing to the fast-paced music. As the song ended, we clapped with the rest of the crowd. The band started in on one of their love songs, a slow two-step. Tristan easily slid us into the dance. "You've done this a time or two, yourself."

I smiled up at him. "Possibly. I have to say, though, I'm extremely surprised to see you here, of all places."

"Why do you say that?"

"I never would have taken you for a country boy."

"I guess I'm just full of surprises."

"Don't you have a show at the theater tonight?"

"Yes. But they don't need me to talk every night. That's only for grand openings and special occasions. I'm not just the master of ceremonies, you know."

"So I hear."

He leaned back and looked at me with raised brows. "Somehow, I sense a lot more behind that statement."

I smiled mysteriously and tucked my head under his chin. Closing my eyes, I inhaled deeply. Under his cologne's crisp, clean smell, I detected a deeper, wilder scent. It was like nothing I had ever smelled before. It reminded me of an impending thunderstorm, where the winds whipped furiously through the trees, and the rain was on the edge of pouring down. A part of me recognized the smell, like a long-forgotten memory, and I found myself thinking of home. Suddenly, I was jolted back to the present when I felt Tristan's arm tense around me. Forgetting about the odd scent, I opened my eyes and looked up at him questioningly. He was staring at the saloon's entrance with a look of feral intensity.

"Are you okay?" When he didn't respond, I looked over my shoulder and saw that two women and two men had entered the bar. They seemed a bit out of place, though I wasn't sure why. They were dressed like everyone else. It was just something about how they carried themselves. Digging deeper into their energy field as I'd been teaching myself to do today, I found they were some kind of Fae—and powerful ones at that. Turning back to Tristan, I lightly placed my hand on his cheek to bring his attention back to me. "Friends of yours?"

His jaw tightened. "Not exactly."

As the song came to an end, I stepped out of Tristan's arms. "Do you...?"

"Tristan, my love. It's been forever." I turned to find the group that had entered the bar standing next to us. The woman who had addressed Tristan had fiery red hair I knew didn't come from any bottle, and bright green eyes. She had the same stature I had come to associate with the Fairies at the theater—a petite, compact figure with an ethereal beauty. She moved forward and pulled Tristan into a hug that implied a close familiarity, confirmed further when she pulled his head down for a kiss.

Tristan quickly disentangled himself from her embrace and took a step back. "Tatiana." He addressed her formally, with no hint of warmth in his tone.

Tatiana pretended to pout and turned to the man standing behind her. "See how he treats me, brother? As if I mean nothing to him."

The man in question chuckled and held out his hand to Tristan. "Ignore her. You know she isn't happy unless she is the center of attention." Beside him, Tatiana huffed and crossed her arms over her chest.

Some of the animosity in Tristan's stance loosened as he clasped the other man's forearm. "Magnus, it's good to see you. It has been a long time, has it not?"

Sadness showed on Magnus's face. "Yes, not since the passing of our dear sister."

I saw Tristan's features tighten with old pain and realized they must be talking about Riona. Looking between Magnus and Tatiana, I saw their resemblance to the small sculpture that now resided in my living room. They must have been her brother and sister. It was no wonder Tristan had reacted the way he had when he saw them come in. Suddenly feeling like I was intruding on a private moment, I stepped back, intending to find my friends. As I turned, I felt an arm encircle my waist and pull me back. Tucking me against his side, Tristan turned back to Magnus and Tatiana.

"My manners desert me. This is Blue. Blue, this is Magnus and Tatiana, my brother and sister..." He paused, seeming conflicted, before continuing. "...in law."

I glanced uncertainly at Tristan, who continued to stare straight ahead before facing his brother and sister-in-law. "It's a pleasure to meet you both."

Magnus stepped forward and, taking my hand, placed a kiss on the back of it. He had the same red hair and green eyes as his sister, but where her eyes held aloofness, his were filled with mischief. "The pleasure is most definitely all mine, *chére*."

After he stepped back, he motioned the other couple they'd arrived with forward. "Tristan, Blue, these are our...friends, Odelina and Aelfric." The way he said *friends* left me with little doubt they were anything but.

I felt Tristan stiffen. "Of the Misty River Clan? Sethos' children?"

I had no idea who that was, but I had a feeling it wasn't a good thing. I could practically feel the hate vibrating through Tristan.

Magnus leaned forward to whisper. "They were at one time, but they have since sworn fealty to the Fernsong Clan. It was because of what happened that they left their clan and father."

Aelfric bravely took a step closer to Tristan and bowed in deference to him. "Your Majesty, we are truly sorry for what happened but know we were just as grieved as you that any of it occurred. Had we been able to stop it, we would have. As Magnus says, we have since disavowed our father and sworn allegiance to Brokk of the Fernsong Clan. We came here tonight to humbly request permission to be able to move through your territory without fear of reprisal."

I felt Tristan take in a deep, soothing breath, then let it out slowly before gathering himself and speaking, looking every bit the King he was alleged to be. "I am obliged to hear of your new loyalties, and you have my permission to go where you will."

Both Aelfric and Odelina moved forward and bowed over Tristan's hand before backing away and moving out the exit, never turning their backs to Tristan. It reminded me of the scene in the play *The King and I* when all his kids were introduced to the new schoolteacher. I looked around us to see if anyone else in the bar was taking in what was happening, but it was as if we were in a bubble. Everyone seemed to move around us as if nothing unusual was happening. I wondered how the Fae did that.

"Thank you, brother."

Shaking his head with a lopsided half smile, Tristan seemed to deflate, then clapped his hand on Magnus's shoulder. "Bold move, Magnus."

Magnus smiled back. "I figured if I did it in public, you would at least behave yourself."

"You know me so well."

"I'd hope so, given how long we've been friends."

"Do you and Tatiana plan on staying in the territory long?"

"For the time being." Magnus shifted a bit uneasily.

Looking at him consideringly, Tristan nodded. "You will stay with me, of course. We'll talk later."

"We would be honored."

Now that all the protocol was over, Tatiana insinuated herself between Magnus and Tristan. "Tristan, aren't you going to ask me to dance?"

Tristan looked down at her briefly. "Not now, Tatiana."

"But..."

Magnus grabbed Tatiana by the shoulders and turned her toward the door. "Come, sister, we have much to do tonight. We will go back to Dock Street and leave Tristan to his evening."

I could hear Tatiana complaining loudly as Magnus pushed her toward the exit. Before they disappeared through the door, Magnus turned back and gave me a wink. Then, with a mighty shove, he forced his sister to continue on her way out.

I turned back to Tristan. He was looking down at me impassively. "Blue, is there somewhere we can go to talk? In light of recent events, I think we need to discuss some things. Privately."

I nodded. "Let me go tell my friends I'm leaving."

He reached up and gently ran his hand along my cheek, softening his harsh look. "I will meet you by the door."

As I walked away to find my friends, I saw Tristan head toward the stage. The band was just setting their instruments down for a short break. As he approached, I saw all the band members put their left fists to their chests and give slight bows. Keane glanced briefly in my direction before turning his attention back to Tristan. Shaking my head, I located my friends at a high-top table just off the dance floor.

"There you are. We were afraid you had been carried off...or, rather, hoped." Brianna giggled. If the glasses in front of her were any indication, she'd had quite a few shots of something in my short absence, and to say she was a lightweight would be a gross understatement. "Christophe said some strange man took you away to dance and neglected to return you."

I laughed. "Actually, he wasn't a strange man. It was Tristan."

My friends were both shocked and excited. "Did he know you were going to be here tonight?"

I shook my head. "No, I don't think so. I'm pretty sure it was just a chance meeting."

Jess looked contemplative. "I'll bet it wasn't. I'll bet he talked to your friend Cedric and learned you'd be here."

I thought about that. "I guess he could have. I forgot I invited Cedric to come tonight." That put this strange meeting into a whole new category. Had Tristan actually planned on running into me here? "Anyway, if you guys don't mind, I'm going to head out with him."

"Mind? Girl, let me give you a push." Brianna giggled again. "Does this mean you're finally gonna get some?"

"Brianna, behave yourself." Caitlin was properly scandalized for me, though I just laughed.

"I don't think so, but if it makes your night, I'll say there is always the possibility."

"Are you sure that's such a good idea?" This question came from Christophe, who was once again talking to my chest, causing me to grimace. I wanted to pull Brianna aside and tell her about him, but she seemed to be having such a good time that I figured I'd leave it for now.

"I'll be fine. I'll call you guys later, okay?"

After leaving my friends, I met Tristan at the front entrance, where he waited for me.

"Ready?"

I nodded, and we went out into the parking lot, where Tristan guided me to a sleek, dark blue Aston Martin. I whistled. "Wow, you sure know how to impress a girl."

Tristan grinned and opened the passenger door for me before moving to the other side of the car and sliding behind the wheel as only a man used to luxury could. "Where to?"

"I figure we can go to my place. That way, we won't be interrupted." I quickly gave him directions, and we set off.

We didn't talk much on the way to my house, and I had to admit I was a bit nervous. I was fairly certain I knew what he wanted to talk about. I just didn't know if I was ready to discuss some things—like his deceased wife.

When we arrived, he took my keys and unlocked the door for me. I stepped around him and began turning on lights, giving him a chance to look around. As I came back into the living room, I found him staring out the back glass at the ocean.

"How much do you know?" His tone was flat.

"Bits and pieces, I guess."

When he didn't turn around and instead remained standing rigidly staring out the window, I sighed and sat on the couch directly behind him. "I know you are Fae, which is a race of otherworldly beings with mystical powers. Your clan, in particular, is mostly made up of fairies, which is a subspecies of Fae, and you are the King of your clan. Speaking of, how is it you don't have a guard detail or something? Shouldn't the King be protected at all times?"

Tristan smiled a bit. "Do not fear. They are not far away should I need them." He paused, seeming to look inwardly. "I thought from the moment I met you that you were more than human, though I wasn't sure what. I could feel your power calling to me from across the room. I couldn't stop myself from bringing you to the ballroom last night, though I had never brought an outsider before. It was almost like I was...compelled to."

"Actually, I believe it was Claude who forced your hand." I laughed softly, trying to lighten the mood. When Tristan didn't respond, I sighed. "I only found out I'm Fae this morning, so I couldn't have compelled you, at least not on purpose. I don't even know what kind of Fae I am. Do you?"

He shook his head. "Something is protecting you, keeping your true self hidden."

I laughed lightly again, this time without much humor. "So I've heard. It figures no one can seem to tell me much about myself, other than the fact that I'm not who or what I thought I was all my life."

Tristan turned around at this and looked at me. "I spoke with Cedric today after he returned from shopping with you." He paused as if expecting a response, but I just nodded. "He didn't intentionally seek me out, just so you know. I smelled you on him when he came in. He was the one who told me where you would be tonight."

"Smelled me? That's kind of weird, don't you think? You're not a Fae Wolf, too, are you?"

Tristan shook his head with a small chuckle. "I could hardly be King of the Fairies if I were a Wolf, now could I?"

"I guess not."

"And to answer your question, there are some types of Fae, though they are rare, that produce a distinctive fragrance. Yours is markedly...unique." Before I could question him further, Tristan's look turned serious again. "Blue, about what happened tonight with Magnus and Tatiana..."

I held up my hand to stop him. "I know about your wife, Tristan."

He quickly moved to sit by me on the couch and took my hand. "But do you? Do you know it was my fault, my arrogance, that got her killed?"

I could see the deep-seated guilt in his eyes. He truly believed it was his fault that his wife was dead. "Tristan, you didn't kill your wife. That other clan did."

"But it was my fault we were at war with them. My fault I didn't have Riona protected better. I should have known they would try to take her. I..." His voice trailed off as he spotted the sculpture on the table in front of us. "What is this?" He glanced at me, then back at the sculpture.

I sighed. I probably should have moved it when I came in but maybe a small part of me had wanted him to see her, to face his feelings. Because if he wasn't over her, there was no point in furthering our relationship.

"This is a sculpture my friend Brody did before your wife passed. He said he originally made it so you would have something to remember her by, but when everything happened, he said you had all of Riona's likenesses removed, so he kept her for fear you'd destroy her."

"Brody? Brody Shimmin? He had a vision about Riona?"

I nodded. Obviously, it was well-known among the Fae exactly why Brody sculpted what he did. "I don't know exactly what the vision was about, but he said he felt compelled to sculpt her after it."

"Why didn't Riona tell me?" Tristan's voice was distracted, his eyes going distant before he focused back on me. "Why do you have it?"

I shrugged. "Brody said these sculptures spoke to him and told him I needed them. He didn't know why, just that they were meant to be with me."

"Sculptures? More than one?"

"One of Riona, one of Iridia." I pointed her out on the other side of the table. "And one...well, one of me." I nodded toward the large statue I'd placed on a small table across the room.

Tristan looked at me in surprise. "You? Brody had a vision of you?"

I nodded uncomfortably. "He said the ones of me have been plaguing him for weeks. He actually didn't even know it was me until he showed me the sculpture today."

"He's had more than one? That is highly unusual."

"So he says."

"What did he see in his visions?"

"Mostly that..." I pointed toward the sculpture.

Tristan got up to take a closer look at it. "It's beautiful. He captured everything about you, though I can't say I've ever seen you look so ethereal—so much like a Fairy. Of course, I've never seen you dance with this much abandon, either. Does Brody believe you are a Fairy, then?"

"He doesn't know. He said the visions weren't ever clear, which is why the sculpture gave him such a hard time."

"He saw you dancing?"

"He said he sees this woman, me, in different places and different time periods. Usually dancing, but doing other things, too. Skilled magic, painting, fighting...Cedric thought it might have something to do with the crowning."

Tristan looked at me sharply and came back to sit by me. "What do you know about the crowning?"

"Only what Cedric told me. About the law requiring you to have a Queen to rule by your side, and how now that your period of mourning is over, it is time for you to take another wife."

Tristan nodded. "He is right, but why would Cedric think Brody's visions have something to do with that?"

"He said something about the Trials."

Tristan shot to his feet as if he had been burned and started pacing. "The Trials. Holy...the Trials haven't been enacted for over a millennium. What would make him think they would happen now?"

I shrugged. "Cedric just said that what Brody described sounded like the Trials."

Tristan ran a hand over his face and through his hair, causing several bunches to stand on end. "The clans have been very unsettled since Riona's death. She was well-loved. You saw that the King of the Misty River Clan was disavowed by his own children over what happened, and at the afterparty, when I was called away, it was due to unexpected visitors from other clans. Even Magnus and Tatiana are here. They are all gathering, waiting to see how this will be resolved. Will I take a bride from within my clan? Will I seek one outside the clan to fortify alliances? Or will I take one from the very clan that killed Riona to bring peace?" Tristan stopped pacing and slumped onto the couch. Staring at the figure of Riona, he sighed. "I'm sorry to have brought you into this, Blue. Now, of all times, was a horrible time to try to start a relationship. It's just...I feel this connection with you. I can't explain it, and I can't seem to get it out of my head, no matter how hard I try." Tristan looked up at me.

"I feel it, too, Tristan."

He nodded, still staring, that intensity from before filling his gaze. "I don't know where we're going, Blue. I don't have a solution to everything that is going on." I nodded as he moved so he sat closer to me on the couch. "I do know I'm having a hard time fighting my growing attraction to you." He reached up and cupped the back of my neck, pulling my face slowly to his. "And I know I shouldn't kiss you because it will only complicate things in the long run, but I can't seem to help myself..."

His lips slowly descended to mine, giving me plenty of time to back off if I wanted to, but I didn't. I felt the same urgency he did. I pushed forward and placed my lips on his, wrapping my arms around his neck and pulling him closer. I opened my mouth to him as he deepened the kiss, our tongues twining. He tasted of hot summer nights and raging storms, which briefly brought to mind his scent from earlier. I wondered if this was what he had been talking about when he'd said that some Fae had a unique smell.

As an explosion of sensations that went far beyond words racked my body, any thoughts I might have had flew out of my head. I felt like I was caught in the eye of a hurricane, being pulled in every direction at once. As he pushed me into a reclining position, I didn't resist, reveling in the feel of his hard body pressed against mine. While one hand was still tangled in my hair, his other hand roamed over my shoulders and down to my chest, where it lingered for just a second before continuing to the hem of my shirt. After a moment's hesitation, again giving me time to say no, he slid his hand under my shirt and up, skirting my stomach and coming to rest on my breast. I moaned softly as he traced my hardened nipple through my bra.

My hands, far from stationary, explored, too. Moving up from his neck, I ran my fingers through his soft curls as I'd wanted to do from the first moment I saw him before moving down to the hard muscles of his back. As I reached the edge of his T-shirt, I slid both hands under the hem. I felt his muscles quiver as my fingers traced from his back to the smooth, tight skin of his stomach and abs, memorizing every crevice and pleasure point. As I reached his nipples, I flicked over them, causing them to harden into pebbles. Tristan's quick intake of breath told me he liked what I was doing. With a nudge from me, he broke our kiss, but only long enough to discard his shirt before his mouth was back on mine, just as hot and heavy as before.

Wanting to feel his skin against mine, I quickly rid myself of my shirt, as well. As our bodies came into contact, I whimpered into his mouth. Wanting more—no, *needing* more—I moved his hand to the front clasp of my bra. With a quick flick of his wrist, he had it open, and Pinky and the Brain fell into his waiting hands. I moved restlessly against him, trying to get closer. He moved his body overtop mine so he was lying between my thighs. I could feel his hard arousal pressing against me through his jeans. Pushing my hips forward, I got even closer, causing him to groan and grind himself against me.

"Oh god, Blue, I can't, we shouldn't…"

"I know."

His hands dove back into my hair, pulling my mouth to his again. His tongue thrust in and out, mimicking what he wanted to do with his body. I wrapped my arms around his back, one hand roaming the muscles that flexed and bowed as I moved over them, while my other hand moved down to his waist to press him tightly against me. He felt so good. It wouldn't take much for either of us to fall over the edge and finish what we'd started.

Slowly, a sound penetrated my lust-filled brain. I was loath to acknowledge it, instead trying to force it into the background. Eventually, though, it managed to push its way through—the phone. The landline I used for my business had been ringing alternately off and on with my cell phone for the past few minutes. Someone was obviously trying to get ahold of me and wouldn't take no for an answer. Tristan broke our kiss and, panting, stared down at me.

"I should go..."

Suddenly, the answering machine kicked on. I was probably one of the last handful of people on earth that had one but I liked the old-school technology. I guessed whoever was calling finally gave up and decided to leave a message. "Hey, Blue, itshme–hic–Brianna–hic–" Her voice was seriously slurred and some of the words were hard to make out. "I hope you're gettin' itonwit your man and thathwhy–hic–you're not ansherin' your phones..." She burst into a bout of giggles. "But I need shomewhere tago–hic–can I come over?" At this point, she started to cry. "That bashtard Christophe...I found him in the ladies' room shrewin' some red shtick! No...red-haired chick." More crying and blubbering.

I sighed heavily and put my hands back on Tristan's chest. "I'd better take this."

Tristan smiled crookedly. "I'd say her timing sucks, but as it is, maybe it's for the best."

I smiled as he sat up. Grabbing my T-shirt off the floor, I moved into the kitchen and picked up the landline. Brianna was talking in garbled sentences and crying into the phone by this point.

"Brianna..."

"I can't–hic–"

"Brianna, it's Blue. Honey, where are you? I'll come pick you up."

"Blue! Oh, thank god! Hic–I'm...I'm...I don't know where I am!" She started to get a bit hysterical.

Well used to Brianna's antics when she was drunk, I sighed. "Brianna, calm down. Look around you, what do you see?"

"Waater...shand...the beach, Don't you live near the beach, Blue? I coulda shworn I wasagoin' to your house."

I groaned. She was right outside somewhere—at least I hoped she was close. "All right, honey, hold on. I'll be right there."

"Donhang up!"

"Honey, I can't stay on the phone and find you at the same time. I'd have to hang up and call you on my cell phone."

"Cell-o-phane?" She giggled.

I looked helplessly at Tristan. His T-shirt was back on, and he was sitting on the couch, trying to appear calm. "Tristan, can you talk to Brianna while I go find her? She's outside somewhere, but..."

He stood and walked over to my side. "You might want to put this back on before you go outside." He expertly re-clasped my bra for me and slid my shirt over my head. "Plus, it'll remove any temptation I have to drag you back to the couch and forget about everything and everyone for a while."

I sighed in regret and handed him the phone. If only....

Going outside, I found Brianna sitting in the sand a few feet from my front porch, facing away from the house. She was a complete mess. Her eyes were all red and puffy, mascara ran down her cheeks in spots, and her normally perfect hair was in disarray. I looked and saw that she'd managed to park her car haphazardly in my driveway without taking anything out. I just hoped everything between here and the bar survived too. Lifting her up under the arms, I finally managed to get her to her feet.

"Blue! Doya know who I'm talkin' to on the phone?"

"Yes, Brianna."

"It's Tristan. He has a shexy voice, doya know that?"

"Yes, Brianna."

"Christophe had a shexy voice, too..." She broke down crying again.

"It's all right, honey, Come on, you can sleep in my guest room."

"You're the bestest friend I could ever have, doya know that?" Her voice cracked a bit as she sobbed.

"Mm-hmm. Do Jess and Cait know where you are?"

"Who?"

"Never mind, I'll call them." I doubted they even noticed her absence yet with as absorbed as they usually got at Ethereal Mutation's performances. As I reached the porch, Tristan helped me get Brianna up the stairs. He and I shared an amused smile as Brianna continued to bemoan her life. When he reached the door, he scooped her up into his arms.

"Weeeeee!!!" She was back to giggling.

"Show me where to put her."

I directed him to one of the guest rooms. Pulling the covers back, I set about finding something to use as a nightgown, and a warm washcloth to take her makeup off with. Tristan carefully laid Brianna on the bed before stepping back. I quickly removed her shoes and changed her into an oversized T-shirt, which I was sure she would be scandalized about once she sobered up—especially since it declared: *So, apparently, I'm dramatic.* Laughing softly, I washed the makeup from her face.

Brianna smiled sleepily at me. "I love you."

I smiled down at her and tucked a stray curl behind her ear. "I know. I love you, too. Don't worry, it will all look better in the morning."

"Donforget if you're shleeping naked again make shure you have a man with you this time." Brianna had barely mumbled this before she promptly passed out, causing me to chuckle.

After tucking the blanket securely around her, I quietly moved out of the room, closing the door behind me. Tristan was waiting in the living room.

"You sleep naked?"

Surprised, my gaze darted to his. How he'd heard that all the way out here was beyond me. "Umm, usually, yes."

Tristan groaned playfully. "That is an image I didn't need as I was leaving. Guess it will be cold showers for me tonight."

I laughed softly and wrapped my arms around his waist. "I guess it'll be cold showers for both of us."

Hugging me tightly to him, Tristan placed a soft kiss on my mouth. "About tonight…"

"Don't. Don't say anything. What will be, will be. We'll just have to figure this out as we go."

He smiled down at me. "Ever the wise counsel."

With a final light kiss, Tristan turned and walked out the front door, closing it softly behind him.

I stood there for a moment with my fingers on my still-moist lips. With a shake of my head, I went into my bedroom for that much-needed cold shower and to make calls to my other two best friends.

# Chapter Five

The next afternoon, found Brianna and I sprawled on my back deck loungers. Brianna huddled under an umbrella, sporting large black sunglasses, nursing her hangover, while I lazed in the sun, wearing a turquoise and green bikini as I soaked up the rays. After a nearly sleepless night, lying in the warm sun and doing nothing felt good. Brianna had already apologized profusely for her behavior the previous evening, but I'd just laughed her off. What were friends for, after all?

"So, what's the deal with you and Tristan anyway?"

I turned my head toward Brianna. I thought about giving her my usual smartass comeback but decided to give her a break. She'd had a pretty rough night. "Nothing at the moment. Why?"

"I thought maybe since you brought him home and all..."

I laughed and shook my head. "No, Brianna, nothing happened. We were just talking."

"I interrupted it, didn't I?"

"What? No." I wasn't a convincing liar, even to myself. Grimacing at the thought, I pushed it away. "Look, it's all good, okay? You didn't interrupt anything that didn't need to be interrupted."

"Ah-ha! You were gettin' it on with him!" She pointed an accusing finger at me.

I rolled my eyes. "Okay, you got me. We were *gettin' it on*, as you like to put it. But honestly, your interruption couldn't have come at a better time. There are…issues we need to deal with before anything like that can happen."

"Such as?"

I sighed and closed my eyes. "He was married at one time, but his wife…died suddenly."

"Oh."

"Yeah, oh. I don't know if he's really over her death, you know? Every time she gets mentioned, he kind of tightens up. I don't know if there's room in there for both of us."

"Wow, that sucks."

"Tell me about it." Thoughts of Riona and Tristan had plagued my sleep last night. So much so that I was sporting dark circles under my eyes this morning. Though I tried to cover them up with a little makeup so my friends wouldn't worry, I didn't think it would fool anyone. I just couldn't go into the whole story with them. I hadn't decided yet how to approach the subject of the Fae. I wasn't sure *I* was even comfortable with it.

"When are you going to see him again?"

"I don't really know."

She bit her lip for a moment. "If you're free tonight, do you want to go out? Make up for last night?"

I smiled, still keeping my eyes closed. "You bet."

"And this time, no guys, just girls." I heard Brianna mumble that bit but decided not to comment on it.

We lapsed into a companionable silence while waiting for Jess and Cait to arrive. It felt good to sit and relax with a friend, thinking about nothing more important than the color of my tan or how much I loved living on the beach. Though in the back of my mind, I knew the worries were lying in wait for when I was alone again.

As I took a shower to prepare for the evening, I thought I heard my front door open and close. Since the girls had all gone home to change, and we were meeting at the restaurant later, I thought it odd.

"Jess? Caitlin? Brianna? Is that you?"

"Wrong on all counts," a male voice drawled, not far from the shower stall.

My heart jumped into my throat. I knew I had locked the doors before jumping into the shower. How had someone gotten in?

"Fae don't tend to need keys."

Uh-oh. He'd read my mind. Not good. Weighing my options, I decided I'd better look to see who was out there. His voice sounded a bit familiar, though I couldn't quite place it. Opening the shower door, I peeked around the corner. As the steam cleared, I saw a man lounging against the bathroom doorframe. After a moment, I recognized him. "Keane?" I knew calling him by his first name seemed to suggest a familiarity I didn't have, but I honestly didn't know his last name. Jess and Cait would be mortified.

Keane, the lead singer and guitarist for Ethereal Mutation, flashed his signature grin at me. This time, I could clearly see his fangs. "The one and only."

"Well, technically, there are a lot of Keanes out there, so you can't be the one and only." Actually, I wasn't sure if there were. He was the first person I'd met with that name, but I naturally retreated into sarcasm when I got anxious. Shit! What was I going to do? I didn't have anything to use for protection. I could hardly smash him over the head with a shampoo bottle. I glanced around quickly. Maybe if I grabbed the toothbrush holder...that was pretty heavy.

Keane reached over and picked it up. "But there's only one Keane like me. And relax, I'm not going to hurt you."

"Sure, that's what they all say right before they attack. Lull their prey into a false sense of security."

He laughed, eyeing me in amusement. "Go on, finish your shower. We'll talk when you get out. That is unless you'd like some company?"

Feeling flustered, I shook my head quickly. "No, go sit in the living room I'll...I'll be right out."

"Suit yourself." His grin widened before he turned and left the room—with my toothbrush holder. I huffed out a frustrated breath as I heard him call from the bedroom. "I'll just hold on to this, so you don't try anything...stupid."

Without other options, I hurriedly finished my shower, wondering what this guy was up to. It wasn't like I knew anything about him other than he was a member of Ethereal Mutation and Fae. It was exceedingly strange that he had just shown up in my house like this. I was quickly beginning to realize that the Fae had their own set of rules.

With a quick peek out the shower door to make sure Keane was nowhere in sight, I grabbed my towel and quickly wrapped it around me. Grabbing a second one, I used it to dry my hair as I walked into the bedroom for my clothes. As I pushed my damp locks out of my face, I let out a frightened squeak when something moved on the bed.

"Jumpy thing, aren't you?"

I let my breath out in a rush. Keane was stretched out on my bed, facing me with his head propped up by one hand. "I thought I told you to go into the living room."

He just grinned unabashedly. "But this is so much more comfortable. Plus, I'm not supposed to be more than a few feet from you at all times."

I frowned at him. "What do you mean?"

His grin widened. "Obviously, Tristan didn't mention me to you, huh?"

"No. Why would he?" Now, I was really confused—though a little less fearful. Why would Tristan have mentioned him? I thought back to the previous evening when I'd seen Tristan approach the band before we left. I wondered if this had anything to do with that conversation.

Keane laughed and rolled over onto his back, tossing my toothbrush holder into the air before catching it. "Isn't that always the way of royalty? Everything is on a need-to-know basis."

I sighed, moving past my fear and quickly approaching annoyed. "Keane, you're talking in circles." I stomped over and tried to snatch my toothbrush holder out of his hands, but he just moved it out of my reach.

"Ah, ah, ah..."

"Give me that back."

"No way. You were going to use it to smack me over the head. I'm not taking any chances here. I'll hold on to it till we're done."

I put my hands on my hips and blew out an exasperated breath. "Seriously?"

Keane eyed my towel as if hoping it would suddenly drop. Not trusting his Fae abilities, I decided to retreat and quickly grabbed my underwear from the bed. After a glance around, I decided my walk-in closet was the best option since the rest of my clothes were in there anyway. Stomping over to it, I shut the door behind me.

I could hear Keane's chuckle on the other side. "Love the matching bra and panties, darling. That is going to have me imagining you in your underwear all night long."

I quickly got dressed, randomly selecting a sundress from the rack and slipping it on. As I came out of the closet, I struggled to get the back zipper up. Before I even saw him move, Keane was behind me.

"Allow me."

I shivered as his breath fanned across my neck. "Ah, thanks."

He grinned, having felt my reaction. After grabbing my white Converse sneakers and my jewelry, I resolutely walked out into the living room with him following close behind. "So, would you care to explain what you meant earlier?"

"Hmm, I was offering my services to scrub your back and..."

"Not that." I frowned in his direction. "Why can't you be more than a few feet from me? And what does it have to do with Tristan?"

Keane gave a one-shouldered shrug. "As far as I can tell, with everything going on within the clans right now, Tristan is concerned about your safety since he's singled you out. And since the Vaimpír act as guardians for the King during the evenings, he asked if I would look after you."

"I see…I think." I ran a hand over my face, wondering what Tristan thought I had to fear.

"No idea, darling."

"Stop that."

"Stop what?"

"Reading my mind."

"I'm not exactly trying here, sweetheart. You're just broadcasting your thoughts loud and clear. It's kind of hard to ignore them."

I was immediately contrite. "I'm sorry. With everything that's happened, I haven't learned how to block them yet."

"No worries. It's really easy, actually. I can't imagine why no one has taught you yet. Just visualize a box or shield around your brain."

"Okay." I did as he told me. "Now what?"

"That's it."

"That's it?"

"Yup. It might take a little time, but as you practice, it will get stronger and easier to do. Eventually, you'll do it unconsciously and maybe even be strong enough to keep an old-timer like me out someday."

"And just how old are you?"

He ignored the question. "Now, if you want someone to see in, you just have to open a little door for them." I narrowed my eyes at his avoidance but decided to drop it. Instead, I closed my eyes and tried what he suggested. "Uh-huh, like that, but just think of that one person you want to see in or anyone can. Perfect. You're a quick study."

I sighed and opened my eyes, rubbing my temples where a slight pounding had started. Still, I smiled gratefully. "Thanks."

He nodded. "No problem. That's something every Fae should know how to do."

"Yeah, well, look at me, as ignorant as a child when it comes to the Fae world."

"So I've heard. Pretty rough intro to have."

"You have no idea. How long do you have to babysit me?"

Keane laughed and shrugged his shoulders. "Until the boss says otherwise. Of course, I don't consider it a hardship. You're a sight easier to look at than Tristan."

I shook my head at him. "You know, I was supposed to be going out with the girls tonight. No guys."

"Hmm, so I gathered." I shook my head again, knowing he had plucked the plans from my brain. "Don't worry, once you girls go into the restaurant, you'll just, by chance, get seated next to this really popular band. Which I happen to know two of your friends are absolutely in love with. It will only be natural that you'll look over, and realize you had been introduced to me last night and had forgotten to tell your friends."

"And just how did I manage to get this introduction?"

"Friends of Tristan's and all. You'll then offer to introduce them to me. I will, in turn, introduce everyone to the rest of the band. They, of course, will be all over hanging with us for the remainder of the evening."

I laughed, knowing he was right. Jess and Cait were going to freak out. There was no way they would pass up an opportunity to be around the members of the band they'd been in love with forever.

"Are all of you in the band Vaimpír?"

"Yup."

A thought occurred to me. "Do you guys really drink human blood?"

Keane nodded. "Yes, we do, though you don't have to worry. I'll make sure all the boys are tanked up before we go out."

Relieved, I asked another question I had been wondering about since Kieran had told me the Vaimpír existed. "Where do you, ah, find donors, if I might ask?"

"You know, that's a pretty personal question."

I was immediately apologetic. "Sorry, I don't mean to pry. Forget I asked."

Keane shook his head. "I didn't mean I wouldn't answer you. I don't mind the questions. Some might take offense, though."

I nodded my understanding.

"Most of my kind have live-ins. Girlfriends, boyfriends, or even just friends. The taking of blood can be a very enjoyable experience for the donor, as our saliva contains an enzyme that promotes pleasure, kind of like the natural hormone humans release when they have an orgasm."

"Oh." That definitely wasn't what I'd expected to hear. "But what about keeping the Fae hidden? Do Vaimpír really allow a bunch of humans to run around knowing about them?"

"No. We can feed off certain other Fae, too. It doesn't only have to be humans. Though human blood gives us the most bang for our buck, so to speak. Those with live-ins have compatible significant others. For those who don't have a live-in, there are places we can go with willing donors who cater to our kind. If all else fails, and we have to take a sip on the run as it were, we merely put a vamp whammy on the human and erase their memories afterward."

"Vamp whammy?"

"Mmm, it's what me and the boys jokingly call it. The best way to explain it is...it puts the human into a trance-like state so they don't get frightened or hurt."

"Gotcha. What about the bite marks?"

"Erased with a little bit of our blood. Another benefit of being with a Vaimpír—healing powers. For example..."

Keane pressed the tip of his finger to one of his fangs. I watched in fascination as a drop of blood welled up. Then he moved over to me and offered me his finger.

"Lick it."

I looked at him incredulously. "Seriously?"

"Trust me."

I hesitated, but then curious enough to try, I leaned forward and sucked the blood off his finger. He shivered in reaction, his eyes turning slightly red and his fangs lengthening.

As my eyes widened, he smirked. "Sorry, that happens when we get turned on."

I could taste his blood in my mouth. It didn't taste coppery like I thought it would, it actually tasted sweet.

"Hmm, that's unusual." His voice was slightly husky.

"What is?"

"That my blood tastes sweet to you."

"It's not supposed to?"

"No. To most, it just tastes like blood. It typically only tastes sweet to other Vaimpír."

I shrugged, not having an answer. "Okay, now what was that supposed to do?"

"Go look in the mirror."

I looked at him quizzically but then got up and looked in the mirror hanging on the wall. "The dark circles under my eyes are gone!"

"See, healing powers. Now, you won't notice it with that small amount, but if you were to take more blood, it would also make you stronger and faster."

"Wow. Do you have a live-in?"

"Offering to fill the position?" He smiled wolfishly while waggling his brows at me but then shook his head. "No. I don't currently have a live-in. I've been relying on a few willing donors."

"How do you become a Vaimpír? Is it like the movie vampires where you have to drain someone and then feed them your blood?"

Keane chuckled while shaking his head. "No, we're born this way. No hope of you ever becoming one of us, love, sorry."

I just shook my head at him and went into my bathroom to put on some makeup. Since I didn't need the concealer, I decided just a little mascara and eyeliner would do. Keane followed me and leaned on the bathroom doorframe, his hands tucked into his front pockets.

"So, what's the deal with you and Tristan?"

Funny, but that was the second time today I'd heard that question. "Nothing, why?"

Keane shrugged one shoulder. "It isn't normal for him to send his personal guardians to watch over just anyone, especially the Vaimpír. It makes me think you're something or some*one* pretty important." He let his sentence hang in the air between us.

I shook my head slightly without looking at him. "I don't honestly have an answer to that, Keane."

He nodded. "Fair enough. So, since I answered some of your personal questions, how about you answer one of mine?"

"You mean besides telling you about my dating life?" He gave me an exasperated look, causing me to laugh. "Sure."

"What exactly are you?"

I smiled tiredly. "Unfortunately, that is another question I don't have an answer to." I turned toward him. "I'll let you know as soon as I figure it out."

"Can I ask a favor then?"

"Sure."

"Can I taste your blood?" I recoiled from him a little bit. "Nothing sinister, I promise. I might be able to tell from your blood what you are. Plus, it'll give me the benefit of being able to track you."

"Track me?"

"Mm-hmm. Once a Vaimpír tastes your blood, they will always be able to tell where you are."

"Always?"

"I mean, it'll wear off over time unless the bond is refreshed, but it takes quite a while for that to happen."

I thought about it and decided the benefits far outweighed any negatives. "O...okay."

Keane straightened and walked over to me. I felt a bit apprehensive about my decision, even though I knew it was the right one. I mean, what did I really know about this guy? He could be a serial killer, for all I knew.

Keane gave me a crooked grin. "Don't worry, I'm not a serial killer."

"Sure, that's what they all say. Then, before you know it, you're six feet under and pushing up daisies." Keane chuckled at my sarcasm but didn't comment on it. Taking a deep breath, I brushed aside my fears. "Do you just need a little bit? Or...?"

"I'll need to take a few sips directly from your life-force point."

"My what?"

He walked around behind me so I could watch him in the mirror. Guess that old adage about vampires not being able to see themselves in a mirror was wrong. Brushing my hair aside, he pointed to the spot where I could see my pulse hammering in my neck. "This is where most beings' life force beats. It's the most potent spot on a body."

I gulped and felt my heart rate accelerate even more. Keane closed his eyes and took in a deep breath. When he opened them again, I saw that they were now a deep red, and his fangs had elongated. "Try to calm your racing heart. I promise I won't hurt you."

I nodded mutely as Keane moved, pressing his body tightly to mine. Tilting my head slightly to the side, I watched in the mirror as he ran his fingers along my neck before bending to kiss the pulse point. I shivered in reaction, though it wasn't from fear. Closing my eyes, I felt Keane wrap his arms tightly around me. I felt his warm breath against my neck, and then his tongue slid along the same spot he had just kissed. There was a slight pressure, and then euphoria filled my body. Had he not been holding me up, I likely would've collapsed to the floor. It only lasted a moment, but it was long enough for me to understand why they had no problems finding willing donors. I could only imagine what would happen if you combined it with sex.

I felt Keane chuckle against me. "Yes, sex does make it much more pleasurable...for both parties." He stared at me in the mirror, letting the suggestion hang in the silence.

Shaking my head, I started to pull away, but he tightened his arms around me. I looked at him questioningly and not without a bit of alarm.

"Let me take care of those holes for you. You wouldn't want your friends to see them."

I glanced down in the mirror and saw two perfectly spaced holes on my neck. I watched as Keane pricked his finger with his fang and rubbed his blood over them. As he did, they completely disappeared.

"Nifty trick. Is this the part where you erase my memory of what happened?"

Keane smiled at me in the mirror and lowered his voice to a seductive growl. "No, I most definitely want you to remember." Leaning over, he licked the residue of his blood from my shoulder, all the while holding my gaze.

Shuddering, I stepped away from him and walked back into the living room, trying to shake off the feelings of desire that lingered in my blood—not knowing if it was from the sharing or the man himself. "Sooo, any luck being able to tell what I am?"

Keane shook his head slightly. "Extremely potent in every aspect, but confusing. You taste like every Fae rolled into one, though there's a strong Fairy resonance."

I sighed, feeling a bit defeated. "It was worth a shot, I guess. Come on, it's time to meet the girls." He immediately looked at Pinky and the Brain with a grin, and I shook my head while trying not to smile. The last thing he needed was an ego boost.

After arguing over whose vehicle we should take, I finally conceded and let him drive, though I wasn't sure how I would explain to the girls why I didn't have my Jeep. He assured me he would take care of it. Stepping outside, I saw that Keane drove a big black SUV with heavily tinted windows. My guess was just in case he and his Vaimpír buddies were out a little too close to sunrise. After holding the door for me, he got into the driver's seat and started the engine. As the stereo came to life, it was naturally playing an Ethereal Mutation song. I looked at Keane, amused, and he shrugged his shoulders. "They're the demo tracks. I like to listen to them so I can make changes for the final cut."

As we drove toward the restaurant, I unconsciously started singing along when a song I knew came on. Keane looked over at me and grinned. "Are you a fan?"

I smiled distractedly in his direction, though I continued to look out the side window. "Mm-hmm."

I wasn't sure what was going on with me, but as I sat there, I thought I could actually *feel* Keane. Not like his physical presence, but something else—something on a whole new level. It was like I could feel his essence within me, like I could feel each move he made before he made it.

Keane looked at me sharply. "You can feel me?"

I turned to him in surprise. "Yes. I...I don't know exactly how to explain it. You're just...there."

Keane shook his head in confusion. "How is that even possible?"

"How is what possible?"

"Blue, that is what Vaimpír feel. We use it to track someone once we've tasted their blood. But Vaimpír can't be felt the same way. We live off the life force of others. We don't have our own signature..."

I was just as confused as he was. "I don't know, Keane. Perhaps because my blood is in you?"

"It's impossible." His look turned contemplative.

We drove the rest of the way to the restaurant in silence, both lost in our thoughts. Keane dropped me at the front door with a promise to see me inside shortly. As he drove away, I felt every move he made as he parked the truck. It was relaxing, in its own way.

Turning, I distractedly headed into the restaurant. As I entered through the front doors, I suddenly collided with someone who must have been exiting. "Oh, my goodness. I'm so sorry. I wasn't paying attention. Are you okay?"

The gentleman smiled at me, and I felt a shiver of apprehension slide down my spine, though I didn't know why. Nothing about him appeared sinister or out of place. He looked like every other young businessman who'd come for happy hour. I took in his dirty blond hair, cropped close to his head, and the slightly blocky build under his suit, which spoke to a muscled physique hidden there. I would put money on the fact that he had been a soldier of some sort at one time. I just couldn't put my finger on what about him put my instincts on alert, but something didn't feel right. I immediately doubled the shield around my thoughts, just in case.

"No harm done. It was entirely my fault." He pinned me with his piercing blue eyes, and I had to check the urge to take a step back. Putting out his hand, he introduced himself. "I'm Lucian, by the way. Lucian Beaumont."

I took his hand reluctantly. "Blue."

"It's a pleasure to make your acquaintance, Blue. Perhaps I could buy you a drink in apology for my clumsy inattention?"

I shook my head, wanting to get away from him as soon as possible. "No, thank you. I'm meeting someone." I really hoped the girls were here already.

He smiled. "Meeting your boyfriend for dinner?"

I could tell he was fishing for information, but I wasn't sure how to deflect him. "Ah, friends."

I tried to step around him, but he moved with me. "Perhaps we could meet for dinner at a later time, then? I would love a chance to apologize better."

"Oh, there is no need, I..." Before I could come up with an excuse, I felt Keane's presence behind me.

"If it isn't Lucian Beaumont." I saw Lucian jerk in surprise and look over my shoulder.

"Keane Rutherman." He practically sneered the name. There was obviously a past between these two.

"What brings you around here? Tired of swimming in your own scummy pond?"

Lucian spoke to Keane through clenched teeth. "None of your business, bloodsucker. Why don't you go find some other innocent victim to inflict your presence on?"

Keane smiled, showing his fangs, and dropped an arm around my shoulders. Lucian looked between the two of us, his eyes narrowing. "That's right, water lily. She's under my protection, so back off."

Keane steered me in the direction of the hostess, pushing Lucian aside as we walked by.

"This isn't over, bloodsucker." With that, Lucian stomped out the door and disappeared into the night.

"I leave you alone for one minute, and you're already getting into trouble."

"Who is he? I take it he's Fae?" I glanced over my shoulder. He hadn't felt like any of the Fae I'd encountered.

"Mm-hmm. A Nixie—or Water Sprite."

I looked at him for a second before starting to laugh. "Hence all the water jokes."

Keane grinned unabashedly and then sobered. "He's also Sethos' number one henchman."

I looked at Keane, startled, my laughter cutting off abruptly. "The same Sethos who killed Tristan's wife?"

Keane nodded. "And I would venture to say he didn't bump into you by accident tonight."

I shivered a little, glad for the first time that Keane was here with me. I wasn't sure how I was supposed to play into everything that was going on, but I sure didn't like it.

As I walked up to the hostess, I noticed she was staring at Keane with a dreamy expression. "Hi. I was supposed to meet some friends here. Three women."

A harried-looking waiter came running up at that moment, interrupting me. "Do you know who is dining here tonight? Who you're seating in *my* section?" The hostess looked at him like he was daft, then inclined her head toward Keane and me. After doing a double-take, he gasped and went running off again.

I raised a hand to my mouth to cover the laughter threatening to erupt. I couldn't look at Keane, or I knew I would lose it, but I felt him laughing, too.

I whispered behind my hand. "You guys cause quite a stir, don't you?"

Keane grinned down at me. "How do you know he was talking about me? He could've been talking about you and your model friends."

I snorted and turned back to the hostess to try again. "As I was saying, I'm meeting three friends here tonight. I think the reservation is under Brianna."

The hostess still hadn't removed her gaze from Keane, and I almost waved my hand in front of her face. Keane turned to look behind him, giving the hostess a minute to gather herself.

"Oh. Ah, yes. They're on the outside patio." She gestured vaguely behind her before leaning against the podium again, sighing heavily as Keane turned back toward her.

I shook my head at her behavior and moved to find my way to the patio. Keane stopped me with a hand on my shoulder. "I'll walk with you."

"I thought you and the guys were going to show up later?"

"Change of plans."

"This wouldn't have anything to do with a certain Nixie, would it?"

"What do you think?"

I shook my head. "This will cause Jess and Cait to really flip."

"Should prove to be an interesting night, then." Keane flashed a smile at the hostess—who sighed again—before putting his hand on the middle of my back to guide me forward. I almost expected her to turn into Betty Boop and say, *What a lucky goyl.*

As we moved through the restaurant, people started to stare and whisper to each other. I just hoped we made it to our table before they started requesting autographs. I saw waiters and waitresses blocking the way so we could walk through. A few flashes went off around us, and I prayed my picture wouldn't end up in any local tabloids or strewn across the internet. For not being in the public eye much, Ethereal Mutation had a pretty huge fan base.

"Do you guys put up with this everywhere you go?"

"Pretty much. Just smile and wave, boys, smile and wave." I grinned as he quoted the penguins from the movie *Madagascar.* Apparently, even big, bad Vaimpír liked cartoons.

As soon as we reached the patio area, I saw my friends sitting in one corner while the rest of Keane's band sat at a table across from them. There was no one else around. Jess and Cait stared dreamily while the band members talked among themselves. I stopped just inside the door. Keane came up behind me and looked around. "What's the matter?"

"Just taking in the calm before the storm."

Chuckling, Keane pushed me into motion again. As he did, everyone turned toward us. My friends excitedly waved me over, not seeming to notice who was guiding me forward, while the band members of Ethereal Mutation looked on in amusement, knowing exactly what was happening. It didn't take long before my friends recognized my companion and stared in shocked amazement. I stood by the table, smiling.

"Hi, guys. What's up?" They continued to look between me and Keane. I pretended to be confused and looked around. "What's the matter?" After a few seconds of their continued shocked stares, I started to feel sorry for them and relented. "Okay, okay. Guys, this is Keane.

Keane, these are my friends: Jess, Caitlin, and Brianna." They all shook his hand in an almost dream-like state.

"Blue..."

I turned toward Brianna, the only one who seemed to have found her voice.

"Huh?"

"Can I talk to you for a second? Privately?"

Keane smiled and looked down at me. "I'll be over here with the guys."

As soon as I sat, my friends pulled me into a huddle.

"Do you want to explain yourself?" Brianna demanded.

I laughed. "Ease up, guys, it's no big deal."

"No big deal?" Jess squeaked. "You just happen to walk into the restaurant being escorted by the lead singer of one of the hottest yet mysterious bands around, and it's no big deal?"

I smiled patiently at her. "Uh-huh."

"Just how did you suddenly become so chummy with Mr. Hot and Sexy, anyway?" This came from an almost sullen Brianna.

My smile widened. "Actually, I met him last night. Tristan is old friends with the band."

"And you neglected to mention this fact earlier because...?"

I shrugged. "I really didn't think about it, to tell you the truth."

My friends were stunned. They didn't seem to know what to think of me or what to say. It was funny watching them floundering for once. They were usually so self-assured.

"Sooo..." I started as innocently as I could, carefully unwrapping my silverware from the napkin without looking at anyone. "You guys wouldn't be interested in meeting the rest of the band, would you?"

I thought Jess and Caitlin might expire on the spot—either that or have an orgasm. "Meet the rest of the band?" They both looked at each other.

"Uh-huh. Keane said he'd be happy to make the introductions if you'd like, but I understand if you don't want to." I changed the subject as they stared at me in utter disbelief. "What are you guys thinking of ordering?" I picked up my menu and pretended like I was deciding on my meal.

"Oooo, she's a mean one, isn't she?" I heard one of the band members whisper, causing me to grin. "I like her."

Brianna incredulously snatched the menu from my hands, and I quickly wiped the grin off my face. "You're thinking of food at a time like this?"

I stared at her, somewhat surprised. I expected this reaction from Jess and Caitlin, but Brianna? "Brianna, I never knew you had a thing for the band. And all this time, you've been pretending to make fun of Jess and Cait for their obsession. Shame on you." I wagged my finger at her playfully.

She guiltily looked around and shrugged defensively. "Yeah, so I kind of have a thing, too, okay?"

While Jess and Caitlin berated Brianna, I stood and walked over to where Keane sat with his band members. He slipped a familiar arm around my waist, and I thought I heard one of the girls sigh, causing me to giggle a little. They were so dramatic.

Keane grinned up at me. "This is the woman I've been telling you about, boys. Meet Blue. Blue, these are my bandmates and best friends. This is Mckile. He plays the bass guitar." Keane pointed to the tall man to his left, whose wavy black hair was so dark it seemed to reflect the light in blues and browns. His cheeks and chin were dusted with the same dark hair, leaving a slight five o'clock shadow, which did little to hide the dimple that peeked out as he smiled. Amused blue eyes met mine as he stood and shook my hand.

"We've heard all about you from Keane, Blue. I can't wait to hear the real story."

Keane slapped his shoulder good-naturedly, then pointed to the guy sitting across from him. "This here is Cullen. He's the drummer." A man of average height stood and took my hand. Height was the only average thing about him. His face was so stunningly perfect it looked like it had been chiseled from marble. He had high cheekbones accented by a strong chin, a wide mouth, and eyes so dark they almost look black.

Like Mckile, he sported a dark five o'clock shadow, making him look both cocky and sexy at the same time.

"Good to meet you, Blue. I can see why Keane wanted to scope you out alone first."

He grinned at Keane in a challenging way, but Keane only shook his head. "And last, but definitely not least, this is Ronan. He plays electric guitar, acoustic guitar, slide guitar, whatever we need."

Keane pointed to the gentleman to his right, who was just as good-looking as the other three men. I wondered if being a Vaimpír automatically meant you were beautiful. He sported curly blond hair that he kept a little long, light hazel eyes framed by long, thick eyelashes, and a crooked smile that was equal parts innocent and devilish. Not to be outdone by his bandmates, he took my hand, turned it, and placed a soft kiss on the back.

"It is a pleasure to finally meet you, Blue. I have to say, I am most definitely looking forward to protecting you."

I blushed under all the male attention. Before I melted into a puddle right there at their feet, I turned and walked back to my friends. Putting my hand on each of their shoulders, I introduced them. The men got up and brought their chairs to sit at the table with us.

I grinned at the girls, only feeling minutely guilty for lying to them. "I trust you won't mind that I invited them to join us."

Jess giggled into her hand. She had situated herself between Mckile and Cullen. "Not at all. This is such a wonderful surprise. Who would've thought I'd be having dinner with the band members from Ethereal Mutation when I got up this morning?"

Caitlin nodded distractedly. She still seemed a little shell-shocked as she sat between Cullen and Ronan. "I hope you don't mind our saying, but we've been fans since you started playing."

"Yeah, they used to drag Blue and me to every release party they could get us into." Brianna laughed while Jess and Caitlin glared at her, embarrassed. I just shook my head and grinned.

After our dinner came out, Keane casually suggested that we adjourn to the Market Street Saloon for some dancing after our meal. My friends all agreed excitedly, completely forgetting we were supposed to make this a girls' night out.

Keane winked at me, having seen my relief at their easy acquiescence. He leaned close to my ear. "See, what did I tell you?"

I rolled my eyes and nudged him in the ribs. "Showoff."

He grinned back unabashedly. "You think that's impressive? Wait until you see my smooth moves on the dance floor later."

# Chapter Six

I t was well after midnight by the time Keane and I made it back to my house. While I assured him I would be fine, he insisted on staying until closer to dawn.

"Really, Keane, all I'm going to be doing is sleeping."

"I have my orders." He spread his arms. "Besides, what if you have a nightmare or something? Someone has to be here to comfort you if that should happen."

I shook my head at him. "Goodnight, Keane."

"What, no kiss?"

I laughed softly as I went into my bedroom. It seemed I needed to find something to wear as pajamas tonight. No way was I sleeping naked with Keane sitting in the next room.

"Hey, I wouldn't mind at all if you slept naked!"

I shook my head and grinned despite myself. I'd have to remember that he could read my mind, even when I was blocking. After digging up a tank top that proclaimed *This shirt is booby-trapped!* and a pair of light cotton shorts, I brushed my teeth before sliding between the cool sheets with a sigh. After not sleeping much the previous night and all the activity today, I was exhausted. I turned onto my left side, tucking my arm under my pillow, and stared out at the ocean. My body relaxed as I watched the waves rolling in and out, but my mind was still moving a mile a minute. It kept running through all the events of the past two days, trying to come to terms with everything—damn ADHD. I wished there was a switch I could use to turn my brain off at night. My thoughts irrevocably kept bringing me back to Tristan and Keane. What was this energy bond I seemed to have with Tristan? What drew us to each other? And what about my reaction to exchanging blood with Keane? And how I could still feel him even now. It was all so confusing. It was hardly a surprise that my dreams were filled with a certain enigmatic Fairy King and a notably sexy Vaimpír when I finally did fall asleep.

A rumble of thunder brought me partially awake. Slitting my eyes open, I saw it was still dark out. I watched sleepily as lightning streaked across the sky, highlighting the waves crashing onto the beach. In the brief flashes of light, I thought I saw a figure standing there. Rising onto an elbow, my hair tangling around my face and shoulders, I leaned closer to the window and waited for the next flash. As the sky lit up again, I saw a man was indeed standing at the edge of the foaming water. He stared right at me, his eyes seeming to glow in the illuminated night. He took a step toward me, and a grin curled the edges of his lips. As the next band of lightning moved over his face, I saw his lips move. A soft, masculine murmur went through my mind, whispering my name. *"Blue."* A gasp escaped me as I scooted across the bed, almost falling off the edge in my haste.

Keane was beside me in an instant. "What is it, Blue?"

I grabbed him and wrapped my arms around his waist, burying my head against his chest. He held me close as I mumbled into his shirt front. "A man. There was a man on the beach. He was looking right at me, and he said my name. But not out loud. It was...it was in my mind." I shivered as I remembered his voice in my head.

Keane looked out the window as he rubbed his hand in slow circles on my back. "I don't see anyone now." He looked down at me. "Are you sure it wasn't a dream?"

I shook my head. "No, it was real." I felt his arms loosen, and I tightened mine. "Don't go. Don't leave me."

"Let me go out and take a look, make sure he's gone." He unlocked my arms from his waist and took my face in his hands, looking directly into my eyes. "I'll be right back. I won't let anything happen to you."

I took a deep breath and nodded. "Just hurry."

I lay down again, still unnerved. It wasn't long before Keane returned.

"Did you find him?"

He smiled reassuringly. "Hush now, nothing to worry about."

Walking over to the glass wall, Keane pulled the tracked curtain panels closed before standing next to the bed again.

"You okay? Think you'll be able to get back to sleep?"

"I don't know. Would...would you lie down with me?"

Keane smiled crookedly. "I knew you couldn't resist me."

I tried to smile but couldn't quite manage it. "Yeah, that's it."

"Scoot." He motioned for me to move over to the other side of the bed, then sank down on top of the comforter. Turning me so I was again lying on my left side, he adjusted the comforter so it wrapped fully around me, then pulled me back against his body and draped one strong arm over my waist. I didn't think I'd be able to fall back asleep, but after a few minutes in his secure embrace, I felt myself drifting off. Just before I fell asleep, I thought I felt his lips press gently against the top of my head, and I smiled softly.

❧

Sunlight peeking through the back curtain panels brought me slowly awake. Opening first one eye and then the other, I rolled over onto my back and stretched my arms.

"Good morning, sleeping beauty."

I jolted upright in bed at the cheerful male voice. Looking through a curtain of tangled hair, I spotted a form lounging in the doorway. "Cedric?" I pushed my hair away from my face as he grinned at me. "What are you doing here? Wait, how did you get in?"

"I'm supposed to keep you company today, and Keane let me in."

"Keane?" I was a little befuddled, my brain still trying to bring me to full wakefulness.

"Yeah, you know, blond hair, blue eyes, sharp fangs?" He held his pointer fingers up to his mouth, crooked at the knuckle, and hissed at me.

I laughed, then sobered when I remembered last night's events. Something must have shown on my face because Cedric uncoiled from the doorway and moved to sit on the bed, taking my hand. "What's the matter, Blue?"

I sighed and told him about the man I had seen last night. Cedric shook his head, not seeming surprised. "Keane told me about that. I sure wish I knew what was going on."

"Me, too. What time is it anyway?"

Cedric glanced at his watch. "Ten-thirty."

"Ten-thirty!" I stared at him aghast. "I had a client scheduled for a photoshoot at eight." I started struggling out of the tangle my sheets had become. "Shit, shit, shit..."

Cedric chuckled as he watched me. "Don't worry. Keane already rescheduled all your appointments for today."

I stopped trying to get up. "But how did he know?"

Cedric shrugged and shook his head.

"Still, you shouldn't have let me sleep this late." I went back to working on the sheets that had me imprisoned.

"Sometimes, your body needs that extra bit to heal itself, and it looked like you could use the sleep." He rubbed a thumb under my eye.

"They're back? I thought Keane took care of them last night?" I raised a hand to my face self-consciously.

Cedric narrowed his eyes. "What do you mean 'Keane took care of them?'"

I waved offhandedly. "Just a demonstration of the power of Vaimpír blood." Finally managing to untangle myself from the sheets, I went into my bathroom and turned on the shower. Walking back into the bedroom, I saw Cedric still sitting on the bed, seeming to mull something over. "So, you're my babysitter for today?"

Cedric looked up at me with an amused smirk. "Yeah, I pulled the short straw."

"Hey!" I put my hands on my hips and glared indignantly at him.

He just laughed. "Just kidding. I actually volunteered to come over. Much to Tristan's consternation." Standing, he headed toward the living room. "After your shower, we'll go out and get some breakfast. I was going to make you something before you woke up, but it seems someone robbed you of all your groceries and only left the ones a little on the green side."

I grinned sheepishly. "Yeah, I'm not much of a cook. I tend to eat out a lot."

Cedric waved me toward the bathroom. "Go on, go take your shower, and then we'll decide where to eat."

❦

An hour and a half later, I slumped back in my chair at the Lost Dog Café and covered my stomach. "I'm stuffed."

Cedric shook his head at me and crossed his arms over his chest, leaning his elbows on the table. "It's no wonder. I've never seen a woman who can eat like you do." He indicated the many empty dishes on our table with a nod.

I looked at him through narrowed eyes. "You'd better mean that in the best possible way."

Cedric uncrossed his arms and raised his hands in self-defense. "I think it's awesome. Most girls I go out with are so afraid of ruining their figures or what I might think they nibble through one or two bites and then claim they're full. It's actually refreshing to eat with someone whose appetite matches mine."

I smiled and patted my stomach. "I'm definitely not afraid of food. But of course, you know there are consequences to eating all of that." Cedric gave me a questioning look, not quite sure where I was going. "Now we have to put in equal amounts of exercise."

Shaking his head, Cedric stood and reached over, pulling me to my feet. "I'm not much for exercise."

109

I eyed him incredulously. "Are you serious?" I looked him up and down. "'Cause it certainly looks like you do something to me."

Cedric grinned down at me. "I'll take that as a compliment. But, honestly, being Fae has its advantages when it comes to one's physique."

I frowned. "Are you telling me you can eat as much as you want and don't gain an ounce?"

He nodded his head, his grin widening. "Yup."

I rolled my eyes toward the ceiling. "Why couldn't I have been born a Wolf?"

Cedric chuckled. "Something tells me you probably don't need to do much of anything either."

"Are you serious? I've worked my butt off since I was a kid to make sure I didn't gain weight."

"Have you ever tried not doing anything?"

I thought about it. "Honestly? No. Growing up, my mom was a bit of a health nut, always making sure I ate right and exercised plenty. And that just kind of moved over into my adult life."

"I'd venture to say if you suddenly stopped exercising, you'd find you don't have much of an issue either. Most Fae have accelerated metabolisms that require higher food consumption and a lot less exercise to maintain."

I furrowed my brow at him, not quite believing. "Are you telling me I've worked my butt off for years to maintain a figure that would've maintained itself?"

"Uh...yes?" He looked at me uncertainly.

Without a word, I stomped past him and off the front porch. "Blue! Blue, wait."

Cedric quickly handed the waitress her tip and ran after me. "Blue, I'm sorry. I didn't mean to upset you."

I swung up into my Jeep and looked at him with a sigh. "You didn't upset me, Cedric. It was more my upbringing. My mom was pretty brutal about my weight growing up, swearing I was getting fat and making me either starve myself or work out like a maniac. Probably more of her own insecurities being pushed onto me. I was never allowed to eat like I wanted—like my body *needed*. I was always too afraid of gaining weight or disappointing my mom to really notice the side effects it caused."

"Like severe lethargy, slow brain function, and muscle cramps?"

I nodded. "Yeah. It wasn't until my mom left and I visited a doctor at my friend's behest. I found out my body needs more calories than most people. I'm wondering now if the guy was Fae and knew what was going on."

"Definitely could have been."

"Even though I figured that part out, I've still been a fanatic about exercise, though I hate every minute of it."

Cedric smiled. "Which, of course, means you have to eat even more to compensate."

I gave him a hesitant smile. "Yeah, I guess you're right. Either way, the exercise is still good for my mind. I find if I don't run, swim, or do something, I can't sleep at night."

"ADHD?"

I looked at him curiously. "Does it show?"

He laughed. "Only a little. Plus, it's very common in certain types of Fae."

Starting up my Jeep, I put it in reverse and backed out of the spot. Before I put it in first, I looked at Cedric. "This conversation never happened, right?"

He smiled conspiratorially. "What conversation?"

Even though Cedric said I didn't need to exercise, I still wasn't entirely convinced he was telling the truth. I managed to talk him into a quick run on the beach. Or perhaps he agreed because he wasn't supposed to let me out of his sight. Either way, it was nice to finally be able to run at a blistering pace and have someone keep up with me. Brianna, bless her heart, was a great partner to talk to, but I always had to slow myself to accommodate her. On the other hand, it appeared Cedric could run forever without tiring.

*Must be a Wolf thing.*

"See, what did I tell you? Don't you feel better?" I put my hands on my knees, taking in deep breaths and wiping the sweat from my face with a small towel I'd brought.

He laughed as he climbed the back steps, hardly seeming out of breath at all. "I don't know if *better* would be the way I'd describe it, but..." His words tapered off as he turned toward the door. It was hanging half-open, the lock on it in shreds. Putting out a hand to stop me, he lightly sniffed the air. "Nixies!" His voice came out as a deep growl. "You stay out here while I check the inside of the house. I don't think they're still here, but better safe than sorry."

"Uh-uh, no way. Have you ever watched a horror flick? It's always the brunette who is the first to die. They never kill the blondes."

Cedric laughed, seeming unable to help himself. Shaking his head, he leaned back and looked at me. "You think of the weirdest things at the strangest times. I never know what you're going to say."

I grinned. "Oh, you don't know half of what goes on in my brain."

He shook his head again and took my hand. "Okay. Together, then. I'll try to keep us alive in the front with my blondness, and you bring up the rear and try not to let your brunetteness get us killed."

I nodded, still smiling. Together, we quietly moved into the house. After the bright sunlight from outside, it was notably darker inside since the shades were still drawn, and it took my eyes a second to adjust. When they did, I let out a small cry of outrage. Someone had taken the time we'd been away to ransack my house. Books and papers were strewn all over the floor. Furniture was overturned. Even my paintings had been taken from the walls and were lying haphazardly about. Letting go of Cedric's hand, I ran over to where the surfboard coffee table had been turned over and frantically searched for Riona and Iridia. Thankfully, I found them a short moment later and let out a sigh of relief. I wasn't sure why, but the thought of losing those two pieces was devastating. Thinking about my sculptures, I turned to where the one of me had been sitting. It was odd, but that table was the only one still standing upright...and it was completely empty. Surging to my feet, I scanned the room, not seeing the sculpture anywhere.

Cedric returned after making a full circuit of the house. He seemed satisfied it was empty of villains and would-be assassins. "I don't get it. What were they looking for?" He righted the couch, which had been turned over. "They didn't touch the TV or the other electronics. They even left our laptops."

Without answering, I went through the house, moving things around, frantically searching, but came up with nothing.

Cedric noted my distress and grabbed me by the shoulders. "What is it, Blue?"

"They stole the sculpture."

"What sculpture?"

"The one Brody did of me." I stepped out of his grip and flopped onto the couch.

Cedric turned to the table where my sculpture had been, his eyebrows drawing together. "Why would they break in and ransack your house, only to steal a statue in plain sight? I don't get it."

"I don't know."

He turned back to me, his hands resting on his hips, and a distracted look on his face. "I called Tristan. He's on his way over now. Maybe he'll be able to offer more insight."

I wanted to put my head in my hands and cry, but I resisted the urge. I would not give in. That's what someone wanted. They wanted to break me, reduce me to a shell. Invading my sleep, my home, my privacy. I wasn't going to stand for it. Not able to sit still, I got up and began putting things back in order. By the time Tristan arrived, I had the house looking almost normal.

He stepped through the door with two men trailing behind him. "Blue." He came over and wrapped his arms around me. "I'm so sorry."

I shook my head. "It's not your fault. Someone has a personal vendetta here. We just need to figure out what it's all about."

Nodding, Tristan stepped back. Turning to the two men who had come in with him, he gestured left and then right, saying nothing. As I watched, the two were suddenly on all fours, hair sprouting from their skin, bones crunching and re-arranging. In a matter of seconds, two large Wolves stood where the men had been. And by *large*, I meant enormous. They had to be the size of grizzly bears. I turned to Cedric, who had walked up to stand behind me.

"Trackers. The best of the best," he told me.

I looked at him in awe. "Is that what you go through to transform every time?"

He shrugged as he watched the two Wolves. "It happens so fast, it doesn't even faze me anymore. When you're young and new to it, it can be quite difficult, but the older you get, the easier it becomes."

Noting the two men—well, *Wolves*—now moving through my house, swiftly seeming to take in everything at once, I could almost imagine Cedric in his Wolf form. The color of the men's hair in human form had carried over to their pelt colors. So, that meant Cedric would be a light blond or white Wolf when he changed.

I looked at Cedric and raised an eyebrow. "Are you going to Wolf out now, too?"

He chuckled in amusement. "Curious? No, not today. As I said, these guys are the best of the best." He pointed to the caramel-colored Wolf snaking his way through the kitchen. "That's Talib. And that,"—he pointed to the black Wolf coming out of my bedroom—"is Olwen."

Both Wolves turned and nodded their shaggy heads at me upon hearing their names, seeming to acknowledge Cedric's introductions. As I watched the Wolves moving about, I noticed how they appeared to work as one. Their movements almost seemed choreographed. When one moved from a room, the other was only steps behind.

"They'll find out who did this, Blue. Don't worry."

I turned at Tristan's voice with a soft smile. "I'm not worried. Should I call the police, too? Or do you think this is strictly Fae politics?"

"Leave the humans out of this for now, if you would. I have a strong suspicion it is Fae-related. More specifically, *Sethos*-related."

I nodded, having thought as much myself. Tristan moved to sit on the couch and shared a look with Cedric, who immediately stepped out the front door, a cell phone already to his ear.

"I want you to come and stay with me for a while, Blue."

Sighing, I sat down next to him. "Do you really think that's necessary?" He arched an eyebrow and looked around the room pointedly. "Maybe this was a one-off thing. Maybe they got what they came for."

Tristan shook his head. "I don't think so. I think someone sent the Nixies who were here for you. When they couldn't find you, they took something that was linked to you so they could use it later for another try."

"What about my friends? Do you think they'll be in danger, too?" I still hadn't managed to broach the subject of the Fae with them, and I'd hoped to avoid it for a while longer.

"I've already arranged for them to be called away for some unexpected work. You should probably be hearing from them soon, telling you they have to leave."

I nodded, relieved that I wouldn't have to worry about them and not even questioning how he had managed to do it. "Do I have time to take a shower before we need to go?"

"Of course. I have a few arrangements to make back at Dock Street before you arrive anyway. I will leave you in Cedric's capable hands." He grimaced after saying that last part, causing me to chuckle. "I'll leave him to watch over you, anyway."

Reaching over, I took one of his arms and drew him closer to me. Leaning forward until my lips were almost touching his, I whispered softly, "You don't have to worry about Cedric. He and I are just friends."

"If I had a dime for every time I've heard that..."

A smile flitted across my mouth as I threaded my fingers through his soft curls, tugging his head down to mine. Our lips met, and the fire that always seemed to consume us when we touched rose. On a moan, Tristan deepened the kiss, sliding his tongue between my teeth to stroke the inside of my mouth. I reflexively tightened my grip on his hair and angled my head to give him better access. One of his arms encircled my back, pulling me tightly against him, while the other slid under my damp hair to cradle my neck. As our lips parted for us each to take a breath, I opened my eyes to gaze into his. His eyes had gone an even deeper blue, appearing almost black now, and his gaze seemed to hold the same overwhelming desire I felt. I tracked a shiver working its way down my spine to pool as liquid heat at my core.

"Do you realize how much I want you?" His voice was a husky growl.

"Probably as much as I want you."

He shook his head. "Blue, I…" He was interrupted as the black Wolf, Olwen, padded in through the back door, followed closely by Talib. Tristan sighed and, with a look filled with regret, dropped his hands and stood. "I must go. I will see you later when you get to Dock Street, won't I?" His question was hesitant, as if he weren't sure I'd want to see him again.

I smiled and nodded. "Of course. I expect you to give me the grand tour when I get there."

Standing, I walked him to the front door. Cedric opened it before we got there, and I saw a black Range Rover parked in the driveway with both the front and back doors open. The Wolves immediately jumped into the back, and a man wearing a pair of shorts, a red graphic T-shirt, and sandals of all things, shut the door. It was such an unexpected sight that I laughed. He winked and waved when he saw me looking at him.

Tristan looked down at me. "That's Paul. He plays chauffer for me sometimes."

"Interesting uniform."

Tristan grinned crookedly. "Yeah, he likes to dress casually. He says it helps him blend in better."

I nodded in amusement. Walking to the edge of the front deck, I stopped by the stairs while Tristan continued to the first step. Before descending farther, he turned to me and cupped the back of my head, pulling my mouth down for a quick, hot kiss. Breathless, I straightened and stared after his retreating figure. He gracefully swung himself into the front of the Range Rover, and Paul shut the door for him. As they drove off, he waved out the open window before shutting himself behind the opaque black glass. I watched until the SUV was out of sight, then turned back toward the house.

Cedric was still standing at the front door, wearing an unreadable expression. "You should probably pack for an extended stay."

I nodded and stepped back into the house's cool interior. Cedric followed me in and shut the door.

"You can use the guest bathroom to grab a quick shower if you'd like. There should be soap and towels in there. And I think I have a pair of sweats and a T-shirt that will fit you. Look in the drawers in the room to the left." As I walked toward my bedroom, I noticed that Cedric had yet to move. Turning back toward him, I gave him a questioning look. "You okay?"

"Are you in love with Tristan?"

"Am I what?" I looked at him incredulously.

"Are you in love with Tristan?"

I sighed. "No, but I don't think it would be hard to do." Without further comment, I went into my room to shower and pack.

# Chapter Seven

The ride to Dock Street was a silent one, at least as far as conversation went. Cedric seemed to be lost in his thoughts, so I let him be. He had insisted on driving my Jeep, so I sat in the passenger seat. My sneakered foot hung out the side, idly tapping out the rhythm of the song playing on the radio on the tube bar, while a soft breeze ruffled my hair like a caress. I was glad we had decided to leave the top down and the doors off. It was extremely relaxing.

I watched the scenery flow by through half-closed eyes, my mind wandering to the two sculptures carefully wrapped in the back seat. I'd insisted on bringing Riona and Iridia along, fearing Sethos' goons would come back and steal them next. Cedric had argued at first but then conceded that they didn't take up much room, so what did it really matter? I didn't know why I felt such a connection to the two Fairies, but I did. It was odd. You'd think with Riona having been Tristan's wife at one time, I would feel animosity toward her, especially since I wasn't sure if he had really gotten over her death. But whenever her sculpture was near, all I felt was a calming influence. Like she was sitting with me and giving me her approval.

I must have drifted off for a bit because the next thing I knew, we were turning into the parking garage near the theater. Cedric pressed the button for a ticket, and when the gate in front of us swung up, he pulled to the right. Instead of going up the ramps as I thought he would, he backed into a parking spot marked *Reserved* along the far wall.

"Wow, front-row parking?"

"Not exactly." I watched as he reached over to a small panel situated next to the Jeep and pressed his palm against it before drawing those weird clockwise circles and swirling patterns with his left hand.

"Just what is that?"

"What is what?"

"What you just did on that pad, with the circles and such."

"Oh. It's a magical passcode of sorts. We magically lock certain places so unsuspecting humans can't accidentally come across our passageways."

"So, if anyone does that pattern, it will let them in?"

"No, it also takes a fingerprint. That's why you have to start it by placing your palm flat."

Just about then, the ground beneath the Jeep jerked and started to lower. "Whoa!" I grabbed the roll bar.

Cedric looked over at me with a grin. "Hang on, we're going down."

"Thanks for the warning." My voice was practically dripping in sarcasm, but he just laughed.

Before long, we faced what was obviously their underground garage. As soon as the Jeep left the metal plate disguised as a parking spot, it began to ascend again. After watching it for a moment, I turned back to Cedric. "Hasn't anyone ever noticed that going up and down?"

"No, it's glamoured."

"Glamoured?"

"Yeah. A spell that hides something's true nature from prying eyes. To anyone passing by, it will just look like a reserved parking spot with an SUV in it that has the theater's logo on it."

"Huh. There's so much I don't know about this new world."

Cedric reached over and took my hand. "Don't worry, you'll get it."

After giving it a squeeze, I nodded and removed my hand from his, putting mine back on my lap. Looking around, it surprised me how bright it was for being underground—it almost seemed like it was lit by sunlight. Cedric, noting I was looking up at what appeared to be skylights, pointed to them. "They're magicked. We're actually about twenty-five feet below ground right now."

"That's incredible."

"Our entire town is lit that way to make it look as though we're not belowground. The light even changes with the natural light outside to show the passage of time."

I shook my head in amazement. It was like I had stepped into the pages of a *Harry Potter* novel. As we approached what looked like an elevator, Cedric slowed to a stop. Putting the parking brake on, he climbed out of the Jeep and grabbed my suitcase, camera bag, and the two sculptures from the back.

"I'm going to leave you here and then go park. That way, you don't have to walk."

I nodded, though I didn't mind walking. I was a bit nervous, actually. This was all so new. Not to mention, the last time I had been here, I hadn't exactly been welcomed with open arms.

Seeming to sense my unease, Cedric came around. After setting my bags and sculptures down, he helped me out of the Jeep. He smiled crookedly down at me, his hands on my shoulders. "You'll be fine, don't worry. Besides, I called someone I believe you are already well acquainted with to escort you."

He stepped aside just as the elevator door opened and, leaning arrogantly against its interior grinning at me, was none other than Keane Rutherman. "Hey, gorgeous."

"Keane!"

His grin widened at my enthusiastic greeting. "Miss me?" He straightened and came over. Reaching down, he ran a thumb under one of my eyes, shaking his head. "Back again?"

I shrugged. "I guess I'm still having trouble sleeping."

With a glance at Cedric, Keane grinned mischievously and leaned closer to my ear. "That's funny because you slept just fine while I was in bed with you last night."

Cedric's expression turned thunderous at hearing Keane's comment, which, of course, had been Keane's intent. "In bed with her? You were supposed to be guarding her!"

I turned to Cedric and shook my head with a smile. "Don't listen to him. He's just trying to get a reaction out of you. It wasn't like that." I pushed Cedric toward the Jeep. "Go. Take care of Orange Blossom. Make sure she gets treated extra special. This being-away-from-home stuff makes her nervous."

"Huh? Who's Orange Blossom?"

"My Jeep. That's her name."

Cedric relaxed and smiled, looking down at me as I pushed against his chest—ineffectively, I might add—trying to get him to move in the Jeep's direction. "Why are you talking about it like it's a living thing?"

"Uh. Don't you dare call her an *it*!" I reached over and hugged the fender. "It's all right, baby."

Keane looked at Cedric and raised an eyebrow. "She talks to her Jeep."

Cedric shrugged, sharing an amused look with Keane. "Makes you wonder what else she's named and given personalities to."

Keane chuckled, and after slanting an impish look my way, he turned partially away. "Ask her about Pinky and the Brain sometime."

"Hey! That's not fair. I didn't even introduce you to them." He only knew about their names due to his little excursion through my thoughts the last time we'd been together.

Keane grinned, then reached down and grabbed my suitcase and the sculptures before handing me my camera bag. "Come on, babe. Tristan is waiting for you downstairs."

I reached over and squeezed Cedric's shoulder before following Keane into the elevator. As the doors shut, I glanced back at Cedric, who was staring after me with that same unreadable expression he'd been wearing a lot lately.

"He's interested in you, you know."

I glanced over at Keane, who was once again leaning against the elevator wall, his legs crossed at the ankles. "Why do you say that?" My eyes were involuntarily drawn to his long fingers, which absently tapped out a rhythm on the handle of my suitcase. I doubted he even knew he was doing it. My hand drifted to my pulse point as I remembered his fingers sliding along the column of my neck. Shivering at the thought, I yanked my gaze away.

"Call it a man's intuition." His voice had taken on a deeper tone, and I felt rather than saw him move. Before I knew it, he was standing directly in front of me. I slowly raised my eyes to his, knowing what I'd see even before I looked. Bits of red were quickly filtering into his gaze, and his fangs had lengthened until they touched his bottom lip.

My mouth went dry as he continued to stare down at me. "What do you think I should do about it?" I knew we weren't talking about Cedric anymore.

"I think..." He lifted a hand and lightly traced it along my cheek before sliding it around behind my neck to pull my lips almost to his. "That you should do what feels right."

Before I could even take another breath, his mouth was against mine, hard and demanding. He wrapped one of his hands around the back of my neck, holding my head still while the other rested loosely on my waist as if waiting. Without thought, I dropped my bag and wrapped my arms around his neck, pulling him closer and fitting my body to his. He growled his approval and snaked his other arm around my back, almost crushing me against his chest. As he slid his tongue across my bottom lip, I opened to him.

He didn't hesitate. He dove in—tasting, taking. His tongue stroked mine, almost demanding a response and causing my heart rate to skyrocket. His breath hissed between his teeth as his heightened Vaimpír senses picked up on it. Bravely, I slid my tongue along one of his fangs. I felt him shiver in response before he guided me roughly backward. I soon found myself pushed against the elevator wall. Never breaking our contact, he reached down and picked me up. I wrapped my legs around his waist and felt his erection press against me through the thin fabric of my shorts. It made me moan into his mouth. He growled in response and pressed harder. Liquid heat immediately pooled between my thighs, and I whimpered. He thrust against my most sensitive part, his hips flexing with each movement. In response, I pushed my hips forward to meet him, gripping him tightly with my thighs. His mouth left mine and trailed a hot path down my neck toward my pulse point. My breath came in short pants and gasps as sensations racked my body and anticipation sang through my blood. I wanted nothing more than to feel him buried deep inside me while his fangs slid into my neck, connecting us in the most intimate way possible. Keane reached between us to undo the snap on his jeans, hearing my thoughts before I could even voice them.

Before he could finish unzipping his pants, though, a beeping alarm sounded, causing us both to freeze. After a second, Keane slumped against me, his forehead resting against the curve of my shoulder. "Shit."

"What is it?" I was still digging my way through the passionate haze that held me.

"To get to Tristan's private quarters, you have to enter a passcode."

I raised my eyebrows. "We're going to Tristan's private quarters?"

"Of course. Where did you think he'd have you stay?"

"I didn't really think about it, to tell you the truth." I mimicked a nasal voice. "Tristan's rooms for wayward Fae, floor two."

Keane chuckled, then groaned when the action brushed his hard-on against me again. "Maybe they won't notice if we hang here for a little longer."

The mention of Tristan had brought me back to my senses. I couldn't believe I had been kissing him only hours ago, and now I was on the brink of having sex with another man. What was wrong with me? Sensing my sudden mood change and the reason behind it, Keane sighed. Lowering me to the floor, he made sure to slide my body against his entire length, holding me there for a moment before stepping back. After adjusting himself, he turned and punched a code into the elevator panel, causing the car to descend again. I hadn't even realized it had stopped.

Keane leaned against the wall with his hands behind him and grinned at me. I avoided his gaze and readjusted my clothing, still trying to come to terms with what had happened. What was it about this man that set my motor running so hot and made me forget about everything, including my morals? Seeing Riona and Iridia on the floor where Keane had dropped them, I leaned down and picked them up.

Shaking his head, Keane straightened, letting me have my way about ignoring what had just happened. "Since me and the boys have to guard both you and Tristan, we figured it would be easier if you were sleeping in the same area, hence Tristan's living quarters."

"I'd forgotten you guys were Tristan's personal guardians." I thoughtfully stared down at the figures in my hands before something occurred to me. "Wait a minute. I thought you were his night guardians. How are you awake at this time of day?"

"Still believing in the myths created by Hollywood?" He grinned. "Unlike movie vampires, Vaimpír don't have to sleep during the day. We do, however, have to avoid prolonged exposure to sunlight. So, working at night only makes sense when we need to move about topside. That doesn't mean that is the only time we are on duty."

"When do you sleep, then?"

"When we need it."

"Do you sleep like normal humans? Eight hours a day?"

"No, we're usually good with sleeping every three or four days for a few hours. Depending on how well we've fed and if we have any injuries we're recovering from."

"Huh."

We rode the few remaining floors in silence. When the doors finally slid open, I grabbed my camera bag and stepped out onto a plush tan carpet, finding we were in a large living area. It was oval and probably big enough to accommodate my entire house. The room had been divided into smaller living spaces using different groupings of furniture and small area rugs. The center of the room contained a cluster of couches and chairs, all done in masculine brown leather, ringing a large oval table made of oak. Directly to my right was a well-used, L-shaped desk with a large monitor mounted to the wall above it. Though there seemed to be a lot of information there, the surface was neatly organized, leaving the main space clear to work on. To my left was a small grouping of oversized chairs and loungers done in cozy browns and greens, all interspersed with soft lighting as if inviting you to sit and read. Behind the chairs were rows of bookshelves that sloped with the oval walls, and each was filled to capacity.

Looking to the far left of the room, I saw a huge slate fireplace with what had to be the largest television I had ever seen mounted above it. The couch was dark blue and easily big enough to seat an entire football team. To the far right was a slightly smaller TV, and by *smaller,* I mean it was probably still twice the size of any television in my house. It sat on a low oak entertainment cabinet with several game systems hooked up to it. Situated on the coordinating leather chairs surrounding the TV were Tristan's personal guardians: Mckile, Cullen, and Ronan, also known as Ethereal Mutation. Battling each other in some shoot 'em-up game, they hollered and called out insults good-naturedly, causing me to smile.

As if sensing our entrance, or more likely hearing the ding of the elevator, they paused in their game and turned toward us. I walked over, needing to put a bit of distance between Keane and me. After looking between the two of us—to which Keane just shrugged—they greeted me like a long-lost friend.

All three enveloped me in bear hugs, which resulted in my feet leaving the floor more than once. After turning down multiple offers to join their game and listening to them heckle me about turning them down, Keane escorted me, still smiling, through a door set back in the wall.

"The bedchambers are through here. There's another door on the other side of the living area, through which are the workout rooms, saunas, and the pool."

"Tristan has a private pool down here?"

"Of course. What do you expect? He's the King."

I kept forgetting that fact. Looking down the long hallway, I saw three doors on either side, with a large set of double doors facing us at the very end. As we passed the open doorways, I glanced in and saw bedrooms in varying colors. "Whose rooms are these?"

"They're guest rooms, though they get very little use. Sometimes, me and the boys use them when we're on guard duty and need some downtime, but otherwise, they're empty."

"Weren't Riona's brother and sister supposed to be staying here?" I remembered that from the conversation the other night at the Market Street Saloon.

"They're one floor up on the normal guest floor. Tristan doesn't like them to be too close."

"Reminds him too much of her?"

Keane shook his head. "No, Tatiana has a way of sneaking into Tristan's bed at night."

"Oh."

"Tatiana always wanted Tristan for herself and was rather pissed when her father married her sister to him instead. She kept her distance while Riona was alive, but since Riona's death...let's just say Tatiana has been quite the handful."

"I take it Tristan has no interest in sleeping with her?"

"No. Definitely not."

By this time, we had come to the door closest to what I assumed was the main bedroom. Keane opened it and stepped back. "You'll be staying here."

As I walked into the room, I instinctively knew it had been Riona's. It was a large chamber painted in a soft brown suede finish, containing a four-poster Queen-size bed done in all different shades of purple from the bedding to the drapery hanging around it. A large white triple mirror stood in one corner with a small pedestal situated in front of it, obviously for fitting the Queen's clothes. A small white writing desk was on the wall closest to the door, paper and writing utensils still neatly stacked on its surface. To the left of the bed was a set of double doors that opened to a huge walk-in closet, which was still filled with clothes, shoes, and accessories as if the Queen were still around.

There was also a closed door to the right of the bed. Keane pointed to it. "The bathroom is through there, though keep in mind you share it with Tristan."

Keane put my suitcase on the bed. "Speaking of Tristan, I'm going to go let him know you're here. If you need anything, just give a holler to any of the guys in the living room."

I nodded absently as I walked around, taking everything in. I wondered why Tristan had decided to put me in Riona's room, especially since there were five other bedrooms. Keane left while I was exploring the enormous walk-in closet. Glad for the distraction as my thoughts were still jumbled with visions of Keane and me in the elevator, I lovingly ran my hands over the custom-made evening dresses hanging there, appreciating the intricacy that had gone into creating each one. They really were beautiful.

Riona hadn't always worn those types of clothes, though, as there were also jeans, slacks, skirts, T-shirts, and blouses in all different colors and styles. On one wall, I saw row upon row of shoes and figured the late Queen had had a bit of a shoe fetish. I noted absently that we wore the same size. Smiling in amusement, I opened a few drawers mounted between the racks of clothes and saw all types of accessories, from sunglasses to hair bands and even some jewelry. One drawer, though, held pictures. Lifting the top one out, I stared at it. It was of a beautiful young man leaning casually against a tree, a lit cigarette clasped loosely in his fingers, the smoke curling up from it to frame his head. He had shining golden-blond hair tossed rakishly over one eye while the other eye, a striking green in color, seemed to stare into the camera with a soulful look. I wasn't sure exactly why, but something about him seemed vaguely familiar.

"His name was Larkin."

I whirled around, my heart jumping into my throat and the picture slipping from my grasp to float to the floor.

"Oh, Tristan. I'm sorry, I didn't mean..."

He stooped down to pick up the picture, a sad smile on his face. After looking at it briefly, he moved to put it back in the drawer. "He was Riona's true love. The man she always wanted to marry. But her father wouldn't let her."

"Tristan, you don't have to..."

He shook his head. "No, I want you to know. You see, Riona was the daughter of the King of the Fernsong Clan, and as such, royalty. On the other hand, Larkin was an orphan brought into their clan as a teenager. While she was all proper etiquette, the perfect Princess, he was a rebel, the ultimate bad boy. It was love at first sight." Tristan laughed softly at the memory. "Riona and I were friends even back then. Having both been brought up under royal flags, we spent a lot of time together. I remember her going to her father and begging him to let her marry Larkin, but he would have none of it. As you can imagine, royal offspring were more often brought into the world to be used as political pawns rather than just to have children.

"Riona was devastated. Larkin tried to convince her to run away with him and elope, but she was too devoted to the people. She wanted to rule one day, to make a difference. So, she let Larkin go." Tristan sighed deeply. "It was the hardest decision she ever made. Angry at her for choosing the people over him, Larkin left the Fernsong Clan and disappeared. It broke Riona's heart to see him go, but she knew it was for the best. After a few years, our fathers proposed a marriage between Riona and me to solidify their alliance. Having already come to care for each other as friends, and knowing we had similar views when it came to the people, we both decided we might come to love each other over time. We were married and eventually crowned King and Queen of the Moon Tree Clan.

"Though we tried, we never really connected on a physical level. Eventually, we decided we would be married in name only and would give each other the space to live separate personal lives if we wanted, hence the separate bedrooms. I think Riona always secretly hoped Larkin would come back to her. Eventually, he did, though she didn't realize how bitter he had become and that his sole purpose for returning was for revenge and not love." Tristan sighed again, this time with disgust. "Larkin had somehow ended up with the Misty River Clan after leaving. A rough and tumble group looking to further their small territory any way they could. Somehow, Larkin convinced Sethos, their King, to attack the Fernsong Clan, not realizing they had allied themselves with us. So, of course, when war broke out, the Misty River Clan was seriously outnumbered. Larkin soon discovered not only was the Fernsong Clan allied with the Moon Tree Clan, but the Queen of the Moon Tree Clan was none other than his former beloved, Riona.

"Angered his plan for revenge had been thwarted, he then concocted a scheme to kidnap Riona to use as a hostage. Not realizing Larkin was now a part of our enemy, Riona welcomed him with open arms. Over the course of several weeks, Larkin wooed her and eventually gained her full trust. So much so that she let him convince her to go out into the woods for a tryst during a time of war without even a single guard."

Tristan shook his head. "I should've seen what was happening. There were so many signs I ignored. I was just so glad to see her happy that I went against my instincts. Sethos' army was waiting in the grove where she was supposed to meet Larkin, and they took her captive. We received the demand to lay down arms shortly after. I couldn't believe it. I sent out our network of spies to find out what had occurred, but by the time they figured it out, Riona was dead. To this day, no one knows exactly what happened. After we defeated the Misty River Clan, we demanded they return her body to us. She looked perfect—there wasn't a mark on her. Our physicians couldn't figure out what killed her. It was like her heart just gave out."

"Perhaps she died of a broken heart."

Tristan smiled derisively. "A sentimental notion, to be sure." He shut the drawer on the pictures and looked at me, his eyes full of self-loathing and guilt. "She died because of my inability to take care of her when she needed me the most. I should have known Larkin was up to no good and made sure she had double, even triple, the guards."

"You know as well as I do that it wouldn't have made a difference. Riona was her own person, and as such, she was going to do exactly what she wanted regardless of what anyone thought."

Tristan shrugged. "Maybe." Turning, he walked out of the closet.

I followed and shut the doors behind us, wishing I could close the doors on the past just as easily. I leaned against them and watched as Tristan walked over to the bed and picked up the wrapped sculptures.

"You brought them with you?"

"I was afraid someone would come back and steal them, too. I don't know why, but something keeps pulling me to them." Walking over, I carefully unwrapped both sculptures and, after looking around, decided to put them on the small nightstand next to the bed.

Tristan stared unseeingly at the sculptures a moment before turning back to me. "How about that tour I promised you?"

Hours later, I found myself sitting in a small café with Tristan, drinking cappuccinos on what appeared to be a Parisian market street. A guard stood unobtrusively along the wall nearby, seeming to watch everything. He wasn't one of the Vaimpír, but something about him seemed just as feral. If I had to guess, I'd say he was a Wolf.

Taking my eyes off the watchful man, I looked at Tristan. "I still can't believe all of this is down here."

He had walked me over only a small portion of the underground world the Fae had created. Just as Cedric had said, there were shops, movie theaters, schools, restaurants, you name it, and each had been magicked to appear as if they were on outdoor streets placed around the world or in malls several floors high. Some were even set in different time periods. All you had to do was step through the right door. I'd actually compared it to the Holodeck they used to have on the *Star Trek: The Next Generation* shows, but Tristan had had no idea what I was talking about.

"I'm going to need a map to find my way around this place." I took another sip of the most delicious cappuccino I had ever tasted. I closed my eyes in ecstasy.

Tristan smiled at my antics. "You won't have to worry about it. You will always have someone with you who is familiar with the layout."

I nodded. He had explained that I was to have a security detail twenty-four hours a day. After hearing Riona's story, I couldn't say I blamed him for being paranoid, though I couldn't imagine what good I'd be for someone to kidnap or why I mattered that much to him. But if it made him feel better, then that was okay by me. The time here gave me an opportunity to explore the Fae culture and their way of life.

Taking the final sip from my mug, I dipped my finger into the bottom and scooped up the last remnants of my drink. Licking it, I grinned at him. "I think I'm in love."

His eyes had darkened, and he was staring at my mouth with barely concealed desire. Blinking, he cleared his throat and brought his eyes up to mine. "Are you ready to go?"

I nodded and stood. As I came around the table, he took my hand and laced his fingers through mine. I smiled at the gesture while glancing at the young girl behind the counter, who sighed dreamily as she stared at us. I winked at her before we headed out the door and down the hallway toward the elevator.

"I'll have to make sure whoever is guarding me knows how to take me there."

Tristan let out a soft laugh and looked sideways at me. "I can always have it delivered to your room in the morning, if you want."

"Are you serious?" I covered my chest with my free hand and rolled my eyes toward the ceiling. "Be still my beating heart. I didn't think it could get any better, but it just did."

He gave a bark of laughter, causing a group bowing and curtsying as we passed to frown at me in disapproval. I smothered a giggle and waved to them as Tristan pulled me into the waiting elevator. As soon as the doors closed behind us, I burst out laughing. "Oh, dear. I think I've managed to offend more of your subjects."

"More? You've already offended some?"

I nodded as I leaned against the elevator wall, my hand over my ribs, catching my breath from laughing. "Yeah, there was this group the night of the afterparty that was really unhappy with me. Especially Celeste."

"Celeste Beaumont?"

"I don't know her last name, to tell you the truth. She was the woman who interrupted our…" I glanced at his guard. "Intrigue that evening."

He nodded, looking amused. "That would be her."

"Wait, Beaumont? Is she any relation to Lucian Beaumont?"

"Yes, cousins I believe. How do you know Lucian?"

I grimaced, thinking about the incident. "I literally ran into him the other night when I went out to dinner with my friends. Don't worry, Keane was there and sent the guy on his way."

Tristan's smile slipped. "Keane didn't tell me you'd had a run-in with Lucian."

I shrugged half-heartedly. "There really wasn't anything to tell. I bumped into him on the way in, he apologized and offered to buy me a drink. Like I said, Keane came in right after, the two of them exchanged some words, then Lucian left, end of story."

"Hmm." He quickly pressed the lower-level buttons on the elevator panel and entered his passcode. "I need to talk to Keane."

I nodded, though I didn't think there was anything Keane could say that I hadn't already. Tristan seemed to be lost in thought, so I kept silent. When we came down to his living area, I stepped through the elevator door first and headed toward the bedrooms. "I'm just going to head to my room and unpack a few things."

He nodded distractedly as he presumably went in search of Keane. Closing the door to my room, I set about hanging my few belongings in the closet next to Riona's clothes. After placing my laptop on the small desk and plugging it in to charge, I stood in the middle of the space with my hands on my hips. What to do now? I didn't have any work that needed to be done. I'd finished editing my last photo session already, and Keane had rescheduled my two from this week for a later date. Looking at the bathroom door, I thought back to what Keane had said about it connecting to Tristan's bedroom. Walking over and opening it quietly, I peeked in and almost fell over in surprise.

The room had been magicked to look like it was situated outside on a private outcropping in some wooded area. Stepping out onto a small tree-covered stone patio, I looked around in amazement. It was like I was in a different world. A double sink had been carved out of a rock face to my left with lots of counter space and two raised sink bowls made of some type of turquoise blue glass. Above the sinks was a large mirror that seemed to be set into the rock itself, and on the counter, spread out haphazardly, was a menagerie of modern-day toiletries, a toothbrush, toothpaste, an electric razor, a hairbrush.

Stepping out from under the tree-made canopy, I saw a huge tub that could easily accommodate four or five people. It was on a raised wooden dais overlooking a waterfall that seemed to plummet hundreds of feet below. After looking over the edge at the dizzying view, I turned around and saw that a large shower had been cut into the wall opposite the sink just outside the canopied area. Two large showerheads hung down, looking like they could produce a small waterfall of their own.

Looking back into the canopied area, I saw that a small alcove had been made for the toilet to give one a bit of privacy. Just opposite the door I had entered through was another door. Walking over to it, I hesitantly put my hand on the knob. Though I had been told I was welcome to go anywhere in Tristan's living quarters, this seemed like such a private thing. I almost turned around and went back to my room when a soft voice urged me forward. What I heard wasn't exactly words, more of a soft rush of breath on the back of my neck. Turning the knob, I let the door swing open without stepping inside. Twice the size of Riona's bedroom, the space before me glowed with soft lighting hidden in recesses all around the room. It flickered every once in a while, giving the illusion of candlelight. A huge four-poster bed was the main focus, situated on a raised platform. It was decorated in differing shades of blue and had to be the biggest bed I had ever seen, easily larger than even a king-size.

Guess they had to have custom bedding made for that thing.

Carefully stepping into the room, I saw a fireplace in one corner with a couch and several chairs around it, all decorated in the same blues as the bed. A flat-screen television was mounted over the fireplace, much like the one in the living area. On the other side of the space, sat a large oak desk, scuffed and stained from years of use. A laptop sat open on its surface, adding its glowing light to the room.

Walking around the bed, I fingered the silky bedspread, imagining Tristan spread out on its surface, his expression gentle in sleep. Suddenly, a light flickered on to my right. Looking, I saw it was in a large walk-in closet. Wondering why the light had turned on, I stepped inside and looked around. It was big enough to have several chairs sitting in it and a free-standing, full-length mirror. Rows of Tristan's suits and tuxes hung to my right, while jeans, slacks, and T-shirts hung on the left. Dress shirts had been carefully folded and put onto shelves with matching ties still around their necks as if they were on display at a store. Shoes hung on a rack in one corner, while yet another corner held a stand full of all types of hats.

Though there were a lot of clothes, the closet wasn't even half full. It had obviously been designed with two people in mind. Poking into the drawers, I saw socks and underwear—he was a boxer briefs kind of guy—as well as various ties and tie tacks, cufflinks, etcetera. As I slid one particular drawer closed, I noticed a small scrap of paper sticking out from between a couple of pieces of clothing. I carefully pulled it out and found it was a photo. One of me. It had obviously been taken from the second floor the night of the theater opening, probably by one of the newspaper reporters who had been there. I was poised halfway up the main staircase and staring down into the crowd, a look of rapt wonder on my face. I remembered the exact moment. When I'd spotted Tristan in the crowd below.

How on earth had he gotten ahold of this photo, and why was it hidden in a drawer in his closet? Shaking my head, I put it back where I had found it and closed the drawer. Just as I turned to leave, I heard the bedroom door open and quickly close, followed by the soft scuff of feet as they crossed the carpeted floor. Too light to be Tristan's tread, I was suddenly concerned about being discovered in his closet, though I didn't know why. Panicking, I ducked behind a rack of suits, making sure they covered me completely. The sound of footsteps came closer to the closet, and my heart rate accelerated.

Just as whoever it was stopped outside the door, and I was sure they would find me, the lights in the closet went off. Letting out a sigh of relief, I scooted out from behind the suits and slid closer to the half-open door, where I could see out into the room. As I watched, a small figure with bright red hair shucked her clothes and slid between Tristan's cool sheets. Moments later, the bedroom door opened again. I instantly recognized the telltale outline of Tristan's form as he entered the room, pulling his shirt over his head as he went. I sucked in a breath as the soft lighting skimmed over his toned chest, highlighting the muscles that dipped and curved all the way down to the waistband of his slacks. Tossing his shirt onto the couch as he passed, he moved over to the desk, where he wiggled the mouse and brought his laptop to life, then sat in the chair before it.

"You can leave now,"—I tensed when I thought he was talking to me—"Tatiana."

The figure in the bed sat up and giggled. "Oh, Tristan, why so cross?"

"I said you can leave now."

"Come on Tristan. You know you want me here. Why do you keep denying us? Is it some cat and mouse game you like to play?"

Tristan sighed, running his hand over his face in obvious frustration. "Don't make me call one of the guys to come and get you again."

Tatiana slid out of the bed in all her naked glory and slunk seductively toward Tristan. "You don't have to play hard to get with me, Tristan, I already want you."

He ran a hand through his hair. "I'm not playing hard to get, Tatiana. I don't want you, end of story." His eyes raked over her contemptuously as if proving his statement.

She pouted playfully. "Oh, I know that's not true. I've seen the way you look at me when you think no one is watching."

Tristan shook his head and sat back in his chair, crossing his arms over his chest. "Is that so? And how do I look at you, Tatiana?" He raised his hand to silence her when she started to speak. "No, let me tell you how I look at you. I see you as a spoiled little girl who can't have what she wants, so she keeps acting out, trying to get it."

"I do not." The pouting lip was out in full force now.

"Yes, you do. Look at that stunt you pulled at the Market Street Saloon with Blue's friend's boyfriend." I started. Tatiana had been the one Christophe had been having sex with at the bar? This was news to me. "You couldn't leave well enough alone, could you? You were mad that I left with Blue, so you seduced her friend's boyfriend, knowing she would go running straight to Blue. I'll bet you even planted the suggestion in her head."

Tatiana smiled smugly. "That was a rather ingenious plan, if I do say so myself. And by the sound of it, it worked."

Now, I was pissed. No one went around playing with my friend's emotions like that. I didn't care *who* she was. Moving back into the closet, I quickly stripped to just my panties and put on one of Tristan's button-down shirts, making sure to leave the top three or four buttons undone. Pulling the elastic out of my hair, I shook it out so it cascaded down my back in a riot of waves and curls. Without a second thought, I opened the closet door and stepped out.

"Tristan, honey… Oh! I didn't realize you were expecting company." I pretended Tatiana being completely naked was normal and walked slowly over to where Tristan still sat at the desk. Wrapping my arms around his shoulders, I nuzzled his neck and placed a small kiss over his pulse point. He hadn't shown any outward reaction when I walked out of the closet, but if his pulse was anything to go by, he was definitely surprised.

He placed his hands over mine where they rested on his chest and smiled up at me. "I wasn't, darling. Tatiana was just leaving. Weren't you, Tatiana?"

I looked up at her from under my lashes and smiled with just a bit of malice. She was seething. I could practically feel the anger vibrating from her.

"You're sleeping with her? A human?" She pointed an accusing finger in my general direction, though she refused to acknowledge me.

"Who I sleep with is no business of yours, Tatiana. Now, please leave." He didn't bother correcting her about the fact that I wasn't human.

She turned her fury-filled green eyes on me. "This isn't over between you and me. He's mine." With that, she disappeared. I stared in surprise at the spot she had been only moments before. She'd disappeared—as in, poof…gone.

"Um, how did she do that?"

Tristan shrugged. "She's a Fairy, of course."

"Oh, *of course*. Well, *that* explains everything." I threw up my hands and walked over to the bed. Perching on the edge, I looked back at Tristan with a slightly annoyed expression.

His lips quirked up at the corners. "Fairies are magic, remember?" Sitting back in his chair, he looked at me curiously. "So, do I want to know why you were hiding in my closet?"

"Oh, you know, the usual...searching for something to wear to bed. When I was unpacking, I realized I'd forgotten my pajamas again." I shrugged, pretending nonchalance.

"And you decided my closet would have your best choices?"

"But of course. There is nothing better than a man's large shirt to cuddle up in."

"And you felt the need to try it on, too?"

"How else was I supposed to find the perfect fit?"

Tristan chuckled and stood, walking over to the edge of the bed. He looked me up and down critically, then shook his head. "I don't know. I would think a button-down might be a bit uncomfortable, wouldn't a T-shirt be a better choice?"

"Ah, but less effective in the given situation."

Tristan moved to stand next to me. "I'll give you that. It was very effective. Though you'll have to watch your back around Tatiana now. She is a very vindictive woman."

I grimaced. "So I heard."

"I'm sorry about that. I would have told you sooner but I just found out myself."

"Honestly, Christophe was a lecher anyway. He didn't deserve Brianna." Sighing, I stood. "Let me go change back into my clothes and get out of your way."

Before I could take a step toward the closet, Tristan was standing in front of me. "You're not in my way." He ran a hand down the collar of the shirt and traced across the edge of the opening, causing my heart rate to spike. His gaze had dropped to watch the progress of his hand, and my breath hitched in my throat. "You know, seeing you in my shirt and knowing you don't have anything else under it is a hundred times more arousing than Tatiana standing there naked."

I was still staring down at his hands, mesmerized as he started to unbutton the shirt. "Is that so?" My voice came out a bit breathily.

He nodded. "It was a good thing I wasn't standing up when you walked out." He got to the last button and, raising his eyes to mine, undid it. Slowly, he reached up with both hands and slid them under the shirt onto my shoulders.

I had to clear my throat twice in order to respond. "And why is that?"

"Because it would've been readily apparent what you do to me."

Never breaking my gaze, his hands slid to the sides and pushed the shirt from my shoulders. It fluttered to the floor, though neither of us paid it any attention.

Tristan looked down and sucked in a breath. "God, you're beautiful, Blue." His hands slid down my arms and back up again, causing goose bumps to spring up, and my nipples to harden under his desire-filled gaze. Reaching up, I put my hands over his and gently slid them down my chest until he could cup my breasts. I moaned softly at the feel of his warm palms against me.

Leaning back against the bed, I moved my hands behind me to support my weight, thrusting my chest deeper into his palms in the process. He ran a thumb over each hardened nipple, causing me to shiver in reaction. With infinite slowness, he slid his hands down my waist to my hips then back up to the girls. My breath was coming fast by this point, my entire body on fire. I wanted to touch him, too, but was giving him time to explore. Seeming to sense my desire—or perhaps he'd read it in my mind—his hands moved behind me and slid down my back before coming to rest on the bed.

Leaning forward, he pressed his chest against mine while capturing my lips with his in a slow, tender kiss that quickly escalated in urgency. Shifting, he put one of his arms around my waist and slid me back until I was lying on the bed. Leaning onto his left side next to me, he took my hand and placed it on his chest, never breaking our kiss. As our tongues explored each other's mouths, our hands wandered over each other's bodies. I couldn't get enough of the feel of his muscles moving and contracting under my questing fingers.

Breaking our kiss, he leaned forward, took a sensitive nipple into his mouth, and suckled. Arching off the bed, I buried my fingers in his hair. He moved to the other one and did the same, causing me to moan and move restlessly against him. Just when I didn't think it could get any more intense, I felt his hand slide across my stomach to cup me between my thighs. Pressing the heel of his hand tightly against me, he rubbed it back and forth. I moaned and pressed my hips forward, whimpering his name. He brought his lips back to mine, thrusting his tongue into my mouth in rhythm to the movements of his hand.

"Tristan..."

Removing his hand, he shifted so he was lying on top of me. I spread my thighs wider to accommodate him, and he pressed his lower half to mine. I gasped and wrapped my arms around him, one hand dipping lower to slip past the waistband of his pants. He moaned as I moved my hand around toward the front, still inside his slacks, slipping it between our heated bodies. As he had nothing on underneath, I easily found my target. He shuddered as I stroked him, pressing himself harder against me.

"Ah, Blue..."

A knock on the door caused us both to stop. "Sir?" It was Mckile.

"Yes?" Tristan called out, his voice a deep growl.

"You wanted me to remind you that you have a dinner engagement in fifteen minutes." Tristan lowered his head until his forehead rested against mine, his eyes closed in frustration.

"Thank you, Mckile. I'll be out in a few minutes." He opened his eyes to look into mine. "It seems every time we get into this situation, we are forever being interrupted by someone." He slid to his left side, sighing in regret. "Had it been anyone else coming tonight, I would've told them to reschedule. As it is, the Elders will not be put off."

"You're having dinner with the Elders tonight?"

"No...*we are* having dinner with the Elders tonight."

That got my attention. "What do you mean *we*?"

Tristan chuckled. "I guess I was a little distracted earlier and forgot to mention it."

"Yeah, I'd say. What am I supposed to wear? Is this a formal dinner?" I felt a bit of panic welling up. I hated being caught off guard.

Tristan considered. "Everything with the Elders is formal to a point. Did you bring anything with you that would work for say, a ball?" He grinned at me.

"You know as well as I do that I didn't."

Standing, Tristan held out his hand. "Come on."

"Where are we going?"

"To pick out something for you to wear." Reaching down, he grabbed his shirt off the floor and handed it to me. "Better put this on, otherwise I'll never be able to concentrate." Laughing, I quickly slipped my arms into it and buttoned a couple of the buttons.

"Where are we going to find something for me to wear?" He had taken my hand and led me toward the bathroom door.

"In your closet, of course." Leading me through the bathroom, we entered Riona's room. Letting go of my hand, Tristan walked over to the closet.

"You expect me to wear Riona's clothes?" I practically squeaked.

"Sure, why not? You're a bit taller than she was, but other than that, I'd say you are about the same size. If we stick with a dress or skirt, it should be fine." He walked into the closet, not even glancing back at me.

After a moment's hesitation, I threw up my hands and followed him inside.

# Chapter Eight

Dinner was a grand affair, at least in my opinion. I was sure the other participants were quite used to this style of dining. After seeing how the other guests were dressed, I was thankful I had let Tristan talk me into wearing the beautifully textured dupioni silk, knee-length sheath dress. I didn't think I'd ever worn anything so fine. Gathered to the left and held by a tonal rosette, it emphasized my small waist, its cap sleeves showed off my toned arms, and the deep sapphire color enhanced my evenly tanned skin.

Tristan had paired it with matching strappy heels that buckled around my ankle. Not favoring heels, I'd argued with him at first, but he won in the end. And I had to admit, they made my legs look long and sleek. I'd quickly talked him out of stockings, my one true enemy, and instead had smoothed on a lotion that added a slight sheen to my legs.

After I'd expertly twisted my long hair into an elegant chignon, Tristan pulled out a pair of dangly sapphire and diamond earrings. Again, I had protested, insisting my silver hoops were fine, but he had only laughed and put the sapphires in for me. Now, sitting here among the multitude of glittering jewels, I was glad for that small bit of shine.

I had been seated at the head of the table on Tristan's right. Given the whispered comments I'd picked up on, it was obviously a place reserved for the Queen or someone of high rank. They all wondered who I was. I felt very ill at ease with all the stares and glances being thrown my way and shifted uncomfortably in my chair. Tristan, however, sat at the head of the table, completely at ease as if he hadn't a care in the world. He was dressed impeccably in a dark blue suit with a white button-down shirt open at the throat. I almost choked on my wine when I realized it was the same shirt I had put on earlier. I recognized the almost imperceptible blue lines shot through the white fabric. Raising my eyes to his, I saw they were full of amusement. He had obviously been waiting to see if I would notice. Turning his head, he pretended to inspect the collar of his shirt before lifting it to his nose and inhaling deeply. He closed his eyes as if in Heaven. Smiling and shaking my head at him, I glanced across the table to see if anyone else had noticed the move. My gaze collided with a pair of very mischievous green eyes as I did. Seated across from me was none other than Riona's brother, Magnus.

He grinned when he caught my eyes on him and winked. My smile widened. Even though I had only been in his company for a few minutes, I found I really liked him. With a slight sense of dread, I felt my gaze drawn to the chair to the left of him. It was blessedly empty. I had fully expected to see Tatiana there, glaring at me. When my attention came back to him, Magnus smiled apologetically and nodded. He was telling me without words that she was supposed to be there. My heart sank. I really didn't want to have a confrontation with her again so soon. Hopefully, she kept to herself with so many people around. Just then, a commotion at the entrance to the dining room brought everyone's eyes up.

Standing framed in the archway was none other than Tatiana herself. She looked gorgeous. Obviously a planned entrance, she paused in the doorway, waiting until she had everyone's attention. Once all eyes were on her, she slowly made her way around the table to her seat. She wore a strapless, floor-length emerald-green gown made of yards upon yards of silk. It was draped artfully around her body, emphasizing every curve. Somehow, it sparkled and glinted every time she moved, though I couldn't see any evidence of anything on the dress that would reflect the light. Long black gloves covered her hands and reached up to her elbows, while emeralds and diamonds sparkled at her neck, wrist, and ears. Looking to the head of the table, she smiled seductively at Tristan, who merely stared back at her, clearly annoyed. Apologizing profusely to the surrounding Fae, she lowered herself into her seat, looking anything but contrite. A smile was upon her lips as she looked around the table—until her eyes met mine. A frown peeked at the corners of her mouth despite her trying to hold her smile. When she realized where I was seated, though, a look of outrage poured over her features, and she started to rise. Magnus put a controlling hand on her lap and pushed her back into her seat. I couldn't hear what he said to her, but I knew it was an admonishment by the flush that crept over her ivory cheeks. She glared daggers in my direction but stayed seated and, mercifully, silent.

When Tristan seemed satisfied there wouldn't be a scene, he arose from his seat. The room quieted down immediately.

"Good evening, my friends. I want to welcome you all to Moon Tree Hall." He paused as a smattering of applause went through the room. "It is a pleasure to have you all here tonight. I hope the business that brought you today can be completed quickly and efficiently, but first, let us enjoy some good food and even better company."

Servers appeared at the door as he sat, carrying silver trays full of varying delicacies. By the time it was all said and done, we had gone through five courses. I personally didn't think I could eat another bite, and that was saying something. Sitting back and sipping my wine, I watched Tristan deftly lord over the table. He was a master at this socializing thing. He asked his guests all the appropriate questions and knew about each of their families and personal lives. All the while, he fielded political questions without really answering any of them. It seemed the main topic—and probably why the Elders were here—was Tristan's upcoming need for marriage.

At the thought of him marrying another woman my gut tightened, as did my grip on the wineglass. I looked across the table at Tatiana, who was shamelessly flirting with every male she could while throwing covert glances at Tristan to see if he was paying attention. Though I didn't think he would ever choose her, the thought of Tatiana being in Tristan's bed every night made me clench my teeth. I supposed he could step down from his position, but that would be a travesty. From what I had ascertained in my short time here, he was wonderful as the King. His people loved and trusted him, and he always put them first. Who knew what they would get if he were to defer the position? No, he would have to make a decision, and looking down the table at the gathered Elders, I had a feeling his deliberation time had come to an end.

Lost in thought, I failed to notice the server standing at my elbow, holding a small silver tray. He cleared his throat practically in my ear, causing me to jump. "Oh gosh. I'm so sorry. I didn't realize you were standing there." I put a hand over my racing heart.

His lips quirked up in a smile, though he fought to keep his face impassive. "A message has come for you, my lady. It was said to be urgent."

"Oh, ah...thank you." Taking the small letter off the tray, I turned back toward the table. Several gazes were turned in my direction, including Tatiana's glaring green stare. Not wanting to read the message in front of anyone, I turned to Tristan, who looked at me with concern.

"Is everything okay, Blue?"

I nodded and smiled reassuringly. "I just need a bit of privacy. Will you excuse me a moment?"

Tristan stood and pulled out my chair for me. Several of the Fae on the other side of me also started coming to their feet. I smiled in their direction and indicated that they should remain seated.

"Do you need me to come with you?"

I shook my head. "No. I'm okay."

Tristan, still looking concerned, signaled to someone at the entrance. "Keane will accompany you."

I nodded and walked toward the door. As I was going down the length of the table, I realized Celeste had also been in attendance for dinner. She was seated next to Cedric, who looked questioningly at me as I passed. Poor Cedric, stuck right next to the very woman he was trying so hard to avoid. I shook my head slightly in his direction to indicate I was fine, causing Celeste to glare at me. I had to force down the grin that threatened to spring to my lips. As I exited the dining room, Keane was waiting patiently outside. He was obviously dressed for work, wearing an all-black uniform that molded to his frame. I saw he was well armed with a 9mm pistol peeking out of his shoulder holster, a long, thin sword strapped to his back, and a myriad of black daggers and knives slipped into his belt—and probably elsewhere if the occasional slight bump in his pants was any indication.

Without asking, Keane put his hand on the middle of my back and guided me into an empty room to our right, closing the door gently behind us.

"What kind of trouble are you getting into now, sweetheart?"

"Who said I was in any trouble?"

Keane grinned. "Because you seem to attract it left and right."

I shook my head at him and held up the letter I'd received. "This was just delivered to me, and they said it was urgent. I didn't want to read it in front of an audience in case it contained something private."

"That's from Kieran."

"Really?" I looked at the envelope in my hand, turning it over. "How do you know that?"

"The seal on it." He pointed to the old-fashioned wax seal holding the flap of the envelope down.

"Huh. I didn't think people used those anymore."

"The Elders are pretty set in their ways." He held up his hands and made air quotes. "This is how it was done centuries ago, so this is how it will continue to be done..."

I looked at the envelope in my hands. "I guess we won't know what it contains until we open it." Breaking the seal on the back, I slid out a piece of folded parchment paper. Looking up at Keane, I lifted an eyebrow.

He shrugged, though I saw he was holding back a grin. "Like I said, set in their ways."

Shaking my head in amusement, I unfolded the letter. It was written in flowing, masculine script. I wondered if Kieran had even used an ink well and a feather quill to write it.

Keane chuckled, having read my thoughts. "He actually prefers fountain pens. Says the old ink tends to splatter everywhere and makes a mess of things."

I quickly scanned the contents of the letter. What was printed there caused my heart rate to pick up. Keane, ever sensitive to it, straightened. "What is it?"

"It seems Kieran found some information pertaining to my parents and says it's most urgent that I meet him." I looked up at Keane. "I hadn't even given it a second thought that he wasn't at dinner. He is one of the Elders, isn't he?"

Keane nodded. "Does he say when he wants to meet you?"

"It just says as soon as earthly possible. That sounds pretty ominous, doesn't it?"

"Indeed. Let me make a call. I remember seeing him arrive this afternoon with the rest of the Elders, so he should be on the premises somewhere."

Keane moved a few paces from me, a cell phone to his ear. I scanned the letter again. I couldn't believe Kieran had discovered something. I wondered if he had spoken to Alannah. My gut tightened at the thought, but I pushed it aside. There was no need to get myself all out of sorts over nothing.

Keane returned. "He's in the library. I'll take you to him."

Unable to get past the lump in my throat to answer, I merely nodded. Keane opened the door and, after looking both left and right, moved into the hallway. He guided me toward the elevators, his hand resting lightly on my lower back. I could tell he had shifted into full guard mode. None of the carefree demeanor I had come to associate with him was evident in his posture or expression. Stepping into the elevator, he quickly punched the button for the floor we needed. I stood there, nervously twirling the opened envelope in my hand.

"Do you want me to call Tristan?"

My head jerked up in surprise. "No. Why would I want Tristan?"

He shrugged. "Just making sure."

I shook my head. "I'm fine. This is personal business."

He nodded just as the elevator dinged, indicating we had reached our floor. Taking a deep breath, I stepped out behind Keane. He led me to a towering set of double doors. Glancing down at me, he hesitated, then grinned that bad-boy smile I'd come to know. "Ready to face your destiny?"

"As ready as I'll ever be."

He pushed the doors open. After scanning the room, he stepped back. "I'll wait out here for you."

I put a hand on his forearm. "Actually, can you come in with me?"

He looked surprised but pleased. "If that's what you want."

I nodded and, screwing up my courage, stepped into the library. Glancing around, I saw that it was enormous. The ceiling was easily fifteen or twenty feet in height, showing exposed wooden beams above. Rows upon rows of shining wooden shelves were spread over the room, towering almost as high as the ceiling. There had to be thousands of books on them, and I distractedly wondered how long it took to amass a library this size.

Keane leaned down to whisper in my ear. "This is the Elder Library. It's actually located in the Isle of Skye, in Scotland."

"Then how are we here? Is the room just magicked to look like it?"

"No, we're there. This is one of those few places you can enter through a portal from Dock Street."

Looking at Keane sideways, I mimicked my mind being blown with my hand and a nearly silent explosion sound. He laughed, smothering the sound behind his hand. I wasn't sure exactly why we were trying to be so quiet. It just seemed the sort of thing you did in a library. Like two misbehaving kids, we made our way to the center of the library, making faces and gestures at each other.

"I am glad to see at least someone is having fun." We both straightened guiltily at the sound of Kieran's voice, causing him to laugh. "Why is it that, even as adults, we feel the need to be quiet in a library? Even our own?" He reached for my hands. "My dear, it is so good to finally meet you for real."

Keane looked at me curiously but said nothing, falling back into his role as my guardian.

"You said you had some information about my parents?"

Kieran nodded, suddenly seeming serious. "I most assuredly do, though whether it is good news or bad, I am not quite certain just yet."

I suddenly wished I hadn't eaten so much. With a feeling of trepidation and a queasy stomach, I followed Kieran to a large table with several books on its surface.

"After speaking with several contacts and looking through old records, I have come to the conclusion that your mother—your birth mother—was a Fairy named Iridia."

"Wait a minute. Iridia? As in the famous warrior Queen, Iridia?"

Kieran looked surprised. "You know of her?"

I shook my head in shock. "Only what she looked like." I fumbled for a chair to sit in. I couldn't believe this. Was this why Brody had been driven to sell the sculpture of Iridia to me, because she was my mother? And why was he now having visions of *me*? Was it all connected?

Kieran shook his head, reading my thoughts but not having an answer for me either. "I had heard Brody was having visions of you. It is most disturbing."

Scrambling for something to use to still my circling thoughts, I grappled with the first thing that came to mind. "Who is Iridia?"

Kieran sighed and sat in the chair next to me. "Iridia is another of my daughters." I looked at him, surprised. "She was, of course, from my Fae wife." I laughed softly at the reference to our first conversation. "She was the youngest of seven and quite unique. You see, her powers did not wait until puberty to manifest. They started when she was only an infant." He paused seeing the shock on my face and nodded.

"By the time she was a couple of months old, she could already do things with magic most Fairies cannot do in centuries—and all before she could even walk and talk." Kieran pressed his lips together for a moment before continuing. "Though her magic was advanced, she grew up as a normal child. Mostly. Since she had to spend a lot of time with tutors, learning to control herself, she had a lot less free time than her siblings. I think that caused a certain amount of animosity, which showed in the form of rebelliousness.

"As a teenager, she was prone to disappearing for hours on end and having outbursts that usually resulted in something being destroyed." Kieran shook his head. "We indulged her, knowing the strain her gifts put on her, but then came the day that changed everything. While exploring the far reaches of our territory, she had the misfortune to come across a band of Witches and Warlocks who were spying on us for a rival clan. Unable to protect herself, even with all her magical abilities, they captured her." Kieran rubbed a hand over his face.

"I think they hoped to use her against our King but a young Warlock, not agreeing with what his fellow clan members were doing, helped her to escape before they could. Once free, the Warlock, whose name was Aiden, decided to stay with Iridia. I guess it was only natural that over time the two fell in love since they spent all their time together. Unfortunately, even though he loved her, a Fairy and Warlock union cannot produce children, so Aiden refused to marry Iridia."

"Why can't Warlocks and Fairies have children?"

"No one really knows the exact reason, but some speculate that Warlocks and Witches are too closely related to Demons, which can only reproduce with each other."

"Huh."

"Anyway, Iridia and Aiden went on that way for some time, during which time Iridia became well known for her skills as both a soldier and a magic user. Usually, Fairies cannot wield Warlock magic, but as I said, Iridia was very gifted. Combined with Aiden's knowledge and tutelage, he took her far beyond any Fairy before. Unfortunately, it had the downside of others hearing about Iridia, including the band of Witches and Warlocks who had captured her.

"Knowing Aiden was the Warlock imparting their secrets to the Fairies, they set a trap. They wanted to punish him and needed Iridia for their own nefarious purposes." Kieran shook his head sadly. "Aiden decided to sacrifice himself so no harm could befall Iridia—his love was that great. He went out to face off with this band of Warlocks and Witches. No one knows exactly what happened, but when all was said and done, they simply disappeared. Iridia was devastated and searched for Aiden for years, but to no avail. Eventually, life moved on, and Iridia married Brokk of the Fernsong Clan—a purely political match, mind you."

"Isn't Brokk now the King of that clan?"

Kieran nodded. "He was crowned King not long after his marriage to Iridia. Some say it only happened because of her, but he has proven to be a strong ruler, even in her absence."

"What happened to Iridia? Everyone refers to her in the past tense…"

"A rumor surfaced some years ago that Aiden was still alive and being held captive. Never having given up on him, Iridia immediately set out to find and free him. Neither she nor the eighteen warriors who went with her were ever heard from again."

"So, no one knows if she's still alive or not?"

Kieran shook his head sadly. "It's never been confirmed one way or the other, but as her father, I certainly hope she is still alive, and living her dream life with Aiden."

"Does that mean Brokk is my father?"

"No, Brokk is definitely not your sire."

"How can you be so sure?"

"For one, Iridia and Brokk were married in name only. Secondly, because of the DNA test."

"What DNA test?"

"Sometime around your fifth birthday, Alannah had you tested for everything under the sun, including paternity."

"Why would she do that?"

Kieran shrugged. "Who knows? Perhaps she did not truly believe Iridia was telling the truth. Nevertheless, the DNA test showed you were Iridia's daughter. The male counterpart samples she used, however, all came up as inconclusive. I am not sure who exactly she tested you against, but my guess is it was several Fae contributors, one of whom was undoubtedly Brokk."

"I guess that makes you my grandfather, then?"

Kieran smiled. "Yes, it does."

"But that still leaves the issue of my father."

Kieran sobered again. "Blue, what we say here must be kept in the strictest of confidence. Your life may depend on it." He glanced at Keane.

I considered Kieran for a long minute and then looked at Keane, who seemed to be asking me if I wanted him to step out. "I trust Keane completely." Keane started visibly, his face showing his surprise momentarily before he wiped it clean.

Kieran nodded, accepting my answer. "I believe your sire was Aiden, in some form or another."

"The Warlock? But I thought you said Warlocks and Fairies couldn't have children. And what does that mean? '*Some form or another?*'"

"I cannot explain it, Blue. But after studying your genetics…you should not exist."

"My genetics?"

"Yes, you have the most complicated DNA of any Fae I have ever seen. It is almost like you are every Fae rolled into one."

I sat back, shocked. "Funny. That's exactly how Keane described my blood."

Kieran looked up at Keane curiously. "You have tasted her?"

Keane nodded. "We thought it would be beneficial to me guarding her. That way, I can track her anywhere."

Kieran nodded his approval. "And you thought she tasted like every Fae rolled into one?"

Keane nodded again. "It was the most intricate blood I have ever tasted, though I could tell Fairy was a top contributor. It was also filled with powerful magic."

"That would make sense since my Iridia was her mother. Your genetics might also explain why you display so many different Fae talents. If you were created with magic…"

I sat forward in my chair. "Wait. Created *with* magic?"

"I believe Aiden did something. Maybe he manipulated his or Iridia's DNA enough that they became compatible. Or perhaps Iridia became so strong in magic that it found a way to conform. Either way, it appears you were born of magic."

I just shook my head. "But what happened to them? Why did Alannah raise me?"

It was Kieran's turn to sit back in his chair. "I do not know. I have been trying to contact Alannah, but she is ignoring all my summonses. I am afraid something might have happened to her."

I immediately tensed at the mention of him having contact with Alannah. Keane stepped closer and put a comforting hand on my shoulder. "If I might interject?" Kieran indicated for him to speak. "Perhaps Iridia contacted Alannah and asked her to raise the child for her. They were half-sisters, after all."

Kieran steepled his hands in front of his face. "But why would she do that?"

"To keep Blue hidden, of course." Keane continued with his thoughts. "What better way to hide an all-powerful Fae than with a human? One who had enough knowledge of the Fae world to keep the child from finding out what she is, hence keeping her powers dormant."

"Until said daughter's powers started to materialize, and said human beat a hasty retreat and dusted her hands of her." There was more bitterness in my statement than expected. I hadn't realized I harbored that much.

Keane squeezed my shoulder and looked down at me. "Alannah was jealous that you were Fae, and she wasn't. That's the reason she left, not because of any shortcomings you had."

Taking a deep breath, I pushed down my insecurities. "So, how do we find out for sure if Aiden was my dad? And if he was, what do we do about it? It's bound to come out eventually that I'm different."

Keane interjected. "Not to mention, Blue will need some serious training if she is to keep a handle on her abilities as they surface. It's a wonder she's been able to adjust on her own so far."

Kieran stared off into space, seeming to contemplate things. When he spoke, he retained that far-off look. "You are right, of course. I will continue to dig into Aiden's involvement. If I could find a bit of DNA from him, we could do another paternity test. Until then, you will most definitely need training. I will have to pull on some of my most trusted confidants to work with you in secret, and I, myself, will need to remain here to monitor your progress." His gaze finally found its way back to us. "Keane, can I trust you to watch over her?"

"Of course. No one will find it odd since she already has a security detail. And when I can't be with her, one of my Vaimpír will be. We won't allow any others to take over."

Kieran nodded. "Very good." Leaning forward, he took me by the hands. "We will figure this out, Blue. Together."

I nodded, suddenly exhausted. Noting it, Keane pulled me to my feet. "I think that's enough for tonight. Blue needs some rest."

"Yes, of course." Kieran rose. "This must be very overwhelming for you."

After a hesitant moment, he stepped forward and hugged me. "For what it is worth, I am extremely glad to have you for a granddaughter. I always wanted my Iridia to find some happiness, and you are proof she did."

I smiled softly before stepping back. "Goodnight... Grandfather."

Keane guided me back to my room in complete silence. I was thankful he understood exactly where I was emotionally. After making sure my room was empty, he stood before me.

"Are you going to be okay by yourself?"

I nodded. "I think so."

"I'll be just outside if you need me."

After he'd left, I put on a tank top with a graphic that said *Fluent in Movie Quotes* and a pair of soft shorts before climbing into bed. I lay there for over an hour but sleep eluded me. I tossed and turned, trying to find a comfortable position. At one point, I heard Tristan outside my door, inquiring about me, but Keane made excuses, saying I was exhausted and just wanted to sleep. It wasn't untrue. I most definitely *was* exhausted. I just couldn't seem to find the sleep part. I heard Tristan moving around in the shared bathroom between our rooms.

For a second, he seemed to hover at the connecting door. I held my breath, but then he went back into his bedroom. Letting out my pent-up breath in a rush, I sat up in bed. It wasn't that I didn't want to see Tristan. I just needed time to myself so I could absorb everything.

Looking to my right, I saw the sculpture of Iridia sitting on the bedside table. Reaching over and picking her up, I stared at her.

"What secrets are you keeping from me? Just what is going on?"

I ran a finger down her cheek, feeling a calming influence flow over me as I did. Setting Iridia back on the bedside table, I yawned and lay down again. I was asleep almost instantly.

*"Carolina…"*

I blinked and looked around. I wasn't in bed anymore. Hearing my name, I turned to find a woman standing before me. She was short and petite with wavy blond hair that cascaded down her back, and large, hazel eyes not unlike mine. She wore a flowing white gown made of layers of shimmering organza that seemed to float and move about, making her appear as a ghost.

I recognized her almost immediately. "Iridia?"

She nodded, smiling.

"What? How?" I frowned. "Am I in one of those waking dream things again?" I looked around, but we just seemed to be standing in nothingness.

Iridia laughed, the sound floating through my head as if she were talking in my thoughts and not actually to me. *"I'm not sure exactly what dream thing you are referring to, but you are asleep, and I am visiting you in your dreams magically."*

"Oh, that's a bit different than before…" I frowned again. "Why are you talking in my head like that?"

*"That is how this works. As I said, I am not actually here, but I am projecting myself into your dreams—hence the telepathy."*

"That's weird."

She smiled and shook her head. *"My little girl, all grown up."*

"So, I am your daughter."

*"You don't seem surprised."*

"I was recently clued in."

Iridia nodded, looking sad. *"I am sorry you had to grow up the way you did."*

I defensively crossed my arms over my chest and stared at her. "What? Now you're here to explain everything to me? Why wait till now? I've been practically on my own since I was sixteen."

She looked stricken by the statement. *"I wasn't able to find you—not until recently. Otherwise, I would've been here a lot sooner."*

I considered that but decided to leave it alone for the time being. "Are you actually alive?"

Iridia nodded slowly, almost like she was afraid to admit it.

"And you let your family think you were dead because...?"

She sighed. *"Why don't you have a seat and let me start at the beginning? It will be easier that way."*

Looking behind me, I realized a couch and chairs had appeared, along with a small table full of hors d'oeuvres. I looked at Iridia suspiciously. I knew that hadn't been there a second ago, and she smiled guiltily. *"I thought you might be hungry."*

"No thanks, I was treated to a sit-down meal with the Elders this evening."

*"Oh, goodness. Five courses?"*

"Yeah." I patted my stomach, though it didn't feel full here in slumberland. "I haven't eaten that much in one sitting in forever."

Iridia laughed lightly. *"I take it the Elders are forcing Tristan to come to a decision about his wife."*

I nodded. "I think that is the idea, though I missed the business part of the evening."

*"Oh, they wouldn't have done business yet. Dinner is usually just part of the preliminaries. Whenever the Elders converge, it is usually a week-long affair. Very tedious, if you ask me."*

"I forgot you were a Queen at one time."

*"I guess that's my queue to start my story."* She seemed to gather herself. *"Let me start by saying I never intended for things to go the way they did. But then, who does? As I'm sure you have heard, I was born extremely gifted in magic. I had a difficult childhood, to say the least. While I tried to be normal, my magical abilities always set me apart. I didn't have any friends because the rest of the clan either feared or revered me. Plus, I had to spend so much*

*time with teachers, forever learning, that I didn't have time to do the normal things most kids my age were doing."*

"Kieran always believed it was rebelliousness that caused you to disappear by yourself."

Iridia shook her head. *"He never wanted to believe my fellow clan members treated me differently, but they did. Even my siblings. And they all avoided me when they could."*

"That had to be hard."

She nodded. *"With little else to distract me from my studies, I spent a lot of time in the woods exploring, finding new places and hidden treasures among the trees. While exploring one day, I spotted a small band of people camped out on the borders of our land. I didn't recognize them or the symbols on their tents. Thinking to spy on them to find out what they were up to, I crept close to their camp to watch. Had I realized they were Witches and Warlocks, I would've kept my distance. I was young and innocent, but not generally stupid."* Iridia shook her head in what seemed to be remembered frustration.

*"Unfortunately for me, they were cloaking what they were magically, so I didn't realize my error until it was too late. They captured me, and thinking to use me against the King of our clan as a bartering tool, they kept me bound and gagged in one of their tents. At first, nothing was done to me. Eventually, though, several members of their band took notice of me as a budding woman."* Iridia shuddered.

*"Those were the most horrible days of my life. I would not wish that on my worst enemy. During that time, the young Warlock who brought me food and water every night started to soften toward me. Aiden was his name. He would untie me for short periods of time when no one else was awake so I could clean myself up, and he cleansed and bandaged my many wounds. I found out he was an orphan and that his guardians treated him pretty much like a slave himself. We quickly became friends, and he vowed to help me escape."*

She seemed lost in thought for a moment. *"It took several days of planning, but we finally managed it. On the night of my escape, Aiden decided to come with me, fearing what they would do to him when they found me gone."*

I cocked my head. "Why didn't you ever use your magic against them?"

"*Unfortunately, they did a spell that crippled me magically. I wasn't able to use it at all.*"

"What happened after you escaped?"

"*Aiden and I traveled back to my clan, where I told my father and the King everything that had transpired. They, of course, went in search of my captors, but all they found was an empty campsite. Afterward, I decided I would not let anyone get the best of me again. I started to train with the warriors—much against my father's wishes—to learn self-defense, martial arts, hand-to-hand combat, swordplay, archery, magical fighting, and anything else that would stop someone from taking advantage of me ever again. I soon found I had an aptitude for it and excelled, rising through the ranks of our military. Aiden was there, too, not only learning beside me but also teaching me things—things only Witches and Warlocks know. Usually, Fairies can't do their kind of magic—*"

I interrupted. Kieran had said much the same thing. "There are different kinds of magic?"

"*Yes, Fairy magic is derived directly from the elements: air, earth, fire, and water. While the Warlocks' magic comes from the ley lines.*"

"What are ley lines?"

"*Lines that crisscross through the Earth, connecting sacred sites that contain high levels of magic and supernatural energies. It allows users to tap into the system and use the magic. It is actually believed by some that Witches are stunted Demons—Demons magically punished during a war between them and the Elves long ago—who were then banished to the Earth. These earthbound Demons found they could harness the magic found in the Earth's energies and amplify it by creating these lines. Nothing compared to their former Demon magic, but it was powerful nonetheless.*"

"Wow, this isn't your average folklore."

Iridia shook her head. "*No. Humans don't know the details of our history. They only know what we've allowed them to know.*"

"I guess I have a lot of studying to do." I turned the conversation back to her story. "Kieran said your unique abilities brought unwanted attention to you. That it pretty much made you famous among the Fae."

*"Yes. Fae used to come from far and wide to see the things I could do and barter for my skills. I guess it was only a matter of time, but the clan who captured me eventually caught wind of my abilities and recognized the Warlock influence. It didn't take a genius to figure out who was helping me. They put up a supposed white flag and invited us to join them to talk. We all knew it wasn't real."*

"Is that when Aiden snuck out to meet them?"

She nodded with a frown. *"When I realized what he had done, I hurried after him, but I was too late. All I found was an area where a struggle had occurred and blood—lots of blood. I didn't know if it was Aiden's or someone else's. I searched for weeks, trying to find him. It proved fruitless. Centuries went by, and I grew to believe that Aiden had been killed. In a weak moment, I agreed to marry Brokk to make an alliance for my father and assure Brokk's ascension to King. I thought if I could perhaps rule as Queen, I could make things better. I'd seen what Tristan and Riona did for their clan and wanted to follow their direction with our clan."*

She took a deep breath. *"Time went on, and I was happy enough—until some years ago when I received word from a trusted source that they had seen Aiden alive and being held captive. With my husband's blessing, I immediately went in search of Aiden to free him."*

"Brokk gave you his blessing to go after another man?"

*"Brokk was a wonderful husband. But what wasn't well known about him, at least at the time, was that he prefers the company of men. As you can imagine, since Fae law decrees there must be one male and one female on the throne, it posed quite a problem for him. When I agreed to marry Brokk, it was with the full knowledge of what his preferences were. Needless to say, we had separate private lives. When the possibility of saving Aiden came up, Brokk was all for me going, knowing I loved Aiden with all my heart."*

"Did you find him? Aiden?"

Iridia smiled widely, saying it all. *"I most assuredly did."*

"So why let everyone believe you were dead?"

*"Among other things...you happened."*

"Me?" I shook my head and asked the thing that had been bothering me since I found out that Alannah wasn't my biological mother. "Why did you give me to Alannah to raise? Didn't you want me?"

*"We wanted you more than anything. We were just so afraid."*

"Afraid of what?"

Iridia sighed. *"You don't realize it yet, but there is great power in you. Something about the way you were conceived made it so you possess the talents of all Fae."*

"So that's why no one has been able to pin down what I am. And why it seems every time I'm around a different Fae, I take on their characteristics and abilities."

Iridia nodded. *"Your talents are coming alive. With your exposure to each Fae, your body responds to their essence and relearns its abilities."*

"Relearns?"

*"Yes. You could utilize them all at one time."*

"I don't remember being able to do anything like I've been experiencing lately."

*"You wouldn't. We worked an enchantment on you to hide your true nature from everyone—including yourself. We didn't want anyone discovering what you were. We knew if they did, there would be wars among the Fae, trying to gain control of you. That is the reason we sent you with Alannah to be raised as a human. I thought if no one viewed you as Fae, and as long as you didn't have your powers, no one would ever realize what you are."*

"Did Alannah know?"

Iridia hesitated as people do when they're caught in a lie. *"She was told you were human—my daughter but with a human father."*

I grimaced. "Like her. So, when I told her what was starting to happen to me, and she realized I was actually Fae, she left."

Iridia nodded. *"So it would seem. I'm so sorry, Blue. Had I known..."* She sighed. *"We still don't know why the enchantment started to wear off. It wasn't supposed to. Perhaps your true nature is just that strong and it can't be contained."*

"What happens now? Will you make a comeback from the dead?"

*"Unfortunately, not yet. There are...circumstances that would endanger you. Please, don't ask what they are. I really can't explain them right now."*

I grimaced. "In other words, I should keep this meeting secret."

She nodded emphatically.

"Will I see you again?" I wasn't sure if I wanted to or not.

*"I will come to you when I can, but it's not always possible. Keep the statue Brody gave you close by. I use it to find you magically."*

"Is that why I feel so drawn to it?"

She nodded. *"When Brody created the statue, a piece of my spirit was somehow trapped inside."*

"Do you think that's why I feel drawn to Riona's statue, too?"

Iridia shook her head. *"I don't know. I only know that whenever you are near my likeness, I can feel your presence. Perhaps even in death, that sculpture contains a small piece of Riona, and she's trying to tell you something."*

This was all well beyond my comprehension at the moment. I covered a sudden yawn. "Uh-oh. If this is anything like my other dreams, that means its wakey time..."

Iridia nodded and moved to sit next to me. *"Know I'll be watching over you the best I can from where I am and will do what I can to help guide you as you become more immersed in the world of the Fae."*

She pulled me into a hug. At first, I was hesitant, then I hugged her back. We stayed that way for a minute before she sat back and smiled, though her eyes were misty with tears. As I watched, she slowly faded away, leaving me alone. I only had enough time to look around once more before waking up in bed. Opening my eyes slowly, I looked toward the bedside table where the sculptures sat and sighed. Life was suddenly so much more complicated than it had been only a week ago.

# Chapter Nine

Tristan was holed up in meetings with the Elders all morning, so I found myself with time to further explore my surroundings. Cedric offered to act as a guide and guard since Keane and Mckile were sleeping. They'd been up for the past four days straight and needed some downtime. That left Cullen and Ronan with Tristan this morning. They weren't too keen on letting me go with Cedric alone, but I assured them I would stay belowground and keep them posted as to my whereabouts.

After a quick stop at my favorite Parisian café for a cup of cappuccino, we set off for a place Cedric assured me I'd love, cameras in hand. When we got to the correct door, he made me close my eyes and promise not to peek. I did and waited as he guided me into place. Finally, when I was standing where he wanted, and a deep silence surrounded me, he told me to open my eyes. I did so slowly and looked around. What I saw made my jaw drop.

"Are we...are we at the Fairy Pools on the Isle of Skye?"

Cedric grinned at me. "We're not actually in Scotland, but it's magicked to look like it. And I figured regardless of whether it's real or not, it photographs the same."

Turning in a circle, I gazed around me. Sights I'd only seen in pictures on the internet surrounded me. "This is incredible."

"I thought you might like it. I spent many an hour here when I was younger. It's still the place I go when I need to get away from everything." He offered me his arm. "Shall we?"

I took it excitedly. "Most definitely!"

We spent the next few hours exploring the area and photographing it. Cedric was a great guide, knowing the best places to take photos, and I taught him all kinds of tricks for capturing the perfect images. By the time the lunch hour rolled around, I was exhausted and more than ready to take a break. Putting my camera down, I grinned at Cedric as he finished capturing his last photograph.

"How about a break for something to eat?"

He nodded and guided us back toward the door we had entered through. At least, I *thought* that was where we were going. It soon became apparent by the changing landscape, that we were headed to a completely new area. The mountains surrounding the pools gave way to large trees that towered high above our heads, almost obscuring the blue sky.

"Ah, Cedric... Where are we going? This isn't where we came in." I looked around a bit nervously. I couldn't say why, but it really felt like we were being watched.

He only laughed. "Come on, Blue. You trust me, don't you?" I nodded slowly and tried to shake off the feeling of unease making its way up my spine.

"Come on, we're almost there." He reached back and took my hand, dragging me forward and almost causing me to fall. Once I regained my footing, I casually took my hand back when he seemed to want to hold on to it. After Keane's comment about Cedric being interested in me, I was being more careful about what I projected to him. While I liked Cedric a lot, I didn't view him as anything more than a friend.

After a few more minutes of walking, during which I seriously considered asking him to turn around, we finally came out of the trees and into an open meadow. A large, red-and-white-checked blanket covered the ground at its center with what amounted to a feast on it.

"Ta-da!" He turned and spread his arms wide. "What do you think?"

"Wow...that's a lot of food."

He laughed while dropping his arms back to his sides. "Hey, I've eaten with you before, remember?"

I feigned an angry huff and swatted at him playfully. He dodged, laughing.

"Is that all you got, Blue? Really, I expected more from you."

Never one to back down from a challenge, I raised an eyebrow. Then, without warning, I sprang at him, hitting him in the chest and taking him to the ground. Rolling, we landed in a heap of camera equipment and combined laughter, me lying half-sprawled on top of him.

"How's that?"

"Damn, girl, I forgot how fast you can move."

I gave him a triumphant grin and started to push myself up so I could stand. Before I got too far, he grabbed my arms and stopped me. Looking down at him questioningly, I saw to my dismay that he wore a look of desire.

"Cedric..." I put my hands on his chest to keep him at arm's length. He merely put one of his arms around me and quickly rolled over so he pinned me to the ground, smiling all the while. Before I could say anything else, he leaned down and tried to kiss me. I turned my head at the last second, and his lips hit my cheek. He let out a frustrated growl and threaded his fingers into my hair, holding my head still as he pressed his lips to mine. I lay there stiffly as he kissed me, not kissing him back. When he realized I wasn't reacting to him, he lifted his head and looked at me with an expression I couldn't read—confusion? hurt? frustration?—before a frown furrowed his brow, and he levered himself up and took off back through the trees.

I sighed and scrubbed my hands over my face. I had hoped to avoid this situation with him. Apparently, my candid indifference wasn't coming off the way I'd hoped. Either that, or he just didn't want to acknowledge it. Dejectedly, I got to my feet and dusted myself off. Turning, I looked at the food laid out, but unsurprisingly, I had lost my appetite. I waited a while, pacing the open meadow, but Cedric didn't return. Finally, I decided to head back to Dock Street. Maybe after he calmed down some, he'd come see me. As I made my way back through the trees, that feeling of unease crept back up my spine. Rubbing my hands over the goose bumps on my arms, I picked up my pace to a jog. I let out a sigh of relief as I stopped in front of the door we had entered through. Reaching out, I grabbed the handle and opened the door. As I was about to step through, someone suddenly jerked me off my feet and roughly pulled me backward, a chemical-soaked cloth slapped over my nose and mouth. Struggling, I tried not to breathe in the sweet-smelling scent, but I couldn't hold my breath forever. What a day to decide not to wear my mother's necklace. As my vision started graying, I thought of Keane and how much he would enjoy scolding me for going out without him. That was if he found me in time.

⁓ℓℓ⁓

I awoke to the tinkling sound of running water. Slowly digging through the fog that encircled my brain, I listened to my surroundings without opening my eyes. What the heck had happened? As I lay there, a soft breeze carried the sounds of birds singing happily in the trees and the scent of wet moss. Grass tickled my face, and I shifted slightly to avoid it. That's when I realized my hands were tied together, as were my feet. Sighing, I remembered the cloying, sweet-scented cloth being shoved into my face. Just great. Only one day with the Fae, and I was already in trouble. Maybe Keane was right. I just seemed to attract it.

Carefully slitting my eyes open, I looked around, trying not to make any sudden movements in case I wasn't alone. All I could make out was green and more green. Not very helpful. There didn't seem to be anyone around, so I opened my eyes all the way. Slowly lifting my head, I saw I was lying under a large willow tree next to what appeared to be a sizable stream. I saw dragonflies flitting about over the water, seeming to play with their reflections in the clear, glassy surface, unperturbed by the woman tied up nearby.

Above me, suspended by the branch of another tree, was a wooden swing. Looking past it and through the trees, I tried to catch sight of the sun. Judging by the light I could make out, I'd only been out for an hour, maybe less, which meant we couldn't have gone far. I was pretty sure I was in one of the many magicked rooms at Dock Street, but it didn't look like the one Cedric and I had been in earlier. Reaching out with my senses, I touched Keane's essence as I had been teaching myself to do. He wasn't far. Definitely still at Dock Street, then. Which meant one of two things: Tristan's enemies had penetrated his inner sanctum, or he had a few traitors in his midst.

Suddenly, I heard voices coming in my direction. Lying back in the same position I had woken up in, I pretended to still be asleep. It took a bit to even out my breathing, but I managed it. As they got closer, I immediately recognized one of the voices. It was Celeste. Damn, I knew she was mad at me, but resorting to kidnapping? Hopefully, this was just over Cedric, and I could easily explain my lack of any designs on his person.

"When will the Elders come to a decision?"

"We should hear shortly." I didn't recognize the second voice, but it was a male. "What do you plan on doing with her?" He nudged me with his foot, and it took everything I had to maintain my ploy of still being unconscious.

"I'm going to take her blood and enter her, of course."

What the heck was she talking about? Enter me into what?

"Why on earth would you do that?"

"Because I want to see her humiliated and brought to her knees in front of everyone."

"But she's just a human."

"Oh, no. She's plenty more than human, though I don't know just what yet. The King even has his personal guardians watching over her."

"Holy shit! You didn't tell me that. They'll be coming after her."

"They will eventually, but by the time they find her, it will be too late."

"I'm not messing with the King's guardians, Celeste. They're Vaimpír, for heaven's sake."

"Oh, hush, Jacob. We'll be long gone before they ever get here."

"But they'll scent us on her and use it to track us." I could tell Jacob was nervously bouncing his weight from one foot to the other next to me.

"No, they won't. You took that potion I gave you, didn't you?"

"Yeah, but—"

"No buts. That will cloak your scent from anything. Now, hurry up. I need to get a blood sample from her before she wakes up."

Jacob leaned down and carefully pulled my bound hands toward him. He adjusted one of my arms to expose my inner elbow. I really didn't want them to get a blood sample from me, especially with what I'd recently learned, but I wasn't sure exactly what to do. Now I knew how Iridia had felt, bound and helpless to do anything.

I decided to remain still and wait for the opportune moment. I'd only have one shot at taking them by surprise, and I wanted to make it count. I didn't think I'd be able to get away, but I could possibly damage whatever they were using to collect my blood. Plus, I had felt Keane getting closer to my location. If I could just distract them long enough, maybe we could catch them.

When I felt Celeste kneel next to me and start to lean forward, I decided this was my best chance. Opening my eyes, I kicked out in her direction with my bound feet. I managed to catch her square in the chest, causing her to fall over backward. Stunned, Jacob did nothing but stare at me. I scrambled to my knees—no easy task with my hands and feet bound. *Thank you, Brianna, for making me take what I thought were useless yoga classes.* I quickly searched the ground for the syringe I'd seen fly from Celeste's hand.

"Get her, you idiot!"

I only had seconds before Jacob came to his senses and grabbed me. I finally spotted the syringe lying by the stream, and in a last-ditch effort, I dove for it. I managed to tip it the rest of the way into the water and watched it slip away with the surprisingly strong current.

"Dammit!" Celeste was on her hands and knees, looking into the water, trying to find the syringe.

Jacob had finally figured out how his muscles worked and grabbed onto me, pulling me against his chest, my knees still on the ground.

Celeste turned her storm filled gray eyes on me. "You bitch!" she cried, slapping me hard across the face. My head snapped to the side with the force of the blow. I felt blood slowly trickling down my cheek, and my mouth filled with it where my lip had split. I turned back toward her and spit it out in her direction.

"Oh, I'm sorry, Celeste. Have I upset some sordid plan of yours?"

"You!" She seemed about to hit me again, but then we all heard a shuffling sound coming toward us through the foliage. "Quick. Wipe her mind and let's get moving."

"But what about her blood?"

"I'll find a way to get it later, just—" She cut off suddenly, a malevolent smile breaking across her lips. "Well, had I known that would do the trick, I would have done it to start with. That was so much more satisfying."

Not sure what she was talking about I flinched when she grabbed my face. Pulling a handkerchief from her pocket, she rubbed it across my cheek and lip. It came away soaked in blood.

"This will do nicely. Now, erase her mind, Jacob. The last hour or so should do."

Jacob sighed but turned me toward him. "I'm sorry about this."

He stared deeply into my eyes, and though I tried to shut them, I couldn't look away. "Whaa...what are you?"

He smiled regretfully. "A Scriosán." Ah, shit, I was in trouble. Again. If I remembered correctly, a Scriosán could erase a person's mind—not that I'd be remembering much soon. I only hoped he didn't accidentally go too far back. "You might feel a bit of a burning sensation." As he continued to stare into my eyes, I did indeed feel a burning sensation. It felt like my brain was being fried over-easy in my skull. I tried to cry out, but my scream seemed to stick in my throat.

I must have passed out, as the next thing I knew, I was in Keane's arms, and he was ladling cool water into my mouth.

"Come on, Blue. Snap out of it, sweetheart." I choked as more water slipped down my throat, momentarily blocking my airway. Keane sat me forward and patted my back, rubbing in slow circles. "Attagirl."

I sat that way until I caught my breath, then turned my attention to him. He was frowning at me, but I saw in his eyes that he was relieved. "You know, I think you're right…" My voice came out dry and raspy.

"About what?

"I do seem to attract trouble left and right."

He chuckled, the sound rumbling in his chest. Standing, he promptly punched me in the shoulder, almost knocking me over.

"Hey! What was that for?" I looked up at him, rubbing my arm.

"I told you not to go anywhere without one of us being with you. You disobeyed a direct order and should be punished accordingly…" He looked at me severely with his hands on his hips before taking my hand and pulling me to my feet, straight into his arms. He hugged me tightly to his chest for a minute before leaning back and lightly tracing his finger along my swollen cheek. "But it looks like someone did that already."

I grimaced. "Yeah, I'm having a bit of an off day today."

Keane stepped back as Mckile came forward and gave me a hug, too. "You gave us quite a start there, girl. See if Keane and I don't chain you up the next time we need to rest."

I laughed. "I'm sorry. I did keep tabs with Cullen and Ronan up until the last move. And I didn't go topside."

Keane growled. "Cullen and Ronan will be getting a dressing down when I get back, too."

I shook my head. "It wasn't their fault. Tristan is their first priority. He is the King, after all. And I was with Cedric…" I trailed off as I remembered what had happened just before all the nonsense started. Hey, wait a minute. I remembered what happened! I looked at Keane in surprise.

"What's the matter, Blue?"

"I remember what happened."

"I'm glad. We'll go over it as soon as we get you back to Tristan's quarters and make sure you're secure.

"No, you don't understand. A Scriosán…"

Keane looked at me sharply. "You had a run-in with a Scriosán?"

I nodded. "But I remember. I know he tried to erase my memories, and it burned like hell, but...I still remember."

Keane shook his head. "This isn't the place to discuss that. I have a theory, but we'll talk about it later." He looked at me pointedly, and I took the hint. It obviously had something to do with my genetics.

As we made our way back to Tristan's quarters with Mckile taking lead, and Keane following, I couldn't keep my mind from wandering to just what Celeste might be doing with my blood.

Tristan was waiting for me as I stepped off the elevator. If the footprints in the carpet were any indication, it looked like he had been pacing the living area. Cullen and Ronan sat in one corner, looking unconcerned. Mckile had explained on the ride down that telepathy was among the Vaimpír's catalog of talents, so they had been in constant communication while looking for me.

"Blue." Tristan folded me into a tight hug. "Thank God. I've been so worried."

"About little ol' me?" My voice was muffled as Tristan pressed my face into his chest. He leaned back to look at me, taking in my cheek, which was starting to bruise, and my already swollen lip.

"Who did this to you? Did Cedric have anything to do with this?"

"Cedric?"

I looked questioningly at Keane, who shrugged. "He was the last known person with you, and he's now missing also."

I sighed. "No, it had nothing to do with Cedric."

"Are you sure?" Tristan gently turned my face toward him. "You're not just trying to protect him, are you?"

"No, I mean it. Cedric and I had a little...misunderstanding earlier, and he stormed off."

"He left you alone?" This came from an indignant Cullen. "I knew I never should've trusted that bastard."

I shook my head. "No, it was all Celeste's doing."

Keane wasn't surprised since he'd already picked the memories from my head, but Tristan seemed floored. "Celeste Beaumont?"

I gave him a half-smile. "I don't think she likes me much."

Keane chuckled while shaking his head. "That's an understatement if I ever heard one."

Tristan guided me over to the enormous blue couch that sat by the fireplace, and everyone followed. "I suppose you ought to tell me exactly what happened."

After I went over everything I could remember in detail, Tristan looked thoughtful. "I wonder what they meant when they said they were waiting for the Elder's decision? The Elders aren't even deliberating on anything yet. Today's meetings were just to present things."

I shrugged. "You got me. What I want to know is why she wanted my blood so badly." Then something from a past conversation occurred to me, making me feel slightly queasy—though that could have been because I was running on a cup of coffee and nothing else. I'd kill for a big ol' greasy cheeseburger and fries right about now. Mmm, I definitely needed some crispy fries. Keane winked at me and walked to the far end of the room, a cell phone pressed to his ear. Shaking my head, I brought my wandering attention back to what I'd been about to ask. "Oh, ah, how exactly are contestants entered into the Trials if they were to be enacted?"

Tristan sat forward on the couch, absently rubbing his hands together. "As the Trials haven't been enacted in over a millennium, I'm only going by the histories, but I believe the Sanguinem Lapis Circuli is used."

"And just what *is* a Sanguinomnom Lap whatever?"

Tristan smiled in amusement. "Rough translation? The blood stone circle."

I let out a harsh breath. "Somehow, I knew it would have something to do with blood."

"The idea is that the Elders set a magical circle in a remote, unknown area that can only be penetrated by a Fae. Inside that circle is a very special stone—the blood stone. All those wishing to participate in the Trials must prove their worth by finding the circle. Once they do, they place a small amount of their blood on the stone contained within. Supposedly, the blood bonds with the stone, entering the person into a magical type of contract from which they cannot be released until the Trials are over."

"What would happen if, say, someone else entered you?"

"I don't think the stone would know the difference."

"Okay, so say this is Celeste's intent." I held up a hand to silence Tristan when he looked like he wanted to argue. "Let's just speak hypothetically." After he nodded, I continued. "Say Celeste did enter me into these Trials and contracted me to the blood stone or whatever. Could I just sit them out and not participate?"

Tristan was shaking his head before I even finished. "The Trials are a sacred ritual for our people. Once contracted, the Elders would require you to participate."

"What would they do if I or someone else backed out?"

"According to the law? Kill them."

I sucked in a breath. "That's a bit harsh."

Tristan shrugged a shoulder. "These laws were written—"

"I know, I know, centuries ago. And laws don't get changed very often." I grumbled, lowered my voice, and gave my best imperial impression. "This is the way it has always been done, so this is the way it will continue to be done."

Mckile barked out a laugh. "Sounds like you've been hanging out with Keane for too long."

I grinned at him. Just then, the elevator door dinged, and all eyes turned in its direction. Standing in the interior was none other than Cedric, who was flanked by one of the royal guards. Cullen was by his side, instantly grabbing him by the collar and dragging him into the room. Truthfully, it was pretty eerie. I hadn't even seen Cullen move.

"Hey! What gives?" Cedric tried to yank his shirt from Cullen's hand by elbowing him, but Cullen held firm.

"You're already on my shit list, buddy, don't push your luck."

"Your shit list? Look, I just came down here to see if Blue made it back okay."

"She did. No thanks to you." Keane stood in front of Cedric, blocking his view of where I sat on the couch. "Because of your carelessness, she was kidnapped, and roughed up in the process."

"What?"

Cedric attempted to step around Keane, but Mckile and Ronan blocked him, creating a wall. Cedric threw up his hands. "Really? It's not like I'm going to hurt her."

"How do we know that? How do we know you didn't orchestrate the whole thing?"

Tristan finally spoke up. "Let him pass."

They allowed Cedric to move forward but immediately flanked him as he came over to the couch. He bowed in deference to Tristan, then turned to me. "Good god, Blue, what happened!?"

"Celeste happened."

"Celeste?"

"Seems she's gotten more possessive. She didn't take kindly to my being with you today." None of the guys flinched at my bald-faced lie. I didn't want to let Cedric know what was really going on just yet—not until I was sure I could trust him.

"I'm so sorry, Blue. Had I known she was around…"

"You would have what? Not run off?"

"Look, I know what I did—*everything* I did—was wrong. I came down here to apologize. If you'll let me." I started to shake my head but not for the reason he thought, causing him to rush ahead. "I don't want to lose your…" He looked around at the assembled company, clearly uncomfortable. "I don't want to lose your friendship over this. I'm really sorry I tried to push you into…things you weren't ready for. And I'm really sorry I left you there alone."

I smiled and shook my head again, causing his shoulders to slump. "It's okay, Cedric. I don't hold anything against you—none of it. I just hope you understand my feelings on the matter at this point and respect them."

He nodded quickly and seemed about to step closer to me. Before he could, Keane cleared his throat, and Cedric held back, looking annoyed.

"I guess I'll go, then."

I stood and walked over to him. "Thanks for coming and apologizing." I gripped his shoulder for a second before stepping back.

Cullen and Ronan escorted him to the elevator. As the doors shut on him, I flopped back onto the couch.

Tristan looked at me, appearing slightly amused. "Do I want to know what things he was referring to?"

I gave a half-laugh and shrugged. "He tried to kiss me. He seems to think we need to be more than friends."

"And what do you think?"

Before I could answer, the elevator door opened again. Three Fae stood inside. I didn't know their names, but I knew they were Elders. After acknowledging them with a slight head incline, I turned to Tristan and mouthed, "I'm outta here."

"Coward." He mouthed back as I quickly scooted through the door that led to the bedrooms.

I wasn't in my room long before a knock sounded on the door. "Come on in."

Keane peeked around the corner. "You decent?"

I laughed. "And if I said I wasn't?"

Keane came in smiling wolfishly. "All the better."

I laughed and relaxed against the headboard where I had been resting.

"I brought you something." He pulled a bag from behind his back, and I felt my mouth start to water. I immediately recognized the black and white logo.

"Is that from The Tattooed Moose?" The Tattooed Moose had the best burger and fries in Charleston, in my opinion, and I was addicted to their namesake burger along with their duck fat fries.

"Mmm, it might be." Bringing the bag over, he first placed a napkin down then upended the bag onto the bed. Two burgers wrapped in foil dropped out, followed by a pile of crispy french fries.

I clasped my hands together at my shoulder and batted my eyelashes at him. "My hero. How did you know I was craving a cheeseburger?"

Keane laughed. "Since it's been practically the only thing on your mind since you walked into Tristan's quarters…"

I laughed then. "Yeah, I guess it has, hasn't it?"

Grabbing one of the burgers, I quickly unwrapped it and took a bite. Moaning as it practically melted in my mouth, I chewed and grabbed a couple of fries. Chef Mike was a true genius when it came to his food. He took even something as basic as a burger and fries to a whole other level.

"Uh. This is the best thing I've tasted in a long time."

Keane smiled and dug into his burger. After a few moments of companionable silence, Keane broached the subject we had put on hold earlier.

"So, the Scriosán wasn't able to erase your memory, huh?"

I shook my head. "He gave it his best shot. I thought it might be working, but I guess my body counteracted it somehow."

"That would make sense given what Kieran told you about your genetics. A Scriosán can't erase the memory of another Scriosán."

I nodded, having figured as much. "I wonder why it burned so badly at first."

"This is the first time you've come into contact with a Scriosán since your abilities started to rise. It probably took a minute for your body to awaken the knowledge."

"Keane…" I was hesitant to mention the meeting with Iridia, knowing she wanted it to be kept a secret, but I thought someone else should know, just in case something happened.

Keane seemed to sense I was about to divulge something important. "What is it, Blue?"

"I had a dream last night…Well, not exactly a dream…" I swallowed. "I met Iridia."

Keane remained silent as I opened my mind with the memory of last night's meeting so he could see it. Nodding, he looked at me. "I think we should keep that between the two of us."

Agreeing, I crumpled the foil my burger had come in and grabbed the last few fries from the napkin in front of us. "The question now is, what do we do about Celeste?"

Keane smiled and gathered our trash. "You leave that to us. We'll find her."

I nodded. "I have no doubt of that. I just hope it happens in time. I have a feeling something else is going on here besides just a woman's jealousy."

# Chapter Ten

Dinner that night was a relatively quiet affair. Tristan was still in meetings with the Elders, leaving me with Keane, Mckile, Ronan, and Cullen for company since they were all off duty—except for Keane. But he was my guard, so...

After some takeout Chinese food from one of my favorite places—don't ask me how they got the things they did so far underground—we sat around playing video games. Well, *they* played the games. I more or less acted as comedic relief.

"Ah!" I threw up my hands, as I was once again blown to bits on the screen. "You guys cheat."

"No, you just really suck at this game." They had been teasing me mercilessly for the past hour about my lack of ability when it came to gaming. Far from being insulted, it only made me laugh because they were so obviously right. Setting my controller down, I wandered over to the small built-in fridge in the corner. After pushing several bags of unidentifiable substances aside, I found an RC Cola and popped the top. I had thought about asking the guys what the bags contained, but in the end, I decided I didn't really want to know. Just as I turned to go back to the game, the elevator opened, and Tristan stepped out. I studied the harried look on his face and knew the Elders had given him bad news. He looked around the room slowly until he spotted me, then headed in my direction. Keane and the guys all stood, immediately sensing Tristan's agitation.

As Tristan reached my side, I eyed him in concern. "What is it? What happened?" He took my arm and led me over to one of the chairs, causing my heart rate to accelerate with dread. I felt Keane lay a comforting hand on my shoulder.

"The Elders called for the Trials."

I closed my eyes. It wasn't really a surprise. I had begun to suspect something like this would happen. But it was one thing to think it, and quite another to hear it. I opened my eyes slowly to look at him again. "How?"

"I don't know. This just isn't how it's done. I'm supposed to be allowed my choice. And *then*, if it's met with disagreement and there is no other alternative, the Trials are called."

Keane leaned forward. Though his voice remained calm, the tightening of his hand where it still rested on my shoulder suggested otherwise. "What reason did they give for calling the Trials so prematurely?"

Tristan shook his head. "None. You know the Elders. Once they decree something, they don't need to answer to anyone. I suspect Sethos had a hand in this, though. Elder Avner was quite smug."

I saw a slight tick in Keane's jaw. "It just doesn't make sense. What possible reason could Elder Avner have voiced that would have convinced the others so quickly?"

Tristan shook his head sadly. "I don't know, Keane. What I do know is that finding Celeste has just become our top priority. The circle is being erected this evening, and the announcement will be made shortly thereafter."

"Tonight?"

Tristan nodded, his expression serious. Suddenly, a keening bell-like sound could be heard, echoing through the room.

"There's the call."

I looked at Tristan. "The call?"

"The call to the meeting from the Elders. It alerts everyone at Dock Street."

"Didn't you just leave them? How did they manage it so fast?"

Tristan gave me a lopsided grin and spread his arms, palms up, shrugging. "Fairies."

I shook my head in pretend disgust, rolling my eyes toward the ceiling causing Tristan to chuckle. "Right, Fairies."

The guys quickly suited up in their gear, weapons and all. "We'll escort you, Your Majesty." This came from Ronan.

"You don't have to." Tristan indicated the other two Fae who had been standing guard for him while he'd been with the Elders.

"Nonsense. With a gathering this large, you need us at your side." Keane had stepped forward to take command. He dismissed the other two guards, and they quickly entered the elevator to make their escape, seemingly not wanting to anger Keane.

I stood. "Where is the meeting being held?"

"In the ballroom."

I nodded and then looked down at myself. I was still wearing my dirty shorts and T-shirt from earlier. "Do I need to dress up or anything?"

"No, you are fine as you are. With this announcement not being planned ahead of time, I'm sure there will be people in all manner of dress. Come."

He offered me his arm, which I immediately took, while the Vaimpír fell into a loose formation around us. As we rode the elevator up, I thought I felt a hand on my shoulder but saw nothing there when I looked. I tried to shake off the sensation, but it stuck with me. I wondered if it was Iridia, somehow. The thought was comforting.

As we entered the ballroom, I saw people standing in small groups, talking quietly. A raised dais that hadn't been there the night of the afterparty had been placed on one end of the room, with several chairs on it. I assumed it was for the Elders.

I looked around for Celeste—not that I thought she'd be here. Something told me she was already on her way to the blood stone circle. As I continued to look over the crowd, I spotted Cedric leaning against the far wall. He had his arms crossed over his chest and one foot planted on the wall behind him. His hair had fallen over his eyes, giving him the look of an insolent teenager who wanted to be anywhere but where he was. It was funny, but in that pose, he looked almost like the picture of Larkin I'd found in Riona's closet.

As if he felt my eyes on him, he looked up. I raised my hand in a silent greeting, and he nodded. Even after I had looked away, I could still feel his weighted stare. I could tell our earlier confrontation had done little to dampen his desire to be more than friends. Shaking my head, I continued to scan the crowd below for the elusive Celeste.

As the gathering spotted Tristan, the room began to quiet. He paused at the top of the stairs. "Good people. Thank you for coming so quickly to this impromptu meeting. The Elders have a special announcement they wish to make. Please, give them the same attention and respect you would bestow upon me." We remained standing on the second-floor balcony above the gathered clan with the Vaimpír flanking us on either side—a security measure, I was sure. Since the Trials hadn't been enacted in over a millennium, who knew how the people would react to the news?

I saw the Elders enter through a set of doors at the very back of the room below us. They moved single file across the floor, looking almost like judges in their dark, ornate robes. People bowed as they passed, staying on bended knees and facing the raised dais. As soon as all seven Fae were seated, everyone rose as one, almost as if it had been choreographed or some unknown puppeteer above had pulled their strings.

I looked at the face of each Elder below me. Most expressions were blank and gave nothing away, except for one man. He had a look of extreme superiority and smugness on his face. It must be the Elder Tristan had mentioned earlier.

From what Tristan had told me, Avner was the representative from the Misty River Clan, hence their belief that Sethos was involved in this breach of protocol. I saw Kieran sitting toward the center of the group. When I caught his eye, he showed the worry and concern he felt for a split-second before wiping his expression clean again. I wondered how they had convinced him to go along with this. I would definitely corner him later to find out.

The small man who sat at the center of the stage stood, and Tristan leaned over to whisper in my ear. "That's Elder Demirtas. He's of the Green Mist Clan...Elves."

"Fae of the Moon Tree Clan, thank you all for coming tonight. I am sure you must be wondering exactly what this is all about. The Elders have come to a recent decision that it is high time we institute some changes." An excited rumble started in the crowd. "And depending on the results, we may decide to establish them throughout the clans."

I felt Tristan stiffen next to me. This was obviously something they had neglected to mention to him during their meeting. Since our hands were below the railing where no one could see, I reached over and took his, giving it a squeeze. He looked down at me for a moment before relaxing his stance and lacing his fingers with mine. I couldn't imagine what he was going through, knowing his future rested on what amounted to a set of games.

Below us, Elder Demirtas continued to talk about change and the betterment of the clans as a whole. After what seemed like hours, he finally paused in his speech. I could practically feel the crowd leaning forward as if knowing he was finally about to announce why they had brought everyone together.

"As you know, the time of mourning for your beloved Queen Riona is at an end." Tristan's hand tightened on mine, and I almost squeaked at the pressure. I saw Keane put his hand on Tristan's shoulder and squeeze. Tristan looked at him questioningly before glancing over at me. Something on my face must have shown the pain. He loosened his grip with an apologetic look before turning back to the Elders below.

"As per tradition, her position within the clan has remained open. It is now time to fill it. Hence why, in two weeks' time, the Elders plan to enact the Trials."

The faint rumble making its way through the crowd below exploded into a roar. Though many looked at Tristan, I couldn't tell if they were excited or outraged. Elder Demirtas, still standing before the people, merely waited as the initial shock flowed over everyone. Once things started to quiet, he raised his hands for silence.

"I know this is unusual, but the Elders have discussed it, and we believe this practice will benefit all the clans. In the past, the Trials have produced strong leaders who went on to lead the clans in great things. With the undercurrents of the situation with this clan, we believe the Trials will provide the best opportunity to select a new Queen.

"Earlier this evening, the Sanguinem Lapis Circuli was put into place. If you wish to participate in the Trials for the chance to be the next Queen of the Moon Tree Clan, you will need to prove your worth by finding the circle and placing your blood on the stone. You have until midnight on the night of the full moon to do so. Do not take this challenge lightly, for it is a most dangerous course. Some have died in pursuit of the prize."

He paused, letting his ominous words float around the room. "We will gather here again on the night of the full moon to announce the participants." With the end of his speech, the Elders stood and quickly exited. I felt the excited energy below start to gather and knew I needed to make a hasty exit before it all came barreling down on my senses. I looked beseechingly at Keane, who understood immediately.

"Sir, I think it's time we make our exit." Tristan nodded, and we exited the ballroom as one, headed back to Tristan's private quarters.

As we rode the elevator down, a sudden wave of dizziness overcame me, causing vertigo.

"Whoa..." I fell back against Keane, unable to stand.

"Blue, what is it?" Tristan took my arm, concerned.

"I don't know. I just feel really dizzy all of a sudden." I rubbed a hand over my eyes, trying to clear my vision. Suddenly, a burning sensation flared on my arm, causing me to cry out. I looked down but saw nothing.

Tristan placed the back of his hand on my forehead. "You might be having lingering effects from the Scriosán."

"I don't think so."

I looked up at Keane—probably not the smartest move when things were still spinning—but we hadn't told Tristan about what I was yet.

We'd only said that whatever the Scriosán had tried earlier hadn't worked for some unknown reason.

Keane leaned over and scooped me into his arms. I laid my head on his shoulder and closed my eyes. I idly wondered if I could communicate telepathically with him like the other Vaimpír could—I'd never really tried. But since I felt him like other Vaimpír, I thought maybe it was possible. Now was probably as good a time as any to try. Thinking of just Keane, I pushed my thoughts toward him.

*"Keane..."*

*"What?"*

I visibly started when I heard his reply in my head and opened my eyes to look at him. *"It actually worked. You can hear me, and I can hear you."*

I felt Keane silently chuckle. *"Of course, it worked. What did you expect?"*

*"I don't know...I just didn't know if I could really do it."*

*"Stop staring at me like that, or everyone will know you're talking to me."*

*"Oh, sorry."* I relaxed against his chest and closed my eyes. *"I think we need to tell Tristan about what I am."*

Keane remained silent for so long that I opened my eyes again and looked at him. Grimacing, he nodded and turned to Tristan. "Sir, there is something we need to discuss once we reach your quarters."

Tristan instantly looked suspicious, clearly having witnessed our silent communication. He could hardly know we had been conversing telepathically, but he kept his comments to himself and only nodded.

The dizziness that had surrounded me slowly dissipated until I felt like myself again. "I think I'm okay now, Keane. You can put me down." The elevator doors opened, and he stepped through them without comment, still holding me in his arms. "Keane?"

"I'll put you down when we get to Tristan's room, not before."

I wanted to argue with him but decided to save my breath. Instead, I crossed my arms over my chest like a petulant child and rolled my eyes, causing him to laugh. After ordering Mckile, Ronan, and Cullen to keep watch, he marched down the hallway to Tristan's bedroom.

Setting me gently on the bed, he stepped back and turned to Tristan, who had followed us, shutting the doors behind him.

Tristan eyed us wearily. "Do I even want to know what is going on?" He had been leaning against the closed doors but now stood and walked over to sit on the bed next to me.

I shook my head at him. "Probably not, but I think it's best if you are fully aware of something I recently discovered."

Tristan glanced at Keane. "And Keane knows about it?"

We both nodded.

"I see."

I took a deep breath. "I found out who my mother is." Tristan seemed about to interrupt, so I rushed on before he could. "My mother is Iridia, the warrior Queen."

Tristan stared at me for a moment. "Your mother is Iridia, the Queen of the Fernsong Clan and one of the most talented Fairies of our time?"

I nodded.

Tristan looked thoughtful. "That means Kieran is your grandfather, and Galene is your grandmother."

"Who is Galene?"

"She's a very high-ranking and powerful Nereid."

I hadn't known that. "Kieran's wife is a Nereid?" Both Tristan and Keane nodded. "But that means she knows I exist."

"What do you mean?"

"My necklace, the one my mother left me, was made by a Fairy and a Nereid. Cedric said it was created with a powerful protection spell."

"It sounds like Galene was well aware of your existence. Protection spells are made specifically for one person only. They're not interchangeable or transferable."

It seemed there were a lot of secrets where I was concerned. If my grandmother knew of my existence, then she also knew that Iridia was alive. I'd have to remember to ask Kieran more about his Fae wife when I saw him next.

Tristan interrupted my musings. "And who is your father?"

I shrugged. "I still don't know that yet. Kieran suspects...well, he thinks Aiden might be my father."

"How is that even possible? Fairies and Warlocks can't have children together."

"I know, but what other explanation could there be? My abilities point to something far outside the realm of possibility."

"What do you mean?"

"I seem to have the powers of all the Fae rolled into one. As I've come into contact with different types of Fae, my powers have awakened."

"Which is why the Scriosán couldn't erase your memories."

I nodded. "And it's why I was able to feel Keane after he gave me a small bit of his blood."

"How many types of Fae have you come into contact with?"

"I'm not sure. Fairy, Vaimpír, Wolf, Ealaín, Scriosán, and Nixie. I may have come across others without even knowing. I have a few abilities I can't really explain."

"You will need training on those abilities."

I nodded. Tristan was taking this surprisingly well. "Kieran will provide a few teachers, and I'm also going to work with him."

I had been leaning back on my arms up to that point, so when I leaned forward and placed my arm on my leg, it was a shock to see a large black mark on the inside of my forearm.

"What the hell...?"

It was an intricate set of Celtic knots with two wavy lines running behind them, almost like a Roman numeral two.

"It's the blood stone mark." I noticed Tristan had gone completely still.

I stopped trying to wipe the mark off my arm and looked up in alarm. I felt as if a noose were tightening around my neck.

"It is the mark of the blood stone union. You are the second participant in the Trials."

I sucked in a breath, remembering the burning sensation I'd felt earlier. "Celeste..."

Tristan nodded. "It would appear you were right about her, after all. About everything."

"What do we do now?"

Tristan looked at me expressionlessly. "Train."

# Chapter Eleven

As I lay in bed that night, unable to sleep, I reflected on my life and the people in it. I was so glad my friends were safely away on jobs out of the country. I loved them, but I wasn't sure how I'd explain everything to them, let alone if I'd let them become involved. At least this way, if something happened, they wouldn't know about it until afterward and wouldn't be hurt. Who knew what lengths these women would go in order to win?

Tristan had promised he would be the one to talk to them if the worst happened. I wasn't sure how he would explain my death if it came to that, but he said if it did, he would make sure nothing in the world of the Fae touched my friends. Trying not to dwell on the possible outcomes of the impending Trials, I got up and out of bed, then wandered into the closet. Pulling out the drawer with all the pictures in it, I carried it to the bed. I started carefully sifting through the old photographs, looking at the snapshots of Riona's life—at least the last few years of it.

There was a bit of everything in the drawer: pictures of Riona, snapshots of family and friends, even events that had occurred over the years within the clans. Some were black and white and so faded they were hard to make out, while others were in color—that old-time color that almost looked like someone had taken a colored pencil to the picture. Eventually, I came across a shot of Tristan buried toward the bottom of the drawer. He was in a lot of the photos, of course, but this one really spoke to me for some reason.

He was sitting on some rocks by the ocean, gazing into its depths as though it would give him the answer to some deep-seated question. The photographer had perfectly captured his look of ponderous thought, and I wondered what had caused that expression. Setting aside all the others, I turned it over to see if Riona had captioned it. There was only a date on the back.

*"That is one of my all-time favorite shots of Tristan."*

I looked up, startled by the voice, but no one was there.

"Uh, hello?"

*"A group of us decided to take a trip to the beach. As a matter of fact, it was in a spot not far from where your house is today, though it wasn't there at the time."*

Suddenly, the bed dipped across from me as if someone had sat down.

"Ri...Riona?"

A shadowy outline started to form before me. It slowly solidified into a person. I stared in shocked amazement at the small figure sitting across from me. She was dressed in a floor-length, regal purple gown and had her hair expertly piled on the top of her head in intricate braids interwoven with pearls and something that glittered. Her feet were bare, and I thought I saw the slight movement of wings behind her back.

*"Hello, Blue."*

"I'm not asleep this time, am I?"

Riona smiled and shook her head.

"Wow, okay." I sat back on the bed, still not quite believing it. "So, are you a ghost or an angel?"

Riona tilted her head to the side in thought. *"I'm not sure what you would call me, to tell you the truth."*

"But you are dead."

She nodded. *"This is merely a projection of my former self. When Brody created the sculpture of me, a small piece of my spirit was captured inside.*

*Because of that, I still have a tie to the earthly plane and can visit in spirit form. This is the first time I've ever been able to appear as anything you can see, though."*

"Why? What changed?"

*"You. You're the one making this happen."*

"How would *I* be doing this?"

Riona shrugged. *"I don't know. I just know your magic allows you to see me."*

I wasn't sure exactly how to take this. It was one thing to talk to a person in a dream. It was quite another to have a ghost sitting across from you, conversing. "So, ah, have you been hanging around for long?"

*"I've been with you since you first touched my sculpture. Don't worry. Your secrets are safe with me."*

I thought about some of the odd sensations I had experienced lately. "It was you, wasn't it? The one who encouraged me to go into Tristan's bedroom that night and turned on the closet light when Tatiana came. And it was your hand I felt on my shoulder earlier this evening."

Riona nodded. *"I've been trying to lend support and encouragement the best way I know how."*

"But why?"

She sighed. *"Among other things, I want to see Tristan happy. I know how my death affected him. I've seen how he's withdrawn and blames himself."* She shook her head. *"It wasn't his fault, any of it. He did everything he could to make me happy, even at the cost of his happiness. It was I who failed him. Failed to be the wife he needed. Failed to provide him the children he deserved. And all because of my selfish obsession with another man."*

I looked at her sympathetically. "We can't help who we fall in love with, Riona."

*"You're right, of course. And I did love Larkin. Even as he betrayed me at the end... I still loved him. But as women we have room for more than one person in our hearts. We don't love everyone the same way, of course, but each love is no less important. I always thought women who said they were in love with two different men were delusional. It took dying to realize it is possible."*

I wasn't sure how I felt about Riona saying she had been in love with Tristan romantically. I had come to view their relationship as more of a close friendship. I was afraid if I viewed it as more than that, I might read more into Tristan's behaviors again. Not wanting to pursue that train of thought further, I veered off in a different direction. "How did you die, Riona? Tristan said there were no marks on your body or indication of who killed you or how."

Riona laughed bitterly. *"It was Larkin."*

"Larkin?"

*"Contrary to what Tristan believes, it wasn't Sethos' guards waiting for me that night in the woods. It was Larkin. We met in that glen exactly as we had planned. We made love under the trees, and afterward, I told him I was pregnant with his child."*

"No..." I covered my mouth, horrified.

Riona nodded sadly. *"He had much the same reaction, though for different reasons, of course. That was when I realized he wasn't the man I thought he was. I was devastated. I tried to talk to him, tell him what a wonderful thing it was. His child would become royalty and one day be heir to the throne. He only laughed at me bitterly and threw in my face that had I loved him as much as I said, I would have married him all those years ago and made him King."*

"What happened then?"

*"He called his guards, some of Sethos' goons, to come and restrain me. They took me to Sethos' palace and placed me in a small cell. Larkin came to me and tried to force me to tell him how to defeat our armies. To tell him what their weaknesses were. He used magic potions and spells to try to make me talk. Of course, I resisted everything he did. I wasn't without magic. In the end, though, hoping to break me, he told me he had never truly loved me and that I had merely been a pawn in his bid to become King."*

She shook her head sadly. *"I saw the truth of it in his eyes. He hadn't loved me at all. As you can imagine, that broke my heart—just as he had hoped. He then brought out a heavily enchanted dagger, and I thought he would use it to kill me. At that point, I welcomed death. I did nothing to resist. I didn't try to save myself or anything."*

She laughed bitterly. *"Unfortunately, I misread his intent. I didn't realize what he truly meant to do until it was too late. He used the dagger to cut our unborn child from my body."*

I gasped. "But why? The child couldn't have been more than a month old. They hadn't even finished developing yet."

*"A Warlock performed a spell that linked my life force to the child's. The Warlock could siphon my years through the tie and give them to the baby. As I took my last breath, my child—a little boy—took his first."*

I was totally dumbfounded. I had imagined many scenarios, but I never could have fathomed something like this. "So...so what happened to your child?"

*"I don't know. Something has always kept him hidden from me."*

I wanted to reach out and hug Riona, but I had a feeling my arms would go right through her. "Riona, I'm so sorry." The words seemed grossly inadequate.

*"It is over and done now. I cannot change what has already happened. I can only hope to help the future."*

"What do you hope to do here? Now? You said you wanted to see Tristan happy, but how do you intend to do that? And how do I figure into it?"

*"Tristan has been waiting his whole life for you."*

I raised an eyebrow in amusement. "That's a bit cliché, don't you think?"

Riona laughed softly. *"Perhaps, but it's true. You know that photograph? The one you felt drawn to?"*

I looked down at the photo I still held in my hand. "Yes?"

*"Do you know what he was thinking about when that photo was taken?"*

I shook my head.

*"He was thinking about you."*

I looked at her incredulously. "How is that even possible? I wasn't even born until years later."

*"Obviously, Brody neglected to mention the very first vision he had of you...one he had over fifty years ago."*

"What are you talking about?"

Riona smiled slightly. *"Brody saw you coming long before you were born, my dear. To be fair, I don't think he even remembers the other vision, let alone connected the two. But I did. Come with me."*

She reached over and, much to my surprise, took my hand. My eyes snapped to hers in astonishment. "I can feel you!"

She laughed softly. *"I told you, your magic brought me to this state. Of course, you can feel me."*

"Would anyone else be able to?"

Riona shook her head sadly. *"No, just you."* She led me into the bathroom and over to the carved vanity. *"Look in the fourth drawer down there on the right."*

I glanced at her curiously before going to the drawer she'd indicated. Inside was a small, black velvet box which I pulled out and set on the counter. I reached to lift the lid but hesitated, almost afraid of what was inside.

*"Go ahead. Open it."*

My hands shook slightly as I raised the lid. Inside was a small silver medallion on a thin sterling chain. I lifted it out and looked at it. On the front surface of the pendant was a small Celtic trinity knot etched with words around it in Latin. "What does it say?"

*"Epigram fata. Intertwined destiny. Open it up."*

I looked at the piece, at first not understanding what she meant, but then I saw a small cutout hidden in the seam where you could put your fingernail. Prying the two halves apart, I saw that the medallion was actually a locket of sorts. Inside was a tiny painting of a woman. Staring at the face, I realized Riona was right. It did look like me, though it was hard to say for sure, given how small the painting was. I wondered how Brody had managed to paint something so tiny and with so much detail.

"You say this woman was in Brody's vision?"

Riona nodded. *"He gave this to Tristan the day that photograph was taken on the beach. Brody told him his destiny was somehow tied to the woman in the painting."*

"Tied how?"

*"I don't know, exactly. I just know Tristan has been looking for this woman ever since. He used to wear the locket close to his heart at all times, but I guess he gave up hope of finding her as the years passed."*

"If it's true, and I am this woman…maybe that's why I felt so drawn to Tristan the first time our eyes met."

*"Possibly."*

"Does Tristan even remember this?" I held up the locket.

Riona shrugged. *"I can't say. He hasn't pulled it out and looked at it for a long time."*

I carefully laid the locket back in its velvet box. I wasn't sure if I would mention it to Tristan or not. I had a feeling there was more to the story than Riona knew. Just as I was about to put the box back in its drawer, the door to Tristan's room opened. I swung around in surprise.

Tristan stood framed in the doorway. "Blue, what are you still doing up?"

"Ah…" I looked toward Riona, but she had disappeared.

He glanced at the velvet box in my hand. "Where did you find that?"

"It was, ah, in one of the drawers here. I was, um, looking for… for…" I stopped and sighed. I didn't know why I even bothered to lie. I was terrible at it. "Actually, Riona showed me where it was."

"Riona?"

I nodded, watching him for the disbelief I was sure would cross his face. I was surprised when he only nodded. "Did she also tell you where it came from?"

I nodded again, this time slower, not sure if he truly believed me. "She said Brody gave it to you after one of his visions. Something about your destiny being intertwined with the woman's in the locket."

Tristan looked at me for a moment before reaching over to open the velvet box. He paused briefly before picking up the locket and opening it to view the painting. "She's right, of course, but there was a bit more Brody told me that I didn't tell her."

Tristan sighed. "According to him, the vision indicated there would be a great upheaval within the clans, one that would affect me personally. He didn't know exactly what, though. Whatever happened would cause a rift that would spread throughout the clans, causing the Fae to take sides."

"Riona's death…"

Tristan nodded. "Exactly what I thought after it happened. Brody said I would experience many trials during the time of discord and that an old evil would resurface to try and destroy me. But not to worry. He said a woman would come into my life, one I would be undeniably drawn to, and one whose destiny was entwined with mine."

He took a breath. "He said she would be more powerful than any Fae we had ever seen, and it would be through her power that the clans would be unified once again." He looked almost longingly at the locket before his expression hardened, and he threw it angrily back into its box, shutting the lid with a snap.

"But she never came along." Leaning over, he put the box back into the drawer I had found it in.

I thought about his statement as I watched his clipped movements. "Tell me, Tristan. Did Brody say you would experience many trials personally or that the clan would experience...Trials?"

Tristan's shoulders stiffened. He obviously hadn't thought about Brody's vision in that way. "You think he meant *the* Trials?"

I nodded. "Why not? It makes sense. It could also be why the woman in the painting hasn't shown up yet. Perhaps she is a participant in the Trials."

Tristan turned and looked at me, a small flame of hope showing in his eyes. "Perhaps."

I felt my body heat up as Tristan's unblinking gaze turned to something deeper, more primal.

When he spoke again, his voice was husky with desire. "Perhaps that is why I feel so drawn to you."

I couldn't speak past the lump that had formed in my throat. Tristan moved forward slowly until he stood mere inches from me, his eyes never leaving mine. Though we weren't touching, I didn't think you could even get a slip of paper between us. His warm breath fanned my cheeks as I gazed up at him.

"I don't know what's going to happen in the future, Blue. And this could be the worst thing I could do, considering what is going on right now, but..."

I placed my finger over his lips. "It's what I want, too. No strings attached." And I did. I not only wanted it, I *needed* it. I needed to lose myself in the tide of passion, let it take me away from the impending danger, and give me a reason for staying alive.

"But…"

I quickly silenced him again by closing the space between us and placing my lips on his. My hands dove into his hair, and I pulled him to me. As soon as our bodies touched, it was like a fuse had been lit. His arms wrapped tightly around me, his tongue diving into my mouth to deepen the kiss. His hands quickly found the edge of my oversize T-shirt and slid up under it. Stroking up and down my back, he pulled me tighter against him.

I felt his hard arousal pressing against my stomach through the thin fabric of my shirt, causing an answering heat to flow down my spine and pool between my thighs. Lifting his head, he looked into my eyes as if searching for an answer.

I smiled saucily up at him. "I certainly hope you've been keeping up with your protection spell."

Taking that as consent, he lifted me off my feet. I quickly wrapped my legs around his waist, and he carried me into his room, laying me gently on the bed, our lips never breaking apart. As I scooted higher on the mattress, I grabbed the hem of his T-shirt with one hand and pulled it up. He quickly got the message and broke our kiss, but only long enough to pull it over his head and toss it to the floor.

When he brought his mouth back to mine and buried his hands in my hair, he kissed me even more urgently than before. I ran my hands down the muscles of his chest, reveling in how they quivered and flexed as my fingers moved over them. Tristan mimicked my motions, moving his hands downward until he was at the hem of my shirt. In one quick movement, he pulled it over my head and flung it aside, letting it fall somewhere on the floor next to his.

Laying me back against the pillows, he cupped my breasts in his large palms, brushing his thumbs over the tips and causing both to stand at attention. He stroked and pinched them, pulling a moan from me. After sliding to lie beside me, he dipped his head and took one taut peak into his mouth, suckling it.

When he nipped at it before gently tugging with his teeth, it felt like an electric shock traveling through my body, headed directly to my core. I buried my hands in his hair on a moan and pulled him closer as he repeated the motion with my other nipple.

He raised his head, and I saw the heat in his eyes. Leaning forward, he took my lips in another intense kiss. As our tongues caressed each other, I moved my hand down his chest to linger at the waistband of his pajama pants. I felt his quick intake of breath as I slipped my fingers past the elastic band and found my target.

Wrapping my hand gently around him, I stroked slowly up and down. He moaned and flexed his hips in time with my motions. As I ran my thumb over his tip, I felt him shudder and reveled in the sense of power that flitted through my stomach. Turning, I slipped his pants down so I could stroke and caress every inch of him with both hands. His breath came in short pants as his tongue moved in and out of my mouth, mimicking the rhythm of my hands. I felt a bead of moisture form as I again stroked my thumb over his tip. Groaning, he pulled my hands away.

"Keep doing that, and this won't last long." His voice was low and heavy with desire.

Rolling onto his stomach, he lay between my thighs. With infinite slowness, he pulled my panties down and tossed them over the side of the bed to join our shirts. Pushing my thighs wider, he flicked his tongue. I gasped as he lapped over me.

He looked up with a wicked grin before leaning down and doing it again. This time, he didn't stop. He continued to lick and suck until I was thrashing on the bed, almost out of my mind from the overwhelming sensations he caused.

Just when I thought things couldn't get any more intense, he slipped one of his fingers inside me. I gasped as he started stroking it in and out, curving it just a bit so it brushed that sensitive spot inside. Then he slipped a second finger in, all the while tormenting me with his talented tongue. I could feel the pleasure buried deep in my core coiling tighter and tighter.

"Tristan, please…"

Seeming to know what I was asking, he straightened and removed his pants. I marveled at the sight of him as he paused for just a second before lowering himself over me. Resting on his elbows, he positioned himself at my opening.

"Are you sure, Blue? Is this what you want?"

I nodded. "I've wanted this since the first moment our eyes met outside the theater."

Tristan groaned and, seemingly unable to hold back any longer, thrust deeply, sheathing himself fully in my waiting heat. I cried out as the pleasure of it flooded every nerve ending, seeming to spark something to life within me. It was like nothing I had ever felt before. It was as if I could feel him on every level, even his pleasure seemed to be reflected back at me. It was extremely overwhelming, yet somehow, my body knew just what to do to adjust.

I opened my eyes and looked directly into Tristan's. I saw pleasure and wonder reflected there, as if he, too, felt what I did. Then he began moving, and it was all I could do to stay coherent. The energy that had built in my center seemed to rise and fall as if moving back and forth between us. I gasped as another wave crashed into me and wrapped my legs around his waist, pulling him deeper.

His groan met my sigh as I tugged his head to mine and kissed him deeply, our tongues dancing in rhythm with our bodies. As the energy between us swelled to unimaginable heights, Tristan took it even higher when he reached down between our bodies and began stroking me. I threw my head back against the pillows and closed my eyes, feeling like I might explode into a million pieces at any given second. Tristan picked up the pace, seeming to sense I was on the edge.

"Look at me, Blue."

I opened my eyes and stared into his deep sapphire depths. Time seemed to slow as I searched his face. Suddenly, a glow lit in the back of his eyes. I blinked, thinking it was a trick of the light, but when I looked again, I saw it was still there, only brighter. Then time snapped back as I found myself riding the biggest wave of pleasure I'd ever felt.

"Oh, god, Tristan…"

He thrust into me harder, pushing me to the very edge of pleasure. I hung there on the precipice for just a moment before falling over the edge crying out Tristan's name as I climaxed. I vaguely heard his shout as he, too, tumbled over the edge, prompted by the spasms rocking my body. I clutched him tightly to me as wave after wave of pleasure cascaded over us, shaking me to the core with its intensity.

When it finally ended, I lay limply in his arms, barely able to move. As our sweat-slick bodies cooled in the slight breeze the overhead fan created, I lifted a hand and ran it through his damp, tousled curls.

It was cliché, but that had been the best sex I'd ever had, hands down. I had never felt that kind of energy connection with anyone before. It was like something within me had been unlocked with the awakening of my Fae powers…and it was a sexual beast! I felt Tristan chuckle and realized I had forgotten to block my thoughts. Pushing onto his elbows, he grinned down at me.

"The best sex ever, huh?"

I grinned, just a bit embarrassed. "Yeah. Don't let it go to your head, though."

He only laughed and rolled to his back, pulling me with him. I snuggled to his side with my head in the crook of his neck, and a thigh draped across his.

"That was the best sex I've ever had, too, Blue." I pushed up onto my elbow and looked down at him with a raised eyebrow of sarcastic disbelief. He shook his head as he lifted a hand to tuck strands of hair behind my ear. "I'm serious. It's never been that intense with anyone before."

I ran my hand over his chest. "Tristan…is it always like that? I mean with other Fae? The energy-pull thing?"

Tristan seemed to consider. "To a point, I guess. Our Fae powers pull on each other, almost like we're sharing them. The intensity depends on the power of the Fae involved."

"Is that what you meant by it never being that way before?"

Tristan nodded. "Even if all your powers haven't been unlocked yet, the power is still inside you. It comes out during sex."

"What about that glow in your eyes?"

Tristan looked at me strangely. "What glow?"

"Your eyes had this strange glow in them at the end."

Tristan shook his head. "Must've been a trick of the light."

He seemed discomfited by my observation. I was about to argue but decided to let it go. It really didn't matter. Lying back down, I curled into his side again with a yawn. Chuckling, Tristan reached over and grabbed the comforter we'd pushed to the side earlier and pulled it over us. I closed my eyes. I should have probably returned to my bedroom for the night, but I was so tired, I didn't think I'd make it. Just before I fell asleep, I thought I heard Tristan mumble. "How will I ever let you go if it comes down to it?"

I awoke the next morning to the sound of someone knocking on the door. Opening my eyes, I looked groggily around, unable to reconcile my surroundings at first. When my eyes landed on the sculptures of Riona, and Iridia, I realized I was back in Riona's bedroom. I didn't remember getting up during the night to come back in here, so I guessed Tristan must have moved me at some point.

I smiled sleepily, thinking about Tristan, and was just about to fall back asleep when a knock sounded on the door again, this time a bit louder. I lifted the blanket and glanced down at myself to make sure I had something on and smiled again when I realized I had on Tristan's T-shirt instead of mine.

Shaking my head, I dropped the blanket back down. "Come in."

Keane poked his head around the door. "Rise and shine, sleepyhead. Time for training."

"Training?" I looked at him incredulously.

He grinned almost evilly. "And wear something comfortable and...durable."

Before I could even respond, he had shut the door. I sat in silence for a full minute, listening to his retreating footsteps before groaning. Rolling onto my stomach, I put a pillow over my head. Maybe if I ignored him he would just go away.

*"You know as well as I do that won't happen."*

I jolted upright in bed at the sound of the voice. Looking around, I spotted Riona sitting at the foot of the bed with her legs crossed under her. I'd almost let myself believe she had just been a figment of my imagination last night. Obviously, not. Turning into a sitting position, I regarded her. She still appeared exactly as she had before with her purple dress and hair piled on her head. Apparently, ghosts didn't get to change their clothes too often. Naturally retreating into sarcasm, I crossed my arms over my chest. "Back again so soon?"

She laughed quietly in amusement. *"I actually never left."*

"Never...you didn't see what went on last night, did you?"

She grinned. *"Don't worry, I gave you two your privacy. Though with the amount of power you two were putting out, anyone within a few miles probably knew what you were doing."*

I groaned again and, flopping back onto the bed, pulled the blanket over my head. How was I going to face everyone if they knew what I had been doing with Tristan last night?

*"You know it's nothing to be ashamed of."* Riona pulled the blanket from my face.

I stared at her for a second and then sighed in defeat, sitting up. "I know, but that doesn't make it any less embarrassing."

She laughed again. *"Come on, get up and get ready. If you don't, Keane will just come back and dump you out of bed. And he'll probably enjoy every minute of it."*

Knowing she was right, I scrambled out of bed and made a beeline for the bathroom after grabbing a sports bra and some underwear. Peeking into the open door, I saw the room—if you could really even call it that—was empty. I quickly showered and took care of the basic necessities. Not knowing how long Keane would give me, I scooped my hair into a messy ponytail, which was no easy task considering my hair was still wet, and skipped makeup. Knowing Keane, I would just be sweating it off anyway.

Since I was supposed to wear comfortable and durable clothes, I had a feeling this wouldn't be an etiquette lesson. Walking back into my room, I stopped short when I saw not one shadowy outline, but two. Riona was seated next to the very familiar figure of none other than Iridia.

"What in the world...?"

Iridia smiled and put her hand lightly on Riona's. "*Riona came to me last night and told me what had happened.*" When I looked at her questioningly and with a bit of alarm, she continued. "*About the Trials and Celeste entering you.*"

"Oh, of course." I breathed a sigh of relief. For a moment, I thought she'd meant that Riona had told her about Tristan and me. Then another thought caused me to become even more alarmed. "Wait a minute, how are you here like this?" I indicated her less-than-solid body. "You're not...dead, are you?"

"*Riona isn't the only one who can venture places in spirit form.*"

"But how?" I looked at her, confused.

Iridia smiled. "*I learned a long time ago, how to separate my spirit from my body to travel to different places.*"

"So, you're not dead, then?"

She shook her head. "*Not dead, just in a trance while I travel incorporeally.*"

"How is that even possible?"

Iridia shook her head. "*It's not something I can explain to you, it just is. In time, I'm sure you'll be able to do it, too.*"

Shaking my head at her, I went into the closet and grabbed my running gear: a pair of three-quarter-length pants and a tank top made out of a sweat-wicking fabric. It would have to do.

"*Don't worry, Blue. We're here to help you.*"

I looked between Riona and Iridia. "No offense, but what can two spirits do for me?"

Iridia smiled patiently. "*A lot, actually. We can teach you all the things the males can't. They mean well, but with the Trials, there is a whole other aspect they won't even consider.*"

"And what is that?"

"*The fact that females are conniving, devious creatures who will stop at nothing to win...even cheat.*"

I nodded. "That is most definitely true."

"*With us watching your back, they'll be a lot less likely to get the drop on you. Not to mention, both Riona and I know this place and these people inside and out. We can tell you your opponent's weaknesses and strengths and make a plan for how to beat each one.*"

I shrugged. "Sounds good to me." I turned to Iridia. "Is it safe for you to stay in this form?"

"*As long as Aiden is there to watch over my body, I'll be fine. He knows how to contact me if something should arise. Don't you worry about me. Worry about yourself right now. Pay close attention to everything, and learn as much as you can from this point on. Even the most insignificant-seeming thing could mean the difference between living and dying.*"

I grimaced. "Aren't you just a ray of sunshine this morning?"

"Funny, I was just going to say the same thing about you."

I spun around at Keane's voice, not having heard him enter the room. "Ahhh... I was just...getting ready."

He nodded, looking at me in amusement. "I can see that. Talking to your sculptures again, too, I see."

I shrugged a shoulder and quickly changed the subject. "You know me. So, what are we doing this morning?"

He looked as though he wanted to say something but only shook his head, seeming to change his mind. "First, we're visiting the gym for a thorough workout: strength, cardio, core, the whole package. Then, we're going next door to the pool to swim laps. Finally, we're hitting the track to run at least ten miles."

I felt my shoulders droop with each activity. This wasn't training, this was torture in the first degree. "Do I at least get breakfast first?"

Keane laughed. "Of course. Do you think I'm heartless?"

I raised an eyebrow and grumbled, "Is that a rhetorical question?"

Punching me lightly in the arm, he opened the door. "Come on, Trouble. Let's get this morning started."

# Chapter Twelve

Over the course of the next few weeks, I worked harder than I ever had. Not only did I have morning workouts with Keane, but I was also closeted away with Kieran and every teacher he could throw my way every afternoon. I had so many new powers developing that I couldn't even keep track of them, let alone learn how to control them. By evening, I was so worn out that all I wanted to do was crawl into bed and let the oblivion of sleep overtake me. But even that was denied me.

After everyone left for the night, my two shadowy spirits showed up for lessons of their own. From Iridia, I learned the art of war. She taught me everything she knew about martial arts, battle strategy, magical defense, and even swordplay—which was a bit tricky when you didn't want to make any noise. I'd finally resorted to covering the blades with foam noodles stolen from Tristan's pool.

On the other hand, Riona taught me the rules and regulations of the Trials, the art of politics, and the dance of Göndul. At first, I had argued about the use of dancing, but then I remembered Brody's vision where he'd seen me doing just that. As it turned out, the dance of Göndul was a large part of the Trials and something that would take the most work. I was a klutz, no question. While I could move my way through a country line dance and maybe even a basic jazz routine, this combined all types of dancing into one complicated mess and then added magic to it.

It was no wonder only a few were able to do it.

After falling on my butt for the fifth time, I stayed on the floor. Rolling onto my back, I covered my face with my hands. "This is impossible. I'm never gonna get it."

At the sound of a masculine chuckle, I peeked through my fingers. What I saw took my breath away. Tristan was leaning against the bathroom doorframe, wearing nothing but a pair of low-riding jeans—even his feet were bare.

"Talking to yourself?"

I glanced toward the two shadowy figures staring in Tristan's direction. "Ummm…"

Shaking his head, Tristan straightened and moved toward me. When he stood before me, he offered me his hand. "Let me just say I thought you were doing pretty good there until that last turn. You seem to be a natural."

Taking his proffered hand, I let him pull me to my feet and into his arms. He leaned down and took my lips in a slow, toe-curling kiss. Due to my training schedule and his meetings, we'd barely seen each other since the night we'd spent together. Pulling back, Tristan looked down at me and smiled. "I've missed you, Blue."

I smiled back. "I've missed you, too."

Tristan stepped back and moved to sit on the bed. I had to cover a giggle as he almost landed on Riona's lap. "How's training been going?"

I shrugged. "Not bad, I guess." Tristan raised his brows, and I grimaced as the lie was clear, even to my ears. "Okay, it's been brutal." I sighed deeply. "Between Kieran and Keane, I've been going nonstop. Keane has been beating me into the ground with workouts, and I've been fast-developing new powers every day as Kieran introduces me to new Fae. It's been rough trying to harness and master my powers as they present themselves, but I guess I'm managing all right." I sighed.

"I have to grudgingly admit that I think a lot of my stamina is due to Keane's physical training. While it's grueling, it really seems to help. I guess that's why he's been so strict about it." Tristan nodded, and I laughed. "Hell, I haven't worked out this much since the time my mom told me I looked like a Macy's Thanksgiving Day Parade balloon in my homecoming dress."

Out of the corner of my eye, I saw Iridia flinch and instantly regretted mentioning my upbringing.

Unaware of my discomfort, Tristan laughed. "I can't imagine you were ever the size of a Macy's parade balloon, even as a child. Most Fae have a metabolism that is hard to keep up with, and since you were raised by a human, something tells me you never had enough calories to even put an ounce on you."

I nodded but didn't say more for fear of hurting Iridia's feelings further. Noting my sudden lack of enthusiasm on the topic of my childhood, Tristan changed the subject. "So, who has been teaching you the dance of Göndul? There are so few adept at it, let alone those who can teach it."

"Ah..." I glanced almost guiltily at the spot next to him where Riona and Iridia were still seated. Tristan followed my gaze before looking back at me and raising his brows.

"You see, it's...well..." I sighed again. "It's Riona. She's been here at night helping me prepare." I didn't mention Iridia also being here. I wasn't sure she wanted Tristan to know she was still alive—at least not yet.

"Are you telling me Riona is here, now, in this room?" Tristan looked around as if expecting her to appear.

I nodded and then smiled. "Actually, you almost sat on her earlier." I did laugh this time as Tristan jumped to his feet and swung to the bed as if expecting to see someone sitting there.

"I see." Tristan glanced at me consideringly. "Can anyone but you see her?"

I shook my head. "No. Riona says it's my magic specifically that allows me to see her, though I can't say for sure how it works..." Before I even finished my sentence, the lesson from earlier today floated through my mind. Suddenly, it all made a whole lot more sense. "You know, I learned something today that might explain it. I wonder..."

Considering the rest of my lesson, I came to a decision. "There might be something I can do so you can see her, too...would you like me to try it?" Both Tristan and Riona looked at me in shocked silence, and I shrugged self-consciously. "I met with a Taibhse today. He showed me a few things." A Taibhse was what the Fae called a ghost whisperer. He could see and talk to the dead. I looked between Tristan and Riona questioningly. Riona smiled, and I knew she wanted Tristan to see her, so I looked at him. "Well?"

Slowly, he nodded. Hoping I could do it, I closed my eyes and concentrated. The Taibhse had taught me how to make a spirit visible. I had almost laughed at the idea, considering I could see the two spirits currently residing in my bedroom perfectly, in addition to the giggling little girl in the corner he was helping me to *see*.

I had briefly considered telling him I seemed to have a natural ability to see ghosts without trying, but I quickly discarded the idea. Better to know how it all worked. Apparently, it was a good thing I decided to listen, considering what I was attempting now. I hoped if I modified what he had taught me, I might be able to make it so Tristan could see Riona.

Going over the spell in my head, I mentally made the changes I thought would work. I felt a light hand on my shoulder and knew it was Iridia without looking.

*"You can do this. I know you can."*

I projected my thoughts to her just as I had with Keane before. *Thanks, I really hope this works. I just don't know if it will also make you visible to him.*

*"Don't worry about me. I can take care of myself."*

I smiled and returned my concentration to the task at hand. The Taibhse had taught me words to say to go along with the magic, but I instinctively knew they weren't necessary. They were more something used to teach young Fae the patterns for what they were feeling. Pushing my senses into my core, I centered my thoughts on the bright gold ball that seemed to reside there. I wasn't sure if it was really gold or not, but that was how I liked to imagine it.

Slowly, I began manipulating and shaping the ball, infusing it with the needed magic until I had what I wanted. Finally, I took a small pinch of the final substance and pushed at it until it seemed flow into my fingertips. With my eyes still closed, I moved to where Riona and Tristan stood. Somehow, I saw them, even behind my closed lids. It was like I was watching their energy moving about in the air in an endless circle. It reminded me of the scene at the end of the last *Matrix* movie, where Neo was blind but could still see everything as if it were all made of light. It made me wonder if someone on the creative team for that movie had been a Taibhse.

Placing both my hands on Riona's shoulders, I let a little of the gold light flow into her. She shook a bit as it seemed to blend with her energy. Turning to Tristan, I gently closed his eyes and then placed my fingertips on his lids. I allowed the remainder of the golden light to leave me and flow into him. He took in deep breaths as my magic rushed through him. Stepping back, I opened my eyes. Tristan was staring at me in shocked amazement.

"That was...incredible, Blue. I've never felt anything so...so...I don't even know how to describe it."

I smiled and gestured toward Riona. "Did it work? Can you see her?"

Tristan turned to where Riona stood and stopped, his eyes widening. "R...Riona?"

Riona looked at him almost shyly. *"Hello, Tristan."*

"I can't believe this. Is it real? Are you actually here?"

She smiled sadly. *"In spirit, yes."*

He moved forward and raised his hand as if to touch her, but Riona quickly stepped back. *"You won't be able to feel me. Only Blue can."*

Tristan hesitated, lowering his arm, but then took another step forward. "At least let me try. Since Blue's magic did this, maybe I can."

Riona stood rigidly for a few seconds before slowly relaxing. *"Okay, but please don't be disappointed if you can't."*

Tristan nodded. Raising his hand again, he slowly reached for her face. I held my breath. Just when I was sure his fingers would pass through her, his hand cupped the side of her cheek. Riona gasped, and I let out my pent-up breath. It had worked. I'd done it.

Tears running down her cheeks, Riona threw herself into Tristan's arms and started kissing him passionately. After a moment of hesitation, Tristan wrapped his arms around her and kissed her back. Feeling like an interloper, I slowly backed out of the room, quietly shutting the door behind me.

Leaning against it, I looked up at the ceiling and sighed. While I was glad they could be reunited like this, it still hurt to see them together. Slowly slipping down, I sat on the floor, pulled my knees up to my chest, and laid my head on my crossed arms.

*"It can't be forever, you know."*

I looked over at Iridia, who now sat next to me in much the same position, though she had her head back against the door.

"I know. But while it does...well..." I stopped and gestured vaguely. What I didn't say was that I now had proof that Riona was definitely more to Tristan than what he'd originally disclosed. People who were *just friends* wouldn't have reacted the way they had.

I wasn't sure I wanted to be with a man who was still in love with another woman, even if she was a ghost. It didn't leave a whole lot of room for me. Though, in the end, it might not be up to me anyway.

*"Are you in love with him, Blue?"*

I stared at Iridia for a brief second before laying my head back down. "Why does everyone keep asking me that? In lust? Most definitely. But in love? No, I don't think so. Honestly, this has all been so overwhelming. Finding out that I'm Fae, being terrorized by some unknown enemy, staying here with the Moon Tree Clan, being unwillingly thrown into these Trials." I left out the part about me sleeping with Tristan, though I had a feeling she knew about it.

"I'm just riding this tide of emotions. When it's all over—assuming I survive—and things calm down, everyone will see it for what it is." I wasn't sure if I was trying to convince her or me.

Resting her hand on my shoulder, Iridia gave it a squeeze. *"Try not to think too much."* I looked over at her questioningly. She smiled. *"Sometimes, it's just better to feel and go with what your heart is telling you. Everything will work out as it should in the long run."*

I smiled and covered her hand with mine. "Thanks, Mom."

I felt Iridia disappear as a pair of shiny black boots slid into my vision.

"Do I even want to know what you're doing sitting outside your bedroom?"

I slowly looked up, leaning my head against the door so I could see the face that went along with the boots—though I already knew who it was.

"Taking in the view?"

Keane chuckled, shaking his head. "Sometimes, I wonder about you."

I grinned. "Sometimes, I wonder about me, too, Keane." Tilting my head to the side, I considered him. Knowing I'd never get any sleep now, I wondered if he'd be interested in a late-night swim. Sometimes, swimming helped me relax on the nights I had trouble falling asleep. I really missed the ocean being in my backyard right about now.

"You wouldn't be interested in a moonlight swim, would you?"

He laughed. "Don't you swim enough during the day?"

"I can't sleep. I think the expenditure of energy might help."

"I can think of a few other things we could do to expend a little energy." He waggled his brows, causing me to laugh and shake my head. "No?"

Suddenly, the image of the two of us together in the elevator drifted across my mind, causing my pulse to leap. I quickly pressed my knees together and squelched any feelings of desire that rose to the surface.

Keane, ever sensitive to my body's shifts, paused and inhaled deeply. His eyes sought mine, but I quickly looked down at my hands. I could feel his weighted stare pushing at me, trying to see what was going on in my head.

Who was I kidding? He didn't need to try to see what was going on, he could just read my mind. I quickly closed the door on my thoughts, though I had a feeling it wouldn't do any good. As a slow smile curved his lips, I knew I was right. "Go grab your suit and meet me in the living area."

I stood and turned as if to go back into my room but then stopped. I vaguely heard the sounds on the other side of the door and knew I didn't want to face what was in there. Turning back to Keane, I shuffled my feet. "Um, how about no swimsuits?"

Keane raised an eyebrow, noting my hesitation. "Something I should know regarding what's happening in your room?"

I shook my head and shrugged as nonchalantly as I could. "Nothing important. Come on, you've got a private spot picked out, right? I'm not shy. This won't be the first time I've gone skinny-dipping."

He seemed about to question me further but then relented with a shrug. "As you wish."

I walked side by side with him down the hall and out into the living area. Once there, we moved across the room and through the door that led to Tristan's private pool. Upon entering the long hallway, he shut the living area door and then locked it. I looked at him questioningly, but he didn't say anything. Moving forward, he walked past the doors leading to the gym and pool, then past the door that led into the sauna.

"Where are we going?"

He grinned mysteriously over his shoulder but didn't say anything. I watched as he walked over to what appeared to be a blank wall. Placing his hand on the surface, he closed his eyes and whispered a few words. Suddenly, a blue glow emanated from hidden crevices in the wall. I blinked as a door slowly took shape, shimmering into existence before me.

"Whoa..."

He grinned as he slowly opened the door. I took a step forward and peered into the room beyond. My eyes widened at the sight before me. "Holy Hera..."

Keane laughed and leaned against the doorframe with his arms and ankles crossed. "What do you think? Is this what you were looking for?"

I continued to stare, still unable to believe what I was seeing. Beyond the open door wasn't the expected pool. No, before me spread a beach with crystal-white sand winking and shimmering in the clear moonlight beaming down upon it. I heard ocean waves gently lapping upon the shore and closed my eyes to let the rhythm soak into my senses. I took a deep breath, letting the air out slowly. I caught the deep, heavy scent of the ocean, and as it filled my lungs, I felt myself relaxing.

I opened my eyes and grinned at Keane. Then, without warning, I took off running across the beach, throwing up sand in my wake. I called over my shoulder to him as I began stripping off my clothes. "Last one in is a rotten egg!"

"Why, you little…"

I felt Keane's essence shift with his body as he took off after me, trying to make up the distance. He was closing in fast, and I picked up my pace. No way was I losing this race. I was down to just my underwear as I hit the surf, and with a quick wiggle, even that barrier was gone. I cried out triumphantly as I dove into an oncoming wave, the cool water enveloping me and washing away the feelings that had been dragging me down only minutes ago. As I broke the surface, I felt strong hands wrapping around my shoulders and turning me.

"You're a cheater, that's what you are."

I just laughed and shifted away from him. "No one said I had to play fair." Pushing off his chest, I struck out into the water, my arms easily slicing through the waves. It felt good to be in the ocean again—real or not.

I always felt like I was connected to a whole other world when I swam in it. And perhaps I was. Keane easily caught up and started swimming alongside me, keeping pace. When we had swum a good distance, I stopped and treaded water, turning to face him.

He wore a grin as big as mine. "Damn, that felt good. I'd forgotten how rejuvenating it is to swim in the ocean."

"Right? My friends think I'm strange for feeling that way."

"Honey, you're a lot of things, but strange isn't one of them. Ready to swim back?"

I nodded happily, and we struck out through the water together. When we reached a level spot on the ocean floor where I could stand, we stopped again. I was slightly out of breath, but he didn't appear fazed at all.

"Do you do this often at home? Is that why you wanted to live on the beach?"

I gave a half-shrug. "You could say that. I have a hard time sleeping if I don't exercise first. Since I can't shut my brain off at night, I have to exhaust my body so I can fall asleep. Plus, living on the water is just relaxing. I've always felt a connection to it."

Keane nodded in understanding. "I can see the draw."

"Something tells me you don't have any trouble falling asleep when you need to."

He shook his head. "No. When Vaimpír sleep, it is only to heal the body. We pretty much just black out until we're rejuvenated, then wake back up."

"Do you dream?"

"No, no dreams."

"Ever?" He shook his head as I stared at him curiously. "Weird."

Keane shrugged with a half-smile. "Maybe to you, but since I've been this way my whole life, I don't know anything different."

"Hmm. An Aisling was working with me the other day and showed me how to initiate Dream Walking. I wonder if it would work on you."

Keane eyed me curiously. "I don't know, to tell you the truth. I've never heard of anyone who's tried with a Vaimpír."

"Challenge accepted, then."

"What challenge?"

"Next time you need to sleep, I will attempt to walk in your dreams."

"But I told you, Vaimpír don't dream."

"Still, how do you know if it will work if no one has tried it? Maybe I can make you have a dream like Iridia did to me."

Keane shook his head but grinned. "Honey, if it's possible, you're welcome to walk in and out of my dreams as often as you'd like. Preferably like this." He leered at me playfully.

Looking down through the clear blue water, I saw that little was left to the imagination. With a grin, I looked at him and shivered slightly as desire raced through my veins. Nope. No imagination needed.

Looking back toward the beach and the trail of clothing we'd left, I considered how best to approach getting out of the water to get redressed. While I had been honest when I told him I wasn't embarrassed about being naked around him, I *did*, however, wonder if I could control myself. I had a serious case of sexual hunger where he was concerned—and just enough curiosity to get myself into trouble. I mean, look what happened in the elevator the first day I got here, and we both were fully dressed at the time. Now, we were completely naked, and I still felt the sting of Tristan's betrayal.

Stopping myself, I backtracked in my thoughts. Betrayal? Where had that thought come from? We'd both agreed to no strings with the sex we'd had, so it wasn't like we were committed to each other. Which was probably a good thing. If he had to marry someone else when the Trials were over... It wasn't like I was going to hang around and be the other woman.

And there was really little chance of me winning. My goal was just to survive. Yet I couldn't help feeling saddened by the thought of never being with Tristan again. Maybe I should just sleep with Keane. Obviously, Tristan didn't have an issue with being with someone else. Maybe that would cure me of the strange draw I had toward him. I looked over at Keane and saw he was watching me carefully, probably reading my every thought as it crossed my mind.

Ever so slowly, he moved closer to me until we stood only inches apart. "Do you always overanalyze things?"

Reaching out, he traced his hand across my cheek and down my neck. I opened my mouth to say something, but before I could, he dipped his head and took my lips in a scorching kiss. I hesitated, trying to hold on to my control, but like before, I felt my good reason slip away as his lips moved on mine, and I tasted him on my tongue. I didn't resist as he pulled my body tight against his.

I gasped into his mouth as skin met skin, and I felt the blazing heat emanating off him, even through the cool water. You'd think a Vaimpír would be cold to the touch, but that was far from the truth. Obviously, that was another Hollywood myth. His mouth moved from my lips to slide down my neck, his teeth grazing the skin. I shivered as he bit down lightly, where my life force beat out a heavy tattoo under his mouth—not hard enough to break the skin but enough to drag a moan from my lips as I remembered the pleasure I'd felt when he last bit me.

As he nipped me again, he pressed my lower half tightly against him, leaving me with no question about what he wanted. And while one part of me wanted to throw caution into the wind and just go for it, the other part was still hung up on my conflicting feelings where Tristan was concerned. I pushed against Keane's chest to try to put a little bit of space between us.

"Keane, we shouldn't…"

He brought his lips back to mine to stop the words. I swallowed my protests as he kissed me again, this time a bit rougher than before. As his tongue danced with mine, I had a hard time remembering why I wanted to stop. I knew having sex with Keane would be explosive and beyond anything I had experienced before, but did I want to complicate things even more? Before I could decide one way or the other, a huge wave rose above us and then crashed down, throwing us in separate directions.

As I swam back toward the surface, I couldn't help but feel that something other than nature had caused the wave. As I broke the surface, I was shocked by what I found. The once-calm water was now full of large, angry waves. And the once-bright moon was obscured by clouds.

What in the world?

While struggling to stay afloat, I searched through the thrashing waves for Keane and found him treading water several feet from me. Just as I struck out to swim to him, another wave hit me, pushing me back under the water. I struggled toward the surface, but something pushed or dragged me back each time just as I was about to break through. I was quickly running out of air and beginning to panic.

Mentally relaxing, I let myself drift to the bottom where I could touch the sand, then with a mighty push, I shot toward the surface using everything I had. I broke through, gasping for air.

*That was close.*

Keane finally made it over to me and tried to say something.

"Blue! Try…." The howling wind quickly whipped the rest of his sentence away, but I got the idea that he wanted me to get to shore. I waited until the next large wave was bearing down on me and launched off the sandy bottom to ride the crest toward the shoreline.

As soon as I hit the breakers, I pushed myself to a standing position and trudged to the beach. It was no easy task with the current trying to pull me back into the water, but I managed. As I hit dry land, I fell to my knees, panting.

"Blue! Are you all right?" Keane ran up behind me and laid a hand on my shoulder.

I nodded. "I think so. What the hell happened? How did the ocean go from calm to a raging storm in seconds? Did something go wonky with the magic used to create it?"

Keane shook his head. "This isn't a magically created room. I actually transported us to a private beach in the Caribbean."

"Okay, that makes it even weirder."

"Something tells me it wasn't a coincidence. Something, or rather some*one*, made this happen."

"But who has the power to do something like that?" I gestured toward the still-raging ocean.

"Someone with friends in high places."

"But why?"

"I don't know, Blue." He looked at me, concerned, and I could practically read his thoughts, though he kept them blocked.

"You think this has something to do with the Trials, don't you?"

Keane hesitated but then nodded. Standing, I started to gather my clothing. My underwear had been washed out to sea somewhere, so I just slipped on my shorts. The more I thought about it, the angrier I got. Someone had just tried to kill me. There was no doubt about it. I clipped on my bra and went in search of my T-shirt. Grabbing it up from the sand, I shook it out angrily.

Someone would pay for this. I just needed to figure out who.

"Blue." Keane turned me to face him. He'd managed to get his pants on and had his other things sitting in the sand next to him. Lifting my chin, he searched my face, his thumb running under my eye. It was only then that I realized I was crying. Pulling me into a tight embrace, he kissed the top of my head and stroked my back. "It's okay, Blue. We'll get through this."

Wrapping my arms around his waist, I clung to him for a few minutes and let the tears fall. It felt good to be held securely in his warm embrace. If only I could sink into it and be absorbed forever—or at least until the Trials were over.

With a sigh, I let my anger and frustration go. They wouldn't help me now. Those emotions would only cloud my judgment. No, what I needed was to be clearheaded and focused. Stepping back, I looked up at him.

"I guess this means no more midnight swims, huh?"

Keane smiled crookedly and shook his head. "Unfortunately, no. It also means you can't go anywhere alone, and someone will be moving into your room to stay with you at night."

I sighed. "Next thing you know, you'll be following me into the bathroom, too."

Keane chuckled and seemed to think about it. "I just might."

I threw my T-shirt over my head. "I don't know about you, but I'm ready for a hot shower."

Stooping down, he picked up his shirt and shoes and moved to the tree line. Holding his hand out in front of him, he closed his eyes and whispered a few words. Just as before, a blue outline materialized—only this time in the air—before a door appeared before us. Turning the handle, he stepped through first, making sure the coast was clear on the other side.

I glanced back over my shoulder toward the surf. As I did, I spotted the silhouette of a man standing by the water's edge. I could just make out his smile, though I couldn't quite see his features. With a wave, he turned and walked into the ocean, disappearing below the waves. I shook my head and followed Keane out. I couldn't be sure, but I was almost positive that had been the same man I'd seen on the beach at my house. I wondered exactly who it was, and what he had to do with everything going on.

Just as we came to the locked door at the end of the hallway, the handle jiggled. Keane pushed me behind him and slowly unlocked the door before throwing it open. Tristan stood on the other side, his appearance disheveled and his expression wary. He first looked Keane up and down, noting his lack of shirt and wet pants before spotting me behind him. Then, he looked between the two of us, his expression changing to one of disbelief. I was sure I knew what conclusion he'd come to, but as I caught a whiff of the scent I had come to associate with Riona, I suddenly didn't care.

Tired beyond belief, I pushed past Keane and tried to pass Tristan. He reached out and lightly grabbed my arm, stopping me, though I didn't turn toward him.

"Blue, can we talk?" He glanced at Keane before looking back at me, a pleading note in his voice. "Please?"

My shoulders sagged, and I nodded before pulling my arm from his grip and walking toward my room. I didn't turn to see if he followed.

Opening the door to my room, I tensed until I saw it was empty—something I was glad about. I wasn't mad at Riona or Tristan. I just didn't want any reminders right now. The fact that it bothered me so much was enough to make me angry with myself. I had been the one to suggest no strings attached, after all. Walking straight through the bedroom, I went directly into the bathroom. Stripping down, uncaring that Tristan and Keane were watching, I stepped into the shower and turned the hot water on full blast.

I heard Tristan and Keane talking in low voices, though I didn't know about what. Leaning my arms against the rock wall, I bowed my head and let the water flow over me. It felt good to rinse away all the salt and sand. After letting the hot water soak into my sore muscles, I washed and rinsed my hair. Picking up a loofa, I put soap on it and carefully lathered up every inch of my body. Before stepping back into the hot stream of water, I glanced at where the two men had been talking.

They were now both staring at me, open-mouthed. I hid a grin. Obviously, neither had expected such blatant disregard for my nudity. I didn't know why since they'd both already seen me naked. It was funny, but my self-confidence had shot through the roof ever since I'd started discovering my Fae abilities. Only a week ago, this would have been unthinkable. Now, it didn't even concern me.

Quickly rinsing off without looking at either man, I shut off the water and stepped from behind the glass wall. Grabbing a towel hanging nearby, I dried off before wrapping it around me and tucking the end neatly between Pinky and the Brain. When I was done, I looked at both men. "Something wrong?"

Keane was the first to recover. "If you'll excuse me, I'll go grab a shower myself and change. Then I'll be back to stand guard tonight." He bowed to Tristan before turning on his heel and leaving. Walking over to the vanity, I slowly brushed the tangles from my hair. As I did, I watched Tristan in the mirror, seeming to wage an internal battle before stepping forward and meeting my gaze in the reflection.

"Blue, I'm sorry about earlier."

I sighed and set the brush down before turning to him. "You have nothing to be sorry for, Tristan. You're a free man. You can do whatever you want with whomever you please, whenever."

"Am I?" Tristan ran a frustrated hand through his hair. "Blue, I know we agreed there were no strings attached to what happened between us, but I can't help but feel it meant something. I've never felt such a connection with anyone before."

I felt my heart leap at his statement but quickly squelched it. I now knew there was no way I would survive with my heart intact if I didn't put some distance between us from now on.

"After Riona and I...after we..."

I held up a hand to stop him. "Don't. Don't do this to yourself or us. You know as well as I do that you can't afford to become...attached to me in any way. With the upcoming Trials, who knows what the outcome will be?"

Tristan started to pace in front of me. "Even if someone else wins, the marriage could be in name only."

I was shaking my head before he'd even finished. "I don't want to be *the other woman*, Tristan. I know that is often how things are in the Fae world, but it wouldn't be fair to you, your new wife, or me."

Tristan looked at me, seeming completely at a loss. "What...what can I do?"

I shook my head sadly. "Unfortunately, only time will tell what the outcome will be. Until then, I think it would be best if we maintained some distance."

Tristan nodded forlornly, knowing I was right. "I just hope you can forgive me for what happened with Riona."

"Tristan, again, there is nothing to forgive. You haven't done anything wrong. She was your wife, after all."

"But I told you there was nothing physical between us…"

"I don't blame you. Especially given the way things ended so suddenly with her death. To see her now, after all this time, well…" I shrugged, leaving the sentence unfinished.

Tristan nodded again, though I could tell he didn't believe me. Stepping forward, he lightly kissed my cheek and stood with his forehead pressed to mine. When he heard my bedroom door open again, he straightened and moved through the door to his room, closing it softly behind him.

I sagged against the counter. It had taken every bit of strength I had not to react to him in any way. Shaking, I moved into my room, closing the bathroom door behind me.

Keane stood erectly by my door in full guardian gear. Exhausted beyond belief, I nodded in his direction before slipping between the cool sheets. I vaguely registered that someone had changed them. I wondered if it had been Tristan or Keane who'd requested the change.

Beyond caring, I closed my eyes and let exhaustion drag me into the sweet oblivion of sleep. For once, no dreams troubled me. It was just welcome blankness. The kind I would later wonder if Keane had anything to do with.

# Chapter Thirteen

The night of the full moon was finally upon us. I'd squeezed in as much training as possible under the watchful eyes of Kieran, Keane, Riona, and Iridia. I couldn't do anything more to prepare myself. During the past week, while remaining ever studious and vigilant, I had become alarmingly emotionless—at least that's what others had told me. To me, it was a welcome numbness, something I needed to remain sane. It was like I was an empty shell, existing only to immerse myself in information and skills and nothing more.

I didn't even feel nervous about the upcoming ceremonies, which I had been told could be very treacherous, especially to one such as I with so little experience using my abilities. As I stood rigidly on what had once been Riona's dressing platform in front of her mirrors, I wondered if this was how soldiers felt before a battle: detached, like they were observing it all from somewhere else.

I looked at the older woman who was busily making adjustments to an ornate cloak draped around my shoulders and wondered who she was. I hadn't even bothered to ask when she came to me earlier. Something about her seemed vaguely familiar, though. I just wasn't sure exactly what.

"There you are, my dear, now it's the right length. It's hard to imagine you're truly a Fairy with that height of yours. It is so rare among our species."

I nodded and stared at her for a minute, still sure I knew her from somewhere but not really understanding why it mattered. "Do I know you?" The question seemed to come from somewhere far off as if someone else had asked it.

The corners of her eyes crinkled as she smiled and looked at me. "My name is Galene."

My eyebrows drew together. I knew that name for some reason. I racked my brain, trying to come up with an answer. Then it hit me. "As in...Kieran's wife?"

She nodded.

"You know who and what I am. Who my parents are." I touched the necklace I wore.

Her smile faded a little as she glanced at it, but she nodded again. "I've known about you since the day you were born." She reached up and smoothed a stray hair from my face, tucking it behind my ear. "How I wish things could have been different for you. You should have been able to grow up with us. Know us. I wonder now if what Iridia and I did was wrong." Shaking her head, she stepped back. "I'm sorry. I shouldn't have said that."

A little of the numbness that surrounded me faded away at the stark emotion in her voice. "For what it's worth, I understand why you did what you did. It couldn't have been an easy choice for either of you."

Galene nodded sadly. "No, it wasn't. But what's done is done. Now is not the time to dwell on the past."

I eyed her curiously, sensing something behind her tone. "Why are you here? They wouldn't have sent someone of your standing just to do alterations."

Galene smiled. "Kieran said you had an uncanny ability for reading people. I see he was right. As usual." She sighed. "I'm here to lift the enchantment that has kept you tied to your human form."

"Why do you need to do that?"

"It will become necessary during the ceremonies tonight in order for you to declare yourself. You are unaligned with any clan, so you will need to swear your fealty to one before you can participate in the Trials."

A glimmer of hope must have shone in my eyes as she shook her head. "No. Not swearing fealty will not get you out of the Trials—at least not in the way you hope."

"What happens to me if I don't swear fealty to a particular clan?"

"You would become an outcast, no longer allowed to associate with the Fae or be under their protection. You would become fair game to any species that wanted to use you. You can understand why that would be a very bad thing, especially in light of what you are."

I felt disappointment crash over me like an ocean wave, and my shoulders drooped from the weight of it. For just a moment, I'd entertained the idea there was an easy way out of this. I should have known better. Sighing, I squared my shoulders. Galene was right. What was done was done, and there was no use dwelling on something I couldn't change. I met her knowing gaze with a determined one of my own. "What do I need to do?"

Galene nodded, all business now. She removed the cloak from my shoulders and laid it across the bed before approaching me. "Remove your shirt and necklace, please." I did as she asked and handed them to her, wondering what they had to do with anything. She laid them on the bed next to the cloak. "Now, close your eyes."

I did so reluctantly as Galene started chanting in a language I didn't understand. As her voice rose from a whisper, getting louder and louder, I began feeling strange. It was like I was hot and cold at the same time. The gold ball I always imagined inside me seemed to dance, following the rhythm and cadence of her voice. As Galene finished her chant with a shout, the ball of magic seemed to explode from my center, bursting forth. I choked back a scream and threw my head back as it flooded my body with its power, seeming to burn all my synapses at once and creating new pathways where none had been before, all while changing those already there into something entirely different.

It stopped as suddenly as it had begun, leaving me feeling weak and disoriented. Sinking to my hands and knees on the dressing platform, I panted and tried to control the shaking that overtook me.

Keane had burst into the room at the first sign of my agitation and now stood transfixed, staring at me.

"Blue?"

I looked up at him through eyes that no longer seemed like mine. He seemed brighter, like he had a halo of white surrounding him. Looking around the room, I saw that everything looked more radiant and sharper. It was like I had been seeing things through a blurry camera lens for most of my life, but now everything was finally in focus. It was a bit overwhelming. Closing my eyes, I concentrated on my breathing, trying to calm my racing heart.

"What did you do to her?" Keane's voice was harsh and angry, but I heard the awe underneath.

"I'm okay." I was surprised when my voice came out soft and a bit raspy as if I had been screaming. I sat back and put my hands on my thighs, still keeping my eyes closed. Everything was just too disorienting to look at at the moment.

I felt Galene's gentle hand on my shoulder, then she handed me a cool glass of something. "Don't worry, the sensitivity is only temporary. Your body needs to adjust to its new form. This will help."

I didn't know what she meant by *new form*, but I willingly took the glass and downed the contents. As the cool liquid slid down my parched throat, it seemed to quell the heat blasting its way through my body and left me feeling immensely better.

"What was that?" I opened my eyes to stare at her. She had a glowing green halo around her now.

"It was me breaking the enchantment. I'm sorry it hurt, but there was no way around it."

I blew out a soft breath. "A little warning would've been nice."

She smiled crookedly. "Would it have?"

I shook my head with a half-smile. "I guess not." I felt Keane's hands resting lightly on my shoulders and patted one of them. "I think I'm okay." I tried to stand, but my legs collapsed under me. I couldn't believe how weak I felt. "Maybe not. Can you help me stand?"

Grasping me under the arms, he brought me to my feet. I wobbled a bit, and he put a steadying hand on my waist. When I finally regained my balance, I stepped away from him. That was when I noticed a light caress against my back. It was soft as silk yet solid. Almost fearing what I'd see, I looked at myself in the mirror. Standing before me was not the reflection I was used to. The person in the mirror staring back at me now looked nothing like me, yet exactly like me. She had wings and small pointy ears—an unexpected surprise, though I didn't know why. Stepping off the platform, I moved closer. The woman in the reflection mirrored my movements exactly.

"Is...is that me?"

Galene stood off to my left, smiling softly. "I know you've never been introduced before. Blue, I'd like you to meet the real you."

I stared in shock at myself. As Keane and Galene did, I now had a soft halo around me. Where Galene's was green, and Keane's was white, mine shifted in a myriad of ever-changing colors. I looked down at my arm but couldn't seem to see it that way. "What is that strange halo of color around each of us?"

Galene sent Keane a confused look. "What halo of color?"

"There is this halo of color around each of us. Yours is a soft sea green, Keane's is a bright white, and mine is, well, a lot of different colors."

Galene seemed to think about it then nodded. "You must be able to see auras." At my confused look, she continued. "They are fields surrounding every living organism in the universe. Usually, the colors represent things about a being, whether it be their personality, or their origin. I may need to talk with Kieran about this. If other people can see auras, your signature may be different than everyone else's and be cause for question. Perhaps we can do something to change or suppress yours."

"Why can't I see it when I look at my arm, but I can in the mirror?"

"I don't know. I really don't have much experience with auras."

Keane spoke up. "Most people can't see their own aura at all. The fact that you can see yours in the mirror is highly unusual. The green you see around Galene represents her being a Nereid. Mine is white because Vaimpír live off the life force of others. And I would guess yours is an array of colors because of you are all Fae rolled into one."

I turned to Keane. "You know about auras?"

He gave a crooked grin. "Of course. Vaimpír can see auras. It's how we know who we can feed from and for how long."

I nodded and looked back at myself. Dealing with one thing at a time, I eyed my pointy ears and grimaced slightly. I turned my head from side to side, touching them. "I guess these aren't so bad."

Keane tilted his head to the side. "Call me biased, but I find your pointy ears quite attractive."

I looked at him to see if he was kidding. He seemed sincere enough, so I looked back at the mirror and took a deep, steadying breath before looking at my back, almost dreading what I'd see there. Sure enough, folded neatly behind me was a pair of multi-layered, iridescent, purple-and-white wings. They seemed so thin and fragile, yet I somehow knew they were riddled with muscles and extremely strong. Like Brody's statue, they glittered and winked as I moved from side to side. I wasn't sure where they were attached but I could feel them twitch somewhere between my shoulder blades.

I glanced at Galene. "How am I supposed to...use them?" I gestured vaguely behind me.

Galene covered a grin with her hand. "They're a part of you. You use them like you would your arm or leg."

I turned back to the mirror, tilting my head. Like an arm or a leg, huh? Easy for her to say. She didn't just discover she had things growing out of her back.

With a determined effort, I concentrated on them, telling my brain what I wanted them to do. After a few seconds, I felt a twitch at my back and, sure enough, a large wing unfolded over my left shoulder and trailed down to my upper thigh. With another concentrated thought, I unfolded the second wing. Glancing over at the side mirror, I saw they weren't just one color like I had originally thought. Purples so dark they were almost black started at my back before slowly fading to lilac and finally shifting into a pure, sparkling white. As I moved in the light, blues, purples, and greens shimmered over the surface, adding yet another dimension to the colors.

I stared at them in awe. They were beautiful. Though now that I had them out, I didn't know what to do with them. I couldn't even begin to imagine taking off and flying, so with another concentrated effort, I folded each one away so they lay flat against my back again.

"Well done!" Galene clapped her hands like I was a small child who had done something exciting.

I grimaced but continued to concentrate on the wings at my back. This time, I tried to unfold them simultaneously. That wasn't quite so easy since they worked as two independent things and kept getting tangled. It took several tries, but I eventually managed to do it. I felt the muscles in my back tightening and loosening, getting used to the previously unknown activity. After folding and unfolding my wings several times, I finally started to get the hang of it. I hoped I'd eventually be able to do it unconsciously. Folding them away once again, I stepped toward the bed to grab my shirt. That was when I realized I had another problem.

"Uh...how on earth do I wear a shirt?"

"You have specially-made ones, of course." Galene reached behind her and pulled out another black shirt. She turned it to the back and showed me where holes had been cut to accommodate my wings.

"And just how do I put that on myself? For that matter, how do you sleep? And what happens when I go topside or see my friends?" I was starting to feel a bit panicky thinking about all the complications wings would bring me. I rubbed a hand over my face.

Keane moved in front of me and put his hands on my shoulders. "Hey, breathe. We'll figure it all out, okay? Fairies have been doing this for all of time, so it can't be that bad, right? Anyway, there are ways to magically make them disappear, remember? That's just something you'll have to learn to do. You haven't seen any wings on the other Fairies the entire time you've been here, have you?"

I shook my head. He was right, of course. I was just letting my nerves get the best of me. Now that the numbness was slowing slipping away, all my anxieties and doubts were returning. I wasn't sure if that was good or bad.

Keane grabbed the shirt from Galene. "Here, let me help you with this." He expertly slipped the long-sleeve shirt over my head and showed me how to maneuver my wings into the holes in the back. I wasn't sure if I'd be able to do it myself anytime soon, but that was the least of my worries.

Galene stepped forward. "You can practice with your shirts later. Right now, we need to get you into your ceremonial dress."

I shook my head. "No dress."

Galene looked at me aghast. "It's tradition. You have to wear the ceremonial white gown."

I shook my head again. "I don't care if it's tradition or not. I am not wearing a dress to something that could break out into a fight at any second. I'll wear the cloak, but I want my fighting gear underneath."

Galene crossed her arms over her chest and looked at me with disapproval.

On the other hand, Keane looked pleased. "That's my girl. Thinking like a warrior already."

Galene threw her hands into the air in exasperation and flopped down into a nearby chair.

I gave Keane a small smile as I changed into my black pants. Keane had had them specially made for me this week. They were modeled after his gear with lots of hidden pockets for weaponry and enough give to fight in any type of situation without tearing. I thought I heard Galene groan as I strapped my lightweight daggers into place before tucking in my shirt and putting on a wide cargo belt. I turned and looked at myself in the mirror. I looked ready for a fight and more than a little badass, if I did say so myself.

I laughed at my reflection before sitting on the dressing platform so I could pull on my boots. They were black, had nonskid rubber bottoms, and were extremely lightweight—another gift from Keane. He'd said being sure-footed was almost as important as knowing how to fight. I laced them up before securing the leather straps that wrapped around them and buckled on the outsides, covering the laces. Standing,

I tested my footing in them to make sure they were secure. Then, with effort, I pulled my wings in tightly and did a few roundhouse kicks and punches. I needed to make sure my newfound appendages wouldn't be an issue if it came down to it.

Galene had explained it was necessary to have my wings on display when I declared myself to prove I was a Fairy. They didn't seem to throw my balance off any, but I would definitely be practicing with them tonight after all this ceremonial crap was done so I wouldn't be caught off guard regardless of my form. Leaning over to the bed, I picked up my necklace and went to put it on.

"Just so you know, the protection spell that was contained in that is gone."

I turned and looked at Galene questioningly.

"It only worked while you were in your human form. Now that I broke the enchantment, the spell no longer works."

I looked at the necklace in my hands, running my thumb over the small Fairy. "I'm still going to wear it tonight, if nothing else so I have a piece of my family up there with me."

Galene's eyes were shiny as she turned away and busied herself, cleaning up the few supplies she had brought with her.

After putting the necklace on and tucking it under my shirt, I grabbed the shoulder harness I'd been using to hold my gun. I'd need to make a few adjustments so it could strap around my wings, but I thought I could make it work.

"Here, give me that. I can fix it." I looked over in surprise to see Galene holding her hand out to me.

"I thought you didn't approve of me wearing my fighting gear."

"I don't, but that doesn't mean it isn't a good idea."

I hid a grin as I handed her the shoulder holster. Picking up my gun from the bed, I dropped the clip out and checked the magazine to make sure it was full before sliding it back into place. I wasn't taking any chances.

Just about then, a knock sounded on my bedroom door. It opened a second later to reveal Kieran. I took stock of his aura, which was a bright gold, and noted his pointed ears.

Kieran came to a stop at the sight of me. "I see you figured out how to break the enchantment that was binding you."

I nodded silently, not looking in Galene's direction. Kieran obviously still didn't know about her involvement. "I just need to know how to hide my wings when I want to."

He nodded, looking thoughtful. "That is easy enough. Do you remember when you trained with Edgar, the Síofra?"

"He's the one that can change bits and pieces of his features, right? He taught me how to change my hair and eye color."

"Correct. You basically use the same spell, only this time, we change it just a bit to remove your wings."

I thought about that. While the spell the Síofra had taught me only consisted of changing something from one thing to another, I could modify it with a disappearing spell.

Closing my eyes, I concentrated on the gold ball of magic at my core. First, I manipulated it into the feature-changing spell, then I added the disappearing magic to it. When I was ready, I took a deep breath and slowly pushed the energy out of my center, directing it to where I felt the wings at my back. At first, there was only a tingling sensation, but then my wings disappeared with a silent pop. I opened my eyes, surprised, and turned toward the mirror.

"I did it!"

"Excellent. You are an even quicker study than your mother was. Now, see if you can bring them back." He eyed me speculatively.

Closing my eyes, I quickly reversed the spell and pushed the energy to my back. Opening my eyes, I was disappointed to discover that my wings were still gone. I looked at Kieran. "What did I do wrong? I did the exact same magic backward."

Kieran smiled patiently. "Making something reappear out of thin air is a bit more complicated than making something already there disappear. Here, let me show you."

Kieran explained exactly how the spell should work, then went about demonstrating it. He had removed his ceremonial robes to reveal his wings lying folded against his back. As I watched, I used my senses to delve into his essence so I could feel exactly what he did. It wasn't something anyone had taught me to do, I'd simply figured it out while trying out the connection I shared with Keane. It had come in handy these past couple of weeks as I tried to understand everything I had been taught. It was also probably why I had excelled as quickly as I had. When Kieran paused in what he was doing, I looked up at him.

"What were you doing just then?"

"What do you mean?"

"While I was demonstrating how this is done, I felt you there, as if you were inside me. How did you do that?"

I shrugged. "It's something I learned a while ago after realizing I could feel Keane like the Vaimpír do."

"You can feel what I am doing inside of myself?"

I nodded uncertainly. "Is that bad?"

"No, just incredible. I have never heard of anyone doing something like that before. Not even Iridia could accomplish that."

I shifted uncomfortably as he continued to stare at me like I was some great science experiment. Shaking his head, he apologized and went back to what he was demonstrating, though I could tell he was paying a lot closer attention to what *I* was doing. It didn't take me long to master the reappearing spell, and after a few times practicing back and forth, I was comfortable with the whole process and ready to get the evening over with.

At Galene's direction, I once again moved to stand on the dressing platform, facing the mirrors. First, she helped me put the modified shoulder holster on, before Keane handed me my gun so I could slide it into place and snap it in. Kieran didn't make any comments about my not wearing the required ceremonial dress or the fact that I was outfitted with enough weapons to start a small war. He merely raised a brow at me, to which I shrugged. "I'm not about to be caught off guard."

Galene moved to carefully place the ceremonial cloak over my shoulders, effectively covering all of what I had on underneath it. The cloak was constructed of bright turquoise tricotine wool with a black silk and velvet lining. There were interlocking black Celtic designs about two inches high stitched around the edges of the large hood and down the front opening, carrying on around the bottom hem. They made a continuous circle around the cloak, and I instinctively knew they were there for more than just decoration. Somehow, they were imbued with magic. The colors and designs represented the Grayson family. Today would be the first day I acknowledged my connection to them in public. Though I would be admitting they were my family, I was keeping how we were related a secret. I didn't need anyone digging into my past and finding out that Iridia was my mother—at least, not yet.

As Galene smoothed the cloak over my shoulders, she met my eyes in the mirror. "This was your mother's, you know. The last time she wore it was on her wedding day."

I smiled at her as she kissed both of my cheeks. "Thank you for everything you've done."

Galene nodded and stepped back. Kieran moved forward and placed his hands on my shoulders. "This is it. No matter the outcome, I am proud to call you my granddaughter."

"And I, you, Grandfather." He kissed both my cheeks and stepped back to his wife. Taking her hand, he guided her out the door, leaving me alone with Keane.

Keane stood, leaning against one of the bedposts. "Are you sure you're ready for this?"

"Do I really have a choice?" He shook his head, and I nodded. "Thought not. Come on, let's get this over with." I started toward the bedroom door.

Keane put out a hand to stop me. "First, we need to change your aura."

I raised my brows. "I can do that?"

Keane nodded. "Most Fairies have gold auras or some variation. Since you have the capabilities of a Vaimpír, I think feeding off some Fairy blood will change your aura to match it."

I wrinkled my nose. "I have to drink blood?"

"You didn't seem to mind it when I gave you a taste of mine. Remember? You said it was sweet."

I nodded. That day seemed like a hundred years ago. "Yeah, but that was different."

I watched as Keane reached behind him on the bed to grab one of the bags they kept down here for emergencies. He must have brought it in with him earlier.

"This is Kieran's blood. He had a feeling this might happen, so he donated some so your aura signature would closely match his, another Grayson."

I grimaced in distaste, looking at the blood. This was so not going to be fun. Keane cut the top off the bag and poured it into a dark goblet. Thankfully, the tint on the glass hid the contents. Shoring up my courage, I prepared to drink, but before I could reach for the glass, Keane tipped it to his own lips and drank. When he was finished, he looked at me and grinned.

"What? Did you think I was going to make you drink it?" I raised an eyebrow, and he chuckled. "Don't worry, your turn is coming. I wanted to make sure this gave you every advantage, so you are going to drink from *me*."

"Won't that defeat the purpose of changing my aura?"

"No. Most Vaimpír auras change to match those they just took blood from—at least for a while afterward."

"Then why is your aura still white?"

"Like I said, *most* Vaimpír."

"What makes you different?"

"Mmm, wouldn't you like to know?" He grinned lecherously before continuing. "Doing it this way will give you the added strength and healing ability my blood provides."

I let him avoid my question for now. "I guess that makes sense. So, how do we do this?"

"First, I want to take a small bit of your blood to strengthen our bond, then I will bite my wrist for you to drink from."

I nodded again, noting that his eyes were already deep red, and his fangs were fully extended. As he had before, he moved to stand behind me. Since my hair was already pulled up into a tight French braid twisted around my head, he didn't have to worry about it being in the way. After setting the Grayson cloak on the bed, he wrapped his arms around me and put his nose into the crook of my neck, inhaling deeply.

"You have the most delicious-smelling blood, Blue. It's like a drug that keeps calling me back to it."

I shivered as his breath and words caressed my skin, desire quickly following. I felt Keane suck in a breath as his ever-sensitive awareness of me detected what I felt. I really needed to get a handle on this lust thing. It had been getting out of control lately. I figured it had something to do with all the Fae powers I was discovering. I'd never been this bad before. Then again, I'd never met anyone like the Fae before now either. I idly wondered if they put out some kind of special pheromones.

"Oh, how I wish we had more time..." Keane brought me back to the present with his whispered words against my neck before quickly sinking his fangs in, pulling me tightly against his warm body. I felt his heat soaking through my clothes as the pleasure of his bite flowed through me. He took more blood this time than he had before, almost seeming to draw out the intense sensations. By the time he released my neck, I was quaking with unspent desire and felt wildly out of control. Before he could even close the holes on my neck, I spun around and jumped into his arms, greedily bringing his lips to mine. Wrapping my legs around him, I pressed my hips to his and ground against him, drawing a moan from both of us.

"Blue, honey...we have..." I kissed him deeply again, causing him to thrust himself against me, seemingly unable to help himself. "We have to go... You need to feed..."

Drawing back, I stared at him. I wanted so badly to feed from him like one of the Vaimpír. It was like some instinct had awoken in me, and now I craved his blood. Closing my eyes, I concentrated. Using one of the spells the Síofra had taught me, I quickly manipulated the magic within me. I wasn't sure if it would work, but it was worth a try. When I felt a tingle begin, I knew I could do it. Sure enough, a pair of sharp incisors suddenly slid through my gums. Opening my eyes, I saw Keane's dark gaze widen as he stared at my mouth.

"Blue, did you just...?"

I drew back my lips, letting the light reflect off the long fangs that now touched my bottom lip. I felt a shiver work its way through Keane's body.

"Fuck, Blue. I can't believe..."

Taking his face between my hands, I kissed him hungrily. He ran his tongue along my fangs, causing me to moan as the pleasure of it somehow radiated down my spine. Who knew teeth could be so sensitive?

"You are incredible, Blue. Do you have any idea what you do to me?"

His voice trailed off as I kissed my way down his throat. When I reached the spot where his life force pulsed, I inhaled deeply. I could smell the blood through his skin. I felt my stomach clench with need. Before I could even think about it, my teeth were sliding into his flesh. As his blood welled and entered my mouth, I moaned. It tasted so sweet, better than anything I had ever tasted before. I felt Keane rumble in pleasure as he placed his hand at the back of my head, encouraging me to drink more. As I did, I felt it quickly coursing through my veins, making me stronger, faster, and more alert than ever before. It also heightened everything. I felt like I did right after Galene had broken the enchantment on me.

Finally letting go of his neck, I gasped. Keane immediately pulled my head down to his and kissed me deeply, the blood mingling in our mouths. I felt like I was on fire, and the only thing that could put me out was Keane. Tightening my legs around his waist, I started to slide myself back and forth across the erection still encased in his pants, drawing moans from both of us. Leaning against the wall, he gripped my hips in his hands and moved me faster.

"Fuck, Blue. We can't...not now... I can't put my scent all over you..."

He moaned, burrowing his head into my shoulder and thrusting his hips even faster. I felt my climax quickly approaching and brought his mouth to mine. He gripped me tightly to him, and I almost felt as if he might snap me in half. As I fell over the edge, crying out his name, I felt him stiffen beneath me and shout, too, as he climaxed.

We stayed that way, both of us catching our breaths, before I slid my shaking legs to the floor. Holding on to him for support, I took a few more deep breaths before looking up at him.

He started to laugh. "I haven't done something like that since I was a horny teenager."

I laughed, too. "I know what you mean. I don't know what overcame me. It was like I couldn't help myself."

Keane nodded, still grinning. "It was the bloodlust. It happens to the best of us. That's why we generally mix the taking of blood with sex."

Closing my eyes, I worked the magic that would make my fangs disappear before turning and walking into the bathroom to quickly wash up. With all the enhanced senses around this place, I didn't need to have that smell lingering on me. After I was done, I brought out a wet washcloth for him.

"Did it work? Is my aura gold now?"

Keane studied me and nodded. "It looks perfect. Let's just hope it stays that way for a while. Here, let me take care of these." After pricking his finger with his fang, he ran the blood that welled up over the holes in my shoulder, quickly healing them.

"What about yours?" I pointed at the wounds in his neck, still unable to believe I had put them there.

Keane grinned. "Oh, no. I'm keeping these babies as a token. The guys will never believe me if I don't have proof."

Shaking my head at him, I picked up the Grayson cloak and threw it back over my shoulders. Then I looked at him expectantly. "Shall we?"

He moved, opened the door, and gestured me out. "We shall."

# Chapter Fourteen

The ballroom was teeming with people, even more than the night of the announcement. I had a feeling that clans from all over had come to see how this would play out. After all, it was the first time the Trials had been enacted anywhere in over a millennium.

Waiting in a private alcove above the ballroom, I idly wondered how many others were hidden among the brightly colored flags that now decorated the top of the room. My competition. As a low drumbeat started below, my grip briefly tightened on the curtain in front of me before falling to my side. It was showtime. I turned as Keane and Mckile entered the alcove, both dressed in their black uniforms and each wearing a turquoise armband to show they were loyal to me.

"That's our signal."

I nodded and pulled my cloak's large hood up to conceal my face. As I walked between the two Fae, I felt like a prisoner being led to an execution. Standing at the top of the main staircase, I heard whispers flowing among the crowd, no doubt those wondering who each hooded figure was. Five women had descended in front of me, all wearing varying cloak colors. A quick glance behind me showed six more, twelve in total. I walked down the staircase on silent feet, looking neither left nor right.

A path had formed through the crowd, leading to the raised dais at the end of the room. I felt my breath hitch as I saw Tristan sitting on a throne at its center, looking every bit the King he was, from his fur-trimmed robe to the crown on his head. I hadn't seen or spoken to him since the incident with Riona, though she had kept me up to date on his movements. He looked tired. I saw dark shadows under his eyes that hadn't been there before, and his mouth was tilted down at the corners in a frown. Riona stood regally at his side, her hand covering his as if she were still alive and his wife. Though I knew she was here to help, she was also a shadowy reminder that no matter how hard I tried, I would always be second in Tristan's affections—should I choose to go down that particular path. She inclined her head in my direction when our eyes met, letting me know she was here for me. I tried to work up a smile, but the all-consuming numbness that had held me earlier started to take over again.

As I reached the throne, I woodenly dropped into a curtsy, refusing to meet Tristan's eyes, though he tried to make eye contact. Rising, I moved to stand with the other women who were positioned in front of the raised dais, all facing the crowd with their heads bowed. Once we were all in place, the drumbeats stopped, and the silence seemed to echo through the room. I felt Tristan stand behind us.

"Ladies and gentlemen of the Fae, welcome to Moon Tree Hall. Today marks a momentous occasion. It has been over a millennium since the Trials were last enacted, but today, by your witness, we will once again usher in one of our greatest traditions."

I heard the insincerity in his voice as he pretended to be proud and excited about the Trials, though I doubted anyone not close to him would have picked up on it. As he continued to speak, I tuned him out and instead let my senses flow through the room. So many different types of Fae were present, and it was amazing to see them all through my new eyes. I quickly located Cedric near the back wall to my left. He stood next to a man I detected was a Nixie. I stiffened in surprise but then relaxed, remembering the Trials were open to anyone, even those outside the clan. So, of course, members of rival clans would be here. They all wanted to see what the outcome of this would be.

My attention was drawn back to the dais as Elder Demirtas took the stage. He seemed to be the mouthpiece for the Elders. He waited patiently as the room quieted without a word from him.

"Good evening, my fellow Fae. It is indeed an auspicious occasion. I would like to start this event by first congratulating these twelve Fae on passing the first of many tests: finding the Sanguinem Lapis Circuli."

Applause broke out all around us. The numbness creeping over me kept me still and silent while the other women around me twittered and giggled in excitement.

When things quieted again, Elder Demirtas continued. "It is now the night of the full moon, and as promised, I will introduce you to your prospective Queens." The Elder moved to the end of the line to a woman dressed in a red cloak. "The first to find her way to the Circuli is someone whose family has always been well known within the clans. They are renowned for their fierce fighting styles and extraordinary ability to control the will of others..." With a dramatic flourish, he pulled back the competitor's hood. "I give you, Celeste Beaumont."

The crowd gasped and clapped, but I wasn't surprised. I had known exactly who it would be. Celeste stepped forward and regally curtsied to the cheering assembly before moving to stand before Tristan, who was once again seated on his throne. She dipped into the required curtsy and bowed her head in submission.

"Your Majesty, I repledge my fealty to the Moon Tree Clan and offer you a token to honor your greatness." Stepping back, she waved her hands back and forth parallel to each other until a swirling cloud appeared between them. Thrusting her hands up, the cloud burst forth and seemed to surround Tristan like a blanket, causing the crowd to gasp in wonder at Celeste's bold display of magic—not to mention her courage at touching Tristan with it.

The cloud slowly solidified and became a bright red cloak embroidered with a large, fire-breathing dragon. It laid itself snuggly across Tristan's shoulders, seeming to take on a life of its own. "The Cloak of Draconem, sewn from the hide of a dragon, said to protect the wearer from any weapon. A piece coveted by many a ruler. I give it to you, my King. I hope my token is proof that my loyalties lay solely with you, so that you would bestow upon me your favor, as well."

Bold move on Celeste's part, not only giving Tristan a coveted family heirloom but also coming right out and asking for his favor. I had learned during my training that the King could indicate his favorites in the competition by giving them something of his to wear, much like in the olden times at medieval jousts where a lady favored her knight of choice by giving him her handkerchief or scarf.

I watched Tristan for his reaction. By the tightening of his expression, he didn't appreciate the move.

"The family Beaumont is ever generous in their support of the Crown. I accept your pledge and your token and welcome you to the competition."

Celeste's mouth immediately turned down in a frown at Tristan's tone and obvious rejection. As she slowly backed away from the throne to stand in line once again with the rest of the women, I saw by her angry expression that she hadn't expected him to ignore her request. Thinking I was next since I was the second person entered by the blood stone, I straightened my shoulders.

"Our next competitor, while not the second to reach the Circuli, is no less important..." The Elder moved to stand behind a woman in an emerald-green cloak. I had a feeling I knew exactly who this one was, too.

"One of royal blood, whose family history is steeped in magic of the first degree. I give you...Tatiana Dermott." He pulled Tatiana's hood back to reveal her striking red hair. A roar rose in the room, including lots of stomping and fist pumping. She was obviously a favorite. No doubt due to her being the former Queen's sister and of royal blood. She moved to stand before Tristan and curtsied, though she didn't bow her head given she was of equal station.

"I have sworn fealty to the Fernsong Clan, but I offer my loyalty to you and yours."

Tristan inclined his head. "Your loyalty is all I ask of you."

"To show our fealty, the family Dermott offers you this..." She spread her arms wide and threw her head back. Chanting, she waved her arms in front of her. Suddenly, a ghostly lion appeared. As it solidified, it first bowed to Tatiana then moved to stand before Tristan. Upon its head was a five-point silver crown studded with diamonds and amethysts. It looked vaguely familiar, but I couldn't quite place it.

The lion bowed low to Tristan, its front paws resting on the dais while its back paws were still on the floor. Tristan reached a shaking hand toward the beast. At first, I thought he feared the animal, but then I realized he was staring in shocked awe at the crown on its head. As he lifted it off, the lion disappeared, turning back into mist.

"Wh...where did you find this? I thought it was lost forever." That was when I realized where I'd seen the crown before. It was the same one on the sculpture Brody had done of Riona. It must have been hers. I looked to where Riona stood and saw the pride and joy in her eyes at Tristan's reaction. She obviously had something to do with its sudden reappearance, and I wondered if her loyalties had just changed from my side to her sister's.

"It was returned to us not ten days ago. Found by a Wizard, though he refused to tell us where he retrieved it from. Will you accept our gift?"

Tristan nodded. "I will. And thank you, Tatiana, you have no idea what this means to me. Welcome to the competition."

Tatiana backed away, looking smug and confident. Her gaze briefly cut to me before she turned back to her adoring crowd. One by one, the others were announced. They each presented themselves and their tributes to Tristan. Four were from the Moon Tree Clan, including Celeste's two cohorts from my first night here. Two others were from the Fernsong Clan, one being Odelina, the daughter of Sethos, which was surprising. Another was from the Misty River Clan, and the final two were from clans I wasn't familiar with. That left me. I was sure it wasn't a coincidence I had been left for last.

"Our final contestant is an unusual case. Entered by another yet contracted all the same."

I stiffened at Elder Demirtas's words. They knew Celeste had tricked the blood stone? I almost glanced toward Tristan but stopped myself. Of course, he had told them. It was his duty.

"As our laws dictate, regardless of how she was contracted, the blood stone accepted her. Therefore, she must compete."

Out of the corner of my eye, I saw Celeste smirk. I felt rage starting to pour through my veins, burning off the residual numbness. It took everything I had to remain still and not lash out at her. I dug my nails into my palms, drawing blood in the process. I didn't know what was wrong with me. I'd never been this angry in all my life. Just when I thought I might burst, I heard a voice whisper through my mind.

*"Relax, Blue. Let it flow out of you."*

My gaze twitched to the side as Iridia appeared next to me. She placed a calming hand on my shoulder.

*"It's your powers. Your body is having a hard time adjusting to all the new Fae in the room. Trust me, I've been there. Take deep breaths and let them out slowly. As you exhale, push the rage out through your fingertips. Imagine it flowing out of you and leaving only calm behind."*

I did as she said, taking my time and concentrating on nothing but letting every last bit of rage flow from my body. As I felt the last bit drop out, I almost sighed in relief. That was close. Who knew what I would have done had I let it take hold of me?

As I refocused on my surroundings, I realized that Elder Demirtas had wound down on his introduction and straightened my shoulders once again.

"From the great family Grayson, I introduce to you an unknown. One who, until recently, had been hidden from herself and us. I give to you...Carolina Blue."

A collective gasp came from the assembly in front of me, followed by silence. As I looked them over, I saw shock and awe on most of their faces. They had all thought me to be completely human. Plus, from what I had learned, the Grayson family seemed to have quite a reputation for producing some of the strongest, most talented Fae. And I, of course, was no exception, though they had no knowledge of that just yet.

As the whispers and speculations began, I ignored all of them and turned once again toward the throne. Tristan sat tensely before me as I stepped onto the platform directly in front of him. Removing my cloak, I handed it to Keane, who was instantly at my side. I heard a slight rumble of disapproval flow through the room when those in attendance noted I wasn't wearing the ceremonial white dress. But I ignored that, too. Instead, I carefully unfolded my wings and bent on one knee before Tristan, my head bowed.

"Your Majesty, as a Fairy of the family Grayson, I wish to pledge my fealty once and for all to you and the Moon Tree Clan. As proven by my unaltered appearance, I give testament to my loyalty to uphold all that is and isn't within the clan forevermore."

Silence greeted my pledge. Glancing up through my lashes, I saw Tristan staring down at me in surprise. I wasn't sure if it was my pledge or my looks that kept him silent. I saw Keane motion subtly to get Tristan's attention, seeming to snap him out of his trance. He inclined his head to me in acknowledgement, though it seemed uncertain at best.

"I accept your pledge and welcome you to our clan." Tristan stood and stepped forward. Taking my hand, he brought me to my feet. Placing his hands on my shoulders, he kissed me lightly on both cheeks. He paused for just a moment, our eyes connecting. "Blue...I..."

I shook my head, indicating that now was definitely not the right time for us to talk.

"I, too, have a token to offer the house of Montague."

Tristan stepped back into his role of King and nodded to me before sitting on his throne once again. Unlike most of the families before me, I had nothing mystical or magical to offer, nor did I have any weapons or special jewelry. I did, however, have one thing most didn't. Talent.

I gestured to Mckile and Keane, who were standing off to the side with my gift. I heard people snicker behind their hands and comment that I obviously wasn't very gifted in magic if I couldn't even conjure something and needed my guards to handle it for me. I almost laughed to myself. People were so easily fooled. Little did they know that I wanted to keep what I could do to myself. It was my greatest weapon in this competition.

Keane and Mckile carried a large, blue-cloth-draped square. It was easily five feet high and three feet wide. They quickly set it up on the dais on an easel another man carried for them. When it was situated, I turned to Tristan, wanting to see his reaction when I unveiled it. "As I have only recently found out who I am, I don't have much to offer you in the way of gifts. I'm sure if I asked Kieran, he would have plenty of things he could let me give you, but I wanted my gift to be something from me alone."

With that, I pulled the cloth away with a flourish. Silence echoed throughout the room as they all took in the photograph that stood before them. It was a beautiful picture of a ghostly Riona dressed in her purple gown, though no one but Tristan and I would know it was truly what she looked like now. I had taken her photo standing in profile before a window, gazing out it with a faraway expression, her hand pressed to the glass as though she were trying to touch what was on the other side.

I hadn't been sure when I took the photo whether she would even appear in the image, but miraculously, she had. I had then used Photoshop to do a bit of manipulation to what she was actually looking at. Through the window, you could vaguely make out the figure of a man playing with a child on the lawn, though they were blurry compared to Riona. Only Riona and I would understand the full meaning of the photograph, but that didn't make it any less moving for those viewing it. I saw several women wiping at their eyes as they stared at the picture. Tristan seemed frozen in place. He gazed at the photograph for a long time before turning to me. His eyes shone in the light, and it took him several tries to speak.

"This…this is beyond anything I could have ever imagined. Your talent goes far beyond any camera or lens. It's as if you can see into the soul of a person and bring it out for the rest of us to view… Blue, I…"

Bowing, I stepped back, wanting to stop him before he said something he would regret. "I'm glad you like it. I hope that even though it isn't some family heirloom, you will accept it as a token of my undying loyalty to you and yours."

Tristan seemed to realize the error he had been about to make and cleared his throat. "I humbly accept your gift and welcome you to the competition."

Once again, I bowed before turning back to the crowd and taking my place among my fellow competitors.

Suddenly, a single person clapping broke the silence of the room. It quickly escalated into drowning applause. At first, I thought it was for all the competitors, but then I realized they were chanting something that sounded strangely like my family name.

"Gray-son! Gray-son!"

I looked out over the people turning to peer behind them to see a group gathered at the center of the room. At first, I was confused about why they would be chanting my name—I had no friends here—but then I saw the color of their cloaks. They were all part of family Grayson.

As I stood there, I suddenly felt a shift in the energy around me. Moving on pure instinct, I slid one of the daggers out of my belt and turned in one fluid motion, stepping back as I did. A blade swung past me, narrowly missing. Had I still been standing where I was, it would have buried itself in my back.

I quickly countered and used the weight my attacker had put into the swing to continue her motion, throwing her off balance, her dress tangling around her legs and dragging her to the floor. She landed in a heap at my feet with my dagger pressed to her neck. After my adrenaline slowed, I blinked my eyes and looked down at my would-be assailant... Tatiana. The room around us was silent except for our harsh breathing.

A slow smile crossed my face as I stared down at her and pressed my dagger just a bit closer, drawing a small line of blood on her neck. It ran down and soaked into the neckline of her white gown. Though she was putting on a brave front, glaring at me, I saw the fear in her eyes.

According to the rules, I had every right to kill her here and now. Leaning forward, I put my lips to her ear so only she could hear me. "I'm going to give you a pass this time, Tatiana, in deference to your sister, whom I have great respect for. But know if you attempt to kill me again, I will end you without a thought."

Stepping back, I let Tatiana regain her feet. As she opened her mouth to no doubt make some snide comment, I drew back my fist and punched her, knocking her once again to the ground. When she didn't immediately move, her guards rushed to her side to assist her. She impatiently threw off their hands and stood. Reaching up, she probed her face—she would have a nice black eye come morning.

After wiping the blood that trickled down from the small cut on her throat, she straightened her shoulders and moved back to her place in the line of women without a word. I'd gotten my point across. I carefully wiped the tip of my dagger on my pants and slipped it back into my belt before returning to my spot, as well.

Tristan, who had gained his feet at the first sign of danger, cleared his throat and turned to the still-silent crowd. "I believe that concludes the presentation part of the ceremonies for tonight. Now, to honor our illustrious competitors, we have prepared a feast beyond anything you could have imagined. Please, eat, drink, and enjoy." As soon as he said this, tables appeared at the back of the room, covered in food. Shaken from their shock, the people cheered and broke apart into groups, starting to mingle and make their way toward the buffet.

I felt a touch at my elbow and looked to see Keane standing at my side. "Your cloak, My Lady."

He bowed in my direction, and I snorted, shaking my head. "Don't go all proper on me now."

Grinning, Keane slipped the cloak over my shoulders. As he did, he leaned close so he could whisper in my ear. "You made me proud tonight. Your instincts were right on, and you moved exactly how I taught you. It was flawless, not to mention a beautiful thing to behold."

I placed my hand over one of his and gave it a slight squeeze. Before I could reply, though, I saw Kieran making his way over to me.

"Blue. Are you all right, my girl?"

I smiled. "Of course. I'd rather say I had everything under control."

Kieran grimaced. "Foolish woman. What was she thinking making a move like that at the presentation ceremony? The way she acted was most certainly not befitting someone raised in a royal house."

I laughed. "Actually, it is *exactly* the move I expected from her, hence why it didn't work. Being predictable won't get you anywhere in these games."

Kieran nodded. "I suppose. Now, enough about that. If you will indulge an old man, I would like to introduce you to our family."

I laughed and shook my head. "*Old man*? Seriously?"

"I am over six hundred years old. I would say that qualifies."

I just shook my head, grinning. Kieran took my hand and placed it on his arm. Guiding me across the room, he deftly made his way toward the individuals clad in the turquoise cloaks, easily sidestepping people wanting to chat and halting them with a word or gesture.

Keane stayed close to my other side, keeping an eye out for any possible attacks. Though the presentation ceremony was done, the night was far from over. It would be even more dangerous now that my identity had been revealed. Before I knew it, we were swallowed up in a sea of blue. Looking around, I saw the similarities in the faces around me. High cheekbones, hazel eyes, and wavy brown hair seemed prevalent. Kieran stopped me as we reached the center of the group.

"Members of the family Grayson, I present to you, Blue, our champion!" Applause broke out all around me.

"Welcome, Blue!"

"We believe in you, Blue!"

"Way to go, Blue!"

"You made us proud up there, Blue!"

Those were just a few of the comments I heard thrown my way.

I smiled graciously and greeted each member of the Grayson family as Kieran introduced me to them. He kept it simple when asked how I was related in the family tree by saying they had yet to discover my exact origins. Most seemed to accept the answer, though some looked speculative.

They asked me many questions about my childhood and upbringing, but following Kieran's example, I kept my answers short and vague. After meeting everyone, I excused myself from the group and moved over to a quiet alcove hidden from the rest of the room. Slumping against the wall, I dropped my head into my hands and just breathed deeply. Keane, who had been following not far behind me, leaned against the wall, too, his shoulder touching mine.

"How are you holding up so far?"

"As can be expected, I guess." I looked up and smiled at him tiredly.

Before he could comment further, a scream rent the air. Moving from behind the wall obscuring us, I looked around. Someone lay on the floor near the buffet tables, clutching their chest and gasping for breath. Upon closer inspection, I realized it was one of the women competing in the Trials. She seemed to be in extreme pain, though I couldn't see any evidence of physical harm. Looking around suspiciously, I saw Celeste standing nearby, a look of concentration on her face. I nudged Keane, and he saw it, too. Debating for less than a second, I struck out across the floor with Keane on my heels.

As I reached the flailing woman, I quickly stepped between her and Celeste, effectively breaking the connection Celeste had forged. The competitor on the ground subsided into quiet sniffles as I faced off with Celeste. I felt rather than saw Keane bend down to attend to the woman and instead kept my eyes on my opponent.

"Still preying on the weak, Celeste?"

She shrugged, not denying it. "What's it to you? One less person to compete with."

"Unlike you, I take no pleasure in being deliberately cruel."

"Aww, does the little Fairy have a soft spot for the weak-minded? Do you really think she deserves to be Queen if I could so easily overcome her?"

"I think it takes a much stronger person to win this competition by fair means, than one who stoops to the level of using cheap magic tricks to force her competitors into submission."

"Cheap magic...? You're calling my abilities cheap magic tricks? How dare you? I'll show you cheap magic tricks!"

As I watched, Celeste's eyes changed to their stormy gray. With a determined expression, she started concentrating on me, using her magic. I almost rolled my eyes, knowing exactly what she would try. It was hard to believe I had once feared her talents.

During my training, I was fortunate enough to meet with an extremely old elemental Fairy who knew all there was to know about air magic. So, as Celeste attempted to use the air in my body to squeeze my heart, effectively shutting down all bodily functions as she had done to the woman on the ground, I merely countered her move and pushed the air back at her, throwing her from her feet and holding her there. Celeste shrieked her outrage and tried to fight against me but was unable to do more than flail about like a fish out of water.

I raised an eyebrow as she cursed me in a different language. "Are you quite through?" Defeated, she stopped struggling and nodded. "Good. I'm going to let you go now. Just remember, if you decide to pull any more of your theatrics, I will most definitely be there to put a stop to it. I may have been ill-prepared for this competition when you so *thoughtfully* entered me into it, but I'm not without resources. Do you understand me?"

She nodded, though I knew this wouldn't be the end of it. With a huff and a flounce, Celeste turned and removed herself from my line of sight. I hated to reveal any of my abilities in front of the others, but they would learn of them soon enough.

After Celeste was gone, and I was sure she wouldn't try anything else, I turned back to the fallen woman who had managed to move to a sitting position. Keane still knelt behind her, checking her vitals to make sure everything was okay, while another Fae, who I assumed was the woman's private guard, stood close by, monitoring the situation. I absently wondered where he had been a few minutes ago when this all started.

Looking back at the woman I took in her aura. It was a multi-colored field that ranged from soft pink to dark brown. I wasn't sure what to make of it, so I gauged her energy field instead. She was some type of shifter, though I wasn't exactly sure what kind. She was also from one of the two clans I wasn't familiar with.

I sat on my knees beside her. "How are you feeling?"

She stared at me in open disbelief. "You just saved my life."

I shrugged offhandedly. "It was nothing. I'm not about to let her gain any advantage in this competition by nefarious means."

"But now you've made her your enemy."

I laughed. "Trust me, I was that long before the Trials began." I reached out a hand. "I'm Blue, by the way."

After a moment of hesitation, she shook it. "Sabrianna."

"It's nice to meet you, Sabrianna, though I wish it were under less stressful conditions."

She gave me a small smile. "I owe you my life, Blue. In the coming Trials, you can count on my help and support."

I smiled back. "I appreciate that."

She stared at me as if taking my measure. "When you presented your gift to King Tristan, you didn't use any magic. We all thought you didn't have any. That was just a ploy, wasn't it?"

I gave a noncommittal shrug and quickly changed the subject. "So, a shifter, huh? Can I inquire as to what kind?"

She shook her head at me but let me have my way for now. "I'm a Shapeshifter. I can turn into pretty much anything."

"That would be why I couldn't figure out exactly what you were."

She laughed. "Yeah. There aren't too many of us out there, so I doubt you've come across one before. Kind of like I've never come across anyone like you before."

Standing, I reached out my hand to help her up. "Mmm. Well, I don't know about you, but after all that drama, I'm starving."

She accepted my hand and allowed me to pull her to her feet. "We will talk about you eventually, you know." She gave me a hard stare for a second before breaking into a grin. "But you're right. Making enemies does tend to work up one's appetite."

"Right?"

Laughing, we moved off to the buffet tables to grab a bite. As Sabrianna and I talked, it didn't escape my notice that Keane and her guard seemed a bit standoffish with each other. Which in and of itself wasn't odd, but it was a bit more pronounced than usual, and I wondered about it. Gauging the man, I realized he was also a Vaimpír. Perhaps that had something to do with Keane's defensive posture. Except for the members of Ethereal Mutation, I had yet to meet another Vaimpír. They seemed to be few and far between, at least in this neck of the woods.

Shaking my head, I turned back to Sabrianna. "Tell me about your clan. I'm sorry to say I'm not familiar with it."

"Not surprising, considering you're pretty new to all this." At my raised eyebrow, she shrugged. "Darrius over there is Keane's brother. Though the two of them don't talk directly, they do speak to their parents, who in turn pass information back and forth."

I looked up in surprise. "That's Keane's brother?" They looked nothing alike. Where Keane was fair-haired and light-eyed, Darrius had dark hair and eyes. They also didn't share any similar facial features, except for maybe their nose.

Sabrianna nodded. "Half-brother, to be exact. They share a sire."

"Why don't they speak to each other?"

"I can't say exactly. Darrius won't talk about it, and I don't know their parents enough to ask."

"Interesting..."

I tried to catch Keane's eye, but he was studiously ignoring me. Deciding to leave him alone for the moment, I returned to my earlier conversation.

"So, the Mossy Earth Clan. Are all of you shifters?"

She nodded. "Mostly, but like your clan, we take in strays." She giggled at her unintended pun, and I laughed with her. "Our King is also a Shapeshifter. His name is Barracus. He's a tough sort, but a fair ruler. You'll probably get an opportunity to meet him sometime during the Trials."

"What about the Fire Cloud Clan? Do you know anything about them?"

She nodded. "They're mostly shifters, too. One of my clan's allies. Their representative, Allison, is a Phoenix. She's one to watch out for. She's quiet but definitely not to be underestimated."

"Thanks for the heads-up. You met the two I'm familiar with. Both Celeste and Tatiana are cunning and devious. They won't hesitate to stoop to the lowest levels to get what they want, which in this case, is the crown. Also, keep an eye on those two." I pointed to where Celeste's two cohorts stood. "They're Celeste's Crabbe and Goyle, if you get my meaning. Not too bright but know enough to get themselves into trouble."

Sabrianna looked at me with amusement. "Crabbe and Goyle? As in the characters from *Harry Potter*?"

I nodded, causing her to laugh. She seemed about to say something further, but before she could, a gong rang, the sound reverberating throughout the room. We looked at each other in surprise and a bit of alarm. The room around us quickly silenced, and everyone turned toward the raised dais.

Elder Demirtas was on the stage. "Good evening once again. I do hope you have been enjoying our feast. Could I please have our competitors make their way back up here?"

With a sigh, I set my drink on the table and moved to where the Elder stood, Sabrianna on my heels. "Something tells me we are about to face our first Trial." I spoke quietly so only she could hear me.

She nodded. "Unfortunately, I believe you are right."

We took our place in front of the Elder, staying as far away from Celeste and Tatiana as we could. There was no reason to take any chances with them. As I stood there, I reached out with my senses to make sure Keane was still nearby. I felt him give me a mental bump and smiled a bit. It felt good to have someone I knew I could trust backing me up.

Sabrianna leaned over. "Wanna share what's so funny?"

I shook my head, still smiling.

"As you know, the Trials were fashioned by our forefathers many centuries ago in the hopes they would generate strong leaders, who would in turn produce stronger bloodlines, thus fortifying our race. As the past has shown us, this has proven true. Thus, it is only fitting that the first task of our competitors will be one of strength..."

Someone cheered, while I silently groaned. So much for an easy night.

"But the strength I am referring to is not one of the body but of the mind." The Elder gave a dramatic flourish of his cloak, causing all the lights in the ballroom to dim as he disappeared from the stage. A hushed whisper made its way around the room as people speculated about what the task would be.

The Elder reappeared on the balcony above, his ghostly voice floating down to us. "I cannot be seen, cannot be felt, cannot be heard, cannot be smelt. I lie behind stars and under hills, and empty holes I fill. I come first and follow after, end life, and kill laughter. What am I?"

I bit my lip. *The dark.*

Suddenly, all the lights went out, leaving us unable to see anything.

Sabrianna grabbed my sleeve. "This can't be good. You got any more of those hidden weapons on you?"

I quickly slid one of my knives from its pocket and handed it to her while palming another myself. Crouching into a defensive position, I tried to use my other senses to see what was going on, but wasn't able to penetrate the fog that seemed to surround us.

Though it felt like a lot of time had passed, I knew it could not have been more than a few minutes. Sabrianna and I stood back-to-back with one arm linked to keep each other anchored in the inky blackness.

Suddenly, a voice came to us through the darkness. It was high-pitched and squeaky. "One path leads to home, the other to the unknown."

"What path? Where are we? What's going on here?" I tried to figure out where the voice was coming from, but it seemed to be all around us.

The disjointed voice just laughed, ignoring me. "One tells the truth, while the other lies."

"One what? You're not making a whole lot of sense here."

"You may ask but one question to discover which path will lead you back home. But be wary, for not all is as it seems." The voice started to laugh. "Good luck." As the maniacal laughter drifted away, so did the darkness. We found ourselves standing in a wooded area on a dirt lane. Strangely, the sun shone brightly. When we left the ballroom, it had been full night.

"Where are we? And where is everyone else?"

I shook my head. "I have no idea, on either account." Straightening slowly but remaining alert, I looked around. There didn't seem to be anything special about where we were, at least not that I could tell. But I definitely wasn't letting my guard down. "I guess we need to find these paths our good spirit told us about. Something tells me that's the only way to get out of here."

Sabrianna nodded, and we started walking the path in front of us. I had a feeling it didn't really matter which direction we went in. We would eventually come upon whatever the unknown imp had spoken of.

Sure enough, after what seemed like miles of walking, both of us lost in our thoughts, we came to a fork in the road. Each path was guarded by what appeared to be an Angel. They didn't have halos, but they did have huge, white-feathered wings spread out majestically behind them.

One of the Angels was a man with golden-blond hair and piercing blue eyes. He wore a pristine white suit and tie that hugged his well-toned body like a second skin. He had his arms crossed over his chest, and his left ankle crossed over his right while leaning back slightly on his wings.

The other Angel was female. She, too, had golden-blond hair and bright blue eyes. She wore a glistening white corset over a short, ruffled white skirt and lace-up Victorian ankle boots. She sat in a chair with her knees pulled up to her chest, her eyes as innocent as a child's. Without warning, both of their wings turned from white to black, their outfits melding with the color change. Their hair darkened to a shining blue-black, and their now-dark eyes emitted a red glow. Their appearances also became more sinister. The man now seemed to ooze sexuality, his stance becoming seductive, as did the woman who had turned to straddle her chair. They gazed at us with knowing eyes.

"Your instincts prove to be dead-on, little fairy. It's almost uncanny what you can sense. We are indeed Angels—of sorts. Though I fear we may be more of the fallen variety than the heavenly ones you are thinking of." The man looked toward the woman, and they both laughed.

"A...a Demon..." Sabrianna sounded a bit nervous. I had never met a Demon, so I didn't know if it was a good or a bad thing in the world of the Fae.

"No need to be so derogatory, shapeshifter. We're not of the same ilk as those you refer to. We are much, much higher on the food chain than that…" He glanced over at the woman again. "…at least one of us is." She in turn, glared back at him.

I wasn't sure I wanted to know, so I turned to Sabrianna, ignoring the two Angels for the time being. "It would seem these are the ones from the riddle we need to ask the question of, in order to find the right path."

"Tsk, tsk. Such forthrightness! We are not merely part of some riddle, we are much, much more. Let us first introduce ourselves. I am Sebastian, and this is my lovely cousin, Lizzy."

"It's a pleasure to make your acquaintances." My tone dripped with sarcasm, though I doubted either of them noticed. "I'm Blue. And this is Sabrianna. But I have a feeling you already knew that."

"Such manners she has, my dear Lizzy. I assuredly like this one. Perhaps we can keep her."

Lizzy eyed me coyly from under her lashes. "Oh, I do hope so, cousin. She's a very special one, she is. She would make a fine addition to our collection."

I barely stopped myself from rolling my eyes, though I mentally carried through with the action. These two seemed to like adding drama to everything they said. I could almost picture them as a sultry pair of characters in an anime series. Even their English accents added to the image. It was hard to believe they had been hired by the Elders to conduct this task for the first Trial. I wasn't sure if either of them knew how to be serious.

"Please, don't underestimate us, my darling Blue. We can be quite the challenging pair when we put our minds to it."

I kept forgetting that Fae had the ability to read minds at will, especially the older generation. And given Sebastian's energy signature, I had a feeling he had been around for a very long time.

"Right you are, *mu kallis*. I am indeed older—much older than even your dear grandfather, though don't tell anyone. We wouldn't want to ruin my reputation now, would we?"

At our continued silence, Lizzy sighed in annoyance. "Ask your question, but you only get one, so make it good." Her eyes twinkled with devilish delight. She seemed to anticipate our eventual failure, which of course only made me more determined to win. It also made me realize they had been conversing with us in the hopes we would ask a question, thus ruining our chance to escape. They were definitely smarter than I had originally given them credit for.

I turned to confer with Sabrianna. "We need to come up with a question that will tell us which path leads out of here."

"And per our mysterious voice, one of them will always tell the truth, while the other will always lie."

"Can they do that, cousin?" A pouting Lizzy addressed her mildly interested partner.

"Do what, Lizzy?"

"Discuss this between the two of them? After all, they are competitors."

"I don't see any reason why they can't."

"None of the others were together. I wonder why these two are."

Out of the corner of my eye, I saw Sebastian shrug. That was a very interesting piece of information. That meant the other competitors who had come through had been alone. I wondered why Sabrianna and I had been allowed to come together. Another puzzle, but one for a later date. Right now, the task at hand seemed a bit daunting.

How did we ask two people in one question what path to take, knowing one would be truthful, while the other would lie? How did we tell the difference between the two? I couldn't glean anything from their energy signatures. They were similar, though I could tell Sebastian was the more powerful of the two. Their demeanors didn't give anything away either. Lizzy was back to being bored and picking at the lace on her skirt, sighing loudly every now and then. While Sebastian appeared as though he hadn't a care in the world, nor any interest in what was going on. He studied his nails, which had turned black along with his clothes. Something about him *was* different from Lizzy, though. I just couldn't seem to put my finger on it.

When his eyes suddenly met mine, I realized I had been staring intently at him for quite some time and quickly looked away. Back to the problem at hand. Regardless of how we viewed it, a liar and an honest person looked exactly the same and would probably give almost the same answer to most questions. Thinking along those lines suddenly gave me an idea. Leaning over, I whispered my solution in Sabrianna's ear. When she drew back, she was grinning. Both Sebastian and Lizzy looked at us with interest.

"We haven't got all day, what's your question?" Now that we seemed to have an idea, Lizzy looked almost sullen. I hoped that was a good sign.

I turned to Sebastian. "Sebastian, my question is for you." He looked intrigued. "Tell me, which path would Lizzy say leads to the way home?"

He appeared confused at first, not quite seeing where my question would lead, but then his eyes widened. "I'd say that Lizzy would choose the left path."

"Excellent, the right path it is, then."

"Wait, why the right path? Sebastian said I would say the left path. How do you know I'm not the truthful one, and he's the liar?" Lizzy seemed quite put out that I'd addressed Sebastian and not her.

I smiled. "It's simple, really. Whether he was the truthful one or the liar, I would still take the opposite path he told me."

"But why?"

She seemed generally confused about my reasoning, though I could see Sebastian understood what I had done. "Well, if Sebastian is the truthful one, then he would tell me you would lie and give me the wrong path, thus I would need to choose the opposite one. If he was the liar, he would also tell me you would pick the wrong path, since he'd be lying. So, it really doesn't matter if he is the truthful one or not. Either way, I need only choose the path opposite of what he says."

Lizzy stared at me, her mouth agape. "How on earth did you figure that out?"

"Elementary, my dear Lizzy."

The *Sherlock* reference seemed to go right over her head, so I just smiled. Together, Sabrianna and I stepped onto the right path. As we did, the darkness started to surround us again. Just before all the light was gone, I saw Sebastian look in my direction, a speculative grin on his face, just before he spoke in my mind. *"Till we meet again, my enigmatic little Fairy. I look forward to furthering our acquaintance."*

I kept a tight grip on Sabrianna as the darkness swallowed us, just in case it was another trick. But as the light returned, we found ourselves back in the ballroom where we had started. As soon as the crowd saw us, a cheer rose. I looked around, a bit disoriented. Keane was immediately at my side.

"Are you okay?"

I nodded. "How long were we gone?"

"About fifteen minutes."

"Really? Time moved a lot slower where we were. How many others are back?"

"None. You're the first."

"But Sebastian and Lizzy said there were others..."

Keane shook his head. "Nobody else has returned yet."

"I wonder what that means."

Sabrianna interrupted us by reaching over and handing me my knife. "Thanks for the use of your weapon, even if we didn't need it."

I grinned at her. "Anytime. Thanks for the tag team on the first task. Seems we're the first to return."

"No, thank you. If it weren't for you, I don't think I'd have been able to figure that one out. I'm not very good at riddles, and that one was pretty hard. How you came up with the solution is beyond me."

I shook my head. "Had it been up to you, I'm sure you would've figured out something equally as clever."

She just smiled as she walked away, throwing over her shoulder, "You just keep thinking that."

# Chapter Fifteen

After all the stress I had experienced of late, you would think I would just fall into an exhausted heap and sleep for days. Unfortunately, that was not the case. As I lay there in bed tossing and turning, I couldn't help but go over and over the day's events, wondering if there was more to what had transpired than what was on the surface. Something just felt off. I was also concerned about Iridia. After the first Trial, she had sought me out to tell me she wouldn't be able to come around for a while. Apparently, things had become dangerous where she was, and she didn't know when she could return. I hoped she was all right, but I had no way of checking on her. I had to trust she could take care of herself and would be back when the time was right.

Hours later, still unable to sleep, I heard Tristan moving about in the bathroom between our rooms and wondered how he was holding up. I was almost tempted to get up and see, but then a scent that reminded me distinctly of Riona drifted by, and the urge quickly passed.

Closing my eyes, I again tried to force my mind to stop the circles it was running around in, but it seemed an almost impossible task. Just as I was about to give up and go see if Keane wanted to work out, I felt a tug on my consciousness. Before I could even react, a familiar dark cloud surrounded me. I wondered if this was another test. Even though the Elders had said we were done for the day, they could have been trying to get us to let our guards down. Relaxing, I let myself be taken to wherever my final destination would be. After all, there was no use in me fighting it.

As the world lightened around me, I wasn't surprised to find myself back in the same wooded area I had been in earlier. Looking left and then right, I saw it was now night here also. A full moon hung high in the sky above me, its light shining down and causing the world around me to glow incandescently. It made everything seem surreal. As I stood there staring up into the sky, I felt him long before I saw him.

"I had a feeling this had something to do with you." I turned my head to look at Sebastian. He was once again dressed in his white suit with his feathered white wings tucked neatly behind him.

"As I said before, your instincts are uncanny."

He gazed at me through half-shuttered lids, and I idly wondered what was going on behind those piercing blue eyes. I was sure whatever it was, he would reveal it to me in his own time—should he choose to tell me. After all, this meeting was of his doing. As a breeze danced across the forest floor, I closed my eyes and lifted my face to the sky. Inhaling deeply, I sighed contentedly, for some reason feeling perfectly safe standing here with Sebastian, though I didn't know why. The breeze carried the sweet scents of the forest and the night, reminding me of long-ago times when my friend's parents would take us all camping. I wondered idly what the girls were doing right now. I hoped they were safe.

Without opening my eyes, I shifted slightly toward Sebastian, reconnecting myself to the present. "Where are we exactly? I didn't want to ask earlier for fear of using up my only question."

He laughed lightly. "Smart girl. That very question tripped up several of the competitors. We are neither here nor there..."

"Nor anywhere?"

"Something like that." He paused, seeming to ponder my question more, probably deciding how much to tell me. "We are in my home. It is not a place you can find on a map or globe. It's not even on the same plane of existence as your Earth is."

"I see."

"Do you?"

Opening my eyes, I looked over and, tilting my head to the side, considered him. After a moment, I smiled softly. "Yes, I believe I do. This place exists somewhere between Heaven and Earth. A fallen angel, you said earlier. You were, of course, referring to status, not morals."

"Your perception of the world far surpasses that of any other being I have ever encountered." He eyed me speculatively. "You may appear to be a Fairy, but I know you are far more than that. Tell me, have you managed to figure out exactly what you are yet?" He seemed genuinely intrigued.

I just shrugged my shoulders in a half-hearted apology. "I don't have an exact answer. I am everything, and I am nothing."

"Interesting." He silently turned back to the sky we had been gazing at and seemed to search it for answers—to what exactly, I wasn't sure, nor did it seem to matter. I once again closed my eyes and waited, content with the quiet of the moment and strangely comfortable with the man standing next to me.

Before long, Sebastian reached over and took my hand, causing me to open my eyes and look at him questioningly. "Come, I want to show you something."

I followed him deeper into the forest, hoping my instincts were right and I could trust him. As we came to a break in the trees, Sebastian slowed. Putting a finger to his lips, he cautioned me to be quiet. I nodded, and together, we moved behind a large oak tree. Peering around its wide trunk, I saw two people in the clearing in front of us, both women. One was definitely Lizzy, but I couldn't quite see the other.

"What the hell happened? You were supposed to imprison her!" I instantly knew the voice. It was Celeste Beaumont. Didn't she ever stop?

"What was I supposed to do? She knew the answer." Lizzy turned petulantly away. "Well, her partner did, anyway."

"How the hell did she know the answer? We had a deal here, Lizzy. You assured me no one would be able to get past this challenge but me. Yet somehow... Wait a minute. Partner? What partner?"

"She came through with another woman. I think her name was a color. Blue or something. Stupid name."

I saw Celeste stiffen at the mention of my name and had to cover my mouth to keep from laughing out loud. "What? Blue? That...that bitch! How the hell did she manage that? This was supposed to be an individual challenge. She must have cheated somehow. I can't believe it. I should tell the Elders and have her punished." I shook my head. Leave it to Celeste to be outraged that I was cheating when she was so obviously guilty of that herself. "Don't you decide who comes to this plane? How could she have hopped a ride with another person?"

"She couldn't have. It's impossible."

"Obviously, she managed it somehow." Celeste began pacing back and forth in front of Lizzy while I glanced speculatively over at Sebastian, who merely stared innocently back at me.

"The master won't be happy about this turn of events. We were supposed to eliminate that shifter by the end of the first Trial. This will set our plans back. Dammit."

"Why does she even matter anyway?"

Celeste's head whipped in Lizzy's direction. "That is none of your business."

Lizzy rolled her eyes and took to the air with a flap of her wings. Landing lightly on a low branch near Celeste, she yawned into her hand. "This is boring. Tell me what I need to do next so you can be on your way."

"During the next Trial, you need to find a way to take out the woman called Allison. I guess I'll have to deal with Sabrianna myself so we don't fall further behind. And you'd better not fail this time, or you can kiss your freedom goodbye."

This seemed to get Lizzy's attention. "Hey! It wasn't my fault they knew the answer today. You can't hold that against me. I could hardly take the shifter after she answered correctly with Sebastian around. He's such a party pooper. He would've reported me to the boss, and then where would I be? Stuck here for another thousand years with just him for company, that's where."

Celeste snorted. "It's your fault you're here to begin with. Had you not gone and messed with one of Poseidon's favorite humans, knowing full well how he would react if he found out…"

"I know, I know. And now I have to stay under the watchful eye of my dear cousin until I can prove myself worthy enough to grace the halls of Olympus again." Lizzy sighed dramatically. "You don't need to remind me."

"How an Angel turned out to be so bad is beyond me."

Lizzy sneered at Celeste. "Like you're such an innocent yourself, first entering into a pact with *Him*, then trying to cheat your way into the crown."

"Enough. I'm not here to debate my motives. Just do your job, and maybe we'll both get what we want."

"Fine."

Sebastian reached over and took my arm, indicating we should leave. I followed him as he led us back out of the woods, lost in thought. Who was this mystery man pulling the strings here? Was he the reason I had been entered into these Trials, not just some jealous revenge on Celeste's part? I looked up at the back of Sebastian's blond head. And why had Sebastian brought me here to show me this? Why did he want to help me? What was in it for him?

As we cleared the tree line, I was surprised to see a small house appear in front of us. Sebastian walked right up onto the porch and opened the door. I stopped just short of the steps. At my hesitation, he turned around. "Is something wrong?"

"Where are we going? Whose home is this?"

Sebastian grinned wickedly, the smile seeming to transform his whole face. "Do not fear, my little Fairy. My intentions are pure." As his wings turned black again, melding with his clothes and demeanor, I arched an eyebrow at him. "Well, mostly pure."

With a wink, he walked through the front door, leaving me standing in indecision. Sighing, I took the steps two at a time and entered the house. What did I have to lose? I'd come this far, after all.

As I entered, what had seemed like a cozy cabin only seconds ago suddenly morphed into a modern high-rise. Sebastian stood in the middle of a sunken living room, a glass in his hand. "Welcome to my humble abode, Blue."

As he saluted me with his drink, I looked around. His home appeared to be a large, open-concept apartment. Besides the enormous living area, there was a kitchen with an island big enough to have its own zip code—along with every modern appliance known to man. A fully stocked bar stood on my right, next to a closed door which I assumed led to a bedroom or two. Everything was done in white and black with small accents of red here and there. I shook my head, smiling at the irony of the décor considering Sebastian's dual personality.

Walking through the sunken living room, I stepped up to the darkened windows. I felt Sebastian walk up behind me as I stared below us. I wasn't quite sure where we were, but it was the strangest place I had ever seen. Clouds floated around the building a few floors below, obscuring most of the view of everything, but I got a few small glimpses of what appeared to be a golden road that ran through a small city.

"Just who are you?" I turned to face Sebastian.

"I told you. My name is Sebastian."

"Yes, I know that, but...what are you? Really? What is your purpose here?"

"I guess you would consider me an independent contractor for the big three."

"The big three what?"

"Gods, of course."

"Gods? What do you mean gods?"

"Poseidon, Zeus, Hades..."

"Are you telling me the gods are real?"

"Of course."

"But they're only supposed to be a myth."

"Come now, you of all people know that within every myth there lies some truth."

"I suppose." Turning away from the window, I moved to sit on one of the cushy couches, idly wondering how he kept them so white.

"What is your involvement with the Fae clans, then? I suppose it has something to do with your bosses?"

"I'm not sure, to tell you the truth. Poseidon just requested my help, so I obliged."

"Poseidon, huh?" I thought back to the incident at the ocean with Keane. He'd said someone must have friends in high places. Could Poseidon really be involved in what was going on? "So now I have to wonder if you're actually for me or against me."

"I did clue you into Lizzy and Celeste's little plan."

Sitting back, I crossed my arms over my chest and considered him. "True, but to what end? To gain my trust so you can betray me later for someone higher up on the food chain?"

"So negative." He clucked his tongue at me while shaking his head. "There are two sides to every coin, you know. I did bring you through to this plane with Sabrianna to keep those two from succeeding in their plans for imprisoning her."

I nodded in concession. After hearing Celeste and Lizzy's conversation, I'd figured Sebastian had been the one to bring Sabrianna and me through together. "And I thank you for that, but perhaps you only wanted to keep Lizzy from gaining her freedom through amoral means. She is, after all, being punished for an offense against Poseidon."

"True."

"Or did you truly care what happened to Sabrianna?"

"It, in fact, had nothing to do with Sabrianna and everything to do with you."

"Then why go to such lengths to save her?"

"Because she will become someone important to you in the future."

"I see, and how do you know this?"

Sebastian smiled secretively. "Working for the big three has its advantages."

I let out a frustrated breath. "I don't understand. Why do *you* care what happens to me?"

"Let's just say I have taken quite an interest in you."

"But, why?" Sebastian only stared at me with a mischievous smile as he refused to answer. I shook my head. "Are you always so vague about everything?"

"Only when it suits my purposes, *mu kallis*." Sebastian moved smoothly to my side and took the seat next to me. Reaching over, he took my chin in his hand and leaned forward, causing my breath to catch. He truly was a beautiful being.

"You, my darling Blue, are a very unique creature, one worthy of a thousand of your kind. Turning my chin, he placed a kiss on my cheek, his lips lingering on my skin. "So soft."

As he leaned back, I let out the breath I had been holding and stared at him. I wasn't sure what to make of Sebastian. His dual nature truly confused me. On one hand, he appeared to want to help me and had already proven he was looking out for me. But on the other, he seemed to be hiding something—something important. I wondered just where he fit into this whole equation. What did he hope to gain by showing me this place and revealing his true identity?

Seeming to sense more questions, Sebastian shook his head and smiled. "I think it is time I sent you back. Your Vaimpír is becoming quite upset by your continued absence."

Standing, Sebastian offered me his hand. I took it, and he gently helped me to my feet. Leaning over, he placed a kiss on the inside of my wrist, his tongue flicking out for just an instant, causing me to shiver in reaction. He glanced up at me, his eyes shining in amusement. "Till we meet again, *Kullake*."

I barely had time to catch my breath before a dark cloud swallowed me up. When the light returned, I was back in Riona's bedroom, sitting on the bed just as I had been before I left. A worried-looking Keane paced the room.

I watched him for a second before crossing my arms over my chest and adopting a sarcastic tone. "What has you so worked up?"

At the sound of my voice, Keane swung in my direction. "Blue! Where have you been? What happened? I completely lost you. I couldn't track you or anything."

"I'm not quite sure what to make of it, to tell you the truth."

"Was it another Trial?"

I shook my head. "Remember the Angel I told you about today?"

"Sebastian?"

I nodded. "He brought me back to his plane of existence, as he called it."

"Plane of existence?"

"It seems Sebastian works for the big three."

Keane visibly started. "The big three? What could their involvement possibly be?"

I was a bit miffed at his ready acceptance of the gods' existence. Was I the only one in the dark about that? "Why is it you're not even remotely surprised they truly exist?"

Keane chuckled, momentarily distracted. "The gods? Honey, you'd probably be shocked and amazed at the things I know. But, honestly, all Fae are aware of their existence."

"Not all Fae." My brow furrowed in annoyance as I crossed my arms over my chest.

Keane sat on the bed and put his arm around me. "The gods aren't what you think they are. They aren't a bunch of deities that rule over all as human myths and legends often show. They are much like the Fae, just a bit more powerful, and they also happen to be immortal. Which explains the humans' fascination with them since the same gods have been a part of every generation since the human race began."

I mulled that over. "So, they're just like...another species?" He nodded. "Then why would they be involved in what is going on with the Fae? With the Trials?"

Keane shrugged. "I don't know. It is a bit disturbing, though the gods and the Fae have always been intertwined. Zeus himself was raised by a Fairy named Amalthea to keep him hidden from his father, Kronos."

Shaking off his arm, I got up and went to the bathroom. When I came back out, Keane was still on the bed, but he'd moved to a more comfortable position and was sprawled out on one side. Putting my hands on my hips, I raised an eyebrow at him.

"Comfortable?" He grinned in my direction before patting the spot next to him. "Aren't you supposed to be on guardian duty? What happens if we're attacked?"

"What better way to protect you than by being right next to you?"

Throwing up my hands in defeat, I crawled onto the bed, making sure there was a comforter wedged firmly between us.

Keane grinned but didn't comment. "Tell me exactly what happened with this Sebastian."

As I did, I noticed a bit of unease come over Keane. "What is it? What's wrong?"

Keane just shook his head. "Hopefully, it's nothing. I don't want to make any assumptions. Let me look into a few things before I say more." I took a breath to argue with him, but he just put up his hand. "Please?"

Nodding in concession at his earnest tone, I snuggled down into the blankets, yawning as I did. Between the events of the day and Keane's warm body next to mine, I was quickly lulled into a deep, dreamless sleep.

⁓ℓℓ⁓

I awoke the next morning to the sound of male voices. They weren't raised in anger, exactly, but I could tell they were arguing. Glancing at the clock, I saw it was a little after nine in the morning. I groaned. Considering I hadn't gotten to sleep until after three, it was still way too early for me. Rolling over, I tried to fall back asleep, but the two voices just outside my room kept intruding. With a sigh, I got out of bed and walked to the door. Throwing it open, I crossed my arms over my chest and glared at the two men standing there. Tristan and Keane froze mid-sentence at my entrance and stared back at me guiltily.

"I really hope you two have a good reason for waking me up so early."

"Blue, I'm sorry we woke you…" Tristan reached toward me as if to touch me, causing me to jump back a couple of steps. I saw the hurt in his eyes at my move, but it couldn't be helped. The last thing I needed was for him to touch me in a caring manner. I had a feeling all the walls

I had spent the last few weeks building up would quickly crumble if he did.

"Go back to sleep, Blue. I'll wake you in a few more hours." This came from an impatient Keane. He obviously wanted to get back to discussing whatever it was he and Tristan had been arguing about.

Sensing that whatever it was had to do with me, I shook my head. "Nope, it's too late for that. I'm awake now. You two might as well come inside and tell me what you're arguing about."

"Really, Blue. It has nothing to do with you."

I snorted, giving Keane a look of disbelief. "Mm-hmm." Walking back into the room, I left the door open. Both men joined me, albeit reluctantly. Leaning against one of the bedposts, arms crossed, I stared hard at both of them. "What's the issue here?"

Keane stood stubbornly with his hands clenched at his sides, refusing to answer. So, I turned to Tristan, who stood in indecision. "It's one of the contestants. She disappeared this morning. She was performing her second Trial when, suddenly, she was just...gone."

That got my attention. "Who? Not Sabrianna."

Tristan shook his head. "No. A woman by the name of Allison." I visibly started at the mention of her name. That had been the one Celeste had told Lizzy to take care of. Tristan noted my reaction. "What is it, Blue?"

I grimaced. I hadn't wanted to tell Tristan about my encounter with Sebastian, but I didn't see any way around it. "It would seem one of the Angels from the last challenge is in league with Celeste in order to take care of some of the competition." I quickly explained what I had learned the other night, of course leaving out the part about the gods' involvement and apparent interest in me. He didn't need to know that right now.

"I see. And when were you going to tell me about this?" Tristan looked angrily between me and Keane.

I shrugged unapologetically. "To tell you the truth, I wasn't. I didn't think it was important. Isn't cheating a part of the Trials? Keane and I will come up with a strategy for dealing with Celeste. It's nothing you need to worry about."

Tristan sighed in frustration. "Blue, I'm not the enemy here. I'm on your side."

I looked down at my feet, trying to hide my churning emotions. "I know, Tristan. I just don't want to burden you. I know how busy you've been." What I didn't add was that I knew how busy he'd been with *Riona*. He hadn't been apart from her since I revealed her to him—this was the first time.

"I am the King here, Blue, remember? And now that you're one of my subjects, it's my job to protect you."

Leave it to Tristan to segregate our positions in Fae society. I looked up at him, my voice edged in anger. "How could I forget, Your Majesty?" I bowed mockingly to him.

"Blue..." He sighed. "I didn't mean it like that."

"Then what did you mean, Tristan?"

"You know Riona and I care about you. We'd do anything for you."

I felt pain slice through my heart at the way he'd said Riona's name and connected it to his like they were a couple again. Why did it have to bother me so much? It wasn't like I hadn't known he was still in love with her. Wiping angrily at the tears threatening to fall, I turned away from him and began looking for my clothes. "Oh, it's 'Riona and I' now? Are you going to make it official again? The King and his ghost Queen? I wonder how that will go over with your subjects..." I huffed out a breath. "I need to get dressed so I can go see Sebastian. He'll know if Lizzy had anything to do with Allison's disappearance."

Running a frustrated hand through his hair, Tristan turned to Keane. "Can you give us a moment, please?"

Keane nodded, though I could tell he wasn't happy about it. Walking out the door, he looked past Tristan to me. "I'll be just outside if you need me. And don't go running off to Sebastian without me this time."

I nodded as he quietly closed the door. Grabbing my fighting gear, I marched into the bathroom, intent on ignoring Tristan. He grabbed my arm and stopped me before I could get far.

"Blue, about Riona and me."

I swung around to face him, unable to keep my emotions in check any longer. "You don't need to feel sorry for me, Tristan. It's obvious you're still in love with your dead wife, and there's nothing I'll ever be able to do to change that. So, stop apologizing. It only makes it worse. Like you said, she was your wife. I understand. But *you* have to understand, that she's dead, Tristan."

He flinched as I spat the words at him. "You can't just pick up where you guys left off because you can see and feel her now. You need to remember that you and I are the only ones who can see her. She's a ghost."

"That's not fair, Blue. I told you that what happened with Riona was a mistake and I regretted it immediately after it happened. We just got caught up in the heat of the moment of seeing each other and all the emotions that were left unsettled between us with her sudden death. I know she's dead. I lived through the pain of it a long time ago. But I got over it."

"Did you really? 'Cause I don't think you ever did, Tristan. I don't think you ever forgave yourself for what happened to her or admitted just how much you loved her before her death."

We stared angrily at each other. Pulling my arm from his grasp, I went over to the vanity and threw my clothes on its surface. Leaning my hands against the counter, I stared at myself in the mirror, hating how I felt. It had been naïve and foolish of me to think I could sleep with Tristan and keep my feelings separate. And even stupider to think I could ever take the place of someone like Riona in Tristan's heart.

I sighed deeply, knowing what I had to do. "Did you know Riona was pregnant when she was killed?" My voice was deathly quiet.

Tristan's face turned white, his anger immediately abating. "No. It's not possible."

I nodded. "She told me what happened that final night. How when she told Larkin, she was pregnant with his child, he rejected her. How he used an enchanted knife to take her life force and siphon it to their unborn child before he ripped the babe from her body." I met Tristan's gaze in the mirror. His expression was one of shock and denial. "That's what killed her, Tristan. She gave her life for that of her unborn child."

"How can that be? She never told me." Tristan shook his head in disbelief. "How long have you known?"

"For a while now."

"And you never told me?"

"With everything going on with the Trials, we haven't really had a chance to talk." I looked down at my hands once more and shored up my courage for what I had to do next. Curling my lip, I looked at him in the mirror again. "Besides, what difference does it make?"

"What *difference* does it make?" I felt the fury simmering just below his words. "How can you be so callous? Riona might have a child out there somewhere, Blue. Don't you think that might be important to me?"

"It's Larkin and Riona's child, not yours. Obviously, Riona didn't think it was important for you to know she was pregnant since she didn't tell you then...or now."

Tristan jerked back as if I'd slapped him.

*"What are you doing, Blue?"*

Turning around, I saw Riona standing next to Tristan, her hand on his arm in a protective gesture. Tristan looked hurt and disbelieving at my sudden turnabout. I almost lost my nerve to continue on, but I knew I had to.

I laughed humorlessly. "In truth, I have no idea, Riona. I'm not sure what cruel twist of fate brought me to this situation, but I'm sure as hell tired of it. I'm tired of being the bearer of everyone's secrets and having to deal with everyone else's emotions and problems. To tell you the truth, I'm tired of this." I pointed at the two of them.

*"What's wrong with you? You're not acting like yourself! You're only hurting him. What possible good can come of this? Are you so self-centered that you would use the secrets I told you to..."*

"You weren't going to tell me about the child, were you, Riona?" Tristan interrupted her before she could go on.

She looked down, seeming caught off guard. *"I...I didn't think it would matter to you, Tristan. He wasn't your child, after all."*

"How can you say that?" Tristan stepped forward and put his hand under her chin, lifting it so she would look at him. "Any child that was a part of you would mean the world to me."

Riona let out a choked sob, and Tristan pulled her tightly into his arms, closing his eyes briefly. I watched them with a heavy heart. When Tristan opened his eyes again, he looked at me over her head. I saw the anger, hurt, and betrayal he felt and had to look away lest I reveal my true feelings. Without another word or a backward glance, they turned and left.

"What good could come of it?" My words were barely a whisper in the empty room. "Now, I might just be able to survive this with at least part of my heart intact." Whatever might have been between Tristan and me would forever have the wedge of Riona and her child between it now. It had been the only thing I could think of to save myself. And though a small part of me would always belong to Tristan, I had a feeling that whatever he might have felt for me had just been dashed away by my callous attitude, even if it hadn't been real. I just wished the pain filling my heart right now would go away, too.

I slumped to the floor, my legs unable to hold me any longer. Laying my head in my hands, I let loose all the feeling and emotions I had been holding back. Deep sobs racked my body as everything poured out in the only way it could.

Keane found me there a while later, a limp body on the floor, empty of everything. Cradling me in his arms, he lifted me and took me back into my bedroom. Sitting on the bed with his back to the headboard, he held me on his lap with my head against his shoulder. Not saying a word, he simply held me close and rocked me from side to side like a child. I lay there unmoving, my arms hanging limply at my sides. I had no more tears to cry, no more words to say, no more emotions to feel. It was like I was dead inside. I didn't know what the future would bring for me, but for now, at least I didn't care.

# Chapter Sixteen

Opening my eyes slowly, I saw Sebastian's unmistakable figure sitting on the end of my bed. Blinking, I stared at him for a long minute. Something about him looked different, but I didn't have the desire or the brainpower at the moment to figure out what it was.

"Welcome back to the world of the living." He grinned at me impishly. "I was beginning to think we'd lost you to a dream world forever." Grunting, I turned over and put the pillow over my head, deciding to ignore him for the time being. I heard him chuckle. "Come now, I'm not that bad to look at, am I?" He lifted the pillow from my head, and I opened an eye to peer at him. "A little birdie told me you were looking for me."

Glancing at the clock, I saw it was well into the evening hours. Since my disastrous encounter with Tristan, I'd done nothing but lay in bed and sleep. Keane had tried to encourage me to work out or go and socialize with the other contestants, but I didn't feel up to either. He'd left a while ago to find sustenance, leaving Mckile standing guard at my door. I assumed he was still out there.

I turned my head back toward Sebastian. "What little birdie?"

He merely smiled at me. "I can't give away my sources, now, can I?"

"Mmm." Propping myself up on an elbow, I looked him over, realizing what was different. "Your wings are missing."

He smiled. "I figured I'd be less conspicuous without them. No need for anyone besides you to know what I really am."

"Don't the contestants all know? You were, after all, the keepers of the paths in the first Trial."

He shook his head. "You and Sabrianna were the only ones who saw us in our true forms. I had no use for anyone else knowing what we truly are."

I nodded, accepting it for what it was. "So, did your little birdie tell you why I was looking for you?"

Sebastian nodded. "That's why I wasn't here before now. I had to look into a few things."

"And?"

"While Lizzy has yet to achieve leaving our plane of existence, she did manage to bring someone through about the time of your Allison's disappearance, though I can't say for sure if it was her. I haven't yet been able to locate where Lizzy sent the person, but given time, I will. I just hope if it was indeed your Allison, that she is still alive when I do finally find her."

"Is there anything I can do to help?"

"In fact, there is, *if* my hunch is correct. But you'll need to slip your leash for a bit to do it." He looked pointedly toward the door where my guard would be stationed.

I considered him, wondering again if I could trust him. "I think I can manage that."

"Excellent. I have some things I need to do to prepare for our little excursion. I'll let you know as soon as I'm ready to bring you through, okay?"

"Okay."

With a last mischievous grin in my direction, he disappeared, leaving me alone in my room. After sitting there, staring at nothing in particular, I decided to get up and get ready. Sneaking into the bathroom, I quickly showered and dressed in the gear I'd left in there earlier. After drying my hair and pulling it up, where it wouldn't be in the way, I went back into my room, thinking I needed to move. There was just too great a chance of me running into Tristan in our current arrangement.

Pursuing that train of thought, I quickly packed my meager belongings. After hauling my suitcase and camera bag to the door, I turned around and looked at the room, making sure I wasn't forgetting anything. As I stood there, I spotted the statues still sitting on the bedside table. Walking over, I stared at them for a minute before picking up only Iridia and setting her with my things. I'd leave Riona for Tristan. Finding a piece of paper and a pen, I quickly scrawled a note on it.

*I think we both know you'll appreciate this more than I ever would. Yours, Blue.*

Sneaking quickly in and out of the connecting doors in the bathroom, I left the statue on Tristan's bedside table. With that, I went to my door and swung it open abruptly, startling Mckile.

He glanced down at my bags before looking questioningly at me. "Going somewhere?"

I smiled wanly. "Though I'd prefer home, I know I need to stay here for now. Any suggestions?"

He nodded in understanding and then leaned down to pick up both my bags. "I have just the place." Leading the way, he surprised me by taking me into the back area where the pool and gym were. Passing everything, he went to the same blank wall Keane had used to take me to the beach. Trusting him, I watched as he placed his hand on the wall and whispered a few words. That same blue light appeared as before, but this time as we stepped through the door, I found myself in a cozy little bungalow.

"Where are we?"

"Keane's place."

"Wait, I thought you guys lived at Dock Street?"

Mckile smiled secretively, like a child introducing his imaginary friend. "We stay there when we're working, but we have our own secluded places for when we just want to get away. We don't have to work all the time, you know."

"Won't Keane care that you brought me here?" I looked around curiously. Though everything had been decorated with a masculine hand, it was tastefully done and definitely reminded me of the man himself. I ran my hand over the couch's smooth leather as I walked by, smiling at the array of game systems hooked up to a huge flat-screen television. These guys sure did like their video games.

"No. Keane anticipated your request and told me to bring you here if you asked."

I nodded, touched that Keane had thought ahead for me, knowing I'd want to move even before I did. Though I was still surprised he had told Mckile to bring me to his home.

"Through here, are two bedrooms and a bathroom." He led me to a hall on our right. "Keane's bedroom is the door at the end of the hall, the bathroom is the one to the left, and you'll be staying in this one."

He opened the door just to the right of Keane's bedroom. Inside was a huge king-size bed, a small desk, and a large dresser with a mirror over it. "This is great." Walking over to the large window on the other side of the bed I gasped. "The ocean!"

Mckile chuckled as he watched my reaction. "He said you'd be excited about that."

"Where is this place?"

"Unfortunately, I'm not allowed to tell you that. In order for this to work, your whereabouts need to be kept strictly secret."

I nodded, figuring he was right. "How do I get back to Dock Street if I need to? Is there some special Vaimpír magic I need to use?"

Mckile shook his head. "Since one of us will be with you at all times, we'll take you through. I'll let you go ahead and get settled. If you need me, I'll be in the living room."

With that, he left. Not sure if Sebastian would be able to find me here, though I figured he could if he wanted to, I set about unpacking what I had brought with me so we could go back over to Dock Street. After I was done, I took a moment to open the window and, leaning against the sill, breathed in the scent and feel of the ocean, letting its gently lapping waves soothe my troubled soul.

An hour later, I found myself back at Dock Street, wandering through the ballroom. It had been set up as a command center of sorts for the Trials. All the points were tallied here, and there was even a large board with all our names on it to show our standings.

Currently, Sabrianna and I were at the top of the board, as we had completed the first task the fastest. Celeste was in second place, followed closely by Tatiana. Looking farther down, I saw Allison at the bottom, listed as *MIA*. She had also completed two tasks. Wondering why I hadn't been given a second Trial yet, I looked up at the list again, seeing that several of the contestants had gone through another Trial, though it appeared as if none had succeeded. I wondered if mine would be coming up soon.

"What do you think happened to her?"

I turned my head to find Sabrianna at my shoulder. "I don't know yet. But I'm looking into it. I hope to have an answer before the day is out."

Sabrianna looked at me quizzically but didn't question how I planned to accomplish that. After searching my face, she smiled and nodded. "If anyone can do it, you can. If you need any help, please don't hesitate to reach out to me. I'll do anything I can, no questions asked."

I wasn't sure where her faith in me came from, but I appreciated it all the same. I smiled down at her. "Thanks. If I need anything, you'll be my first call."

We exchanged numbers before she nodded and walked away, her guardian Darrius not far behind her. I watched the pair, noting how Darrius almost unconsciously moved closer to her and took her elbow as she climbed the stairs to keep her steady. I had to wonder if his feelings toward her were more than just those of a guard and his charge. Not that anyone could blame him. Sabrianna was a beautiful woman with her long, curly dark hair and large expressive brown eyes. Petite in every way, she turned many a head as she walked by.

Turning to leave the room myself, I suddenly came face-to-face with none other than Lucian Beaumont.

"Well, well, well, if it isn't the lovely Miss Blue."

Inwardly, I cringed. Of all the bad luck. I'd known he was here somewhere as he was the acting guard for Trulia, the Misty River Clan's representative. I had just been hoping to avoid any further confrontation with him. Not showing any of the discomfort I felt, I smiled widely.

"Hello stranger. Fancy meeting you here. Not planning on running me down as you exit the room this time, are you?"

My jovial attitude seemed to set him back a step. "Ah…no."

I forced a laugh. "That's a relief. So, what brings you here without Trulia?"

"I came to find you."

"Oh? I'm flattered. I was just about to head out, but what can I do for you?" I felt Mckile move closer to me, just as suspicious as I was.

"You can tell your guard dog I mean you no harm." He looked pointedly at Mckile, who in turn stared back. Hard. "I'm here on behalf of my King."

"Your King?"

Lucian nodded. "He requests the honor of your presence, if you could spare him a few minutes of your time."

This was interesting. Though I was a bit nervous to meet the infamous Sethos, I could hardly turn down such an opportunity. "I would be honored."

Mckile immediately put a hand on my shoulder. "Blue, can I speak with you a moment? In private?"

Nodding, I looked back at Lucian. "Will you excuse me for just a second?" He nodded as I walked away.

Mckile pulled me into a secluded corner just out of Lucian's earshot. "Are you out of your mind?"

"What?" He gave me an annoyed look, which I answered with a pointed stare. "Look, Mckile, what's going to happen? What better place to meet him than right here under your watchful eye, in our own territory?"

"A lot can happen. Did you forget about the incident with Celeste that got you into this position in the first place?"

I cringed at the reminder but refused to back down.

"Why do you need to meet him anyway? What would Tristan think?"

My expression hardened at the mention of Tristan's name, annoyed Mckile had even brought it up. "Honestly, Mckile, I don't care what he thinks. He may be my *King* but that doesn't mean he gets to control everything I do. If I want to meet with someone, then I'm damn well going to." I walked away from Mckile, leaving him frustrated but trusting he would do his duty and follow me.

Walking back up to Lucian I smiled widely. "Sorry about that, Lucian. Shall we?"

Lucian nodded looking smugly at Mckile. "Right this way."

As Lucian led us from the ballroom, I hoped we didn't have far to go, as I was sure Mckile was sending out an SOS to the other guys already, some of whom were currently with Tristan. Sometimes, having a guardian with supernatural powers sucked. Not that I wasn't glad for the backup. I was extremely nervous about this meeting, but something told me if I wanted to put an end to all the things happening, I needed to do this. And having it brought to a halt by Tristan's entourage wasn't in my plans.

After entering the elevator, we went up several floors. When the door opened, I saw we were at the main theater. Surprise must have shown on my face as Lucian chuckled and looked down at me. "You didn't think he'd be allowed down into the inner sanctum of the Moon Tree Clan after what happened, did you? The only reason I'm allowed there is because I'm escorting Trulia and Elder Avner."

"I suppose you're right."

Walking through the silent theater lobby was a bit unnerving. I'd never been in here when nobody was around. One almost expected a ghost to pop up around every corner. I laughed to myself. If there were ghosts here, I'd have no problem seeing them. I had more to fear from the living than I did the dead.

Lucian led us up to the second floor and into none other than box five. It was hard to believe that the last time I'd been in this very spot, I had been a completely different person with no knowledge of the whole other world that existed around me and how I was about to become a part of it.

"Thank you for meeting me on such short notice, Miss Blue."

I turned toward the voice and was surprised to see an older, heavyset gentleman sitting in the front row of the box. He was probably in his late sixties, had completely gray hair, and stormy gray eyes. Standing, he smiled and offered me his hand. I felt Mckile twitch behind me, but I put a soothing palm on his arm. Stepping forward, I bowed before taking the man's hand.

"It's a pleasure to meet you, Your Majesty."

"Oh, please, call me Sethos."

I nodded and sat in the chair next to his. I was completely at a loss. I couldn't seem to reconcile this old man with the cold-blooded killer he had been painted as.

"Strange isn't it? The perception we receive from others?"

Not surprised that he'd read my mind, I decided to be completely honest with him. "You can understand my confusion. I know not all is as it seems most of the time, but the fact remains that Riona was killed under your authority."

Sethos nodded sadly. "You are completely right. And though I had no knowledge of what really happened that night until it was too late, I was just as much at fault for not questioning my subjects' motives or monitoring their actions."

Watching his eyes, I saw the truth of his statement in them. That's when I noticed something else, something strange. Sitting back, I stared hard at Sethos. As I did, I saw a bit of a waver in his appearance. Smiling, I sat forward again. Just as I thought. His appearance was magically enhanced projected—to put me at ease, no doubt.

Sethos smiled again, his eyes crinkling at the corners. "Well done, my dear. Very few can see past my glamour." With that statement, he dropped it to reveal his true self. He was a handsome man, looking to be in his early thirties. He still had the same stormy gray eyes, but now he sported dark black hair and a wiry build. His face was thin and narrow, his chin almost coming to a point. This version better fit the dastardly image that had been painted of the man. "What gave it away?"

I considered. "It was something about your eyes. For a moment, I saw a shimmering halo around them."

"I can see the rumors about you are true. Another powerful Grayson on the rise."

Not wanting to pursue that line of conversation, I instead steered it back to the reason he'd asked me here. "So, what can I do for you, Sethos? There must be a reason you invited me here—something other than to test my abilities."

"Naturally. I need your help."

"Oh? And what could I possibly help you with?"

"You see, Blue, things in my clan are becoming very volatile. It's gotten so bad I've even sent my children to another clan for protection."

"Your children? Do you mean Odelina and Aelfric?"

Sethos nodded.

"But I thought they disavowed you because of your involvement in Riona's death."

Sethos sighed. "A necessary lie, I'm afraid. It was the only way Brokk would accept them. I knew Tristan would never take them in, but I needed them to be safe from harm, and Brokk's clan is the next strongest and allied with Tristan's."

"Harm from what, exactly?"

"In order to tell you that, I need to go back to the beginning." Sethos scrubbed a hand over his face before sitting back and closing his eyes. "It was before the tragedy that took Riona's life. A young man traveling through our territory stopped and requested sanctuary. We, of course, welcomed him in as we do all travelers." He shrugged.

"Now this particular young man had quite a charismatic personality. He easily drew people to him, making them feel special and needed. It was quite a talent. After watching him for several weeks, I came to realize it wasn't just his personality that caused the phenomenon, it was his gift. I thought it would be a great asset to our clan. I mean, what King wouldn't want an advisor who could so easily charm others? I invited him to my home one night for dinner to see if he would be interested in swearing fealty and joining our clan. When I asked him where he came from and why he was wandering, he broke down in tears. He proceeded to spin a tale for me of forbidden love, corruption, and a tyrant King." He shook his head.

"I have to admit, I was drawn in to his magic just like all the rest. I was outraged that a King of the Fae would use his position to manipulate people's lives the way the he described. I instantly vowed that if he joined our clan, I would stop at nothing to avenge his treatment at the hands of this supposed tyrant. Little did I know that he had just manipulated me into starting a war." Sethos opened his eyes to look at me.

"I still don't know how he did it, or how I didn't see it for what it was at the time since I already knew what his talent was." Sethos sighed and closed his eyes again to continue his story.

"As I'm sure you guessed by now, his name was Larkin, Riona's once beloved. In the coming weeks, we raised an army and attacked the Fernsong Clan, only to find out they had allied themselves with the Moon Tree Clan, one of the strongest to ever exist. I wanted to retreat and call for peace negotiations, but Larkin would have none of it, especially once we found out that Riona was the Queen of the Moon Tree Clan. He said he had a plan, one that would have us conquering both clans.

"Naturally, I was intrigued. What King wouldn't be, especially one with as small a territory as we had at the time? So, I agreed to the plan. He went about infiltrating the Moon Tree Clan, using Riona's love for him to open doors. Once inside, he manipulated people and found out as much inside information as he could, which was actually very little, considering. In hindsight, I think Tristan kept a very close eye on him, knowing what his gifts were. Anyway, when he couldn't get what he wanted from where he was, he decided to kidnap Riona to use as a bartering tool. Until he found out she was pregnant with his child, that was. I don't know what happened to him, but something seemed to snap. He was a man possessed." A look of sadness crossed his features.

"He tortured that poor girl, and I stood by and did nothing to stop it. I was on the front lines when I got the message that she was dead. I rushed back to find out what had happened since it definitely had not been part of the plan. Larkin merely laughed and said she didn't matter, that he had what he needed to bring the clans down without any more fighting.”

He opened his eyes, but kept his gaze downcast. “I was overjoyed. There had been too many unnecessary deaths already. He then showed me a child, a boy of about two or three. I was so confused. Who was this child? He then gleefully told me about what he had done, and how he had used black magic to siphon Riona’s life force to put into their unborn child. I was horrified. It went against everything I believed in. I couldn’t fathom that I had allowed it all to happen.”

He wiped a hand down his face. “I immediately recalled all our troops and sent up a white flag. Of course, by that point, it was too late. Events had already been set in motion that would bring my eventual downfall. Within a month, Larkin had complete control of my clan, though he continued to let the outside world believe I was still in charge and behind all the death and devastation that had been wrought. I was merely a pawn, and if I didn’t do exactly what he wanted, he threatened to kill my family.”

“Which is why you sent your children to the protection of another clan.”

Sethos nodded.

“What of your wife?”

He shook his head. “She is completely enthralled by Larkin.”

I considered everything he had just told me, wondering if it was all true or if this was just an elaborate story concocted to win my sympathies.

“There is something else I haven’t told you. The child, Riona and Larkin’s…after I discovered his existence, I knew what Larkin planned to do. He wanted to use the boy to claim the Moon Tree Clan throne. I couldn’t let that happen, so I…I stole him. I took him to the one place I knew Larkin couldn’t touch him.”

I felt my heart stutter in my chest and my eyes widen. “Cedric.”

Sethos was genuinely surprised. “How did you know? He doesn’t even know who his real parents are. I just told the woman who took him in that his mother had died, and his father didn’t want anything to do with him.”

My hands were shaking in my lap, so I clasped them together to get them to stop. "I found a picture of Larkin. I thought he looked familiar, but it wasn't him I was seeing, it was Cedric."

Sethos shook his head, bemused. "You have an uncanny perception, my dear."

I smiled slightly, thinking of Sebastian saying the same thing. "So I've been told. What happens now? Why tell me all this? What help can I possibly be?"

"I have to disappear. Larkin finally figured out I took Cedric, and if I stay, I will surely be killed. For the sake of my children, I can't let that happen. I would like to see one of them on the throne someday, but if I'm dead, there is no doubt Larkin will assume power."

"Why hasn't he before now? If he's as formidable as you say, I would think he would've already made the move."

"He needs my influence and contacts to do what he wants."

"What contacts? You said he's almost unmatchable when it comes to manipulating people. Wouldn't he just charm anyone he needed?"

Sethos laughed humorlessly. "People, yes. Gods, no. His powers have no effect on them whatsoever."

I was taken aback. "The gods?" Then I looked at him suspiciously. "It was you, wasn't it? The one who tried to have me killed when I was in the ocean?"

Sethos shook his head. "That was Larkin. He fears you."

"Why would he fear me? I don't even know him."

"He's afraid you're the Fae Brody saw in his vision, the all-powerful one who is supposed to end the strife and unite the clans once again."

"How did he know about the vision? I thought it was given to Tristan."

Sethos gave me a lopsided grin, making him look like a completely different person. "Brody is a member of the Misty River Clan, of course."

That surprised me. Though I didn't know much about the clan, what I did know made them out to be a ragtag bunch of thieves and villains. Perhaps like the perception of Sethos, that was also wrong. Plus, what did I really know about Brody other than the fact that he sculpted beautiful things that helped him deal with the visions he had—both good and bad?

Sethos shook his head but didn't comment on my internal battle. "As I said, I have to disappear. But I wanted someone to know what I do and realize what is really going on."

"But why tell me?"

"Because, my dear, you *are* the one Brody's vision showed. Of that, I have no doubt. It will be by your hand that Larkin is brought down and peace will be restored within the clans. You have already proven your worth by allying yourself with not one but three clans in your short time here."

"Three?" As far as I knew, I hadn't allied myself with any but the Moon Tree Clan.

Sethos smiled and ticked them off on his fingers. "Obviously, the Moon Tree Clan, who you are now a member of. The Mossy Earth Clan, by saving Sabrianna, who is a favorite of Barracus, their King. You will forever have his support. And the Fernsong Clan, because you are the daughter of Iridia, their Queen."

I sat back, shocked. How did he know who my mother was?

"You have her look about you, my dear. And who else in the family Grayson would be powerful enough to have a daughter with your abilities? Don't worry, your secret is safe with me, but be sure others will figure it out pretty quickly."

Knowing he was right, I got back to the question at hand. "But what can I do? What do you expect from me?"

"You must defeat Larkin before he brings the very fabric of the Fae world crashing down. If he gains control of the Moon Tree and Fernsong Clans, it won't be long before he has control of the rest. And once that happens, he plans to kill the Elders and become ruler of all." Shaking his head, Sethos looked at me. "If that happens, we are all doomed, as is the world around us."

Lucian reappeared in the box. "Your Majesty, we must be going. We have stayed too long already."

Sethos nodded. "One more thing, Blue. These Trials were Larkin's doing. Everything about them is designed to bring about your eventual death." Standing, Sethos looked at me sympathetically. "I'm sorry to drop all of this on you, but I believe you are the only hope the Fae has."

I stood when he did and bowed in deference. "Thank you, Sethos. I'm still not sure what to make of all of this or how I can ever hope to accomplish what you expect of me, but I appreciate that you took the time to tell me, even though it put you at risk. And for what it's worth, I don't believe you had a hand in Riona's death, at least not consciously."

Surprising me, Sethos reached over and clasped my forearm as an equal would before moving to leave the box. At the top of the stairs, he turned to me. After a moment, he tossed me something, which I easily caught. "If you are ever in danger and have need of me, simply toss this into the water."

Opening my hand, I saw he had given me a strange-looking gold coin. It wasn't like any currency I had ever seen, and I wondered what it was. With the question on the tip of my tongue, I looked up to ask him, but he was gone.

Slowly sitting back down, I stared at the strange coin in my palm before slipping it into one of the concealed pockets in my fighting gear. What was I going to do? Who could I trust? I had never felt as alone as I did now. I sat there staring into nothing until I felt Mckile come to stand beside me.

"Are you ready to go?"

I looked up at him. "Did you hear any of that?"

Mckile shook his head. "No, Sethos put up a shield around you so your conversation would be kept secret."

I saw the disapproval on his face. "Did you tell the others I was here with Sethos?"

Mckile shook his head again. "I just let them know we were going topside for a bit. I figured if you wanted them to know, you would tell them."

"Thank you for that, Mckile." I stood and, preceding him, made my way out of the box.

# Chapter Seventeen

I was sitting in one of the many magicked parks, taking photos of the playing children, when I finally got the mental call from Sebastian that he was ready for me. I had almost forgotten about him. Unfortunately, Keane was back on duty. I would have been able to easily slip away from Mckile, but Keane was another story. For him, I would need a little help. I shot Sebastian a mental message to stand by, then pulled out my cell phone and quickly texted Sabrianna.

"Something you want to talk about?"

I looked up from my phone and toward Keane. I knew he could easily read my mind and find out what I was thinking, but ever since the Tristan incident he had been giving me the courtesy of my privacy. Hopefully, I could use that to my advantage.

"Did you ever have something everyone believed to be true, through and through, only to find out it wasn't? What are you supposed to do with that kind of information? Keep it to yourself and let everyone continue to believe as they have, or rock the boat and try and show them differently?"

Keane seemed to consider this. "Does this have anything to do with your secret meeting today?"

I arched an eyebrow at him. "Secret meeting?"

"Come now, Blue, you didn't think you could just disappear with someone as notable as Lucian Beaumont and not have anyone notice. Were you even going to mention it to me?"

I laughed and crossed my arms over my chest. "Ah, I see now. The big, bad Lucian. Perhaps, he only wanted to buy me that apology drink…"

Keane gave me a deadpan look.

I smirked. "And no, I wasn't going to mention it—at least not yet." Mckile had obviously kept his word and not mentioned who I had really met with. Turning away, the smirk slid from my face and I gazed unseeing across the playground. "Remember how, not long ago, you wanted to look into things before you said something to me about your concern over my meeting with Sebastian?"

I saw Keane nod out of the corner of my eye. "This is one of those things. I need to look into it first before I can tell you." I turned back and looked him in the face. "Okay?"

He seemed about to argue, but his cell phone interrupted him. He answered it brusquely, obviously annoyed. "Rutherman. What? I'll be right there."

"Something wrong?" I tried to appear concerned, though I knew full well what the phone call had been about.

"It seems your friend Sabrianna has disappeared. That was Darrius on the phone. He's frantic. He left her in her room not five minutes ago, but now she's gone."

Darrius calling Keane directly surprised me. I had expected it to be routed through other sources. "I thought the two of you didn't talk."

Keane grimaced. "We don't…usually. If he's calling me, this obviously has him extremely upset."

"Why don't you guys speak to each other?"

Keane turned away from me, ignoring my question. I smiled behind his back. "We need to go over there and help in the search."

"Let's get a move on, then." I jumped up and took the lead so he wouldn't see my face. I knew the jig would be up if he did.

We took the elevator to Sabrianna's rooms and found Darrius inside, pacing back and forth. By the look on his face, I was now sure what he felt for Sabrianna was way more than just duty or responsibility. His expression and the fact that he had called Keane directly when there was obviously friction between the brothers confirmed it.

"Keane. Thank God. I didn't know who else to call. What do we do? Where do we look? What could have happened? Who would take her?"

"Calm down, brother." Keane put his hands on Darrius's shoulders to get him to hold still. "We'll find her, I promise."

Darrius nodded, shaking. "We've got to, Keane. We've just got to."

I helped Keane and Darrius begin searching rooms and areas they thought Sabrianna might be in. I felt a bit guilty for putting Darrius through this, but perhaps some good would come of it, and he would finally tell her how he felt.

As they went through yet another door to search one of Sabrianna's favorite spots, I made my move. Staying behind, I slipped back down the hallway we'd come up and went to the end. When Keane didn't come back for me, I shot a mental message to Sebastian. As the darkness surrounded me to take me to Sebastian's plane, I felt Keane jerk in surprise as he realized what I had done. Anger drifted through the connection between us. I knew there would be hell to pay when I got back, but for now, I needed to concentrate on finding Allison. I had told Sabrianna to give me about a fifteen-minute lead, so she should be reappearing shortly, which would distract them again. Hopefully, they wouldn't give her too hard of a time for helping me.

"Well, hello, beautiful." I blinked into the bright sunshine that greeted my eyes, seeing only Sebastian's outline.

Moving into the shadow of a tree, I sighed. "How is it that it's night at Dock Street and still day here?"

Sebastian laughed. "Time flows a lot differently here. You know that."

I grunted. "Had I remembered, I would have brought my sunglasses."

"Where we're going, you won't need them."

"You found her?" I looked up at him, surprised and hopeful.

Sebastian nodded. "It's not going to be easy to get her back. My dear cousin was playing for keeps."

"Where is she?"

"It seems Lizzy gave Allison to Poseidon as a gift to get back into his good graces."

"A gift? Who gives a person as a gift?"

Sebastian looked at me quizzically. "You really don't know how things work, do you?"

I wrinkled my nose and stuck out my tongue at him. "Okay, so then tell me. Why would Poseidon want Allison?"

"Because of what she is, of course."

"A Phoenix?"

Sebastian nodded. "She's very rare, even among the Fae. And Poseidon collects rare things."

"I hardly consider a person a *thing*." I shook my head, not understanding the world I had been dropped into. "So, what are we going to do?"

"Oh, you know...nothing too extravagant. Just sneak into Poseidon's territory undetected, break into his home, steal the *gift* he just received, get out again without being caught, and then return here alive."

"Is that all?" I let out an annoyed breath. I had no idea how we were going to accomplish this. It seemed like an impossible task.

Though I knew I wouldn't like the answer, I asked anyway... "So, where exactly is Poseidon's home?"

Sebastian grinned. "In the middle of the Aegean Sea, of course."

"Oh, of course. Why not?" I allowed the sarcasm to drip from my words before I continued. "I don't know if you've noticed, but neither of us is a fish."

"True, but we could be."

I looked at Sebastian, not quite understanding what he was getting at initially, but then I began thinking about it as he looked on speculatively. "I can become a fish, can't I? A Nereid, Mermaid, or something like that? I've come into contact with a shifter and have proven I can turn myself into a Vaimpír, so why not something else? But what about you?"

"No need to worry about me. I can hold my own."

I nodded. Now, how to go about it?

I'd naturally had the talents of the Vaimpír. All I'd had to do was create the teeth. How did one go about creating the gills and lungs of a Mermaid or Sea Nymph?

"If I might interject?" I looked questioningly at Sebastian. "Perhaps it is simpler than creating each difference. What if you merely changed yourself on the whole?"

Tilting my head to the side, I considered what he'd said. Strangely, it made sense. After all, what did I know about Mermaid or Nereid physiology? Now, which one? A Mermaid would give me a tail, which would help for movement, but if I remembered correctly, the Nereids were the ones who helped Poseidon, so I could probably get in and out without detection much easier that way. Making my decision, I closed my eyes and concentrated, using Galene as my mental model. After I had what I wanted, I carefully pushed the golden energy out from my center to fill my body. I felt the change start slowly as things moved and shifted within me. When it was finally done, I opened my eyes to look at Sebastian.

"Well?"

"You are simply amazing, my dear."

Looking down at myself, I realized my clothes no longer fit me since this new form was much shorter and more petite. Even Pinky and the Brain had suffered a downsizing, though I absently wondered if I could make that a more permanent thing. Sighing, I looked down at myself again. I didn't know any magic to adjust my clothing.

"Allow me." Sebastian waved his hand, and I soon found myself wearing what could only be described as a harem outfit—layers of multicolored scarves wrapped around my neck and crisscrossed my chest to cover only the essentials before encircling my waist and then falling to create the illusion of a skirt. When I felt a breeze through the bottom, I quickly made sure Sebastian had included a pair of panties to go with the ensemble.

I looked down at myself before looking back at Sebastian and raising both eyebrows. "Seriously?"

"Trust me, it's what they wear."

I nodded, though I wasn't entirely sure I actually trusted him—at least in this. Walking around, I tried to adjust myself to the new form. I never realized five inches would make such a difference.

"You may want to change your hair and eye color, too, just in case someone down there was at the presentation ceremony."

"Good idea." Closing my eyes again, I concentrated until my hair changed to a fiery red, and my eyes turned bright green. I'd always secretly wanted red hair but never had the guts to dye it. Now was my chance.

Sebastian nodded his approval. "You look good as a redhead."

"What about you?"

"I'm your ticket in. I have free rein to go where I will down there."

"Won't Poseidon suspect something if you show up right before his gift disappears?" I put as much derision as I could into the word *gift*.

"That really bothers you, doesn't it?" He seemed genuinely curious about my apparent dislike.

"More than I can express in words."

"Interesting." He continued to stare at me, making me feel decidedly uncomfortable.

"Shall we get a move on? The last thing I need is the cavalry appearing during our rescue mission and screwing things up."

Seeming to shake himself, he smiled. "Of course. Time is of the essence."

Without another word, he led the way into the woods. Not quite sure where we were heading, I stayed close behind him, which was definitely a challenge, considering I didn't have any shoes on. I managed to stub my toe more than once as we walked. I only hoped Sebastian could quickly retrieve my clothes from wherever he'd sent them if I needed to change forms again to fight. I felt very uncomfortable heading into what I considered enemy territory without a weapon.

Sebastian slowed, so we walked side by side. "I would hardly say you're walking into this unarmed."

"But you took all my weapons when you changed my clothes." I held up my arms and then patted myself down. I noticed he eyed my exposed skin as I did and quickly stopped.

He just grinned at me before turning serious. "Don't you realize that what's inside you is greater than any weapon you could physically wield?"

I couldn't refute his statement. I did have a lot of power and skills, but was I ready to use them all? Could I use them effectively? Or would I end up like Iridia, trapped with no apparent escape? It was a sobering thought.

As we came to the edge of the tree line, I heard the distinct sound of water lapping against a shore. My heart beat a little faster as I thought of having to go under to take a breath and hoping my spell held so I could truly breathe underwater.

"Um, Sebastian? Just how are we going to get to the Aegean Sea? We don't have to swim all the way there, do we?"

Sebastian chuckled and shook his head. "Oh, ye of little faith. Of course not. Once we're in the ocean, I can transport us there, of course."

"Right, *of course.*"

Shoring up my courage, I followed Sebastian into the surprisingly warm water. He immediately dove under the surface, but I was decidedly nervous. Walking all the way out until the water was up to my chest, I took a couple of deep breaths before closing my eyes and dunking under the surface.

I held my breath for as long as I could before letting all the air in my lungs out and tentatively taking a breath. I fully expected to choke on the water that rushed into my nose and mouth. When I didn't, my eyes opened wide in surprise, and I found myself looking at the bottom of the ocean in a whole new way. Everything was magnified and beautiful. I saw reflections bouncing around from the light above, and there weren't any dark corners or cloudiness you usually had when you opened your eyes underwater. I took another deep breath, surprised all over again as it easily flowed in and out. Sebastian stood not far away with his arms crossed over his chest, a smirk on his face.

*"Confidence. You need to have more confidence in yourself."*

I tried to talk to him but found only a muffled sound came out. Then, realizing he had spoken to me telepathically, I readjusted. *"That's easy for you to say. This life is all you've known. I, on the other hand, was brought up in a world that believed these kinds of things were merely fiction."*

*"Touché."*

Without another word, he turned and led the way through the many rocks and bunches of coral that littered the ocean floor. I wondered idly where we were. After we had walked a few feet, he stopped and put his hand on a large patch of coral. With a few whispered words, a hole opened, creating a tunnel. Sebastian gestured for me to precede him. I did so cautiously, having no idea what to expect.

As we came out the other side, I stopped suddenly, causing Sebastian, who had been following closely behind, to bump into me. *"What's the matter?"* I just shook my head, unable to speak. Sebastian peered over my shoulder and then pushed me forward, chuckling as he did. *"Quite a sight to behold, isn't it?"*

Before us stood what could only be described as a magnificent castle made of shimmering gold. It had many towers and sweeping lines that seemed to touch the water's surface before tapering down to the castle below. Swimming in and out of the gates and around the area was a multitude of marine life, including Mermaids and Mermen.

*"Come on. We need to keep moving so we don't attract more attention than we already will. Just act like you belong here and guard your thoughts as carefully as you can "*

I nodded and followed him along the ocean floor, doubling the shield around my thoughts. As we reached the front gates, a pair of Merman guards stopped us. Both had shining gold tails that matched their breastplates. Upon their heads were golden Corinthian helmets, and they both carried tridents as weapons. They were intimidating, to say the least.

Remembering what Sebastian had said about appearing to belong, I raised my chin a notch and stared imperiously at them both. I wasn't sure if the Nereids held a higher position in this society, but I had to believe they did since they were Poseidon's handmaidens. After a brief exchange with the guardsmen in a language I didn't understand, both males bowed to me before gesturing for me to enter. When we were out of earshot—or mindshot in this case—I moved closer to Sebastian.

*"What did you tell them?"*

*"That I was escorting you here at Poseidon's urgent request."*

*"Why did they bow to me?"*

*"Because I told them you were none other than Leukothea, also known as Princess Ino."*

*"Royalty, huh?"*

*"Once upon a time. She was a mortal Princess who incurred Hera's wrath when she fostered the infant god, Dionysus. In retaliation, Hera drove Ino's husband into a murderous rage, which caused him to kill their firstborn son. In order to save herself and her younger son, Ino took him and jumped off a cliff into the sea."*

*"Oh, that makes perfect sense, To keep your murderous husband from killing you, just jump off a cliff so you can drown instead."*

Sebastian chuckled. *"The marine gods had an affinity for Ino. So they changed her into a Sea Nymph upon her death and renamed her Leukothea. They also changed her son into a Nixie and renamed him Palaimon. Though these days she goes by Thea, and her son goes by Paul."*

By this time, we had reached the palace doors. Striding forward as if he owned the place, Sebastian pushed the doors open and turned to hold them for me. I moved through, trying to maintain my air of superiority, though it was becoming more and more difficult by the minute. As I stepped into the entrance area, I glanced quickly around. While quite a few people were moving about, none paid us a bit of attention. They all seemed to have their own tasks. Sebastian guided us down one of the many hallways that branched off the main room.

*"Do you have any idea where they might have Allison?"*

*"If I'm correct, she'll be caged in the trophy room."*

*"Caged?"*

*"Of course, how else would you hold a Phoenix?"*

Grumbling, I moved along behind him, following as he led us down hallway after hallway. I liked Poseidon less and less at this point. How did one simply take someone and cage her, all for their personal enjoyment? And what did he do with her now that he had her? Put her on display? Ugh. If it was the last thing I did in my life, I would make sure Allison was released and kept out of the hands of the likes of Poseidon.

After what felt like the millionth staircase, Sebastian finally went down a wide hall and came to a stop in front of a set of large doors. *"Ah, here we are."*

I had no idea how he even knew where *here* was, let alone which room to enter. This palace seemed to have thousands of passageways that all led to nowhere. Sebastian opened the doors in front of us, revealing a room full to the top with every treasure imaginable. There were golden statues, fine works of art, glittering jewels, massive vases, pottery...and that was just what I could make out through the entryway.

As we stepped through the doorway, I felt a wash of magic move over us and looked down quickly to make sure my disguise was still in place. I wouldn't put it past a god like Poseidon to have a security system that would reveal an intruder. My guise was still perfect, and I looked around, wondering just what that bit of magic had done. That was when I realized we were once again breathing air. That explained how a Phoenix could survive under the ocean.

Looking around cautiously, I made sure no one else was in the room before relaxing my stance. "So, this is Poseidon's trophy room, huh?"

Sebastian glanced sideways at me. "One of them. He has...a few."

"How many is *a few*?" I narrowed my eyes at him.

He grimaced in return. "I don't know the exact number, but it has to be in the—"

I quickly put my hand over his mouth, shaking my head. "Never mind. Forget I even asked. Just answer me this: How did you know this was the one Allison was being kept in?"

"Because I told him, of course." I straightened in shock as a very familiar voice flowed over me. It was the same one I'd heard in my mind all those weeks ago. Turning slowly and looking up, I found myself staring at the same man I had seen on the beach at my house, and again at the ocean attack with Keane. He stood on a walkway above our heads, leaning nonchalantly against the railing. He had short, wavy red-brown hair, a close-cropped beard and mustache, and brown eyes so dark they were almost black. He was extremely tall with a very muscular physique, which he showcased by not wearing anything but a draping piece of fabric that wrapped diagonally across his chest and encircled his waist to flow down like a skirt, toga-style. I couldn't help but notice he had really nice legs.

Shaking my head at the wayward thought, I shot an accusing glare at Sebastian, who just shrugged. Call me the fool for trusting him. I should have known it was all too easy.

The man above us laughed. "I sense you somehow have this wrong. Let me introduce myself before you get mad at Sebastian. My name is Triton, son of Poseidon." That took me back a step. The confusion must have shown on my face as Triton laughed again. "No, I'm not Poseidon, though some say I favor him in my looks, much to my mother's consternation. Poor Amphitrite."

"But...you were the man I heard and saw on the beach at my house and again in the Caribbean."

Triton nodded sadly. "Yes. I am sorry for those two incidents. It wasn't my intention to frighten you."

"Frighten me? You tried to kill me!"

Triton shook his head. "No, I wasn't trying to kill you. I was there doing what I could to keep you alive."

"What do you mean?"

"That first night at your house, a group of mercenaries were sent to kill you. I used my powers to bring up that storm and drive them back to their hole, though from what I understand, they came back later. I tried to warn you, but I think I frightened you. Your guardian, Keane, came out, and I spoke briefly to him."

That was news to me. Keane had never mentioned speaking with Triton. I would have to take him to task for that little oversight.

"As to the incident at the beach in the Caribbean, I was there also to merely keep you alive. It seems someone convinced Thetis you were a threat to Poseidon. As the leader of the Nereids, her duty is to protect him and remove the threat. I got wind of the attack just before it happened and rushed over to make sure you weren't killed."

Someone wanted me dead. Bad enough to make it look like Poseidon was after me. Was this the same person pulling Celeste's strings? Or was Larkin really behind all of it as Sethos had insinuated? I was starting to get a very bad feeling about being here in Poseidon's castle. Something told me Allison being brought here was for more than just being a *gift* to the god. Someone wanted me here, too. But for what?

"Why would you want to help me? What am I to all of you?"

I looked questioningly between Sebastian and Triton, truly confused.

"You, my dear, represent the future. And as such, you are to be protected."

"The future? What do you mean by that?"

Triton shook his head. "I'm afraid I can't reveal that to you at this time. Just know there are those who are set to protect you and keep anything from happening to you at all costs. Even if that weren't the case, you are far too precious to me to let anything happen to you."

I was dumbfounded. Who did he think I was? Before I could ask any more questions, an alarm sounded.

"What the…?" Triton looked around, seemingly as surprised as we were. "Someone must have triggered the alarm. You must get Allison and get out of here. Now! I will do what I can to distract the guards. Go!"

He ran down the stairs and flew out the door, leaving both Sebastian and me standing there in shock. Sebastian was the first to gather his wits. "Come on, Blue, we have to hurry." He ran over and grabbed my hand, dragging me farther into the room.

"Why didn't you tell me about Triton?"

I saw Sebastian smirk. "Would you have come with me if I had?"

I gave a half laugh. "Probably not."

"Exactly."

I shook my head as I ran along with him, having no idea where we were headed. How was it that this man—or Angel, rather—knew me so well? Was I that obvious?

As we wove in and out of aisle upon aisle of treasure, trying to locate the illusive Allison, I heard Sebastian muttering to himself about

Poseidon's hoarding tendencies. There were things here from all over the world, spanning centuries. I caught glimpses of Greek statues, famous paintings I would bet were originals, and even modern-day sculptures. Scattered among the large items were gems that could put the Crown Jewels to shame, strings of pearls, and even some really odd-looking boxes and trinkets that didn't seem like they would be worth anything.

Finally, we reached the back of the room and a ring of cages. Inside were all manner of birds: parrots, cockatiels, lovebirds, and some I couldn't even identify. In the center of the ring was a large, gilded cage set on a high pedestal. Inside was an extremely large red-and-gold-winged bird, a Phoenix. Allison was truly beautiful in her animal form. I could see her natural grace in how she held herself and the arch of her neck as she stared down at us.

"Allison, is that you?" She cocked her head at us as if listening carefully. "Allison?" She didn't seem able to understand me, so I decided to try to speak to her telepathically. *"Allison, it's Blue, one of your fellow competitors in the Trials. We're here to rescue you."*

*"Blue? You don't look like the Blue I remember."*

*"It's a spell to change my appearance..."* I figured since they already knew we were here, it didn't matter what I looked like. I quickly changed my hair and eye color back to normal.

*"Blue. It is you! You need to get out of here. It's a trap."*

I shook my head. *"We're not leaving without you."*

*"You'll never be able to get me out of this cage in time. It's set up with some type of lock that can only be opened by a Nereid."*

*"I guess it's a good thing I'm a Nereid at the moment, then."*

She stared at me in shocked silence, her brilliant golden eyes assessing me. Without waiting for further comment, and a boost from Sebastian, I scrambled onto the pedestal's edge. Eyeing the lock, I saw it would take some type of scan to open. You'd think being magical beings they would have some convoluted magical contraption for a lock, but apparently modern technology worked just as well for them as it did for humans.

Taking a deep breath, I held it as I placed my palm on the reader and prayed it worked. At the touch of my palm, the reader came to life, and a green light traveled up and down my hand, scanning it. For a second, everything was silent, and I thought for sure it hadn't worked. But then the cage door beeped loudly and swung open.

I glanced in at Allison. *"I'd suggest turning yourself back into your mortal form since we'll have to traverse the sea."*

*"What difference does it make? I can't breathe underwater, even in my other form. You'll never get out of here alive with me coming along. Just go."*

*"Let me worry about that. Just change."*

With a frustrated huff, Allison closed her golden eyes. I watched in fascination as she quickly transformed. The whole process really was a beautiful thing. Unlike the Wolves, there were no bones crunching and rearranging, it was just a smooth transition, like sliding a silk dress over your head. When she was done, I hesitated. She didn't have any clothes on. Looking around, I spotted a bolt of cloth not far away. Jumping off the pedestal, I grabbed it and, using the point of a nearby sculpture, ripped a large chunk off. Running back over, I handed it up to Allison.

"Here, wrap this around yourself." After she tied it the best she could, I took her hand and helped her down. "Okay?" She nodded. We started running back the way we had come, praying Triton had been able to misdirect the guards long enough for us to get out. If they caught us in this room, it was over. Approaching the main door, I saw it was still closed, and the vestibule was blessedly empty. As I reached for the door handle, I felt magic tickle my hand and realized I hadn't made it so Allison could survive underwater. Thinking fast, I stopped and turned to her.

"Give me your hands. This might feel a little weird."

"Oookay."

I closed my eyes and concentrated on that gold ball within me. Manipulating the magic faster than I ever had before, I took the spell I'd used to turn myself into a Nereid and changed it slightly so I could pass it on to Allison like I had with the spell I used so Tristan could see Riona.

Thinking about Tristan caused a spike of sorrow to jolt through my heart, but I quickly pushed the sensation aside. Now was definitely not the time to think about him or the troubling feelings that went along with it. I pushed my energy into Allison, being careful not to overwhelm her. I felt her shiver as my magic coated her and seeped into her. Opening my eyes, I found her staring at me with shock and awe.

"What are you?"

I grimaced. "Unfortunately, I don't think there is anything in this world or the next that can explain that. Let's just say I'm different."

"Ladies, we really don't have time for this." I looked at Sebastian, who was impatiently tapping his index finger on the biceps of his crossed arm, and knew he was right.

Cautiously opening the door, I peeked out. The hallway seemed empty as far as I could tell. Slipping out the door, I gestured for Sebastian to precede me. I knew there was no way I could find my way back through all the winding corridors we had taken to get here.

Pressed tightly together, we moved quickly down the hall on silent feet. My heart raced as I expected to come face to face with a bunch of guards—or worse, Poseidon himself—around every corner. I shuddered to think what he would do to us if he found us stealing his latest treasure. As we came around the next corner, Sebastian came to a skittering halt.

*"Bloody hell! Turn around and go the other way, it's blocked. We'll have to detour through the kitchens."*

Not needing to be told twice, we quickly went back to the other hallway we had passed on the way here. After several twists and turns and a couple of additional detours, we entered what looked to be a large dining hall. Several long tables were set up across the room with low benches running the entire length on either side, while a raised dais at the front of the room contained another table with five ornate chairs behind it.

As we started moving down the length of the tables, we heard a commotion outside the door we had just entered through and froze, all of us crouching low below the table's edge in case someone threw the door open. A deep, booming voice cut through the walls, causing us to sink lower, not daring to move a muscle for fear of making a sound.

*"I don't care what you have to do, find them! And bring them to Poseidon's throne room as soon as you do. Somebody's head is gonna roll for this. How did someone breach our security? Get me Theodon and Apostolos. NOW!"*

We heard a bunch of scrambling as the guards moved to do their captain's biding. After a few beats of silence, we started inching our way toward the far door I hoped led to the kitchen and eventually out of this place. Just as we reached the exit, it swung open to reveal a servant. She froze, her eyes widening as she spotted us before she opened her mouth and let out a loud scream. Moving on instinct, I grabbed her before she could run back into the kitchen and quickly knocked her unconscious. Unfortunately, her scream had been enough to alert the guards, and we could hear them scrambling in the halls, moving quickly toward us.

*"In the dining room. It came from in there. Quickly!"*

My head whipped to the door. *"Shit, shit, shit! We need to move fast!"*

I turned and pushed through the door in front of me. Taking a quick inventory, I found we were indeed in a large kitchen. There were two lines of workstations covering the length of the room, as well as two big cooking stoves, and a massive fireplace. I would wonder later how on earth a fire could be lit underwater.

Between us and the exit were also about two dozen servants. They looked up from their work, seeming only mildly curious about our presence. Hearing fellow servants scream obviously wasn't an oddity to them—a reflection of what went on in this palace, I was sure. Hoping they all stayed where they were, we raced across the room. Just as we were about to reach the back door, it banged open to reveal two Mermen, armed to the teeth.

Scrambling backward, we made to backtrack across the kitchen but soon found it blocked by more guards spilling in through the dining room door. We were in serious trouble now. There was no way I'd be able to take them all down without one of us getting hurt or killed.

Turning to the two Mermen blocking our entrance, I crouched into a defensive position. Since we weren't getting out of this without a fight, I figured these two were my best bet, though I wasn't sure I could take them on. Drawing on Iridia's training, I threw up a magical barrier behind us I hoped would hold for the time being, though I was certain it wouldn't last long.

It would take most of my magical ability to hold that large of a barrier, so it looked like I would have to fight the Mermen hand to hand.

The warriors in front of me laughed.

*"And what is this? The little sea urchin thinks she can take us? You should just give up now, little girl, before we have to hurt you. Poseidon will want you alive so he can punish you properly."*

I ignored their taunting and instead concentrated on building the magic in my center that would enhance my strength and endurance. *"Sebastian, I need my gear back. Now."*

He nodded and, with a wave of his hand, I had my fighting gear, thankfully now sized to me. Quickly unsheathing several of my daggers, I prepared to take on two of the toughest opponents I had ever faced. This was nothing like the sparring I had done at Dock Street. These Fae were skilled fighters, taught to kill. There would be no leniency.

*"I guess the captain won't be too disappointed if we soften her up a bit for him, will he, Apostolos? He just said she had to be alive, not what condition she had to be in."*

*"Right you are, Theodon."*

They both laid down their tridents and unsheathed large Greek swords, and short Spartan Lakonia blades. While I was familiar with what they were and how they were used due to Iridia's tutelage, I had never fought against either.

*"Keep Allison safe while I deal with these two, Sebastian."* I saw him nod out of the corner of my eye. I stood my ground, waiting to see what the Mermen would do. The bigger of the two, the one called Theodon, swaggered forward, a smirk on his face.

*"So, you think you can fight, little sea urchin?"* He raised a brow when I didn't back down. *"Let's see what you've got, then."*

He swung his large sword around his head and, turning in a quick circle, lunged, narrowly missing me. I quickly danced to the side to avoid the sharp blade before dropping and rolling when he made to jab at me with his short sword at the same time. Taking advantage of his forward momentum, I stayed low and used my small-but-exceptionally-sharp daggers to slice a cut across the wrist holding the Lakonia sword when I sprang up.

He dropped his small blade, letting out a cry of pain and outrage. Not stopping to see what he would do next, I quickly thrust my second dagger, burying it deep into his side before dancing backward. As I moved, I scooped up the dropped Lakonia sword. Rotating it back and forth a couple of times to get the feel of it, I stayed out of arm's reach of the male in front of me. He hadn't moved from where I had stabbed him. Instead, he stared at me incredulously.

I heard a bark of laughter before the other Merman's voice carried from somewhere nearby. *"Need some help there, big guy? The little sea urchin too much for you?"*

*"Shut it, Apostolos."* Theodon yanked the dagger from his side. He grimaced and then threw it down, his gaze narrowing in my direction. *"You're going to pay dearly for that one."*

Baring his teeth and snarling at me, he charged, his sword held high above his head, blood oozing from his wrist and side. I met him blade for blade. I felt the vibration of our swords connecting making its way down my arms and almost lost my grip. It was unlike anything I had ever felt. Gritting my teeth, I held back, keeping my attacker's blade just inches from reaching my shoulder. He practically pressed his face into mine.

*"Your time is up, little one."*

My strength clearly no match for him, even with his wounds, I looked around wildly before spotting my saving grace. Letting him push me backward until I bumped into one of the workstations, I turned and let go of the sword while ducking to the side. As the full force of his blow ricocheted through the metal table, I used the precious few seconds I had to grab the cast iron frying pan sitting on its surface. With all my strength, I brought it down on his head. He stared at me in disbelief for just a second before his eyes rolled up, and he fell unconscious to the floor.

I let out a small sigh of relief, hoping he stayed down. Quickly turning to face my other opponent, I knew I was in for an uphill battle. The Lakonia sword had slid across the room and out of my reach, which left me with only a frying pan and a small dagger. I had used up most of my strength on Theodon and wasn't sure I could take much more. The Merman called Apostolos moved forward, an arrogant smile on his face.

*"You may have bested Theodon by sheer luck, but you'll never be able to take me. I'm going to teach you to show a Merman some respect, girl."*

He came at me fast and hard, thrusting both swords. I dodged and deflected as many blows as I could, though he managed to cut me in several places. I knew if I couldn't get my hands on the blade lying a few feet away, I was done for.

Summoning what magic I could, I pushed forth a burst of light, momentarily blinding my opponent. He cried out but continued to swing and hack with his swords. I dove to the floor, sliding across it on my knees. Scooping up the small Lakonia blade, I stood and turned in one fluid motion, just as a large sword came at my head. Feinting backward, I readjusted my footing just as Iridia had taught me, then went on the attack. I managed to land several hard blows that sent Apostolos staggering backward.

*"Well, well, seems I might have underestimated you a bit."*

I stood in a defensive position, catching my breath. I didn't know how much more of this I could take. I'd tried everything I knew of to get through his defenses, but I'd barely managed a scratch. Now, he was slowly circling, seeming to assess me. Without warning, he sprang forward and grabbed me by the hair, throwing me back into one of the massive ovens. I hit my head hard against the glass but managed to stay conscious and keep a hold of my weapons. A small line of blood trickled down into my vision from a cut just above my eye. Apostolos wrapped my hair around his hand before I could move and put the edge of his blade against my neck. He leaned in until I felt his watery breath fan my cheek.

*"You're a very fiery woman, I like that. Now, if you could just learn some respect."*

With that statement, he punched me hard in the stomach. I fell to my knees, gasping for breath. As I knelt there on all fours, clutching my side, I heard the shield holding the other guards back starting to crumble. I knew my time was quickly coming to an end. If I didn't do something drastic right now, it would be over, and they would capture us.

I just couldn't let that happen.

As I felt Apostolos lean over, no doubt to grab me by the hair again, I suddenly swung my head up and headbutted him. Blood spurted, and I quickly rolled to the side and out of his reach. When I regained my feet, I looked toward Apostolos and saw he was clutching his nose, which bled profusely.

*"You little bitch, I'm going to kill you for that. I don't care what the captain says!"*

He advanced on me, swinging every which way with his large Greek sword, which I deflected...though barely. I just didn't have the strength. He had picked up a dagger somewhere along the way and used it to make small, painful cuts across my arms, slicing through the fabric of my shirt. After a particularly hard clash of our blades, I felt pain flair in my side. I wasn't going to make it. There was no way I'd be able to hold out if he hit me like that again. Just when I was about to admit defeat, I heard a voice floating through my thoughts.

*"Get down and hold on to something."*

Not questioning it, I dropped and rolled to where Sebastian and Allison stood, yelling for them to get down. We all grabbed on to one of the metal table legs bolted to the floor and waited. Seconds afterward, what felt like a tidal wave of force rolled through the ocean water, scattering servants, guards, equipment, and most importantly, Apostolos, away from us. It was all we could do to hang on. As soon as I felt a lightening in the sensation, I looked up at our exit and saw it was blessedly clear. Grabbing Allison by the hand and trusting Sebastian to follow, I raced toward the door. Bursting through, I found we were in a small garden. As I hesitated, not sure which direction to go, Sebastian ran by at full tilt.

*"Follow me!"*

We took off after him. Looking back, I saw the soldiers struggling to their feet, trying to pursue us. Apostolos was in a rage, roaring at the top of his lungs. I just hoped that had given us enough of a head start to get through the portal to Sebastian's plane, because I was sure if Apostolos caught us, we were dead.

As we ran, I felt another sharp tug in my side but didn't stop to investigate. Pushing onward, we quickly found the coral tunnel Sebastian had opened earlier. He went first, followed by Allison. Just as I was about to enter, I heard that same voice from earlier float through my thoughts.

*"Congratulations on your achievement in rescuing the Phoenix and besting two of my top warriors. This Trial has truly been enlightening. I will definitely be keeping a closer eye on you in the future."*

Though I didn't recognize the voice, I knew who it was. Poseidon. Why had he helped me back there? What did he mean by this was a Trial? As soon as we were back on Sebastian's plane and out of the water, I turned angrily to him.

"This was all a part of the Trials? You put both our lives in danger for some stupid game?" I pushed at him to emphasize my point.

"I didn't know, Blue. I was as much a pawn in this as you were."

"Ugh! Why did I ever trust you?" I started pacing. "Whose side are you on?"

"I told you it was a trap, Blue. I didn't get a chance to explain further down there." I stopped and turned to Allison, who looked contrite. "I failed my last Trial. I was captured during it and brought to a wooded clearing somewhere around here. My captor told me I was her golden ticket to freedom, whatever that means."

"Lizzy..."

"Yeah, I think that was her name. She called Poseidon and presented me to him as a gift. He only laughed and said something about no gift atoning for what she had done. I think he would have gladly sent me back home right then and there, but a hooded figure appeared and asked Poseidon to take me to his palace, as I was going to be a part of another Trial. I don't know the specifics. They stayed mostly in the shadows, whispering."

"Did you recognize the newcomer?"

She shook her head. "I didn't see their face. They stayed fully robed with their hood up the entire time."

"This just makes no sense. Why would the Elders send me somewhere I would almost surely be killed? If it hadn't been for Poseidon…" I trailed off as I remembered what Sethos had told me: that the Trials had been designed to bring about my death.

I sighed. This was getting out of hand. The slight throbbing in my side that had been nagging at me suddenly seemed to match my heartbeat, bringing my attention to it. I put a hand on it and winced. As I pulled my fingers away, I saw they were covered in blood. My wet, black clothing had been hiding it until now.

Sebastian stepped over to me, his face showing concern. "You're hurt. We need to get you back to Dock Street immediately."

I was starting to feel a bit woozy. "Okay, Sebastian, I…whoa…" All of a sudden, I couldn't see straight, and my body felt heavy. "We…we need to get Allison back safely…" A black circle started creeping into my vision.

"Don't worry about Allison. I'll take care of her."

"Thanks, Sebastian. Sorry that I…that I didn't trust…"

"Shhh. It's okay, Blue. I understand. Don't talk now. Save your strength."

As the blackness overtook me, I felt Sebastian's arms slide around my waist to keep me from falling. "Don't worry, Blue. I'll take care of you." His voice was a mere whisper in the overwhelming darkness.

# Chapter Eighteen

I felt like I was floating on clouds, not really here or there. I could hear voices all around me, talking in hushed whispers. I wasn't sure exactly what they were saying, but I knew something serious was going on given their tones. I tried to open my eyes, but my lids felt like they weighed a million pounds. Giving up, I pushed my senses out and located Keane not far from my side. He seemed tense. At least I knew Sebastian had held true to his word and brought me back to Dock Street. Hopefully, Allison had made it back safely too.

I tried to talk to Keane telepathically, but I couldn't seem to penetrate the strange fog surrounding my head. Giving up, I tried to figure out who else was there. I didn't recognize the signatures of three of the others surrounding me, but I could tell they were older. The fourth and final person was Tristan, and he seemed angry and worried. I wasn't sure, but it sounded like he was arguing with someone. Sighing, my meager strength depleted, I let the oblivion of sleep claim me once more.

Something tickled my nose. I tried to move back from it, but whatever it was followed me. Aggravated, I swiped at it. My efforts only produced a male chuckle. The tickling continued. With a sigh, I dragged my heavy eyelids open so I could glare at my antagonist.

Keane was lying on the bed, practically nose to nose with me. "Wakey, wakey, eggs and bakey."

I merely glared at him.

"Did you know you snore?"

I narrowed my eyes.

"No, seriously. You make this little snuffling noise when you sleep. It's rather endearing."

I rolled my eyes, which caused him to laugh.

"You're really not much of a morning person, are you?"

I gave an annoyed sigh and shook my head slightly.

"I suppose getting stabbed, beaten, and almost dying doesn't help." I felt the anger vibrating through him.

I remained silent.

"Not going to apologize for disappearing on me, are you?"

I shook my head again.

He sighed this time. "Then I'm afraid you'll just have to be punished."

My eyes widened in alarm as his hand rose over me. I knew he wouldn't hurt me, but I wasn't sure what he had in mind.

"For the crime of disobedience and putting oneself in extreme danger, the punishment is...a thorough spanking."

He brought his hand down hard on my backside. I yelped, more from surprise than pain. He swatted me a few more times, each time with a little less force. When he was done, he caressed my burning cheeks.

"And now, your reward for coming back alive."

My heart rate accelerated as I watched his eyes turn dark red and his fangs lengthen. He held me still, twisting his hand into my hair as his mouth lowered to mine. My eyes drifted closed as his lips delicately traced the outer edge of my mouth. He flicked his tongue out and ran it along my bottom lip, followed by the slight scraping of one of his fangs. I shivered as the sensation radiated through my body, moving straight to my groin.

A whimper escaped my parted lips. He growled and pressed his lips hard against mine, his tongue immediately invading my mouth. He kissed me hotly, almost angrily, before softening it. Removing his hand from my hair, he slid it down to the middle of my back, where he pressed, bringing our bodies tightly together. I felt his erection pushing against me, and an answering heat surged to my center, liquefying and pooling between my thighs. Just when I was about to surrender to the lust flowing between us, a throat cleared not far from the bed.

"I'd say I hope I'm not interrupting anything, but I can see I am…"

Startled, I pulled back from Keane, who growled a bit under his breath before raising his head and looking at where the voice had come from.

"You have impeccable timing as always, brother."

I looked up and saw Darrius standing at the foot of the bed.

"I do try my best where you are concerned. I just came to relay a message from King Tristan. He humbly requests your presence in the war room at your earliest convenience."

"And you felt the need to deliver the message personally?"

"I was to stay and watch over the unconscious patient, but I can see she is quite awake now."

A smile flitted across my face at his sarcasm. He was more like his brother than either of them would likely admit. It was probably why they weren't generally on speaking terms.

Keane sat up and slid to the edge of the bed, grumbling under his breath. After locating his boots, he slipped them on and then stood, strapping on his weapons, which had been sitting on a nearby chair. As he did, I noted we were in the room he had lent me temporarily at his place. I was both surprised and grateful that I wasn't lying in some sterile hospital bed—especially considering what I had just been about to do.

"What are you still doing here?" Keane directed his abrupt question at his hovering brother.

"I'm to stay and guard Blue until you get back, of course."

"You'll do no such thing."

"Oh, I'm sorry. Did I miss the part where they made you King?"

I giggled as the two of them continued to argue like teenage boys. Who knew Keane had such a childish side to him? When it seemed like it would come to blows, I carefully sat up on the bed, first making sure I had something decent on before drawing their attention with an earsplitting whistle.

They both stopped and turned to me in surprise. "Now that's enough out of both of you. Keane, go and see what Tristan wants. Darrius, I'm perfectly fine here by myself. Go on and look after Sabrianna like you should be."

I immediately saw the relief in Darrius's eyes, though he made a half-hearted attempt to dissuade me. "But King Tristan said..."

"Don't worry about Tristan. If he says anything, send him to me. I'll be more than happy to let him know I don't need a babysitter. Go on."

With a last glare at his brother and a nod in my direction, Darrius turned on his heel and left the room, leaving me with an irritable Keane.

Keane turned to me. "Don't you dare even think about leaving that bed. Not only are you still healing, but I'm not finished with you yet."

With that, he stalked out of the room, following in his brother's wake. I just shook my head. No way would I be lying here when he got back. I didn't trust him—or myself, for that matter. What I really wanted was to get back to Dock Street, check on Allison, and find out what the hell was going on with the Trials. Were the other contestants being given similar Trials? If they were, did the Elders really have any idea what they were putting us through?

I waited a few minutes until I was certain Keane had left before swinging my legs over the side of the bed. I was still sore, but not enough that I didn't think I could move around. Using the headboard for balance, I slid off the mattress and tentatively put my weight on my feet. I was definitely hurting everywhere from the beating I had taken, but nothing a few ibuprofen wouldn't cure.

Moving slowly, I made my way out of the room and shuffled across the hall to the bathroom. Once there, I started the shower and moved to stand before the full-length mirror on the back of the door. Removing my shirt, I looked down and saw that my middle had been wrapped in white gauze. I was pretty sure I wasn't supposed to remove it, but I had to see it for myself. After carefully unwrapping the many layers of gauze, I threw it onto the sink and, taking a deep breath, looked into the mirror. My body was a riot of color. My right temple, where Apostolos had slammed my head into the oven, boasted a lovely purplish red patch, while my left shoulder and neck were an array of yellows and greens. Across my ribs, I saw dark bruises where I had been punched, as well as some small healing cuts where a blade had landed several blows. I avoided looking at my side and instead moved down to my legs, which, other than a few scratches, didn't fare too badly.

Moving my gaze back to my side, I was shocked at the wound. It was still an angry red but well on its way to healing. I didn't have any stitches, and while tender, it didn't provoke any major feelings of pain. I wondered just how long I had been unconscious. Perhaps Fae healed differently than humans did. I couldn't really remember a time I'd had a major injury before to compare this to. Deciding not to dwell on it, I climbed into the now-steaming shower. I needed to decide on my course of action. Did I confront the Elders directly? Or maybe I should just talk to Kieran first, although I still wasn't sure why he had agreed to this whole mess in the first place. Every time I had tried to bring it up in the past, he had answered me evasively and quickly changed the subject. It was all so confusing. If Larkin was behind all these attempts on my life, how was he doing it? How was he controlling the Elders, not to mention the gods?

After my shower, I decided to get dressed so I could go and see if I could get myself back to Dock Street. On my previous visit to Keane's place, I had Mckile with me to open and close the portal, but now I was here alone. I wasn't sure if I could manipulate the magic that was needed, but it wouldn't hurt to give it a try. Walking into the living room, I went over to the wall they used. Closing my eyes, I concentrated on the space, looking for any residual magic. In one of Kieran's many lessons, he had taught me how to trace a magical trail. Normally, the technique was used for the police by a Fae called a

Detektip to determine how some magical mishap had occurred. Now, it was coming in handy so I could see how the boys had been moving back and forth. I finally located the small blue line that created the portal in my mind's eye. Mentally twisting it around, I reversed the spell so I could see how it worked. It was easy enough, not unlike what the Fairies used to create the portals at Dock Street, but it required a passcode of sorts. It was like a signature imprint from only a select few people—which I obviously was not. Sighing, I opened my eyes. Damn Keane and his impenetrable security measures. Wandering back into the kitchen, I decided to see what—if anything—was available to eat while I mulled over the problem at hand.

Not having any culinary skills to actually cook something, I settled on a peanut butter and jelly sandwich. After putting together my meal with some potato chips, I sat at the kitchen table and turned the problem of the signature imprint over in my mind. It wasn't like I could just change my fingerprints or turn myself into a Vaimpír to get through it. The imprint was almost like a DNA test. It was probably why Keane had left me here by myself. He knew there was no way I could get through the barrier on my own. I rolled my eyes at the thought. Insufferable man. So, how to get back to Dock Street without him knowing? I was sure he would deny any request I made for him to take me there.

As I sat staring at the room across from me, the wall suddenly lit up with a blue line. Someone was coming through the portal. I was instantly on alert. There was no way Keane had been able to meet with Tristan and returned that fast. It was probably one of the other Ethereal Mutation members coming to check on me. I was sure not many had access to Keane's private lodgings, but I looked for a viable weapon just in case. Finding none close at hand, I ducked behind the counter in the kitchen and watched surreptitiously as a figure slowly emerged from the portal. It was a woman I didn't recognize, and a Vaimpír to boot. This was definitely a curious turn of events.

Staying hidden, I watched as the newcomer quietly made her way through the bungalow toward the bedrooms. She was obviously acquainted with the layout as she moved unerringly towards the room

I had been lying in only moments ago. Seconds later, a harsh expletive floated down the hall.

"Shit! She's gone! Damn bitch is going to make me look bad."

She came running back down the hall, glancing back and forth, trying to locate me, no doubt. Using my magic, I quickly cast an invisibility spell. While it didn't truly make me physically invisible, it did make me undetectable to others, more like a shadow. Even still, I tried to make myself smaller, pressing against the cabinets as she leaned over the island to check the kitchen. I wasn't sure how powerful or old she was.

"Dammit!" She lowered her voice to a persuasive tone. "Uh, Blue? Are you here? Come on out, sweetie, I won't hurt you. Keane sent me to check on you." When she didn't immediately get a response, she dropped her sweet tone. "Blue! Where the hell are you? Stop playing around and get out here! That's an order!"

I kept silent as she moved around the bungalow, checking several other places. With an angry huff, she went over to the wall where they'd made the portal. I heard her whispering the words to unlock it and thought fast. I only had a few seconds after she went through where it would remain open. I just needed to get through without her seeing or sensing me.

Decision made, I readied myself for the quick dash. Thank goodness I had decided to get up and get dressed. As the Vaimpír stepped through the portal, I ran as fast as I could behind her. I managed to make it through just as it snapped shut. Who knew what would have happened if I had been caught halfway? I shuddered as I thought of the consequences.

Moving on light feet, I followed closely behind the unknown Vaimpír. We had emerged in a hallway I wasn't familiar with, and I hoped she could lead me to the elevator, at least. Suddenly, she stopped a few feet ahead of me and cocked her head. Then, in a lightning-fast move only a Vaimpír could accomplish, she turned and stood as if ready to battle. I froze in place, still hidden in the shadows. While I was technically *invisible* to her, I wasn't chancing accidentally giving myself away with a sound or even a thought. She stayed perfectly still for what seemed like forever. I was beginning to think I would have to risk moving past her when she swung around and started walking down the hall again.

I slowly let out my breath. That had been agonizing. I didn't think she would hurt me, as it appeared Keane had sent her, but I also didn't want to be sent back into exile wherever Keane's place was located. Who knew when I'd get another opportunity to escape?

I almost laughed out loud but managed to stop myself. I was acting like a prisoner. I knew if I put up enough of a fuss, Keane would take me wherever I needed to go, but that didn't mean I wanted the extra aggravation it would require. As we rounded yet another corner, the woman suddenly stopped before a door. Knocking, she waited until she was told to enter.

"Pardon the intrusion, my lords, Your Majesty, but I have an urgent message for Keane."

Creeping forward, I peered into the room, careful not to reveal myself. It appeared to be a large conference room with about a dozen flat-screen TVs mounted to the walls, showing various information and images, though I couldn't make out exactly what. Tristan sat at the head of a large oval table with Keane standing at his side, while the Elders sat around it. Various guards were posted at intervals against the walls. With this many important individuals in a gathering, I was surprised they hadn't posted guards outside the doors.

Keane looked annoyed at the intrusion, though Tristan and the Elders appeared merely curious. "What is it, Jasmine?"

"I'm sorry to bother you, but could I speak with you?" She didn't sound sorry for interrupting at all. In fact, she appeared to preen before so much male attention.

"What you have to say can be heard by any of the ears here, whether we are in the room or not. So, please just tell me."

I heard chuckles from several of the Elders, and Jasmine flushed angrily before placing her hands on her hips and glaring at Keane. There was definitely some history between the two.

"Of course." Her lip curled in a small sneer before she answered. "I hate to inform you, but your miscreant of a charge has managed to give you the slip and is not where you left her."

Keane let out an annoyed sigh. "Jasmine, I told you to be extremely careful where she's concerned, didn't I?"

She snorted. "Yes, but she wasn't even there."

Keane merely shook his head and looked exactly where I was standing in the shadow of the door. "Blue, stop skulking in the hall and come in."

Jasmine turned toward the door in surprise, but since I hadn't removed the invisibility spell, she still couldn't see me. She turned back to Keane and eyed him coyly. "Really, Keane, is this some sort of joke? You do so love to tease me." She moved closer to him and placed her hand on his chest.

Keane shook his head in disgust and pushed her away from him. "Blue not only managed to hide from you, but you also allowed her to follow you through the portal. Had you not come straight here, who knows where she would have ended up? I knew I shouldn't have trusted you with such an important task."

Jasmine looked as though he had slapped her. "Really, Keane, what does it matter? She is just some nobody who wishes to raise herself from obscurity by competing in the Trials. Everyone knows she doesn't have an ounce of talent and has only succeeded so far by pure luck. Why they have you, a Vaimpír of your ranking, looking after her is beyond me."

Keane ignored her seemingly by force of will and turned back to the door. "Blue, you know I can feel you."

I sighed and stepped into the room, releasing the invisibility spell. I should have figured he could sense me—our bond had become that strong.

Jasmine looked back and forth between us, her eyes narrowing before she turned to me, a look of stunned outrage slowly overtaking her features. "It's not possible. You're not Vaimpír! How could you have…? There has to be another reason. Come here." Jasmine jumped toward me. I had no idea what she had in mind, but I figured by the enraged look on her face that whatever it was couldn't be good.

Quickly maneuvering around the table, I kept just out of her reach as she continued to spew profanities at me.

"You bitch! If you have soulbound him, I will kill you."

Soulbound? What the hell was she talking about? I looked at Keane, who appeared annoyed but not overly concerned. Then I caught the look of utter surprise on Tristan's face. I shouldn't have let myself become distracted because, at that moment, Jasmine leapt forward and tackled me. My head slammed against the floor, causing my vision to swim. This probably wasn't the best activity for someone just out of the hospital for a head injury. Regardless, I tried to keep my wits about me as she loomed above me, her fangs extended.

Thinking fast, I manipulated the magic within me to create a binding spell. It was a simple one that Iridia had taught me and should make my opponent's muscles simply freeze up. I hoped it worked like she'd said it would, as I had never actually tested it. Such things didn't tend to work on ghosts.

Using the spots where Jasmine's skin touched mine, I pushed my magic into her. I felt her shudder and then freeze. I tentatively pulled at my arm, and her stiff fingers fell away. Sighing in relief, I shimmied from under her and left her kneeling awkwardly on the floor. It seemed she could only move her eyes and they were currently blood-red and full of hate.

I sidled up to Keane. "Uh, you want to explain what that was all about?"

"Go ahead and release her, Blue. I will deal with her."

"Not going to answer me, are you?" I sighed when Keane raised a questioning eyebrow. "Fine." Moving to stand behind Jasmine, I quickly did the counterspell and then leapt back when she made to grab me again. One of the other guards immediately grasped her by the arms and held her back.

Sure, *now* they wanted to help.

"You bitch! I will kill you if you don't release him to me."

Confused, I just shook my head. "Jasmine, I have no idea what you're talking about."

"I don't believe you." She looked around at the group of Elders. "You see what an abomination this is, don't you!? You won't allow this to continue, will you?"

With a signal from Keane, two guards took charge of Jasmine and escorted her, still screaming, from the room. When everything was silent again, Keane returned his attention to the Elders and Tristan.

"I do apologize for the disruption, my lords." He bowed to them and then to Tristan. "My King."

"While that was rather diverting, Keane, would you mind explaining to me why Jasmine believes you are soulbound to Blue?" Though Tristan appeared calm, I sensed his underlying tension and wondered at it.

Keane looked at me momentarily before turning to Tristan. "That would be because we are." There were audible gasps from around the table while Tristan's eyes widened. "It was quite by accident, I assure you."

Tristan frowned. "I would certainly hope so, especially considering it doesn't seem as though Blue even knows what that *is*."

"But how is that even possible?" Elder Demirtas—always the one to speak for the Elders, it seemed—asked the question.

After a short nod from Tristan, Keane addressed the Elders as a whole. "As you know, Blue is of the family Grayson." Keane looked at Kieran, who also nodded to him. "What you may not know is that her mother is none other than Queen Iridia."

Murmurs rose around the table, and I heard some quickly whispered words between the Elders before Elder Demirtas spoke again. "So, you are telling us that Blue is not only a Grayson but also one of royal birth?" Keane nodded. "And one imbued with Iridia's powers?"

"Her powers and more."

"And who would her father be, then?"

Keane shook his head. "That, we do not know. Without Iridia to ask, we have no way of knowing at this point."

Elder Demirtas seemed to consider that. "So, how is it that she, a non-Vaimpír, was able to bind your soul to hers?"

Keane sighed. "Blue isn't your average Fairy, as I'm sure you have seen by her Trials. She actually exhibits several different talents of the Fae." He left out the fact that I could mimic them all, something for which I was glad.

"One of her talents is to become one of the Vaimpír, leaving us to, of course, wonder if her father was one."

*Nice deflection, Keane, keep them off the real scent.*

"It was during this discovery that we...accidentally bonded."

Elder Demirtas nodded. "I see. And do you intend to honor this binding?"

Keane looked at me for a long moment. "I do."

"So be it, then. We will give our blessing on this union. From this point on, you are strictly Blue's guardian. You will no longer bear the duty of keeping King Tristan safe. Blue will be your one and only concern. You will, of course, explain to her all the...duties involved?" Keane nodded and bowed in the Elder's direction.

I finally piped up. "Don't I get a say in this? I don't even know what it all means."

Elder Demirtas chuckled and looked at me. "I am sure Keane has some explaining to do, but know it is a great thing in our eyes, especially considering your birth line."

"But..."

"Blue, I feel it best we leave the King and Elders to their discussions." Keane moved forward to take my elbow.

"But I need to talk to them about the Trials. I need to tell them—"

Keane continued to pull me toward the door. "Don't worry, I've already told them everything they need to know."

"But you don't understand..."

"Not now, Blue. We will discuss this privately."

I allowed him to pull me from the room, though I was far from done with my discussion with the Elders. I was, however, very curious as to what this soulbinding thing was. By how the Elders had acted, you would think they had just married us. I hoped that wasn't the case. While I wasn't opposed to Keane, I *was* averse to someone making my life decisions for me, and that was a big one.

"It's not exactly what you're thinking."

I glanced at Keane. "Oh, and just what is it I'm thinking?"

Keane only laughed and continued to lead us down the hall toward an elevator. I sighed in relief when I saw the lift doors, I thought he might be taking me back to his house.

"What, you don't like my place now?"

I gave him a disgruntled look. "It's not that I don't like it. It's just that I don't have the freedom to leave when I want. I was starting to feel like a prisoner there, held against my will."

Keane looked amused. "I was merely trying to keep you safe the best way I knew how."

"Mmm, perhaps you should have started by talking to me about it first to see what I wanted."

He seemed to consider that, but then shook his head. "Nah." He guided me onto the elevator and then pushed the symbols for the floor he wanted.

I mumbled under my breath about controlling men, causing him to chuckle. "Where are we going anyway?"

"To get something to eat."

"Oh, good. I didn't get to finish my sandwich before Miss Dark, Toothy, and Obviously Still Hung Up On You interrupted me. Speaking of, you wanna explain what your relationship with her is? Especially if she has access to your private quarters, where I don't."

Keane sighed. "She won't have access any longer, don't worry." When I just raised an eyebrow at him, he rolled his eyes at me. "Fine. We were betrothed at one time, some years ago."

"Um-hmm. A light is beginning to glimmer. Do go on."

Keane gave me one of his annoyed huffs, to which I just grinned and made a rolling gesture with my hand.

He shook his head at me but continued anyway. "I thought myself in love with her, and she with me. But on the day we were to marry, I found her in bed with another man."

"Oooo, yikes. I'm...sorry." I tried to sound sympathetic but knew I likely wasn't pulling it off. By my way of thinking, Keane had dodged a bullet on that one. Jasmine seemed to fit into the category of super deranged bitch to me, but that was just my first impression. I was sure she had a lovely personality buried somewhere under there...deep, deep down. Trying to make light of it, I danced around the confines of the elevator and gave him a few pretend punches in the arm. "I'll bet the guy who you caught her with didn't fare too well after that."

Keane crossed his arms over his chest and leaned against the elevator wall. "I never did anything to him."

I stopped and stared at him. "Nothing?"

Keane shook his head. "No. It was my brother."

My jaw dropped. If it hadn't been connected, I knew it would have hit the floor like in the cartoons. "Darrius?"

Keane nodded.

"So, *that's* why you guys don't talk anymore. Wow...umm...I don't know what to say to that."

Keane snorted. "There's a first."

"Hey!" I punched him in the arm again, this time hard. He merely laughed and turned, walking out the elevator doors as they opened and leaving me to follow him. I chewed on my bottom lip as I considered everything while following in his wake. Not one to think quietly, I of course did it out loud.

"So, if she was sleeping around with your brother, why would she still be hung up on you? I mean, she was practically foaming at the mouth back there when she thought we were soulbound."

"She claims she was under some spell when she slept with Darrius. That someone wanted our relationship over."

"Is it possible?"

"I suppose. But he claimed she had been pursuing him for months before he finally gave in. He actually warned me about it."

"And you believed him over her?"

Keane stopped and looked down at me, his expression serious. "Though I don't condone what he did, I would never doubt his word. If he were to lie to me, I would know it. I would feel it. In here." He tapped his chest, before he turned and continued down the hall.

I stood still and watched him as he walked away. I could feel all the old emotions churning inside him. Even though he was glad that

Jasmine's true nature had been revealed, it still hurt him—what his brother had done. Shaking my head, I jogged to catch up with him. It was strange how I could feel his emotions now. I wondered if that had anything to do with the soulbinding.

Before I could ask, Keane stopped before a brightly colored door. "I hope you like Mexican food. This is one of my favorite places." When he opened the door, the most delicious aroma wafted out to greet me. I felt saliva start to pool in my mouth with just a whiff. I groaned. Keane chuckled at my response. "I'll take that as a yes."

Guiding me forward with a hand at my back, Keane led me into a small but tidy restaurant. The walls were all painted in different bright colors, with small mementos and photos hung on them. A bar was set off to the right side, where a man I assumed was the bartender took a nap, perched precariously on the back two legs of his stool, a hat pulled over his eyes. Tables were spread across the main floor, and a few other patrons were happily ensconced in the chairs before them, eating and talking.

The restaurant's main focus, however, was a large deck overlooking the ocean. Over the railing, I saw boats on the water, bobbing up and down as the waves flowed past them. My soul was immediately calmed. As we approached what I assumed was the host stand, I saw a small, squat man with graying black hair sitting behind it, reading a newspaper. He was dressed casually in dark slacks and a long-sleeve white dress shirt, open at the throat. As soon as he spotted Keane, he jumped up, throwing his paper aside, and ran around the podium with huge smile, his hands outstretched.

"Señor Keane! What a wonderful surprise. So good to see you." He shook one of Keane's hands with two of his. "Ooh, and you brought your *novia* to see us. Wonderful, just wonderful. And so *bello*!" He gave Keane a sly glance.

"Señor Alejandro. It is good to see you, as well. This is Blue." I noticed Keane didn't dispel Alejandro's idea that I was his girlfriend, and I frowned over at him.

Alejandro turned to me and took my hand, bringing it to his lips. "Your *novio* is a very lucky man, yes?"

I smiled at him. It was hard not to. The guy just had an infectiously happy nature. "I am so glad to meet you, Señor Alejandro, but I must tell you I am not Keane's—" A feminine squeal of happiness interrupted me.

"Ooh! Señor Keane! *Mi amor.* You have finally come to see me again. It has been so long. I was beginning to think you didn't like me anymore. *Estoy tan feliz.*"

I turned as Keane caught a young woman up in his arms, twirling her around before setting her back down and holding her at arm's length. She was a beautiful little thing, probably in her early twenties. She wore a long, black, layered skirt embroidered with colorful flowers and a matching white, off-the-shoulder blouse that showcased her overflowing assets.

Keane gave her an affectionate smile. "Mariana Rodriguez, look how much you've grown. I swear the last time I saw you, you were only knee high."

The young woman blushed prettily while eyeing him coyly. "It has not been that long, Señor, but I have, how do you say, grown more in certain areas." She shook her chest back and forth suggestively.

I had to choke back a laugh, covering it instead with a cough. It was obvious this girl wanted Keane in a very bad way. The noise I made, of course, drew her attention to me. She turned angry brown eyes in my direction. "Do I amuse you, *mi amiga*? Or perhaps I can help you with something, like finding the door?"

Alejandro immediately jumped forward. "*Hija!*" Grabbing his daughter by the arms, he turned her away and started speaking to her in rapid-fire Spanish. He gestured several times while Mariana threw angry glances in my direction.

I looked at Keane, who gazed at me, clearly amused. He mouthed the word *troublemaker* to me. I pointed at my chest and mouthed back, *who me?* He nodded, and I shook my head while crossing my arms over my chest. By this point, Alejandro had turned back to us, obviously having sent his daughter elsewhere.

"I am so sorry, Señorita. I do not know what came over Mariana. She is not usually so impolite."

I shook my head. "No need to apologize, Alejandro. It was no big deal. She was just excited to see Keane and thought I was making fun of her. I didn't mean to insult her. Please tell her I'm sorry."

"You are so very kind to say so, and so very tolerant. What she did was unacceptable, and she will be punished accordingly."

"Please, don't punish her. No harm was done." I took his hand in both of mine turning him toward me. "Please?"

He searched my eyes for a moment before giving in. "Very well, but I will make her come apologize to you at the very least." When I would have argued, he put up a hand to silence me. "No, she must do this. If anything, for her own good."

I nodded, though I wasn't very happy about it. I really didn't want to cause any friction between Keane and his friends here. Alejandro gave my fingers a slight squeeze. "You are not the one causing friction. And it is good for Mariana to see she cannot always have what she wants. I spoil her way too much." I had obviously forgotten to block my thoughts. I sometimes forgot that no matter where we went at Dock Street, I was in the presence of some sort of Fae.

Alejandro showed us to a table located on the deck, right next to the ocean. He pulled my chair out for me, and after I sat, placed a napkin on my lap with a flourish before pushing my chair back in.

"Now, what can I start you two off with?"

As there was no menu, I deferred to Keane for our choices. He seemed to know what I liked most of the time without me telling him, so I figured he'd know what to order.

"I'll have my usual times two."

Alejandro bowed to Keane and, with a wink at me, took off to take care of our order.

"Sooo, what *is* the usual?"

"You'll see. Trust me, there is nothing here you won't like. After you taste Alejandro's food, you'll want to come back again and again."

"I do trust you. Speaking of, how about you explain this soulbinding thing to me?" I sat forward, placed my elbows on the table, and my chin in my hands, appearing the eager student, causing him to laugh.

"As I am sure you have already figured out, a soulbinding is usually done between two Vaimpír. It is something that makes a Vaimpír couple very strong, as it combines the power of two into one. Have you noticed that you're able to feel my emotions in addition to my essence now?" I nodded as I had most definitely noticed. "You will also be able to read my thoughts more easily, though with as new as you are to this, and as old as I am, I can still keep you out most of the time. The one exception would be if we were to have sex."

At my raised brow, he just shrugged. "The joining of the two soulbound bodies would create such an intimate link, there is no way I would be able to keep you out." I put this little tidbit of information on the back burner of my mind, something to definitely think about later.

"With our link, we can also share each other's power. For instance, if you were in trouble, I could lend my strength and healing abilities to you, and you, in turn, could do the same with any of your many abilities to me. Though we do have to be on the same plane of existence." A frown overtook his face, and I knew he was thinking about my battle down in Poseidon's castle.

I immediately steered the conversation back. "When did this happen? I don't remember doing anything that would have bound you to me."

Keane smirked and pulled down his shirt to reveal two marks from what had been perfectly spaced holes on his neck, though the wounds themselves were gone. I felt a blush creep up my cheeks. Those looked suspiciously like the marks I had left on him when I decided to drink his blood like one of the Vaimpír the night of the presentation ceremony.

He nodded, his grin widening. "When your instinct to drink my blood took over that day, it must have awakened your full Vaimpír powers. Though you didn't consciously do it, when you bit me, your magic bound my soul to yours. Your bite mark is proof of your claim on me."

My eyes widened. "Are...are the marks permanent?"

Keane nodded with a smile. "The mark is there as long as we are bound, however, it is up to me whether I want it visible or not."

I eyed his neck before raising my eyes to his. He just continued to grin at me. "So, how did I bind you to me? I mean, you've bitten me several times, and you didn't bind me to you that way."

"A normal bite won't soulbind someone. First off, it has to be between two Vaimpír, of which you weren't fully until that moment. Second, it is a very specific magic. It happens while you are connected to the other person by their life force point. Essentially, your soul reaches out through that spot and tethers the other person's soul to yours, connecting them to you."

"How would I have done that accidentally?"

"How do you do anything you do?"

"Mmm. Okay, so what did Elder Demirtas mean when he said something about my duties?"

Keane's smile slipped a bit, and he started squirming in his chair, looking discomfited. "Well, umm…."

He was saved from having to answer when Mariana came up to the table with a tray in her hands. It had two bowls of soup, a plate of some type of fried rolls, salsa, queso, and what looked to be guacamole. She also had two bottles of cold beer. I could feel the saliva start to flow again as the spicy smells drifted toward me, and it almost distracted me from what I had asked Keane. Almost.

After placing everything on the table, Mariana folded the tray against her side and turned to me. She curtsied but refused to meet my eyes. "Señorita, I wish to apologize for my rudeness earlier. It was uncalled for, and I am ashamed of my outburst."

I could tell she was only doing this because her father had said she must. I saw no remorse in her, only resentment. I sighed. "It's okay, Mariana. I shouldn't have laughed. I meant no insult. You just took me by surprise."

Mariana executed another little curtsy, then with a sideways glance at Keane to see how he perceived the interaction, took herself back to the kitchen.

I shook my head at her retreating figure. "Something tells me she will learn nothing from this encounter, contrary to what her father hopes."

"She is definitely strong-willed. She will make someone a fine wife someday, though she will be a handful."

I took a spoonful of the delicious-smelling soup in front of me and nearly melted. "This is divine."

"I told you you'd like it."

Still needing an answer to my earlier question, I gave Keane a pointed look while I continued to eat. "So, about those duties?"

He sighed, knowing he couldn't avoid the question. "Normally when two Vaimpír are bonded, they provide each other with...sustenance. The blood is obviously obtained from another source, but they do not engage in the act of the bloodletting from another physical body. That way, their powers are perfectly in tune to each other's at all times."

I stared at him, one of the fried rolls poised halfway to my mouth. "So, let me get this straight, since you are bonded to me, you can only drink my blood? And since I'm not technically Vaimpír and don't need blood to survive, that means it will just be my blood that keeps you alive?"

He nodded, seeming afraid to say anything else until he gauged my reaction. I took a bite of my food and sat back in my chair, chewing thoughtfully as I mulled it over. "I guess that's not so bad." Keane seemed to deflate in relief before tensing at my next question. "What happens if I'm killed during these Trials? Does that automatically release you from our bond?"

Keane sighed. "Always worried about others, aren't you? No, it doesn't. Sometimes, there are no ill effects for the Vaimpír left behind when the link is severed. But other times...it kills both of them."

"Keane—"

He put up a hand to stop me. "Since I am bonded to you and not the other way around, if something were to happen to me, nothing would happen to you—that is unless I complete the soulbond by binding your soul back to mine, which I'm not going to do. So, it is only my life that is in question. And since it is my life, it is up to me if I want to take that chance."

"Keane..."

"Nothing you can say will dissuade me, Blue. I have made my choice."

I sighed. "Keane, I don't know what to say. Why would you give your life for me? Why would you even consider taking that chance? We've only known each other for a short time."

"It only took me one glance across a crowded bar to know there was something special about you, Blue. From the moment our eyes met, I knew our fates would forever be connected. I didn't know how then, and I still don't now, but I do know I want to be a part of your life. I have to. Only time will tell in what capacity, but for now, if it is only to protect you with my very life, then so be it."

I stared at him in shock, not only because of his words but because of the emotions churning through him. I couldn't believe one person could feel that strongly about another in such a short period of time. It was beyond anything I had ever encountered, even with my best friends. Reaching across the table, I took his hand and interlaced my fingers with his. I had no words to explain how what he'd said and felt made me feel. I figured I'd let our connection do the talking. He smiled softly and took my other hand, interlacing those fingers too. As he caressed the side of my hands with his thumbs, I closed my eyes and let the tide of emotions flow over me. I shivered at the intensity before letting them envelop me.

The sound of a tray full of dishes shattering brought my eyes quickly open. I turned to see Mariana standing among the broken shards of what had probably been the rest of our lunch. She was shaking in suppressed hurt and fury.

"You have chosen her for a soulmate? She is not even Vaimpír! Or of the seven houses." I saw an energy starting to build in her aura and knew there would be trouble.

Keane stood slowly, not making any sudden moves. "Now, Mariana, you need to relax. Blue and I aren't…"

"Oh, but you are. I can see the connection running between you when you touch. It's so strong. How could you? How is it even possible?"

She turned her fury-filled gaze on me. Her eyes were now blood-red. Huh, little Mariana was apparently a Vaimpír, or at least partly. I didn't see any fang as of yet, though. What was it with these female Vaimpír and Keane, anyway? You would think there weren't any other male Vaimpír out there, the way they all fought over him. First Jasmine, and now Mariana. Not that Keane wasn't a tasty morsel and all, but he was just like any other Vaimpír, wasn't he? Maybe I was right in thinking there weren't a whole lot of them out there.

"You mean you don't even know who he is?" Shit, I'd let my guard around my thoughts slip again. If it was possible, her voice rose higher, and her hair started to float. I was in deep trouble if she loosed whatever spell she was building around her. I had a feeling it was set to kill. I started building the magic in my center, just in case I needed to throw up a protective shield around us.

Alejandro appeared from out of nowhere. "Mariana, stop this at once. You must contain yourself. Regardless of your feelings on the matter, Keane has made his choice, and it was not you."

Mariana had not taken her eyes off me. "You will not have him. You are not worthy!" Before anyone could stop her, she spread her fingers in my direction and loosed her spell. Just as fast as it crawled over the floor, leaving scorch marks in its wake, I put up a shield around Keane and me. I watched as the power slithered and burned across my shield as if searching for a weak spot. When it found none, it continued its path until it fell sizzling into the ocean at our backs.

I kept my eyes firmly on Mariana. I didn't want to hurt her, but I needed to find a way to bring her down before she ended up killing someone. The other patrons in the restaurant, while looking wary, hadn't moved from their respective seats. I guess they figured they had a front-row seat to this fight, and unless things started flinging their way, they weren't going anywhere.

Thinking fast, I remembered a spell Iridia had taught me. It was the same one that had been used on her by the Witches and Warlocks to cripple her magically. Working fast, I built up the magic it required. This would take a lot out of me, so I only had one shot. Keane moved up behind me and put his hand on my shoulder, lending me his strength and magic.

I barely acknowledged him, but I saw that his touch enraged Mariana further. She started to sway and chant, and her aura became engulfed in a fiery red. Just before she reached her peak, I dropped my shield and threw my spell at her. It hit her so hard, it lifted her off her feet. She lay on the floor unmoving, steam rising all around her as my spell quickly put out whatever she had been creating.

I sighed in relief when I tested the air and felt that all her magic was gone. It was safely locked away in her center where she wouldn't be able to touch it until I released her. After a moment, she sat up, looking dazed.

"Whaa...what did you do to me?"

I sat in the chair behind me, a wave of fatigue overtaking me. "I have simply locked away your magic so you can't hurt anyone with it."

"You can't do that!" Mariana was back on her feet, and I eyed her wearily. "You will release me at once."

I just shook my head. "Not until you calm down."

Without warning, Mariana lunged at me. She managed to take everyone by surprise, even me, and caught me square in the chest, toppling us both to the floor. I landed on my back with her looming over me. Her eyes had turned red again, and she now sported a set of fangs.

Well, wasn't that just great?

I could feel the iron strength in her arms and legs where she held me down. I tried to conjure up the same freeze spell I had used on Jasmine earlier, but my magic reserves seemed to be depleted, not to mention my head was spinning again. My poor brain had taken quite a beating in the last few days. It was a wonder I didn't have permanent brain damage.

"If I can't kill you with magic, then I will suck you dry!"

As she leaned over, no doubt to slice into my neck with her razor-sharp fangs, I felt Keane shift into action. Grabbing her by the back of her neck, he physically lifted her off me and held her squirming in the air—quite a feat with only one hand if you asked me, which of course no one did. From my position on the floor, I watched as Alejandro and another male—the bartender I assumed—took Mariana. With a few choice words from Keane, they removed her still-screaming form from the room.

"Blue, are you all right?"

Keane was leaning over me, but I couldn't seem to bring him into focus. I giggled. "Are you going to hold up your fingers and ask me to tell you how many there are? Because I don't think you have enough to cover that."

"Shit." Leaning down, he scooped me off the floor and into his arms.

I closed my eyes and held my head, hoping it would stop the world from spinning. "Can we stop this merry-go-round, 'cause I'd like to get off, please."

Keane strode forward, at least I think he did. To me, it seemed as if we were walking in circles. I heard him briefly confer with Alejandro before moving on. Since I couldn't hear or smell the ocean anymore, I assumed we were back in the Dock Street hallways.

"Rutherman, where are you taking me now?"

"Rutherman, is it? So formal."

"Mmm... Is Mariana going to be all right?"

"Still worried about everybody but yourself."

"Keane..."

"She will be fine in time—and with some counseling. We'll have you remove your magical binding after we've sorted her out some. For now, I think it's good for her. Where did you learn to do that, by the way?"

"Iridia."

I felt rather than saw Keane nod. Looking just hurt too much right now.

"Keane, what did she mean when she said I didn't know who you were?"

"Hush now. Just try to relax."

"Are you avoiding the question?"

"Aren't I always? We'll talk about all that later when you're feeling better. I'd hate to have to explain it twice."

I tried to reply, but it seemed my mouth had stopped obeying my commands. I idly wondered if I'd ever get a straight answer out of him.

# Chapter Nineteen

I must have passed out because the next thing I knew, I was lying on a comfortable bed with a very familiar blue comforter wrapped around me. A strong arm lay across my waist while a second was settled on my hip. As they came from two different angles, I had to assume they belonged to two different people. I wasn't sure exactly what had happened since I'd passed out, but by the looks of things, it was something very interesting.

"Get your mind out of the gutter, Madam Blue," a deep voice rumbled alongside me.

"*Madam*, is it? So formal." I turned my head toward Keane, but he still had his eyes closed.

"Stop stealing my lines."

I giggled.

"You know, some people are trying to sleep here." I turned my head the other way to see Tristan lying on my other side. Before I could retort, my stomach rumbled loudly. I clapped my hands over it to keep it quiet, but it wasn't cooperating. It just grumbled louder, causing both men to laugh.

"I guess that's that, then. No one will be able to sleep with that racket." Keane propped himself up on his elbow, and Tristan followed suit. I peered up at both of them.

"Hi." I meekly looked between the two.

"Hi, yourself." Keane smiled. "How are you feeling? Besides hungry." He patted my stomach, which had let out another loud growl.

I thought about it for a moment. "Surprisingly well rested."

He shook his head. "It's actually not surprising, considering you've been asleep for two days."

"Two days!" I was aghast.

Tristan nodded. "We weren't sure if you were going to come out of it."

"How...what...*why* was I asleep for two days?"

"My guess is your body was trying to recover."

Keane nodded. "You really did a number on yourself this time. Between getting beaten up while saving Allison, getting poisoned by a Merman's blade, and using all that energy to stop Mariana, your body just gave up. If it hadn't been for Tristan's healing magic..."

I stared at Tristan. "You healed me?"

He nodded, looking a bit embarrassed. "It was a combined effort between Keane and me."

Keane pushed himself up and off the bed. "Don't sell yourself short, Your Majesty. You just used my connection with her. It was all your magic's doing. Now, what sounds good to eat, Blue?"

I was shocked that Tristan had used his healing magic on me. From what I had learned from Kieran, it was a rare gift. He had told me someone with that talent could bring a person back from even the brink of death, so long as their soul was still attached to their body. The healer essentially had to give a part of themselves to whomever they healed, connecting them, which was why a Fairy with that talent did not use it lightly.

I shook myself from my thoughts. "I ah...what time is it?"

"Just after seven."

"I guess some breakfast food, then."

"At night."

"At night?" I bit my lip. "How about some of that Mexican food I missed out on?"

Keane nodded and turned away. "Your wish is my command. I've been meaning to go and check on Mariana anyway. Do try not to get into any more trouble while I'm gone." He slipped into a pair of jeans. Grabbing his shirt off the couch, he threw it on and went out the door, leaving me alone with Tristan.

The sound of the door shutting echoed through the room, and I was suddenly ill at ease. I hadn't been alone with Tristan since the whole bathroom incident. I glanced uncertainly at him. He stared intently back at me.

I quickly looked away. "I should probably get up and take a shower."

I started to shift out from under the blanket.

"Blue..."

Stilling at his tone, I stopped refusing to meet his eyes.

"Look at me, Blue."

Unable to help myself, I slowly raised my gaze to his. He stared unblinkingly at me, causing the intense energy that always seemed to flare between us when he was around, to skitter across my skin. I sucked in a sharp breath and held it, trying to quell the rising heat slowly making its way through my treacherous body. His arm tightened around my waist as if sensing my inner struggle. I saw that strange green flame flicker to life in the back of his eyes and again wondered at its cause. I wasn't sure why, but I was pretty sure it was something significant.

My voice dipped to a whisper. "I...I really should go."

"Blue, when I healed you, I felt...I saw..." He took a shuddering breath. "I know why you did what you did. I know you were just trying to keep me at a distance so you wouldn't get hurt, and I understand."

"Tristan—"

He held up a hand to stop me. "Hear me out, Blue. It doesn't matter. Any of it. Not the Trials, not Riona or her child, none of it. It doesn't change how I feel or my connection to you. I thought I'd lost you the other day, and it was almost more than I could bear."

I shook my head sadly. "It's not like we can just cancel the Trials, Tristan. Not even you have that power."

He sat up against the bed's headboard. "I know. When you came in the other day half-dead, I told the Elders I wanted to put a stop to them. That something was wrong. But they wouldn't hear of it. They couldn't seem to comprehend what had occurred. Even Kieran. It was like they were brainwashed. They seemed to think you were just merely sent on a simple seek-and-find mission. They swore no real danger was involved and said they were merely testing your ability to think and manipulate your magic. They even refused to believe you were really injured or poisoned. What happened to you...it was insane. No normal person, even a Fae, should have been able to survive, let alone heal from the injuries you received."

He shook his head. "I still don't know how you did it. The blade that stabbed you was tipped in a very unique poison with no known cure, yet here you sit with barely a scar to show for it. It just doesn't make sense, any of it."

Needing space to think, I slipped out from under the covers and paced in front of the bed. Tristan's gaze followed me as I moved back and forth.

"Tristan, there is something I should tell you, but you have to promise not to get mad or overreact."

He was immediately suspicious, his brows drawing together. "Nothing good ever came from a preemptive statement like that."

"True." I took a deep breath and pushed ahead. "I had a meeting with Sethos the other day."

"What?" Tristan sat up straight, practically vibrating with rage. "Are you really that foolish? He killed my wife!"

"No, he didn't." I quickly told Tristan the story that Sethos had relayed to me, leaving out the bit about Cedric being Riona's son. I wasn't sure if I wanted anyone to know about him just yet. "So, you see, Sethos is as much a pawn in this game as you are. Maybe even more so."

"You expect me to believe that?"

"He was telling the truth, Tristan. I know it."

"So, you think this was all a plan concocted by Larkin to get revenge?"

"And as a way to take over the clans. According to Sethos, Larkin wants to rule all the Fae."

"But how is he accomplishing it all? Even with his charm talent, how could he control the Elders from here?"

"I think I have an answer to that." While we were talking, Keane returned with several bags of food. My belly let out another loud rumble as the savory smell hit me. "But first, sit and eat before you starve to death." He pulled out the desk chair and then set about getting all the food out of the bags. Tristan slid out of the bed and joined us, pulling up two other chairs for them to sit on.

"How's Mariana?"

Keane shrugged. "As good as can be expected. Furious with you and vowing vengeance for what you did."

I grimaced. "I dread the day I need to restore her powers."

"Don't worry about it. That's a long way off. Her father and I talked, and we agree that she needs some time to..." Keane coughed lightly. "...*adjust* to the most recent changes in her life. Not being able to act out and hurt someone with her magic will be good for her while she's coming to grips with things." Once again, I wondered just what sort of role Keane played in the Vaimpír world and *who* he was.

Once we were all seated and had started eating, Tristan again broached the subject of Larkin. "How could Larkin be controlling the Elders? It's not like he could have snuck into Moon Tree Hall. Our security is too tight."

"He had inside help, of course." Tristan, his mouth full, made a rolling motion with his hands for Keane to continue. "You said yourself, it seemed like the Elders were brainwashed. While Larkin's talent definitely has some controlling aspects, he was never able to change people's memories like it seems has happened to the Elders. That would require the services of someone with master skills at mind manipulation."

"Such as a Vaimpír."

"Exactly."

"But who?"

"Celeste." Both men turned to stare at me. "She has the ability. Combine her talents with those of her cohort, Jacob, the Scrionsán, well…"

Tristan shook his head doubtfully. "I don't know, even with her talent, these are the Elders."

"They may be the Elders, but they are still just men—albeit, Fae."

"But why?"

"There's the million-dollar question."

We continued to debate the possibilities as we finished our dinner.

"Is there a way to see if the Elders' minds have been altered?"

"Perhaps, but we'll need to do it discreetly. There's no reason to alert whoever is doing this that we're on to them."

After cleaning up our dinner, we went our separate ways. Tristan left to see if he could corner one of the Elders, Keane went to do whatever he did when he wasn't on duty, and I set off to clean up and dress.

Just as I finished my shower, a knock sounded on the bathroom door. After ensuring I had a towel wrapped securely around me, I bade whoever it was to enter. Cullen popped his head around the door.

"Sorry to disturb you, Blue, but you've been summoned to the ballroom immediately."

"Any particular reason?"

He shook his head. "No, but they've summoned all the competitors, so I assume it has something to do with the Trials. Once you're dressed, I'll escort you. Keane said he'd meet us there."

I nodded, a bit anxious at the turn of events. Who knew what my tormentors had up their sleeves this time? Dressing quickly, once again in fighting gear, I made sure I had all my weapons before following Cullen into the elevator. Once in the ballroom, I made my way up to the front by the stage and Sabrianna.

"Hey, girl. Any idea what's going on?"

She turned toward me with a smile and gave me a hug. "No clue, but damn, it's good to see you up and about. I was getting worried."

"Ah, you know me, I always seem to bounce back from these things. Hey, I never got a chance before to thank you for your help getting Allison back."

She shook her head. "No thanks necessary. I didn't do anything."

"Sure you did. You distracted the brothers long enough for me to slip over to where I needed to be. Without your help, I seriously doubt I could have gotten away."

"Mmm, maybe that would have been a good thing? If Keane had come with you…"

I shook my head. "I never would have made it into Poseidon's castle if I hadn't been alone."

She looked at me strangely. "Poseidon's castle?"

"Yeah, that's where they were holding Allison."

"That's not the story the Elders gave."

I shrugged. I really didn't want to burden her with what was really going on. Before she could ask any further questions, the Elders entered the room, wearing their ornate robes. As they took their seats, Tristan moved to the front of the stage. In contrast, he was still wearing his jeans and T-shirt from earlier, and boy, did he make it look good. The thought floated unbidden through my mind. Shaking my head, I returned my concentration to what he was saying.

"Welcome everyone, thank you so much for coming here this evening. Due to unforeseen circumstances, there have been a few changes to the Trials that you should be made aware of. Elder Demirtas…"

"Thank you, Your Majesty." The Elf bowed slightly in Tristan's direction before turning back to the crowd. "As you can see by our leaderboard, we are down to eight competitors from the original twelve. Considering we are only on the second Trial, that is a pretty drastic downsizing. The last Trial was a very difficult one, which led to a few…injuries."

I grimaced while absently rubbing my side. That had to be the understatement of the year.

A slight rumble made its way through the room as people whispered to each other. It quieted down again as the Elder continued. "Due to the difficulties encountered in the last few individual Trials, we have decided to change things up a bit. The rest of the Trials will now be group challenges conducted in full view of the Elders. As an added bonus, they will also be broadcasted here for you all to watch."

Thunderous applause greeted Elder Demirtas's words. He waited patiently on the stage for the crowd to settle down. Once they did, he continued. "As such, the next stage of the Trials will begin tomorrow at eleven o'clock sharp."

As the Elders left the stage, I was disappointed they hadn't revealed just what we would be doing tomorrow. While I was glad the Trials would now be conducted in full view of all the clans and were being presided over by the Elders themselves, I was also nervous that it would allow my would-be tormentor the opportunity to track my movements and cause an accident I wouldn't be able to recover from. Shaking my head, I looked at Sabrianna, who was still in the running.

"What do you think? Good or bad?"

She tilted her head and considered. "A bit of both, I suppose. It all depends on just what they expect us to do."

I nodded in agreement. As I spotted Keane talking quietly to his brother Darrius, it brought something else to mind. "Sabrianna, you said you know Keane and Darrius's parents, right?" I gestured to where the brothers stood.

"Sure, they've been friends of my family's for years, hence how Darrius became my guardian."

"I had a bit of a run-in with two female Vaimpír. They were very upset about my relationship with Keane."

"I'll bet, considering who Keane is."

"Just who *is* he? I thought he was just one of Tristan's royal guardians."

Sabrianna shook her head. "Keane is...for lack of a better term, he's the Dark Prince."

"A Prince? He never mentioned that fact."

She shook her head. "No, he probably wouldn't. I'm sure it's a novelty for him to come across someone who has no idea what his position in society is. You see, in the Vaimpír community, there are seven dominant families."

"The seven houses. Mariana mentioned that."

Sabrianna nodded. "Those not directly related are always trying to marry into them. Of those houses, one is higher than the rest. The family Rutherman. They are the ruling family of their kind."

"So, do the Vaimpír have their own clan like the Moon Tree Clan? And if so, why are Keane and Darrius members of other clans?"

"They don't have a clan, per se, just a ruling family. And none of the Vaimpír are actually sworn to a particular clan. They are just accepted as part of whichever one they stay with. Which is why they are considered guardians. You see, large groups of pure Vaimpír living in one place tend to cause problems. Their natures are aggressive, domineering, and very territorial."

I snorted. "Yeah, I know those traits well."

Sabrianna laughed and nodded. "Because of their nature, most purebloods tend to be loners."

"But Ethereal Mutation..."

"Is the exception. Probably due to Keane."

"Huh. What does that make Keane's role in life?"

"He's the next in line to be King, of course, but he's also considered one of the most powerful Vaimpír of our time. He's said to be even more powerful than his grandfather, one of the Elders, though he doesn't currently serve on the Council. Keane's word holds a lot of sway with all the clans. Whoever marries him will become a powerful woman, indeed."

"Ah, I think I'm beginning to see. So, if Keane were to say be...accidentally soulbound to someone not of the seven families?"

"The Vaimpír in question would pretty much have a target on her back unless he was to marry her."

"Wow, okay. That's not good news and complicates things a bit more."

Sabrianna looked at me, the shocking truth dawning. "You're not saying you are soulbound to Keane, are you?"

"I, well...maybe a little."

"But how? You're not Vaimpír, are you?"

"It's...complicated. Suffice it to say I have the abilities of one, and while testing out my newfound powers, I accidentally bound him to me."

Sabrianna pulled me into a more private corner of the room. "Blue, this is a very dangerous thing. If others were to discover..." She shook her head, not finishing. "Can you reverse it?"

I shrugged. "I don't honestly know much about it, and Keane hasn't had the chance to explain it fully. I do know the Elders blessed the union and encouraged me to keep it. God, that makes it sound like I married the man."

Sabrianna shook her head. "It probably would have been safer for you if you had. Although being stuck in these Trials with the possible outcome of becoming Tristan's Queen, and now being soulbound to Keane..."

I threw up my hands. "I know, I know. Like I said, it's complicated."

She huffed out a breath. "That's an understatement. Who were the women you had a run in with that discovered your connection to Keane?"

I grimaced. "They don't know for sure, but both guessed at it and were pretty upset."

"Who?"

"Mariana Rodriguez, but she doesn't currently have any magic powers to do anything against me—unless she acts without it. And Jasmine. I don't know her last name."

"Keane's ex-fiancée?"

"Yeah."

"Not good."

"I think she's currently locked up somewhere due to her outburst in front of the King and Elders."

"Let's hope so. You don't need to add the trouble it will cause you once word gets out on top of the Trials."

"Tell me about it. Promise me you'll keep my secret? Even from Darrius."

Sabrianna nodded. "You can count on me."

Just about then, Keane and his brother came up to us. "And just what are you two whispering about over here?"

"Just girl stuff."

"Mm-hmm. Come on, Blue, let's get you back to your room. I don't want you overextending yourself before the next Trial tomorrow."

I nodded as Keane took my arm. As we walked away, I saw Darrius watching us with a strange look on his face and wondered if he could discern our connection like the two female vaimpír had. I wasn't sure if it was something they could all sense or just those of the opposite sex. I'd have to remember to ask Keane later.

❦

The next few days passed in a whirlwind of activity. The Elders threw everything they could at us. Trials involving art—painting and drawing. Etiquette—pouring tea and greeting little-known cultures from across the world. Hand-to-hand combat—tournament style. Magic usage—creating, changing, and disappearing. Politics, poetry, history, and just about anything that had to do with anything. As Brody had predicted, it all happened in different places and time periods, taking us to rooms all across Dock Street. I didn't think there was a corner we hadn't visited.

By the end of the week, we were down to just five of the original twelve: Celeste, Tatiana, Sabrianna, Odelina, and me. We were running neck and neck in points, so it was anybody's game. I'd done everything but cheat to get Celeste out, but she seemed to be two steps ahead of me each time.

While I had inched ahead of her in most categories, every time I seemed to get the upper hand, the Elders would change something and throw things in her favor. It was frustrating, to say the least.

Add to that, we had yet to uncover proof that Celeste and her cohorts were manipulating the Elders. Whatever or however they were doing it, was beyond any type of detection or tracing we were capable of. Aside from setting twenty-four-seven surveillance on them, I didn't know what else to do.

After the last Trial, which had involved a lot of dirt and mud, I decided to clean up in Riona's room since Keane wasn't there to take me to his place yet. Stripping down to just my underwear, I went into the bathroom to take a long, hot shower. After making sure the room was empty, I turned the water up as hot as I could stand it and tossed the rest of my clothes to the side. Climbing under the scalding waterfall, I stood with my arms braced against the wall and let the hot water ease my sore and tired muscles.

"If I were an artist, I would paint you just like this."

I swung around at the strange masculine voice. "Who the hell are you?" Planting my hands on my hips, I suddenly realized I wasn't wearing anything. I started to slide out of the shower to grab a towel but stopped when the man revealed he had a gun pointed straight at me.

"I'm no one important, merely a delivery boy."

"Oh? Tell me, what could be so crucial that you would risk your life by breaking in here like this?" I crossed my arms over my chest and pretended nonchalance, when in reality, I was racking my brain, trying to figure out how he had managed to slip past the guards undetected and just how to take him out if it proved necessary.

I tried to throw a mental message out to Keane, but something blocked me.

The man before me smirked. "You won't be able to contact any of your friends. It's just you and me till I say so."

I studied him carefully, trying to figure out what he was and how he could block my mental connection with Keane.

The man casually leaned against the countertop. "You're not really what I expected."

I arched an eyebrow at him. "And what is it you expected?"

He scratched his chin thoughtfully. "Someone hard and unyielding with quick reflexes and a sharp mind. You're too soft and feminine to be any real threat. I mean, look how easily I snuck up on you. It's a wonder you've survived in these Trials as long as you have. I really don't see the threat everyone thinks you pose."

I shrugged. "Things are rarely what they seem."

"Perhaps. Regardless, now I have you at my mercy." He waved his gun in my direction. "You are hardly in a position to do anything."

"So, it would seem." I wasn't about to enlighten him as to my many magical defenses. Just because I didn't have a physical weapon on me didn't mean I was helpless. Sebastian had taught me that. Stupid, stupid man. "Why don't you just go on and deliver whatever it is you came to deliver and be on your way before my friends figure out something is wrong and come looking?" I kept my voice even and bored-sounding.

"Still hoping your friends are going to save you?" I just shrugged. "I could do anything I want to you right now, and they would be none the wiser." He leaned forward and leered at me. I tensed, waiting for him to make a move in my direction. "However, you're hardly worth the trouble it would cause me in the end."

As he straightened from the counter, I vaguely wondered if I should feel insulted or grateful that I wasn't worth the trouble. Hmm.

Walking toward me, he grabbed a robe off one of the hooks on the wall and threw it at me. "Put that on, and let's get on with business."

"So, do you want to start with who sent you? Or is that a secret?"

Walking toward the edge of the room, the man cocked a hip up and sat on the ledge of the giant tub.

"I'm sure you know exactly who sent me."

I sighed. "Something tells me it was Larkin."

The man nodded with a smile. "Smart girl."

"What does the infamous Larkin want?"

"I'm sure you know the answer to that, too."

"While I do have a notion, what I don't understand is what I have to do with it."

"Hmm, that is a good question, but it's not something I'm privy to. Like I said before, I'm just the delivery boy."

"You keep saying that, but you have yet to deliver anything."

He laughed evilly. "Well, now, I didn't say to whom I was delivering what to, now did I?"

I started to get a bad feeling. Slowly backing away while keeping a close eye on him, I tried to come up with the best escape route—one that wouldn't end with me getting shot. Though I couldn't get through telepathically to Keane, I had a feeling this guy wasn't aware of our other connection. I allowed all my anxiety and fear to pulse through the bond. Sure enough, a knock sounded on the door a second later.

"Blue, everything okay in there?" I heard the knob rattle as Keane tried to open it.

The unknown man looked up at the door, surprised, then glared suspiciously at me. "Aren't you just full of surprises? I guess that means I'll have to move things up a bit." Standing, he shifted toward me. I immediately shuffled back out of arm's reach and closer to the door, causing him to chuckle. "You don't really think I'm going to let you escape me, do you?"

Before I could react or say anything, he raised his gun and pulled the trigger. I felt a stinging in my leg and grabbed it, falling to one knee. Looking down, I saw a dart sticking out instead of a bullet hole. Ah, shit. I immediately started to feel woozy, and it took everything in me to stay upright.

Keane and my other guards were trying to break down the door, but the man had put a magical shield in place, not unlike the one I had used in Poseidon's castle. I heard them yelling my name, but I couldn't even answer. My tongue felt like it was swollen in my mouth.

The man came to stand over me. "Just relax, there's no use fighting it. The sedative in that dart is fast-acting and more powerful than any anti-spell you can come up with."

I struggled to stay conscious. He was right. I'd already tried at least three counterspells, and nothing worked. But again, he underestimated me. Reaching out to Keane through our connection, I siphoned off some of his healing powers. I instantly felt my head clear and my muscles start to regain feeling. Remaining on the floor where I was, I waited as the power flowed through my body, pushing the rest of the sedative out.

The man above me furrowed his brows. "Well, hell. You should've been down for the count by now." Just as he raised his weapon to no doubt shoot me again, I made my move. Plowing forward, I grabbed him by his waist and drove him into the floor. He was completely thrown off guard, and as he hit, the gun flew out of his hand, skittering over by the tub. While he was still dazed, I scrambled to my knees and crawled toward it. Just before I could reach it, though, large hands grabbed my ankle and yanked me back. I let out a cry of frustration, stretching my arm farther, my fingertips just brushing the grip.

"You little bitch. You're lucky the master wants you unharmed."

As he regained his knees, I turned onto my back and blasted him with a momentum spell. It propelled him into the vanity, shattering one of the sink bowls. Shaking the glass out of his hair, he growled and came toward me again, barely seeming affected by my spell.

Working the magic again quickly, I threw a freeze spell at him. He batted it to the side with a spell of his own, lights sparking where our magic collided. I scrambled backward around to the other side of the tub, grabbing the tranquilizer pistol from the floor as I went. I leaned against the edge of the basin and pointed it at him.

He laughed. "You're more than welcome to shoot me with that, sweetheart. I happen to have immunity to the drug."

I shot him anyway. His shoulder jerked back as the dart sank into his arm, but he kept coming at me. I emptied the rest of the darts into him, five in all. He still kept moving forward. Guess he had been telling the truth, but at least he couldn't shoot me with them now. I tossed the gun over the side of the waterfall. I threw two more defensive spells at him, hoping to knock him out of the way so I could make a break for the door, but he easily knocked each one aside.

"You're going to have to do better than that, poppet." Twisting his hands in a peculiar motion, he threw a spell my way. I put up a shield to block it just in time, stopping the magic before it connected. Instead of just disintegrating like most spells, it kept pushing me back, putting me precariously close to the edge of the cliff.

I used my magic shield and backed it with a fire flash spell, sending both his spell and my flaming shield at him. He cursed and dove to the side just before it hit him. I darted around the tub, making for Tristan's door. Before I could grab the handle, I spotted a spark of green out of the corner of my eye. Shifting my weight, I quickly spun away while throwing up a protection bubble. I heard a loud grating sound and a harsh snap. Turning back toward the door, I gaped. It now sported a metal cage over it with a large lock. Grumbling in frustration I turned back toward my antagonist.

Narrowing my eyes, I concentrated on him and used the air in the room to batter him, pushing him closer and closer to the edge of the waterfall. He tried to counter me but he clearly wasn't versed in air magic. Using that knowledge, I pressed my advantage. While I didn't want to kill him, I *did* want him incapacitated. I decided to use the air in his body to shut him down like I had seen Celeste do to Sabrianna the first night of the Trials.

The man fell over, gripping the edge of the tub for support. I pushed a bit more air at him, trying to get him to pass out. I was concentrating so hard on the amount of air I was using that I didn't notice him sinking his hand into the tub. Suddenly, a torrent of water came barreling at me. I lost my concentration as it smashed into me and pushed me back, pinning me against the wall. I struggled against the weight of it, trying to keep it from drowning me. When the first rush finally settled, the water moved until it covered me, keeping me where I was. Every time I tried to move, it just added more pressure to keep me still.

The man gasped for air, trying to catch his breath. "What...the...hell...are you? You can manipulate magic like a Warlock, communicate telepathically like a Vaimpír even through a magical block, and use air magic like an elemental Fairy."

I let a smirk slip onto my face. "And that's not all I can do." Summoning my Nereid powers, I used them to peel the water off me and push it back at him. His eyes widened in shock before he went over the cliff, screaming into the open air where he dropped like a stone into the endless water below.

I had no idea where the drop ended, but at this point, I didn't care. I fell to my knees, panting. Just about then, the door crashed open, the magic holding it releasing with the man's sudden disappearance.

Keane ran over to me while the others searched the room. "Are you all right, Blue? What happened?"

I opened my mind so he could see what had gone down. It was much easier than explaining it all.

"Fiorian." Keane ground out his name, and I raised an eyebrow. "He's Sethos'…I guess *Larkin's* bounty hunter."

"I'm guessing I was the bounty this time." I slowly got to my feet.

"How the hell did he get in here undetected? Not to mention how was he planning on getting back out with an unconscious woman?"

Shuffling over to the edge, I shook my head. "I was wondering the same thing." I looked at the foaming water below. "Where does this go?"

Keane joined me. "Through drainage pipes and out to the ocean."

"Judging by his command of water, my guess would be that is the way he got in and planned to get out."

Keane nodded his agreement. "I'll have some of the Water Sprites loyal to the Moon Tree Clan check it out. We don't need another attack like that happening in the future." He turned away to confer with Mckile and Ronan, who were standing by. He instructed them on what needed to be done. Keane may not be a royal guardian any longer, but Ethereal Mutation were more than loyal to him and would do his bidding without question.

While he was talking, he reached over and grabbed one of the towels hanging nearby, throwing it at me. I figured that was a hint to get dried off and dressed. Chuckling, I took a step toward Riona's room. As I did, something snagged on my robe. Before I could turn to untangle it from whatever it was stuck on, I found myself catapulted over the edge of the cliff. I screamed as I found myself in the open air, hovering over the water far, far below me. Though I expected to plummet at any second, I somehow hung suspended in midair. I couldn't see behind me or even move my head to look. I was paralyzed and stuck in some sort of bubble.

"Put her down, Fiorian, and you just might live to see another day."

"Rutherman. How nice. I'd heard you were assigned to the chit here. I have to say, I'm sorely disappointed. Word of your prowess and abilities has spread far and wide, yet here I am, with the upper hand." He tsked.

"Know this, Fiorian, if even one hair on her head is damaged, I will bring the wrath of the seven houses down on you."

"So much drama for a single woman. Better be careful, or I'll begin to suspect she means more to you than being a mere charge."

With that statement, he jumped from where he hung on the cliffside and grabbed me by the waist. We fell toward the water. I heard Keane's roar of rage from above and felt his anger and desperation through our connection. I didn't have long to dwell on the feelings, though, as the water below quickly approached. I covered my face and took a deep breath just as we hit the surface. It was like hitting a brick wall. The impact knocked the breath from my body, and I just barely hung on to consciousness. Just as I was about to use my magic to turn myself into a Nereid, I felt a bubble slide over us. The water receded, and we were left sitting in a pocket of air.

"Damn. Larkin is going to pay three times as much for this one. Who knew one little woman could be so much trouble?" He paused and looked down at me, then laughed softly, his body relaxing. "Although, I have to admit, you've got gumption, poppet. It reminds me of someone in my past."

He used his magic to push the bubble forward like some kind of weird boat. My last thought before I passed out was: *I don't know where he's taking me, but I know wherever it is won't be good.*

# Chapter Twenty

I wasn't sure how long I was out, but when I came to, I was still lying at the bottom of Fiorian's bubble with my hands and feet bound by some type of magical rope. I pushed my senses out to see if I could break the bonds but found they were somehow magicproof. Deciding it was in my best interest to remain still, I silently tracked our progress across the water, catching glimpses of the shoreline here and there, though it was impossible to tell exactly where we were.

Before long, he turned the bubble, and we headed up a small tributary. After about half an hour, he finally slowed when we came to a marsh. Unlike most stereotypical visions of a swamp, this one was beautiful. Trees grew out of the water, standing hundreds of feet tall with Spanish moss hanging from their branches like the most delicate lace. The water was clear and free of the pond scum you would expect to find, and wildlife moved everywhere you looked. The light from above shone through the canopy of trees, creating tiny rainbows and shafts of gleaming light beams that dragonflies and birds alike played in.

Fiorian steered the bubble around some small islands and trees, taking us deeper and deeper into the swamp. Finally, we came to a stop in front of the largest tree I had ever seen. Its base was easily a hundred feet across. Peering through my slitted eyes, I couldn't make out how far it stretched up without moving my head, but I had to imagine it was up there. Pulling up as close to the tree as he could, Fiorian reached out with his hand. Carefully placing it on the tree's rough bark without penetrating the bubble, he closed his eyes. I saw his lips move as he recited whatever spell he needed to unlock the entrance to wherever we were going.

When he was done, a large opening appeared, and he steered us into its dark depths. I tried once more to contact Keane telepathically, but Fiorian was still using his magic to block me. As soon as we were through the opening, it closed behind us. The knot that had been growing in my stomach tightened. I didn't know how I would get out of this alive, but I knew I would do everything I could to survive.

We pulled up to a dock built along one wall of the great tree. Leaning down, Fiorian scooped me up and threw me over his shoulder like I didn't weigh a thing. Leaping from the bubble, which popped as he moved through it, he easily landed on the wooden boards and started marching forward. From where I hung, I saw paths leading this way and that within the tree's structure. He moved purposefully from one path to the next, throwing out greetings to people as we passed. Though I received a few curious glances, no one questioned why Fiorian was walking around with a strange unconscious woman slung over his shoulder.

After he had climbed a few sets of stairs, he stepped into an out-of-the-way elevator. Punching in the code to get it to move, he casually leaned against the wall.

"You, my little girlie, are going to fetch me a handsome price. Maybe even enough that I can take a few years off. I could use a nice little vacation." He patted me on the backside and chuckled. It took everything in me to remain still when all I wanted to do was swing up and punch him in the face. Thankfully, the elevator came to a halt just about then, stopping me from giving myself away.

As the doors slid open, Fiorian stepped out into what appeared to be an old-fashioned throne room of a medieval castle. The walls were old gray block stone with banners depicting all types of ocean-based mythology hanging on them. I rolled my eyes. Leave it to Larkin to be so cliché. Fiorian strode up the center of the room, unceremoniously dumping me onto a rug on the floor in front of him. I silently grunted as my shoulder dug into the stones beneath.

The first chance I got, I was so kicking this guy's ass.

"My lord." He bowed to the figure I had glimpsed sitting on the throne. My head wasn't turned that way, so I couldn't see exactly who he was talking to. "I bring you the prize you covet."

"You have done well, Fiorian. And much faster than I expected."

Fiorian smirked. "She was no challenge."

"Mmm, somehow, I don't believe you in that regard. If the bruises on you are any indication, she put up quite a fight."

Fiorian's mouth tilted down at the corners. "You didn't warn me about her magic."

"Magic?"

"She can command several different forms—not only two elements, but also that of a Warlock and Vaimpír."

"Indeed. It would seem our little prize has a few secrets. Would you care to explain yourself, Miss Carolina?"

Fiorian smirked and nudged me with the toe of his boot. "She can't answer you. She's out cold."

"Hardly. My guess is she has been awake for quite some time but was just pretending to be out cold so she could track where you were taking her." I heard the grimace in Larkin's voice.

Fiorian shook his head. "That's not possible. I would have felt her awaken."

"Clearly, you have underestimated her. Please remove her bonds. This is no way to treat our guest." Fiorian grumbled but did as he was told. "Now, Miss Carolina, if you would please get up off the floor. It is a most undignified position for someone of your station."

I sighed and slowly levered myself up, stretching out the kinks as I went. Once standing, I first looked at Fiorian, who stared in astonishment. "You really shouldn't underestimate me. I told you before that things are rarely as they seem." Then, ignoring him, I turned to Larkin.

Bowing to him, even though he wasn't really the King, I kept my eyes on him. "Really, if you wanted to meet me, all you had to do was ask, my lord. All this cloak and dagger nonsense really wasn't necessary."

"Talented *and* a sense of humor. This should be a delightful evening." Larkin stood and offered me his arm. "Welcome to the Misty River Clan. Shall I give you the grand tour?"

I decided to play the docile prisoner for now. Better to get the lay of the land before trying anything. "That sounds delightful."

Fiorian sputtered behind me as I took Larkin's proffered arm. "Bu...but...what about my fee?"

Larkin turned his head. "Oh, you will get your fee, Fiorian, don't you worry. And don't even think about asking for more than the offered price. I was quite concise in my notice of what it would be—no more, no less."

With a last glare in my direction, Fiorian bowed to Larkin and then stomped out of the hall the way he had come. I was sure there would be further words about his *fee* later.

Larkin looked down at me. "I do apologize for the way he treated you. I did request that whoever collected the bounty be very careful with your person. I will make sure he is reminded of just how a woman should be treated."

Larkin's voice was smooth as silk, and I could tell he was trying to use his charm talent on me. Though it wasn't working, I figured it best to pretend to be enslaved. For now. "Oh, don't worry about it. It's already forgotten. I have to say, I'm very flattered that you went to such lengths to bring me here. I never would have thought to merit such attention. After all, I'm only a mere Fairy and one not that familiar with the Fae world at that."

Larkin smirked, thinking he had charmed me as he had all his other followers. "My dear, you do yourself a disservice. You are far too valuable a player here not to be the center of attention. I have heard a great many things about you. Mostly rumors, I am sure, but one has to wonder what truth may lie within them."

I smiled secretively and allowed him to guide me out of the room via a passage hidden behind his throne. As we emerged through the curtains, I saw we were in a small antechamber tastefully decorated in greens and golds. There were mirrors all around the room, giving the illusion that it was bigger than it really was. Noticing movement in one of the mirrors, I turned my head and saw a woman sitting on a small divan in the corner.

She was gorgeous. The lighting around her glinted off her hair, making it look like spun gold, and her eyes sparkled like two large, blue jewels. Her skin was pale but had the perfect blush of youth to it. She had no doubt carefully chosen where she sat to show herself off to her best advantage.

"Ah, Astra. I was wondering where you had wandered off to. Please allow me to introduce our guest, Miss Carolina."

Astra rose slowly from her seat and approached as though gliding on air. "It's a pleasure to make your acquaintance, Carolina." She held out a perfectly manicured hand. I took it, figuring it would be rude not to. Her glamour wavered in my mind's eye as soon as our hands touched, and I saw her for what she truly was. While still attractive, she was hardly the bombshell she portrayed to the world. I smirked a bit and dropped her hand, causing her to look at me suspiciously.

"Astra is my confidante and advisor, among other things." I had no doubt as to what the *other things* entailed. "Astra, could you please have a room made up for our guest? The one right next to mine should do."

"But the room next to you is reserved for your special dignitaries. Don't you think one of the other many rooms would better suit?"

Larkin gave her a stern look. "My guest deserves the best we have to offer. Do as you are told." With a last glare at me, Astra glided off angrily. I seemed to have that effect on a lot of people lately. "I do apologize for her behavior. She can be quite stubborn at times." He gave an indulgent smile. "Now, allow me to show you around our humble home."

Their home was much like Dock Street in that it was much larger than it appeared. While the hollow of the tree housed a great many areas, most of their territory was accessed through magicked doors. I was surprised that Larkin showed me so much. He obviously thought his powers were that great and figured there was no chance I would be immune to them. I tripled the shield around my thoughts. I'd have to be very careful about leaving my mind unguarded.

After our tour, Larkin showed me to an opulent bedchamber.

"Why don't you take some time to refresh yourself? I took the liberty of having a bath drawn for you, and in the closet, you will find several sets of clothes. I am sure you will be able to find something to your liking. I do hope you will join me for a small meal when you are ready. Just ring the bell, and one of my servants will escort you to the dining hall." Larkin indicated a corded red rope near the door and exited the room with a bow.

As soon as he left, I heard the door being locked from the outside. I laughed quietly to myself and shook my head. So much for being a *guest*.

Looking around the room, I saw it was like most of the bedchambers I had come to associate with the royal families. A large bed with fancy draperies, a couple of bedside tables and dressers, a separate dressing area, plus what looked like a walk-in closet and an attached bathroom. There were two large windows, one on either side of the bed, showing the swamp outside. Walking over, I touched my hand to the warm glass. Just as I had suspected, it was just magicked glass frames made to look like windows to the outside. I wondered if they showed the actual movement of time like the ones at Dock Street did. If that was the case, then it appeared I had been gone for most of the day already.

I tried to speculate what Keane and the others were doing back at Dock Street. Would they know where Fiorian had taken me? I shook my head. Of course, they knew where he had taken me. He was, after all, Larkin's bounty hunter. But there was no way they would be able to gain access to this place, at least not without causing another war.

Concentrating, I tried to tap into Keane's emotions like I had been able to do even through the block Fiorian had put up, but I couldn't feel anything. Whatever magic surrounded this place was some heavy-duty stuff—either that or the distance was too great. I had a feeling I was on my own for this daring escape.

Keeping my movements casual, I made my way around the rest of the large room, touching things and appearing interested in all the textiles surrounding me. While it would appear innocent to anyone watching, I was using my magic to check for any bugs or magical traces that would indicate a surveillance system. I found several listening devices around the nightstands, two microscopic cameras by the would-be windows, and one by the door. They appeared older, yet still high-tech.

Leaving them be, I made my way to the closet to see what Larkin had provided for me to wear. Being caught in just a bathrobe was definitely a disadvantage I didn't want to have again. To my surprise, there was actually a rather expansive collection of clothes, though to my disappointment, nothing resembled my fighting gear. I decided on a pair of well-fitting black crop pants with multiple convenient cargo pockets down the sides, a black tank top, and a flowing sheer turquoise blouse. I figured flexing a few feminine wiles wasn't out of the question if needed, not to mention it would help to hide the bulk in my pockets if I could find some weapons.

The next chance I got, I was definitely making sure Sebastian taught me how he hid my clothes and weapons and brought them back on command. Taking my outfit into the attached bathroom, I found a bath had indeed already been drawn and was filled with steaming bubbles. Giving it a light sniff, I detected lavender and sandalwood. Nice choices.

Laying my new clothes on the sink, I slipped off my robe and slid into the waiting warm water. Though I didn't want to let my defenses down for too long, I took the opportunity to let the warmth of the bath leach into my sore and overused muscles. Fiorian had interrupted my previous shower, and though I had been doused in more water than I cared to think about during our fight, I still felt dirty and tired. Closing my eyes, I luxuriated in the quiet calm the bathroom provided. Knowing I needed to get moving so I could find out all I could about my captor and his intentions, I sighed, opened my eyes, and reached for the soap.

After finishing and getting dressed, I wandered back into the closet to find some proper footwear. With little choice, I grabbed a pair of turquoise flats. While not ideal, they would provide me with some light, no-slip tread. To my delight, I also found some jewelry that had probably been left by the last occupant. A long, thick silver chain that hung almost to my belly button with an attached shorter chain that rested just between Pinky & the Brain. Appealing, yes, but in my mind, it could also double as a makeshift weapon. Finding nothing else of use, I made sure everything was back in its place and pulled the corded red rope by the door.

⁓ℓℓ⁓

I sighed inwardly while mentally rolling my eyes for what had to be the hundredth time. I had been listening to Larkin go on and on about himself and all the wondrous things he had done in his life for the last hour. I wasn't sure how much more I could take. Meanwhile, across the table from me, Astra glared daggers, not even trying to hide it. I wanted to stick my tongue out at her but resisted the urge.

Fiorian watched me with a thoughtful scowl from a little farther down the table. I wasn't sure what to make of it but I sure as hell didn't want to look too closely. He was probably trying to figure out how best to kill me after his punishment from Larkin. Bad enough that I couldn't roll my eyes for real. I was even being denied the fun of poking at the pair of them. Apparently, that pleasure would have to wait for another time.

We were currently seated in Larkin's dining hall at the head of an enormously long table. It was so long I was pretty sure the person at the end wouldn't be able to hear me even if I yelled. I hadn't been introduced to anyone else in the room, so I figured they all must be a part of Larkin's court, as it were, which meant they knew exactly who I was. We had long since finished dinner, a relatively simple fare, and were now conversing. I had yet to learn anything other than the fact that Larkin was a pompous ass who clearly thought highly of himself. He had not revealed his reasoning for why he had kidnapped me and brought me to the Misty River Clan, nor had he said what he planned to do with me moving forward.

As Larkin launched into yet another story, no doubt about how he had saved some other clan from plague or sacrificed himself for some poor child, I decided I'd had enough and determined I needed to churn the water, so to speak. Slowly leaning forward, I lightly traced my fingers over the hand he had placed on the table closest to me. The entire gathering of occupants seemed to lean forward and hold its collective breath as Larkin turned to look at me. I smiled seductively and slid my fingers under his in a flirtatious manner. Out of the corner of my eye, I saw Astra's face turning red with anger as she watched me, and a smile quirked the corners of my mouth before I could stop it. Turning my full attention back to Larkin, I lifted his hand and brought it to my mouth for a kiss. Larkin's expression turned to one of supreme smugness, and he placed his hand on my cheek.

Ugh, this was so gross. I swore if the man leaned down to kiss me, I was going to blow my cover. Thankfully, he leaned back in his chair again, placing his hands in his lap.

"Tell me, Carolina, have you discovered your origins yet?"

His question caught me off guard since he had done nothing but talk about himself all evening. "Uh, sorry? What do you mean?"

"Your parents. Have you been able to discover who they are?"

Sethos knew who my mother was, so I was pretty sure Larkin had been able to track down the same information. "Oh. We believe Iridia Grayson was my mother, but we have no idea who my father was." Thinking fast and wanting him to believe I was imparting all my knowledge and not holding back, I remembered what Keane had told the Elder Council. "Though we do have reason to believe he was some sort of Vaimpír."

"Now, why would you think that?"

"Oh. Well, because I have some of the powers of the Vaimpír."

Larkin nodded, looking thoughtful. "From what Fiorian said, you have quite a few powers to behold."

I lowered my head modestly. "I don't really know what I am capable of, to tell you the truth. Like my mother before me, I do have the ability to command several elements."

A slow smile slid across Larkin's face. "Interesting. Very interesting, indeed." Sliding his chair back, Larkin stood and reached out a hand to me. "Why don't we take a private little walk together? What we have to discuss doesn't need to be heard by all the ears here."

Nervous but glad to finally be getting somewhere, I took his outstretched hand, and we moved toward the balcony exit. Astra jumped to her feet behind us, her voice bordering on shrill. "My lord, don't you think you ought to take some guards with you? Or at least Fiorian?"

Larkin turned back toward Astra. "Now, Astra dear, whatever do you think I need protecting from? Surely not little Carolina here." He looked down at me with an appraising stare before turning his attention back to Astra.

"Of course, not. But a surprise attack would not be unheard of. Especially with you...distracted as you are. You know you must be protected at all times, my love. If anything were to happen to you, I don't know what I would do." Astra had moved to Larkin's other side and was staring at him beseechingly, her hands clasped together in front of her, though she managed to throw a few glares in my direction when Larkin turned back toward the table we had just left.

"Very well, my dear. You are right, of course. Fiorian, my good fellow, why don't you join us on our walk? As you have experienced Carolina's powers firsthand, you might be a good reference."

Fiorian came up behind us, and Larkin turned to Astra. "There, dear, does that allay your fears some?"

She lowered her head and nodded. "Yes, Larkin. Thank you. Do you...do you wish for me to join you, as well?"

Larkin smiled tolerantly. "No, not this time. I will see you later this evening, of course." He lifted her hands to his lips and stared deeply into her eyes. I could practically see the waves of his magic washing over her as she sighed and dipped into a low curtsy.

Releasing her hands, Larkin once again turned to me and, with a smile, gestured for me to precede him out of the balcony doors. Expecting to go through a magical door, I was surprised when the exit led us to the swamp instead. Moving side by side, with Fiorian keeping a few steps behind, we walked out over the bridge that had been built between three large balconies. When we reached the center, we stopped and leaned on the railing overlooking the water, standing shoulder to shoulder. The swamp was a beautiful sight with the moon gleaming on the sparkling surface below. Little islands of plants and trees floated calmly in and out of the light beams, adding an almost surrealness to the picture.

"It really is beautiful here. And peaceful." I was surprised. I actually meant it.

Larkin smiled. "I'm glad you like it."

"Why have you brought me here, Larkin?" I kept my gaze turned toward the swamp so he believed my question was just one of mere curiosity.

He laughed softly. "Would you believe I want to help you?"

I turned slightly toward him. "Why would you want to do that? What do you want to help me with?"

"I want to help you discover who you are, Carolina. What you can do. I can feel this power in you. It's brimming just below the surface, waiting to break free. I want to help you realize your true potential."

"But why? What good can all this supposed power do?"

"I don't want you to end up like me, Carolina. I don't want you to have to fight and claw your way toward everything you want. To be told you're nothing and can never *be* anything, when in reality, you should have everything you ever wanted at your fingertips. And…I need your help."

I turned fully toward him. Now, we were getting somewhere. "What could I possibly help you with? I'm no different than anyone else, other than having a few extra powers."

Larkin turned his back on the swamp and leaned against the railing. Crossing his arms over his chest, he stared up at the night sky. "I don't believe that, Carolina. I don't believe you are no different than anyone else. The world of the Fae has changed in recent years, and not for the better. Corruption and a blatant disregard for the old ways has become the norm. The intermixing of species within our clans has gotten out of hand, and the very blood of our races is being diminished, tainted.

What I need your help with is something no one else can do. It is something that has been predicted over and over again by shamans, psychics, and wisemen. No, my dear Carolina, what you were created for, what you were born for, was to save the Fae species."

I couldn't help it, my mouth dropped open. Even knowing the story Sethos had told me about Brody's prediction and hearing Tristan tell me something similar hadn't prepared me for what Larkin said. I expected a declaration of war, a desire to destroy the other kingdoms, the Elders. I didn't expect Larkin to want to save the Fae species.

Then, as I thought about it more, even without his Fae talent of charm, I knew he was a far more dangerous man than I had ever thought possible. With one sentence, he almost had me believing him—believing that he, the man who had slaughtered the only woman he had ever loved in a bid to win the kingdoms, wanted a better world.

But then I began to read between the lines of his words, looking more at his tone, his emotions. He didn't want to save the Fae species out of some sense of betterment. No, he wanted to *save* the Fae species by conquering them. By using my powers to kill all who opposed him and bring the rest to grovel at his feet. That was what he *really* meant by *saving* the Fae. I quickly turned away from him lest he read something in the emotions I was sure showed on my face.

Gripping the railing hard, I bowed my head. Let him think I was in disbelief over his wholesome goodwill. Let him think I likened him to a god for wanting to save the Fae—because that is what he was thinking. Though I couldn't read his mind, I saw it in the uptilt of his smile, and the way he leaned toward me as if to hug me close. I quickly allowed a small tear to slip past my lids, then another, slightly turning my head away from him as if in shame of my awe. He reached over and wiped one of the tears away, staring at it for a moment as it lay suspended on his thumb.

"I'll leave you to your thoughts for now. We will discuss things further in the morning." He started to walk away with Fiorian at his side but paused after a few steps. "And, Carolina..." I turned my head slightly in his direction. "Don't believe everything you have been told up to this point. As you like to say, not all is as it seems." He smiled at me again, just a small upturn at the corner of his mouth, before walking away and leaving me alone on the bridge.

I stood there for a long time. I considered trying to escape but quickly realized that while I seemed to be alone, I was far from it. Best not to blow my cover just yet. Let Larkin continue believing I was deep under his spell.

I put my hand in my pocket and turned to go, but felt something in there. Confused, I slowly pulled whatever it was out. When I opened my hand, I was shocked to see a small stamped gold coin with strange writing on it. How on earth had that gotten in this pocket? I was sure it was still secured in my fighting gear back at Dock Street. I'd had nothing on in the shower when Fiorian attacked me, and only a bathrobe when I got here. Flipping the coin over in my palm, I watched as the light struck it and seemed to make it glow. Slowly closing my fist around it, I considered. Sethos had said to use it if I ever needed his help. Could it be that he knew I needed him now? Would it work if I threw it into the water here? This was, after all, Sethos' home. I deliberated a moment more before leaning back on the railing. Using my senses, I searched around me to see how many were watching and gauge how powerful they were. Not sensing anyone that would be a threat, I turned and faced the water.

I held the coin tightly in my hand for a second before tossing it over the railing. I stayed there for a few more minutes so my actions didn't seem suspect, then made my way back to my room. As the lock clicked on my door, I hoped whatever magic Sethos had imbued that coin with could make it through whatever seemed to block the magic here.

# Chapter Twenty-One

As the following day wore on, one hour seemed to bleed into the next. I spent my time either on my own exploring the tree, under close watch of Larkin's guards, or with Larkin and one of his Warlocks, being tested and questioned about my abilities. I kept most of my powers to myself, only allowing them to see what I had inadvertently shown to Fiorian. Yet I kept even those talents low-level, so they had no idea how powerful I really was. Larkin seemed especially aggravated with my seeming lack of progress.

"There has to be something we can do to awaken her dormant powers. I can feel them sitting there untapped." He ran a frustrated hand through his hair.

"Well, my lord, perhaps if we put her into…"—he glanced at me—"compromising situations, it would cause them to awaken."

Larkin looked intrigued while my stomach dropped with dread. "What type of situations do you propose?"

The Warlock glanced at me again. "Perhaps we should discuss this in private. If she knows what is coming, it might not have the same effect."

Larkin looked back at me as if he'd forgotten I was sitting there. "Of course." He approached me and took one of my hands. "Carolina, my dear, why don't you go rest? It has been a long day, and we have been pushing you pretty hard." He smiled cajolingly while pouring out some of his charm talent so I would acquiesce.

I nodded, afraid I would give myself away if I spoke. Getting up off the examining table I had been sitting on, I quietly left the room, shutting the door behind me. I walked about twenty steps away before tiptoeing back. Looking around to make sure I was still alone, I put my ear to the door.

"What do you have in mind, Tolem? The potion we slipped into her food last night hasn't seemed to do anything."

I was taken aback. I hadn't realized they had given me anything. No wonder I hadn't been feeling myself. I'd felt heavy and sluggish, and my brain hadn't seemed to be able to keep up with me. I'd just attributed it to the stress I was under, and the fact that I hadn't slept much before or since arriving. I would need to be very careful what I ate moving forward. I wondered if there was any prepackaged food in the kitchen that I could get my hands on. I refocused on the conversation on the other side of the door.

"I still can't figure out why it hasn't affected her. Whatever was done to her in her youth to cloak her from the world of the Fae must have been strong, indeed."

Larkin snorted. "Considering who her family is, I suppose it should not be surprising she is so resistant. What is this more aggressive approach you have in mind?"

"I believe putting her in danger may be the answer we are looking for. I noticed a very slight increase in her abilities when she felt uncomfortable."

A sound down the corridor had me standing up straight and turning away from the door. A familiar voice floated down the hall to me as I took a few steps away.

"Blue? Is that you? What on earth are you doing here *ma chérie*?"

I turned to find Brody Shimmin walking toward me and smiled. "Brody? Oh my god, you have no idea how grateful I am to see a familiar face."

Brody's brow crinkled in concern. "Blue, what is going on? Are you okay?"

I glanced at the door before quickly taking his arm and steering him down the hall toward the outdoor balconies.

"Oh, I'm okay. Just learning more about the Fae world. Larkin has...umm...invited me to stay here as his, uh, guest."

He looked at me strangely. "As his guest? Blue, not to pry, but aren't you in the middle of the Trials at the Moon Tree Clan? Did King Tristan approve this?"

I looked long and hard at Brody. I wasn't sure if I could trust him. What if this was just some test of Larkin's? Brody's face only showed confusion and concern, causing me to sigh. It wasn't like everyone here at court didn't already know. "Honestly? Larkin had me kidnapped and brought here."

"What? Is he out of his mind? What reason could he possibly have for kidnapping you? Doesn't he know this could be considered an act of treason?"

"I hardly think I would merit such attention from the clans."

"Blue, you are a participant in the current Trials for the crown of the Moon Tree Clan. While contestants are allowed to do pretty much anything, there is to be no interference from the outside."

I almost laughed, thinking of some of my most recent troubles. If only he knew. I shook my head and, with a look around, lowered my voice. "Brody, I think this has to do with your prediction."

He looked taken aback. "What prediction?"

"The one you gave to Tristan about the woman you painted in the locket for him."

Brody's look turned thoughtful. "So, Larkin believes you are this all-powerful Fae?" I nodded. "And why would he care? Unless he's the reason for...?" He trailed off, his eyes going wide.

"Yes, he's the reason Riona's dead, for all the dissent between the clans and for the Trials. I don't know exactly what he's planning, but I know it isn't good. He wants to use me somehow. I can't let that happen, Brody. Will you help me?"

He stared at me for a long moment before shaking his head slightly. "I don't know what I can do. I can't just take you out of here without him knowing. We would be stopped long before we got anywhere, and if we were both captured, then where would we be? I don't have anyone here I would trust with this information." He turned away from me and walked to the balcony's edge, seemingly deep in thought.

Suddenly, he straightened. "Wait, there is someone. Someone who just so happens to be at Moon Tree Hall, even as we speak. Lucian."

"Are you sure we can trust him?"

He turned back to me, taking my hands. "We have to, Blue. It is our only option at this point. I will get in contact with him. Meanwhile, I will start making my way to see King Tristan myself. I can leave today. This act cannot go unpunished. Will you be okay here by yourself?"

I smiled sadly. "Do I really have a choice?"

He drew me into a tight hug. "I will be as quick as I can. Stay safe, Blue." I nodded as he walked briskly away, his steps determined.

With a sigh, I turned and made my way back to my chambers. I really hoped my trust in Brody wasn't misplaced and he would be able to alert the cavalry. I had a terrible feeling about what Larkin had planned to bring out my powers. I needed to get out of here sooner rather than later.

∼ele∼

The following morning, I found myself alone in the breakfast room with Astra. She seemed to have gotten over some of her jealousy and was sitting quietly across from me, eating. It was a bit unnerving.

"Good morning, Astra."

She nodded in my direction as she continued to eat. "Carolina." A servant placed a plate loaded with eggs, bacon, pancakes, and hash browns on the table in front of me as I sat. I stared at it suspiciously. "Eat up. We have a big day ahead of us."

"Oh?"

"Larkin has requested I take you under my wing and teach you everything there is to know about running a clan—from a Queen's perspective, that is. I know you have had experience working with King Tristan, but you must know that a Queen's work is much, much different."

I was a bit taken aback by her sudden turnabout. "Uh-huh. To tell you the truth, Astra, I never took any lessons from Tristan. Why would I need to know how to run a clan?"

"Aren't you a participant in the current Trials happening at the Moon Tree Clan? Isn't the outcome of that to become Queen."

"Well, yes, but I don't intend to win."

Astra's head snapped up, and she stared at me disbelievingly. "Why ever would you enter a dangerous competition like that and not try to win? Was it just some narcissistic thing, wanting to show off your skills and prove yourself?"

I laughed. "Good heavens, no. Someone else entered me."

"Someone else? How can that even happen?"

I shrugged my shoulders. "I have no idea, but there you have it. Someone with a grudge against me took some of my blood, a rather lot of it if I recall correctly,"—I rubbed my jaw absently, remembering the sting of Celeste's backslap—"and contracted me with the blood stone."

Astra shook her head in astonishment. "I didn't even know such a thing was possible."

"You and me both."

I could see my words had given Astra something to mull over. She withdrew into her corner of the room and seemed to be contemplating something. I pushed the food around on my plate, afraid to eat it.

"Be that as it may, I will still teach you *everything* I know." I looked up at the change in her tone of voice. The way she looked at me was different than previously, too.

Slowly lowering my fork, I tilted my head. "Astra?"

She waved a hand in front of her face and shook her head. "We'll get started as soon as you are finished. There are a few things I need to prepare before we begin."

Without another word, she got up from her chair and practically ran from the room. I watched her as she went. I couldn't be sure, but I would almost say Astra had come back to herself for a moment there. She had looked at me with eyes clear of Larkin's influence. Interesting.

Hours later found us in the Queen's personal salon. She had been going over the best way to handle a dispute among the staff when the smallest Water Sprite I had ever seen popped up in the fountain flowing in the corner. She was no bigger than the palm of my hand. A dark shade of blue, she was completely naked and had large, luminous black eyes.

"Your Majesty."

Astra's head snapped up sharply at the sound of the tiny, high voice. "Sorcha. Finally. I was hoping someone would come."

The little Water Sprite nodded. "She sent a message to Sethos via the Drachma." She pointed to me, but I just shook my head.

My heart started pounding. I slowly rose to my feet, ready to fight Astra and subdue her so I could escape before she could raise an alarm. She waved me back to my seat. "Relax, I am trying to help you."

I stayed standing, still alert. "How do I know that for sure? How do I know you are not just trying to trick me?"

"Blue, I don't know how it happened, but something you did snapped me out of Larkin's control. One minute, I was in a haze, hardly knowing what was going on. The next, everything was clear. What Larkin has done, what he is still doing: the Trials, Sethos, my children, everything." Tears filled her eyes, and her tone was like earlier in the breakfast room. "You have to believe me, Blue. Look into my eyes. Use your power to search my mind and soul. I will open them to you."

Her use of my nickname was enough to give me pause, as no one had used it since I had arrived. I quickly glanced toward the door to make sure no guards were coming, then closed my eyes. Reaching out with my senses, I searched her mind, which she had indeed opened for me. I ran through days of things that had gone on. Stuff Larkin had forced her to do all with his talents. I saw how she had tried to fight him and all the small things she'd set in place to keep those she loved safe and away from him. I saw the conversations she overheard and the things she learned about Larkin's intentions. He had been working with Elder Avner, Celeste, and Jacob to control the Elders.

It seemed Elder Avner also had quite a bit of ambition, though it appeared that Larkin planned to double-cross him in the end. That explained why Celeste and Jacob could subdue someone as powerful as an Elder to perform the magic needed to control them. I saw Larkin's final plan, using the Trials as a cover for killing all the Elders, and how he planned to subjugate the clans and bring them under his control. It was all so perfectly timed and planned out, except for one thing. The one thing he hadn't been able to affect or control...me.

I snapped back to myself and considered everything she had seen and what they still planned to do.

Astra lowered her head in shame. "I can make no apologies for my part in all this, Blue. I have done horrible things for him."

"It's not like you had a choice."

Astra shrugged. "Didn't I? Couldn't I have fought harder against him? Or was it just easier to allow it all to happen?"

I put a hand on her shoulder. "When this is all done, we'll make everything right."

Sorcha interjected, dancing from one tiny foot to the other. "Your Majesty, time is of the essence. If we are to get her to the secret passage and into the labyrinth, we must move fast."

Astra straightened her shoulders. "You are right, Sorcha. Blue, you are the most important thing here. Larkin cannot be allowed to get his hooks into you. I don't know how you've been able to resist him up to this point, but we can't take the chance that you won't be able to continue. If you are who they think you are, that could be catastrophic for all the Fae." Astra stood and quickly shut and locked the outer doors. Then, moving quickly, she led us across the room and into her bedchamber, closing and locking those doors too. Astra stopped me as I went to add a barrier to give us some time to escape.

"Leave them free. I will tie myself up once you are gone to throw them off where you are. Sorcha here will lead you to the secret passage and safely through the labyrinth."

I gripped her arm. "You aren't coming with us?"

She shook her head sadly. "No. I need to stay here to do what I can. As long as I am clearheaded, I will work to unravel some of the things that have been done." When I went to argue with her, she put up a hand. "We all have our parts to play in this game. This is mine."

I nodded, though I wasn't happy about it. I watched as Astra reached into a large cupboard near her bed. The cabinet swung away from the wall with an almost inaudible click, opening just wide enough for me to fit through.

"This is the secret way out of this room. If you follow the passage straight, you should find a door that will let you out into the corridor on the other side. Good luck, Blue. We're all counting on you."

As Astra moved away from the opening, a very distinct smell wafted to me through the secret entrance. It was the scent I associated with Riona. Knowing Riona was tied to her statue, it couldn't be her, which meant another ghost was nearby. Sure enough, the figure of a man formed in front of me. I didn't know who he was or if he was friend or foe, but he looked oddly familiar.

*"You must hurry! The guards will be here shortly. I'm not sure who alerted them, but someone did. Hurry! Hurry!"*

Astra, noting my stare, looked at me strangely. "You can see him, can't you?"

I turned to her, not even denying it. "Who is he?"

She smiled sadly. "I think it's my twin brother, Astron. Larkin killed him not long after Sethos left. He was trying to protect me. I have felt his presence at times and hoped he was still here somehow."

Thinking of Riona, I knew there was one thing I could do for Astra to help protect her in the coming days. Quickly manipulating the magic within me, I recreated the spell I had used for Tristan.

I reached out a hand toward Astron. *"There is no time! We must go!"*

"Yes, there is. This will only take me a minute, so hold still." As I touched him, just like with Riona, my magic flowed through his spirit. Then, I reached out to Astra. "Close your eyes." I placed my fingers over her closed lids.

She drew in a deep breath as my magic washed over her. As Astra opened her eyes and took in the figure of her deceased brother now standing in front of her, they filled with tears. "Astron?"

He looked between me and her. *"She can see me now?"*

"And hear and feel you."

After a look of disbelief, then hope, Astron reached out to his sister and pulled her into a tight hug. Looking down, he wiped the tears now streaming down her face. *"There is so much I want to say, but we will talk when I get back. First, I must help to get her out of here. Larkin knows the layout of the labyrinth and has laid traps throughout it. But I know how to get around them. I have not been idle even in death, sister dear."*

Astra nodded. "Go help her."

Stripping down to just the black tank top and cargo pants I had taken to wearing, I started to slip behind the cupboard. When I was halfway through, Astra grabbed my hand. "Blue. I almost forgot. Here are some small daggers in case you run into trouble. And thank you. You have no idea what you have returned to me."

Taking the weapons, I slid them into my pockets. As I did, I heard knocking and voices on the other side of Astra's outer door. Quickly slipping into the darkness, I gave Astra one last look as she pushed the cupboard back against the wall. I only hoped Larkin wouldn't kill her when he found me gone.

With nothing to light my way, I reached out a hand to try to find a wall or something to guide me. I shouldn't have worried as Astron jogged into view.

*"This way."*

I had forgotten how bright ghosts were in dark rooms. He was like a beacon. Reaching down, I scooped up the Water Sprite and placed her on my shoulder. "Hang on." Then I took off running, trying to keep up with Astron. I really hoped he didn't forget that I couldn't walk through walls.

As Astra's room was on one of the outer walls of the tree, we didn't have far to go until we found the secret entrance to the labyrinth. Our good luck held, and I'd only had to slip past three guards on the way. Now, looking down at the dark hole before me, I prayed my saviors were truly friends. I was about to jump into a very long, very dark hole with no bottom in sight.

Sorcha jumped ahead of me, and taking a deep breath, I slipped over the edge. Keeping my arms and legs tucked in tight for fear of hitting a wall or ledge, I fell and fell some more. Just when I feared there wasn't a bottom, I hit the water. Not being prepared, it was a bit of a shock as I slid into the cold depths. Quickly swimming to the surface, I took in gulps of air as I bobbed around. I couldn't find either Astron or Sorcha in the dark around me.

"Astron? Sorcha?" My whispered words echoed back at me. For a moment, I thought they had left me to my fate, but then a little form bobbed up next to me.

"So sorry. I forgot you were an air breather. This might be a problem. Larkin has had most of the tunnels flooded well past the normal air pocket points."

Astron appeared just below me in the water and beckoned me on. Thinking quickly, I did the magic that transformed me into a Nereid. It was really starting to become a habit. The only unfortunate side effect to this form was that the size of the clothes I had been wearing was now way too big. While I could work with the tank top and sports bra, the pants were just too much. Quickly pulling the daggers from the pockets, I kicked free of them. Holding the weapons by their straps in my teeth, I awkwardly tied knots in the sides of my underwear so they stayed in place—no easy task when you were trying to tread water at the same time. Thankfully, the daggers Astra had given me had come equipped with their own sheaths made to snap around a belt and the thighs. I quickly clipped the snaps around the knots I'd made in my underwear and wrapped the leather straps around my thighs to secure them. Not perfect, but it would definitely do.

"Okay, where to?"

Sorcha just blinked her luminescent black eyes at me. "I don't think I have ever seen anything of your like in my lifetime, and I've lived a very long time."

I grinned. "Nor will you likely ever again. Lead the way, water breather."

She just shook her head and dove beneath the surface. I followed suit, using Astron's soft glow to guide me through the watery tunnels.

⁓·ℓℓ·⁓

As we passed yet another empty chamber, I was exceptionally glad I had Astron and Sorcha as guides. The many tunnels and rooms down here branched off in every direction, and each one looked just like the next. There was no doubt you could become lost for days down here—if not forever—and with all the traps, I probably would have died or ended up captured by Larkin again without Astron.

As we neared another branch, Astron put his finger to his lips and signaled me to slow down. Reaching out with my senses, I felt what he did. There were about six beings somewhere up ahead. They seemed to be moving slowly and cautiously, but there was no way of knowing if they were friends or foes. It could be that Larkin had sent soldiers to come at us from the other end to try and cut off our escape. Though I had yet to hear anyone actively pursuing us from the rear, there had been indications that we weren't alone down here. I pulled both of my daggers from their sheaths and signaled for Astron to scout ahead.

Carefully looking around the corner, I saw we had reached an incline. It looked like the tunnel was moving us upward again, probably toward the surface. As Astron moved away, taking his glowing light with him, I put my side against the wall to keep myself grounded. The last thing I wanted to do was accidentally get turned around and head back into the labyrinth behind us.

Sorcha stayed with me as we slowly made our way up the incline. At the top, I saw we had indeed reached where the tunnel let out. Sunlight played over the surface of the water about seventy-five feet above us, and I saw shadows moving back and forth. I kept to the sides of the tunnel in a dark corner lest whoever was above look down and spot me.

I started getting nervous when Astron had yet to return after ten minutes. I didn't think it would be a good idea to stay here much longer for fear of being captured from behind. I had already felt waves moving through the water that weren't there before. Something told me Larkin's forces were getting closer. After another few minutes elapsed, I decided to chance climbing out of the tunnel alone.

I knew using my invisibility spell underwater would only partially hide me. There was too much movement in the water to make me completely unnoticeable, but it would have to do. With a loud clanging somewhere in the chambers behind, I decided to make my move. I quickly put away my daggers so my hands were free. Keeping tight to the wall, I scaled it to the top, dodging in and out of the shadows. When I reached the ledge, I looked at Sorcha.

"Thank you for bringing me this far, my friend. I understand if you need to bow out now. Who knows what is waiting for us out there?"

"I promised King Sethos I would get you to safety, and I'll not break that vow. We do this together."

I nodded. Planning my attack, I prepped the magic that would change me back into myself as I propelled out of the water. It was a risky move, as I would be vulnerable for a few seconds, but it was a chance I was willing to take. Being a Nereid may work for underwater battles, but on land, my normal form was definitely the strongest. Taking a deep breath, I gripped a ledge just below the surface of the water. As a cloud covered the sun, I made my move.

With all my strength and an added boost of magic, I thrust myself straight up out of the water. As soon as my hands were free, I pulled my daggers from their sheaths, simultaneously pushing the magic I had prepared out through my body. I barely had time to register the five surprised Fae standing around the entrance before someone knocked me to the ground from behind and pinned me there with my arms above my head. Screaming, I tried to flip my opponent off me. There was no way I was going down like this.

"Blue! Blue, stop. It's me. It's me."

Something about my opponent slowly registered in the deepest depths of my body. I knew that feeling. I knew that scent. I knew that voice. I stopped struggling and focused my eyes on the face not inches from mine.

"Keane? Keane!" Letting go of my daggers as he let go of my wrists, I wrapped myself around him. "Oh my god, Keane. It really is you." I could feel him on every level again—his essence, his emotions, all of him. I hadn't realized how much I'd missed that piece of me until it was taken away. I had gotten so used to having him there alongside me that it was like a piece of my soul was missing when he wasn't there. Now that he was back, I felt whole again. I knew I was crying and shaking like an idiot, but I didn't care.

"Shhh, it's okay, Blue. You're okay. Relax, honey, I've got you. I've got you." Somehow, Keane managed to stand without letting go of me before sitting back down on a nearby tree stump. I straddled his lap with my legs still tightly wrapped around his waist and my arms encircling his neck. He placed small kisses on the top of my head while rubbing my back. When his hand reached up to hold the back of my head close, he inadvertently awakened the thirst I had come to associate with the Vaimpír. It had been a while since I had shared blood with him, and suddenly, I knew I needed to refresh the bond we had formed, however accidentally.

With a quick shot of magic, I brought my sharp incisors out and pulled back in his embrace. Staring into his already blood-red gaze, I knew he felt the same. Standing with me still in his arms, he moved farther back into the tree line to give us a bit of privacy. Leaning his back against one of the smooth, angled trees that grew here, he balanced me on his hips and cupped my cheek with his free hand. Rubbing his thumb over my lip, he pricked it lightly with one of my fangs and spread the blood over my bottom lip. My tongue dipped out to taste it before pulling his thumb in to suckle.

Keane moaned with pleasure, as did I. Trusting me to hold on, Keane let go of me so he could cup my face between his hands. Leaning slightly forward, he brought our lips together in a fervent kiss. I knew our time was limited, and we really needed to get moving, but I also knew I needed this moment. I had been living on adrenaline and instinct for days now, and it was all crashing down around me.

Pulling back, I searched his gaze once more before leaning forward and running my nose along his neck. He tilted his head a bit to give me better access. When I reached his shoulder, I licked the spot I knew was the sweetest. As Keane quivered beneath me, I sank my teeth into him. His blood poured into my mouth, sweeter than ever. I couldn't believe how good it tasted.

Likely unable to wait any longer, I felt Keane's fangs pierce my skin. I loosed a guttural moan as we exchanged blood. It felt more than incredible. With all our emotions tangled together, along with our blood, it was more intense than ever.

Keane pulled back first, breathing like he had just run a race. It was the first time I'd ever seen him that way. I was breathing hard, too. Unlocking my legs from around his waist, I slid slowly to the forest floor, though I remained lying on his chest. I needed to feel him close to me for just another minute as I came down from the blood high.

I felt Keane reach over and close the wounds on my shoulder, then his. Closing my eyes, I retracted my teeth. I was simultaneously worn out and exhilarated.

Finally feeling like my legs would support me, I stood and moved back from Keane. He remained reclining on the tree, looking at me.

"I thought I lost you this time." His voice was a soft whisper. "I couldn't feel you, any of you, once they took you into the Bog Tree. I thought for sure Larkin had killed you, and I was nearly out of my mind. Then we received word through Lucian of all people that you were alive. Tristan thought I was foolish to believe anything Lucian said, but I didn't care. If there was even a slight chance you were alive, I was taking it. That's when Odelina stepped up. She told us about the secret labyrinth between the Bog Tree and the forest beyond. We had all heard rumors, of course, but no one outside the royal family was privy to its exact location. Odelina gave us detailed maps on how to get here and how to get through the labyrinth safely. Tristan refused to send any extra guards, said he couldn't put anyone else at risk. He even threatened to relieve my team of their duties if they came."

Keane shook his head. "Like that would stop any of us. We would have been here sooner, but little did anyone know that Larkin had laid extra traps around the entire area. We were just about to start exploring the underwater sections when you made your exciting entrance."

I shook my head. "It's a good thing it was you guys. You overpowered me so easily."

Keane chuckled, lightening the mood some. "Honey, if you thought that was easy, I have some news for you. It was just pure luck that I was on your backside when you came flying out of that water hole. Had I not been, there is no way we would have gotten you down before you attacked. And when your body changed from one form to the other, the released power was incredible. It took everything I had to hold you down. I honestly don't think I could have done it if we weren't connected. You have become very powerful, whether you realize it or not."

I shook my head in disbelief. "To me, it just seemed like you plucked me out of the air and pinned me to the ground."

"You, *ma moitié*, need to start seeing yourself for what you really are." Stepping forward, he pulled me into a tight embrace. "As happy as I am to see you, we really need to get moving. We have stayed too long already."

I pulled back. "I know. Thank you for coming after me."

"Blue, I will always come for you."

I turned to go back toward the others, but Keane stopped me. "Um, Blue, as much as I enjoy the view, I think we need to do something about your wardrobe."

I looked down at myself and laughed. I had completely forgotten that by changing back into my usual form, the adjusted underwear barely covered anything, especially with the dagger sheaths doing their best to drag them down. Reaching down, I unclipped the sheaths, then went to work on the knots I had put in the underwear. Being they were wet, it wasn't going well.

Keane laughed and moved past me. "Wait here. I brought some stuff with me, just in case."

I sat on a nearby log to wait. As I did, the ghostly figure of Astron appeared. "Astron. There you are. I was getting worried. When you didn't come back, I thought something had happened."

*"I am so sorry, Blue. I don't know how they did it, but somehow, they set up a containment field that trapped me. I couldn't get out. I am so glad you are unhurt. I thought I had failed you, and you were captured."*

I smiled. "No. Thankfully, these guys are on our side. I'm glad you are unhurt, as well."

Astron laughed. *"Blue, I'm a ghost."*

"Yes, but there are ways to make even that existence unbearable. Thank you so much for your help, Astron. If it weren't for you, I never would have made it out of that labyrinth."

*"You would have done the same for me if our roles were reversed, I am sure. I would really like to return to my sister now if it is okay. I am sure Larkin has discovered her duplicity, and who knows what he has done to her."*

I nodded. "Yes, please do what you can for Astra, and tell her...tell her we will do what we can to get her out of this. If it weren't for her, I don't think we'd be standing here now."

Astron nodded and disappeared just as Keane reappeared through the tree line with Sorcha seated on his shoulder.

"Another of your friends?" He nodded to where Astron had just been standing. I knew he couldn't see him, but he could sense him because of his connection to me.

"Sorcha. I am so glad to see you unharmed." She jumped off Keane's shoulder and moved to stand on the log next to me.

"No thanks to those bloodsuckers out there." She spat on the ground, and I laughed.

"Don't be too mad at them. They didn't know if we were part of Larkin's forces. Are you all right?"

She nodded. "Yes, they just captured me in an aqua bubble. Powerful little things. Has Astron gone?"

"Yes, I sent him back to try to protect Astra."

"Here you go." Keane tossed me a pile of clothing.

I was overjoyed to see Keane had not only brought my fighting gear with him but had also thought to include fresh undergarments. As I changed, I quickly explained to Keane everything that had gone on since my kidnapping, including what Larkin had been attempting to do to me, who Astron was, how Queen Astra had helped me, and the things I had seen in her mind.

As I told my tale, Keane's eyes turned a deep red, and I could feel the anger rolling off him in waves. "I promise you, Blue, when the time comes, I will make that bastard Larkin pay for what he has done. As for Fiorian, his death was already in the cards the minute he touched you." He took a deep breath and let it out, trying to calm his raging temper.

"I am not surprised Elder Avner has been helping Larkin. That man is slimier than an eel. Always seems to have some type of hidden agenda. Once we get back to Moon Tree Hall, we will have to find a way to oust him and the others. Even though Celeste is behind some of this, she is still contracted to the blood stone, and as such, can't be removed from the competition."

I couldn't believe that with everything that'd happened and all we now knew, I would have to go back and compete in the Trials. Hopefully, without the influence of Elder Avner and Celeste and Jacob's powers, we'd be able to put an end to the stupid games.

After getting dressed, I moved out of the tree line and greeted my rescuers—all the members of Ethereal Mutation, of course—along with Darrius and Cedric. I was surprised to see the last two, considering things.

"Darrius, as good as it is to see you, who is guarding Sabrianna?" I clasped his forearm like I had seen many of the other Fae do for those they held in high regard.

"Do not worry. She is in good hands. King Barracus himself is with her, plus his guards. I could not turn away when Keane needed help."

"Even with your history, you prove to be a loyal brother. I appreciate your loyalty and dedication, Darrius. Sabrianna could not do better." I paused and gave him a meaningful stare. "Just remember, there is an expiration date on that kind of thing. So, if you're going to make your move, I would suggest you do it soon." I winked at his shocked expression and turned to Cedric. "Hey there, Wolf."

"Hey."

"What brings you to these parts?"

Cedric gave me a crooked grin, sensing the forgiveness and acceptance in my voice. "Oh, just a pleasure cruise at night through eel-infested waters."

I grinned at his reference to one of our shared favorite movies, *The Princess Bride*. "Planning on going for a swim with the shrieking eels, too?"

"Hey, dogs love to swim."

I laughed and gave him a one-armed hug. "I'm glad you came."

"Me, too." Looking around, Cedric seemed to be making sure our conversation was private. As the Vaimpír packed their supplies, no one was paying us much attention, though I knew they were listening. "What's with you and Keane?"

I raised my eyebrows at him. Not again. "What do you mean?"

"He was out of control when you were taken. Stalking the halls, yelling at anyone who came too near, picking fights with his fellow Vaimpír. It was strange." He shook his head. "Then, when you appeared ready to fight, he was able to subdue you with a few words. And then you disappeared with him into the forest. I tried to go after you two, but the other Vaimpír built like a wall and wouldn't let me pass. They said it was their duty to protect you and Keane."

I barked out a laugh. "I guess that cat is out of the bag."

"What cat?" Cedric had a perplexed look on his face.

"Look, there are some things going on that I can't talk about. Just know it is all good, and trust that things will work out."

Cedric looked annoyed at my cryptic answer, but let it go. "Listen, Blue. I haven't really gotten a chance to talk to you since our incident all those weeks ago."

I must have looked panicked enough at the direction the conversation was going because Mckile immediately came over and threw a large canvas bag at Cedric. "Here, pup. Time to pull your weight around here."

"My weight? What about all that tracking I did to get us in and around those traps? Ungrateful bastards." Mckile winked at me from behind Cedric's back, and I had to muffle the laughter that bubbled up.

"All right, guys, time to move out."

"We'll talk later, okay?" I patted Cedric on the shoulder before moving up to where Keane stood.

Keane raised an eyebrow at me, and I just rolled my eyes, causing him to chuckle.

We spent the rest of the day carefully making our way out of the Misty River Clan territory. It was too dangerous to open a portal for fear they would track the magic to us, so we had to go on foot. It got a bit dicey at one point when we came across one of Larkin's patrols, but with Cedric's help, we maneuvered around them without any bloodshed. By nightfall, we finally reached the border of the swamp and moved into the Fernsong territory.

Though we weren't completely safe, we all breathed a sigh of relief. We spent the night in several massive, hollowed-out trees the Fernsong Clan had to welcome visitors. The members of Ethereal Mutation took turns keeping watch so I could get some much-needed rest. Keane, of course, stayed by my side, refusing to even let me out of his sight to go to the bathroom—a novel experience, to say the least. As I snuggled up in an oversized sleeping bag beside him, I thanked whatever gods had helped me escape today. I knew Sethos didn't have the power to orchestrate what had happened, so he must have called in one of his favors with the gods. I'd have to remember to ask him who when this was all over.

# Chapter Twenty-Two

I t took us another day to make our way back to Dock Street overland. Being wary of the water, we decided a boat voyage was too dangerous. Thankfully, we didn't have to walk the whole way. Members of the Fernsong Clan provided us with ground transportation. I'd never been so happy to see the brick façade of the theater. Though I had only been living there temporarily for a short time, it already felt like home.

After dropping Cedric off on his floor and Darrius on his, the rest of us continued to Tristan's private quarters. As the elevator took us down, my mind was drawn back to the last time I had made this voyage. Glancing over at Keane, I saw that he, too, was thinking about it, if the grin on his face was any indication. Shaking my head, I laughingly pushed him away when he made to pull me into his arms.

"You stay on that side of the elevator, and I'll stay on this one."

"What...why ever would I need to do that?"

"Let's just say I don't trust you."

Keane placed a hand over his chest. "You cut me to the quick, Blue."

Everyone laughed at our theatrics. It was a much-needed release. We had all been on edge since leaving the Misty River Clan's territory. Something just didn't feel right. Not that my rescue had been easy, but it almost seemed like Larkin had let me go. But why would he have done that? None of it made sense.

The elevator reached Tristan's quarters and opened with a ding. As soon as I stepped out, he swept me up into a warm embrace and kissed me thoroughly.

When he finally stepped back, I was breathless and more than a little confused. "Blue, I have been beside myself with worry. We thought, I thought... Oh, god." He moved as if to grab me again, and I stepped back.

"Thank you, Tristan. I appreciate your concern."

Tristan looked as if I had slapped him, but I couldn't help it. He was hot one minute, then cold the next. And if what Keane had told me was true—and I had no reason to doubt it—Tristan hadn't even wanted to go after me.

"Blue, I...what...?" He ran a frustrated hand through his hair, making it stand on end. "Can we talk privately?"

I sighed. Seemed the conversation couldn't be avoided, though I wished it could. "Lead the way." Tristan hesitated but then preceded me to his bedroom. Keane started to follow, but I put a hand on his chest and shook my head. "Better to get this out of the way now. You stay out here."

"Blue..."

"We'll be fine. You can remain just outside the door if you want, but this is something that needs to be done between the two of us."

Keane searched my gaze, then nodded. "I'll be here if you need me."

Slowly shutting the door, I leaned against it. Tristan paced before his bed.

"Blue, when you were taken, I wanted more than anything to go after you."

"But...?"

"But, for the sake of the clan, I couldn't. I couldn't in good conscience drop us into a war that would probably get many people killed, all for the life of one person, no matter how much that life means to me."

"I understand, Tristan."

"No, you don't."

"Yes, I do. As the King of this clan, you need to put the well-being of all your subjects first. I wouldn't expect anything less. It's what you are supposed to do. It's why you were made King. Because you put everything else before your wants and needs. You weigh everything against the good of the clan. I can't fault you for that, and I don't hold it against you."

"But..."

I laughed softly as he turned my word back on me. "But I can't, in good conscience, be with a man who is unable to be there for me. To protect me no matter the cost. And I know it's not that you don't want to. It's that you can't."

"So that's it? All or nothing?"

I shrugged my shoulders. "You can't change who you are, and I can't change who I am. It just wasn't meant to be, Tristan, no matter how much we thought it was."

"But what we had together, what we still have...this pull."

"I believe that was the universe's way of bringing us together. We needed each other, we *still* need each other, just not in the way we originally thought."

Tristan suddenly turned and pulled me into his arms, kissing me hard. I kissed him back with everything I had, knowing it would probably be the last time. Pulling back, he searched my gaze, seeing my resolve.

He sighed heavily and rested his forehead against mine. "It's Keane, isn't it? Are you and he together?"

I pulled away from Tristan and leaned against the couch with my arms crossed over my chest, a little annoyed he had brought Keane up. "Keane's and my relationship is...complicated. If you're asking if we are keeping the bond, then yes. For now, at least. I don't know what the future holds there, but something about it just feels right. If you're asking if it's because of Keane that I don't think we'll work, then no."

"So there's no chance you will change your mind? I know you feel as strongly for me as I do for you."

I sighed. "You're right. I do feel strongly for you, Tristan, and I probably always will. But there are other things to consider."

Tristan turned his back to me and leaned heavily on the bed. "I want you to know I disagree with your decision. I think there is a chance for us."

I shook my head, even though he couldn't see it. "I won't say anything as cliché as I hope we can still be friends. But, Tristan, I hope we can still be...something." When he didn't say anything else, I slipped out the door and closed it softly behind me.

Keane wasn't standing on the other side as I thought he'd be, but I could hear him talking to Cullen and Ronan in the living area. I wondered how much he had heard. Shaking my head, I went out to ask him to take me to his home to get some rest and escape all the drama. I felt drained in ways that had nothing to do with my ordeal, and if I hoped to even make a showing at the next Trial, I needed to get some downtime. While I knew I didn't want to win, I also didn't want certain other individuals to either.

I also needed to see the Elders to explain the real danger Larkin posed. I didn't think anyone realized how extensive his plans were.

✦✦✦

The next few days brought a return to normalcy. Well, as *normal* as things could be when you were fighting against four other women for something you didn't even want. The Elders had started the Trials again, barely acknowledging my kidnapping. They wouldn't even consider what I had to say about Larkin. They told me it was just the stress of the Trials and my overactive imagination. I wouldn't be surprised if Elder Avner had gotten Jacob to wipe it from their memories. It was frustrating, knowing something would happen but not having any power or control over it. And with Tristan not speaking to me unless absolutely necessary, I had no idea what the Elders were even thinking at this point.

That was why it was a surprise when we were suddenly summoned to the ballroom. Having already completed the Trial for today, it was definitely unexpected. Keane and I glanced nervously at each other as we made our way to the ballroom, though we didn't say anything. On our way, we met up with Sabrianna and Darrius in the elevator.

Sabrianna moved in close to my side. "What do you think is going on?"

"I don't know, but it makes me nervous. Hopefully, they are just going to make a decision and announce it today, putting an end to these infernal things."

"Not likely. We're all pretty much tied at this point. If they were to make a decision, it would look like favoritism."

"True."

As we walked into the ballroom, I immediately noticed something was different. All the point boards had been removed, and the room had been reconfigured.

I heard Sabrianna gasp and turned my head toward her. "You okay?"

"It's the final Trial, the dance of Göndul."

I looked back at the new layout, then back at Sabrianna. "Are you sure?"

She nodded. "I've seen drawings of the setup in the archives. This looks exactly like them."

I took a deep breath and let it out slowly. The final Trial, the dance of Göndul, something I had been dreading since the beginning. Fighting, magic, arts, those were things I knew and had proven to be good at. But dancing was completely foreign to me. Not only that, but I also hadn't worked with Riona in weeks due to everything that had been happening. I wasn't sure I could even accomplish it now or had even managed it once in the time I had been working with her.

It may sound silly, and I was sure most people would laugh it off, a dance? As the final Trial after all the dangers faced so far? But that was only because they had never seen it. Not only was it an intricate set of steps and moves, there were also very particular spells that had to be laid and executed while you were dancing. Very few could accomplish both simultaneously. It took every bit of focus to execute the complicated dance moves, let alone concentrate on doing advanced magic. As we descended the steps, I saw the Elders had already made their way onto their raised dais at the far end of the room. The crowd parted for us as we made our way to the front to join our fellow competitors.

Celeste turned her head toward us with a sneer, then whispered loudly to Tatiana. "Always late to the party, aren't they?" They both snickered.

Sabrianna seemed like she was about to make some retort, but I put a hand on her arm and shook my head. "It will only encourage them."

About that time, Elder Demirtas raised his hands for quiet. "Ladies and gentlemen. Your attention, please. As we are nearing the end of the Trials, I am pleased to announce that we have five strong competitors left in the running, each having her own special set of skills. Any of them would make a strong Queen. We, the Elders, have decided it is time for the final Trial. This event will decide the outcome and who will be named as your new Queen. I know you have all been anticipating this. Tomorrow, we will present each of our finalists in the most cherished tradition of our people... The dance of Göndul!" Tremendous applause and shouting broke out all around us.

I was sure they were all looking forward to this. The crowd liked nothing more than seeing someone fail epically. "Ladies, would you please step forward to draw numbers for the order in which you will dance?"

Celeste and Tatiana, of course, ran forward to be the first to pull while the rest of us followed sedately behind. I could tell Sabrianna and Odelina were just as nervous as I was. Celeste pulled fourth, and Tatiana pulled second, much to her disappointment. Odelina pulled first, which left third and last for Sabrianna and me. We bumped fists in solidarity and decided to draw at the same time. Holding my breath, I pulled the stick out... Fifth. I would be dancing last.

I wasn't sure if it was an advantage or a disadvantage at this point. I could see Celeste and Tatiana arguing with the Elders about their placement, but as it had been witnessed in front of the entire clan, there was no changing it. With all the excitement over, the crowd dispersed.

As I made my way up the stairs, I felt the air stir around me. "Hello, Riona."

*"Hello, Blue. I know we haven't seen much of each other recently, but I thought, considering the events happening tomorrow, perhaps you would like to practice?"*

I nodded. "I would appreciate that."

Keane, well used to me conversing with ghosts all the time, kept watch around us but didn't intervene.

*"Shall we meet at the gym in Tristan's quarters in say, fifteen minutes?"*

"Let's make it an hour. I really need to get something to eat to refuel my body before I start again."

Riona nodded and drifted back to where Tristan stood.

"Let's go visit your friends at the Mexican place, hmm?"

Keane looked at me sideways. "Are you sure you're ready for that?"

I laughed. "At this point, it doesn't really matter what I'm ready for. If I've learned anything in the past few months, it's to just keep rolling with things as they come. Besides, I've been dying for some of Alejandro's soup."

Keane chuckled, knowing that wasn't my real reason for visiting Alejandro's restaurant. In my research, I had found that Mariana was one of the few Fae in recent years to successfully complete the dance of Göndul with an almost perfect score during competition.

Wasn't that just the way my luck seemed to slide these days?

As we rode down in the elevator, Keane stood in his usual seemingly uncaring position. What few realized, and what had taken me a while to notice, was that he stood that way on purpose, loose with nothing encumbering him. He always kept one foot raised so he could plant and go in whatever direction he needed to, and his arms, while crossed, were poised and ready to pull any weapon he had on his person. Staring at him now, I could appreciate his calm, even if it was just a practiced façade. On the inside, I could feel his emotions roiling—even his foot tapped slightly.

"Stop that."

"Stop what?"

"You're worrying."

He snorted. "I don't worry."

"Of course, you do. But, hey, you don't have to worry about Mariana attacking me. I can handle her."

"Of that, I have no doubt, *ma moitié*. It isn't Mariana I am worried about and you know it."

"I thought you said you weren't worried." I grinned at him while he gave me an annoyed look. "What does that mean, by the way?"

"What does what mean?"

"*Ma moitié?*"

"It's French. It roughly translates to my other half. Why?"

"That's the second time you've called me that, and I wondered if you were cursing at me or something."

Keane chuckled. "No, just an endearment we Vaimpír use for our soul partners."

I nodded. "Better not let anyone else in the Vaimpír community hear you say that. If it gets out that we are soulbound, I have a feeling all kinds of shit will hit the fan among your kind."

"Not if, *when*."

I gulped. "When?"

"Blue, I am not going to keep it a secret forever. I just thought it best while you were involved in the Trials. After they're done, I plan to let everyone know."

"Oh, shit."

"Are you ashamed of our connection?"

My eyes widened. "Good heavens, no. But considering your position within the Vaimpír society..."

"My positi—Blue, who have you been talking to?"

I could see he was getting tense, and I instantly regretted bringing it up. "Um... well...I asked Sabrianna about you and Darrius, and, well..."

"I see." Keane's tone conveyed his burgeoning anger.

"Keane. I'm sorry. I asked you several times about it, but you always deflected me. I thought it was important considering our new...relationship, the reaction of the Vaimpír females, and...and...well,

I'm sorry. I should have waited until you were ready to tell me. Can you forgive me?"

Keane let out a loud breath, his anger draining away. "No, it is I who am sorry, Blue. I should have told you much sooner, especially considering our new relationship. You had a right to know. I just enjoyed the fact that you didn't know, I guess. You can imagine how differently I get treated when I'm around those who know who I am."

I nodded. "I can understand that. Don't worry, it doesn't in any way change how I view you." I smirked. "Your Highness." I gave him a mock curtsy.

"Why you little…" Keane grabbed me and started tickling me.

I giggled and laughed. Trying to avoid his tickling fingers, I danced and rolled around the interior of the elevator but couldn't get away. "Stop! Stop! I give! Uncle! Uncle!"

Just about then, the elevator doors swung open on our floor. Standing at the entrance was none other than Cedric and a woman I didn't know. As I was currently flat on my back with Keane straddling my hips, we must have looked a sight. The woman giggled at the sight of us.

"Uh, hi." I pushed at Keane's chest to get him to move.

He just laughed and kissed me on the tip of my nose. "To be continued." He pushed himself up off the floor, reached down, and pulled me to my feet.

I stepped past Cedric and the young woman waving as I went. "Good to see you, Cedric."

As the elevator doors were closing, I heard the woman giggle again. "They make such a cute couple, don't they?"

I blushed, and after taking quick inventory, dusted off my pants and pushed my hair back into its ponytail holder. The last thing I wanted to do was present myself to Mariana as a woman who had just been rolling around on the floor with the man she had once hoped to marry. That would certainly get things off on the wrong foot. Keane just walked ahead of me with a huge grin on his face.

I ran to catch up. "Hey, seriously, back to our original conversation. Who you are in the Vaimpír society has no baring whatsoever on how I see you. You're still the same overbearing, egotistical, has-to-have-his-way-all-the-time Vaimpír you've always been." I grinned at his profile.

"Overbearing, egotistical, and has to have his way, huh?" Without warning, Keane turned and pressed me against the wall with his body while pinning my arms above my head with one hand. His face was inches from mine.

I nodded mutely, more turned on than I'd ever admit to him with his show of domination.

"If that's the case..." He licked his lips, and I held my breath. Leaning forward, he nuzzled the side of my neck, and I had to contain the moan that threatened to escape. "Since you now know who I am, perhaps I should punish you for such insolence." His free hand moved to my waist before sliding down to cup my rear while his lips moved to my ear and suckled, causing a shiver to run through my body. "Or perhaps I should teach you a lesson on just how the Dark Prince is supposed to be treated." His lips moved over my cheek until they reached mine, where he sucked on my bottom one, leaving me wishing he would kiss me hard.

"Mmm, such a sweet mouth." My arms ached to be released so I could touch him, but he was having none of it and held them firmly in his steely grip. "You, my dear, are a smartmouthed, headstrong, and infuriating woman, which is why..." His grip tightened on my rear, and one of his fangs pricked the inside of my mouth, causing me to whimper. "We make the perfect pair. And I wouldn't have it any other way."

He stepped away, leaving me a quivering mess of arousal. I leaned heavily against the wall behind me, trying to bring myself back under control.

Keane smirked, knowing exactly what he had done to me, and walked toward the door that would take us to Alejandro's restaurant. Taking a few deep breaths, I moved to stand beside him. "That was playing dirty."

"Oh, sweetheart, you haven't seen dirty yet." He winked then opened the door, gesturing for me to precede him.

As I moved past him, I made sure to rub my entire body against his. "Two can play that game."

A grin crooked his mouth. "That's what I'm hoping."

Alejandro was in his usual seat when we entered. As soon as he saw us, a smile lit up his face, and he jumped up to greet us.

"Blue. Keane. What a wonderful surprise." After shaking Keane's hand, he held me by the shoulders and lightly kissed both my cheeks.

I returned the gesture. "It is so good to see you, Señor Alejandro. How have you been?"

"Good, good. Business has been busy with all the excitement of the Trials going on and so many Fae staying here. I see you have been doing very well in the competition. I look forward to seeing you dance tomorrow."

I grimaced at the reminder but nodded as he led us to the table we had sat at before, the scorch marks still etched into the floor. I allowed him to pull out my chair and put my napkin in my lap before mentioning the real reason for our visit.

"Thank you, Alejandro. That actually brings up one of the reasons we're here—besides your wonderful food, of course." I smiled at him. "I wanted to...well, I was hoping I could talk to Mariana about the dance. I heard she is very accomplished at it and even managed an almost perfect score in competition."

Alejandro puffed his chest out proudly and smiled. "*Sí. Mi hija* is very talented. She has been dancing the Göndul since she was a *niñita*."

"I just wasn't sure if she would talk to me because of...well, after what I—"

Alejandro shook his head. "She will talk to you, do not worry. You are Keane's *alma gemela*. She must show respect to Príncipe Keane, which means she must show respect to you."

I grimaced. I was pretty sure she wouldn't take too kindly to being forced to talk to me or being told it was her duty. I had a feeling this would be a wasted effort on my part.

"I will get her for you. But first, to eat?"

Keane ordered for us again, this time going with something completely different but no less delicious-sounding. After Alejandro walked away, Keane sat forward in his chair, seeming a bit tense again.

"Blue."

"Hmm?"

"What are your plans after the Trials?"

I turned from where I had been watching the water to look at him. "You know, I really haven't thought about it. I've been so caught up in what has been going on day to day that I haven't even considered the future." I mulled it over. "I guess I'll move back into my place in Folly Beach and pick up with my photography again. I have quite a few sessions I put on hold that I need to reschedule."

Keane nodded but still looked tense. "Do you plan to travel with the fashion company again?"

I shook my head. "Not for a while, at least. It's not like I have to work, I just do it because I want to."

"What...what about our arrangement once you leave? Will you still keep our bond?"

I smiled softly. "Is that what this is about?"

Keane nodded, and for the first time since I'd met him, he seemed unsure of himself. "I wasn't sure. You know, especially since you now know who I am. And if you aren't planning to stay here..."

"I have no intention of letting you off the hook just yet, *ma moitié*." I placed my hand on his arm and squeezed.

"Isn't this just sweet?"

I turned toward the new voice dripping with sarcasm and sighed. So much for starting on even ground. "Good evening, Mariana."

"What are you doing here? Come to take something else away from me?"

"No, Mariana. You know I am very sorry for what happened previously, but you were just as much to blame for the outcome as I was."

She placed her hand on her hip and frowned at me. "I don't see how."

I let out an exasperated sigh. This type of conversation wouldn't get me anywhere. She obviously still hadn't grown up any. I glanced at

Keane, but he just shrugged, leaving it up to me. "Did your father tell you why I wanted to speak with you?"

"Of course. But what's in it for me? Why should I help you when you took everything from me?"

"Mariana, I didn't take anything from you. You still have your magic. You just can't use it right now. When your father decides it is time, I will release the binding spell." I took a deep breath to curb my anger and then let it out slowly. "I didn't come here to discuss the past, what I came to talk about is the dance of Göndul. I heard you are one of the best at it."

"So I am. What of it?"

"I came here to humbly ask for your help. I have had little training when it comes to this dance and need any advantage I can find to get through the last Trial. While I have no intention of winning, I do not want to see someone like Celeste or Tatiana take the throne, either. I think that would be detrimental to all of us."

"What makes you think I care who is on the throne of this clan? As Vaimpír, we are above the clans."

"Then what do you care about, Mariana? What is it you want in order to help me?"

"Him." She nodded toward Keane.

"Him?"

"I want you to release him from your soulbond. He is supposed to be with me, a real Vaimpír of the seven houses, not some lowly Fairy like you. I don't care how powerful you think you are. You are not worthy." She spat on the floor at my feet.

I sighed. "That is something I cannot grant you, Mariana. I'm sorry."

"You bitch. You act as though you are already Queen of both the Fairies and the Vaimpír. You cannot have both. I will tell everyone who will listen about your treachery. How you used your magic to enslave Príncipe Keane and probably King Tristan. I will find a way to undo what you have done."

Suddenly, Keane slammed his hand on the table, causing us both to jump and look at him. "Enough! I will not have you treating Blue this way, Mariana." He stood and rolled his shoulders back, showing his regal bearing. "You will show Blue the respect she deserves, not only as my other half, but as the royalty she is."

Mariana sneered. "Even if she is royalty, she is not of the seven houses or even a Vaimpír. She should be nothing to you. You are the Dark Prince, the one above all others. And I should be your other half, your partner, and eventually your Queen. I have been raised to hold that position, It is mine, and I want it."

Keane took a step forward and stared angrily down at her, causing her to wilt under the intensity of it. "I am tired of you looking down on everyone and thinking you are better than others because of your family name. You are not and never will be my other half, my partner, or my Queen, Mariana. As a matter of fact, you are no longer welcome in the Rutherman household. You will never again set foot through our doors or hold any honor previously bestowed upon you by your family. You are nothing."

Mariana burst into tears and dropped to the floor. "No. No! Do not do this, Príncipe Keane. Do not shut me out. She is not worth this. She is just a treacherous snake, a whore trying to take all that is supposed to be mine. You will see in time. She will reveal herself to you, and you will come back for me—"

"*Hija*! What have you done?" Mariana's father came running over, hearing the exchange escalating. "I am so sorry, Príncipe Keane. This is my fault. I have raised her to be an arrogant, spoiled child. Please, do not take your wrath out on her, punish me instead."

Keane shook his head. "No, Alejandro. Mariana is an adult now. She must be held accountable for her actions. I am sorry."

Turning, Keane grabbed my hand and pulled me to my feet. I looked sadly at Mariana, who sobbed in her father's arms. She turned angry, water-filled eyes up at me.

"I will never forgive you for this, do you understand? I will find a way to kill you and take back what is mine."

Keane looked dispassionately down at her. "No, Mariana, you will not. If you touch so much as a hair on her head, or any other she cares about, you will forfeit your life. You have my word on that." He turned to Alejandro. "Señor, if you would allow, I would like to have an enchantment done on Mariana so she can neither speak of this nor act on any of her threats. I want her bound by it.”

Alejandro nodded sadly. “As you wish, Príncipe.” He motioned forward two men I hadn’t seen earlier. They took Mariana by her arms and started dragging her forcefully away.

“Papa! No! Do not let them do this. Papa!!”

“Know that her words and actions hold no bearing on you or the rest of your family, Señor Alejandro. Her actions are her own.”

Alejandro nodded again. “Thank you for your kindness, Príncipe. I know you could have done far worse.”

“I will have someone come back to pick up our food. I think it best we leave now.”

As we made our way out, every patron and employee bowed to Keane as he passed. I hadn’t realized they were all Vaimpír. A few even reached out to brush my hands or legs from their crouched positions, which I thought was odd.

*“It is a sign of respect for you, Blue. Please allow them to touch you.”* Keane projected his thoughts to me so no one else knew of my lack of knowledge. I nodded and continued to move forward as if nothing were going on.

When we exited the room, I sighed. “I guess our secret is out.”

Keane smiled and shook his head. “Not likely. All those present in there were of the Rodriguez family. They are very loyal to the Ruthermans. Mariana was not far off when she said she had been raised to become my wife. Each of the seven families has one chosen woman they all put their hopes in, that I will someday choose.”

“Damn, no wonder Mariana wants to kill me.”

Keane’s expression darkened. “That will not happen. Now that Mariana is disgraced, Alejandro will remove her from the family and send her somewhere remote, most likely with humans. When enough time has passed, she will be allowed to return, but she will never be allowed the accolades she had as one of the chosen. It will be a good life lesson for her. While I hadn’t planned to choose her regardless, I did allow her to stay in her position to reap the benefits. Clearly, she has abused that position.”

"Will her father have me remove the magical bond?"

Keane shook his head. "No, she is much too dangerous with all her magic. Until she learns to live as she should with it, she will live without it."

I nodded and moved toward the elevator. "I guess I can't put this off any longer, then. We will have to see what Riona can teach me." With feet that felt like lead, I made my way down to Tristan's quarters and the workout room where Riona waited patiently for me.

# Chapter Twenty-Three

I waited in the same private alcove I had started the Trials in, high above everyone else. However, this time, I knew who was hidden among the brightly colored flags covering the top of the room. It seemed fitting somehow for things to end where they'd begun. We had been forbidden to watch the other competitors perform so we wouldn't be given any advantage over each other, though the course was supposedly rearranged for each dancer so no two were the same. I could hear the *ooohs* and *aaahs* of the crowd below as each woman took her turn. Though I couldn't see what was happening, I could clearly tell that no woman had managed to complete the dance to the satisfaction of the people. Of course, that didn't mean they hadn't managed to finish, it just meant they hadn't finished with any type of flourish that pleased the crowd.

Riona and I had practiced well into the night, and while I had managed the dance and magic separately, I had not been able to combine them successfully. I just hoped I would at least beat out Celeste and Tatiana. I had decided instead of concentrating on the dance and magic as a whole, I would instead veer from tradition and mix things up. While I would hit the required main points, I wouldn't necessarily do them in the order originally written. It was risky, but I figured I didn't have much to lose at this point.

Keane approached me. "Are you ready?"

I laughed up at him. "Is that a trick question?"

He shook his head, smiling slightly. Reaching down, he took my hand and brought me to my feet. "Just be you. Don't worry about the specifics. Pull the dance from your heart, and there is no doubt you will succeed."

I took a deep breath and let it out slowly. "I'm glad you have such confidence in me."

"Sweetheart, I believe you can do anything you set your mind to." He pulled me into a tight hug, which I returned.

After a few minutes, we broke apart. "I guess it's time to Fairy up."

Keane chuckled and stepped back. Closing my eyes, I concentrated on my magic as Kieran had taught me and brought my wings and ears back into the here and now. I still wasn't completely comfortable with either, but since they were a part of me, and this dance was all about inner strength and defining one's true self, I figured it best I honor them. Opening my eyes, I sighed. "That was much easier to do *after* my clothes were in place."

Keane laughed lightly in amusement. "Live and learn. You look gorgeous, Blue. Even your skin takes on a luminescent glow when you become a Fairy. I don't know why you always try to hide it."

"That coming from someone that doesn't have strange appendages growing out of his body—and, no, your teeth don't count."

He just grinned and shook his head, knowing there was no winning this argument.

I did a few stretches with my wings, making sure I was comfortable with folding and unfolding them. Some of the moves Riona and I had come up with relied on me being able to do it fluidly. I adjusted my filmy white dress. While I had wanted to wear my fighting gear, Riona had convinced me that it would be in my best interests to go with something more ethereal. Instead, she had chosen a white body suit injected with shots of ever-changing color and paired it with a filmy white dress overlay that sparkled every time I moved. As the fabric surrounded me, I had felt the magic imbued into its very fibers. I didn't know where she had gotten it, but I had a feeling it had been made by some very old and powerful Fae. I just hoped they were on our side.

"It's time."

Keane stood by the entrance to the alcove, holding out my Grayson cloak. I slipped it on and moved to stand between him and Mckile. Just like the first time, they escorted me into the ballroom with my hood raised and whispers in my ear. As we made our way down the stairs, I reached out with my senses. They moved over the room, and I took note of who was there to watch. It was definitely a mixed bunch from clans all over. As I came across one particular signature, I was so surprised that I almost tripped.

Keane, following behind me, moved forward a bit. "What's wrong, Blue?"

"Nothing, it's just...Sebastian is here."

Keane nodded. "I felt him, too. I wonder what he is up to."

I shook my head and fell silent again. Moving to stand before the raised dais situated in front of the dance floor, I dropped into a low curtsy. Tristan was seated at its center, with the ghostly Riona at his side while the Elders were spread out on either side of him. I glanced briefly at Kieran, and he nodded in my direction. I tilted my head at him slightly in acknowledgment.

Tristan stood, and I quickly lowered my head again. "Members of the Fae clans, we have come to the final competitor for this evening. Honoring the family Grayson and the Moon Tree Clan is Carolina Blue, better known as Blue to her friends. Throughout this competition, she has proven to be strong and resourceful, overcoming many obstacles to stand before you now. Her magic is just as profound as we have come to expect from one of the Grayson family, and we look forward to seeing her skills put to this final test." I felt Tristan's gaze shift to me, but I didn't look up. "Blue, you may take the floor in competition."

I dropped into another curtsy without meeting his eyes, then moved to stand in the middle of the floor, still cloaked. I took in several deep breaths to calm my racing heart. I could do this. The music I had chosen started out as a low beat that slowly escalated. I began moving along with the it, working up my magic. Twirling and moving slowly around with lots of accented choreography, I conjured a dark blue sparkling mist, letting it settle across the entire dance floor and shroud the many raised surfaces and poles surrounding me. As the music escalated, I moved with it, conjuring the first required spell. As the peak of the music hit with a beastly roar, I sent fire balls through the hoops to my left and right while simultaneously shedding myself of my cloak and unfurling my wings in a dramatic spin.

The crowd went nuts, cheering and stamping their feet. Taking a deep breath and tuning them out, almost terrified of the next move Riona and I had come up with, I jumped and spun in the air, letting my wings catch the breeze I created and turned into a tornado-like swirl. It carried me almost to the roof before letting me slowly float back down. As I descended, I brought up my water magic and allowed a small torrent to join the circling wind. The picture it made was stunningly beautiful, inspiring vocal appreciation from the crowd. Before I reached the ground, I quickly manipulated the magic and froze the swirling water in mid form, creating an ice spiral in the middle of the floor. I slid down the last few feet of it, following the beat of the music.

Twirling and dipping my way past several of the raised surfaces, I ran my hand softly along them. Almost immediately, flowers sprouted in my wake, growing and blooming slowly before everyone's eyes. The crowd gasped, as with another caress, I turned the blooming flowers into hundreds of butterflies that shrouded the entire dance floor before melding in with the blue mist. While not exactly what the dance outlined, I was, in fact, demonstrating each of my skills in my own way. I had showcased all the elements, along with a little transformation magic.

Continuing to move about the dance floor and keeping my movements fluid, I made sure to utilize the raised surfaces and poles. Demonstrating more magic, I shifted and raised the platforms with me on them, incorporating it all into my dance.

So far, so good. As I prepared my next big spell, I suddenly felt an odd magic floating through the room. I noticed several groups turning their eyes toward the balcony and starting to point and whisper. I tried to tune them out, but it quickly became impossible. The room seemed to quake before it quieted bit by bit, until even my music turned off. All eyes were glued to the balcony behind me. Slowly turning, almost dreading what I would see, I looked up.

There, silhouetted by the spotlights pointed toward the stage, stood none other than Larkin. He was flanked by Celeste and Jacob on one side, while Fiorian and a man whose name I didn't know stood on his other. He leaned on the railing, looking down over the crowd with malicious intent.

"Well, well, well, what an occasion." His sugary-sweet voice grated on my nerves as a rumble of discontent poured through the people around me, though they remained quiet.

Tristan, still on the dais, surged to his feet. "What is the meaning of this? You are not welcome here. Guards, seize him!"

Larkin laughed. "Sit and be quiet like a good, obedient servant, won't you, Tristan? This is no longer your court."

Tristan seemed to freeze in place, then sat woodenly. I couldn't figure out how Larkin had managed it until I saw Elder Avner standing at the end of the dais. One of his talents was the ability to control others, whether physically or mentally.

Several of the other Elders stood to protest, and they, too, were quickly overtaken with Celeste's help. She had moved down the stairs to stand at Elder Avner's side. Tristan glared up at Larkin. "You will pay for this act of treason."

Larkin laughed. "You are hardly in a position to do anything, *Your Majesty*." He gave a mocking bow before standing and moving to the top of the stairs. "So, you see, my good people. Even though you look to them for guidance, your royalty, your Elders, are nothing if not mortal. Controlled and manipulated the same way every man is." Larkin swaggered back and forth, remaining on the balcony above, lording his control over everyone.

While a few tried to make a move against him, they were quickly subdued. It seemed Larkin had a throng of followers positioned throughout the crowd. Seeing no way out of the current situation, most settled into their seats to see where this would go.

"That's better. Now, if we are done with the resisting..." Larkin was back to leaning on the railing. "I am here to tell all of you that from this day forward, I will be your supreme ruler. Every clan, every species, will look to me from now on."

There was a grumble of protest among the people.

"You will all obey me in everything. And things are going to change."

As Larkin continued on about his greatness and what he would do for the clans as their new supreme leader, my gaze circled the crowd. While I was in the middle of the arena, I was also hidden slightly by shadows. There had to be something I could do to put a stop to this. I had warned the Elders over and over that this was coming, but they hadn't prepared anything for even the possibility.

A slight movement to my left brought my attention around. It was Keane. He had managed to make his way to the far side of the room, along with the rest of Ethereal Mutation. It looked like they were going to try to sneak up on Larkin and his guards. He motioned for me to stay where I was.

Looking at the shadows on the other side of the room, I felt rather than saw Cedric, Darrius, and two others mirroring Keane's pattern. They were going to try to scale the wall in the shadows so they could surround Larkin and his people. Knowing others were spread throughout the crowd who were loyal to Larkin, I didn't think they'd make it without a bit of a distraction. Without second-guessing myself, I jumped from the raised platform I had been standing on and moved smoothly to the center spotlight.

"My lord!" I loudly interrupted his monologue and dipped into a deep curtsy. "It is indeed a pleasure to have you here at last."

I felt Keane freeze, and anger drifted through our connection. "*What are you doing, Blue?*"

"*Hush. I'm giving you the distraction you need. Don't worry about me, I can take care of myself. Go!*"

I heard him mentally growl but I just ignored him. Standing, I smiled widely at Larkin. In turn, he stared down at me. I could tell he was annoyed by my interruption, but he was also intrigued.

"If it would please you, my lord, I would like to continue my dance for you."

"There is no more need of these Trials. Why would you want to continue?"

"To prove myself worthy of you."

He seemed surprised. Then, he smiled widely. I felt his magic flowing around me as he tried to use his talent to charm.

"You ran away from me once. Why would you want to prove yourself worthy now?"

"I let others influence what I was thinking and feeling before. I realized once I came back here that I had been wrong to leave you. You are the only one who can unlock what is hidden deep inside of me."

Everyone around me seemed to hold their breath, waiting to see if Larkin would accept or punish me for my insolence. I even heard a few calling me a traitor. Let them think what they wanted. This might just save their lives.

Suddenly, Larkin let out a loud bark of laughter. "Life will never be boring with you, Carolina, that is for sure."

I wasn't sure what he meant by that, but I let it slide.

"It would please me greatly for you to dance for me." Larkin signaled to a few of his followers in the crowd and indicated that he wanted a chair brought up to him. They quickly moved to obey him and took the throne Tristan had been sitting in, leaving him standing, though thankfully under his own control. Once Larkin was comfortably ensconced in his seat on the balcony, he waved his hand at me to proceed.

I curtsied again and walked toward one of the tall poles in the middle of the floor. In my mind, I quickly changed up what I had been doing, removing all the spells I had been taught and replacing them with bigger and more dramatic ones—anything to keep Larkin's and his guards attention solely focused on me.

As my music started once again, I created my sparkling mist, this time using the center pole as my focal point. Swinging around it, I was glad Keane had made me do so much upper body training. Hoping it would help distract Larkin, and his followers, I decided to make things much more sexual. Using moves I taught my models in my boudoir studio, I slowly stripped the filmy dress from my body, following along with the music until I was just in the white body suit. The colors interspersed through it glowed to life with a little push from my magic, accenting all my generous curves.

I pulled myself up onto the pole and gracefully made my way up about halfway. Hanging upside down with just my legs supporting me, I created the same fire spell I had used before, but this time, I sent it out in spirals, keeping it circling me as I slid seductively to the floor.

Under the cover of flames, I quickly ripped my dress into lengths and rose, using them as dancing scarves. Wrapping one of my legs around the pole, I leaned back and circled the scarves around me. As I did, I pushed my wind and water magic out together to slowly follow the spiral of fire surrounding me and snuff it out, leaving only the water still flowing in the same pattern. I pushed the water higher and tighter above me until it was a spinning ball, all the while keeping my movements seductive.

As the music reached another peak, I caused the water ball to explode in a shimmer of sparkling blue and green. I arched my back as it rained down on me and allowed my magic to change the color of my suit to match the color of the droplets. Sliding across the floor on my knees, I turned and moved with the music before sitting and spreading my legs suggestively, my toes pointed upward. I winked at Larkin with a wicked grin before bringing my legs in to my chest and bending them at the knees. After a few kicks, I slid down into a split before drawing myself back to my feet and mounting one of the raised surfaces.

Standing, I lifted my arms above my head and pulled once again on my wind and fire magic. It swirled around me, completely drying my clothes and changing the color of my suit again, this time to red and orange. As I leapt from the raised surface, I used my wings to slowly twirl me around until I landed in a perfect split on the floor before rolling to my back and drawing one knee up. I used the brief slowing of tempo in the music to run my hands seductively up and down my body while arching my back. I made sure to make eye contact with Larkin, whose gaze was riveted on me. Using my peripheral vision, I tried to see if I could spot Keane and the others, but they seemed to have vanished. I hoped that meant they had at least gained the second floor and were closing in.

Rolling back to my stomach, I slowly gained my knees and stretched my arms above my head. This was turning into quite the R-rated show. It was a good thing my friends had insisted on me taking all those stupid pole dancing classes with them for *exercise*. I laughed to myself.

Following the music, I slowly got to my feet, and as the tempo increased, so did my speed around the dance floor. During one of my longer spins, I used my magic to allow my hair to fall free of the pins that held it so it spread out and floated around me. As the pins hit the floor, they burst into little sparklers, lighting up the area I was dancing on and mixing with the blue mist almost appearing as a night sky reflected onto the floor.

I unfurled my wings and used them to lift me up to the nearest platform. As I did, I noticed something I hadn't before. There were long, billowing sheets of fabric attached to the ceiling and tied back at intervals along the wall. Using my magic, I unclipped two of them from the wall as I was dancing so they floated delicately into my hands. Another fad my friends had decided to get in on, scarf aerobatics, and I had been pretty good at that one.

Using what I had been taught, I slowly ascended the scarves, dipping and flowing with the music and all the while praying they held. As I executed one of my moves, I glanced toward Larkin just as one of Keane's men grabbed Fiorian and dragged him behind one of the curtains. They had been busy. Only Larkin's right-hand goon still stood at his side. It looked like my display had worked to distract them, as no one seemed to notice the missing guards. Continuing with my aerobatic dance, I heard my song coming to its close. I hoped they would be able to grab the last goon before I finished.

Using my wind magic, I manipulated it to swing me widely around the room, each move bringing me closer to the floor. As the music ended, I smoothly slid down and hid within the confines of the fabric.

Larkin was immediately on his feet, applauding along with the surrounding crowd. He started down the stairs, not even glancing back to see that all his guards were missing.

"Bravo! Bravo! You are indeed a treasure. Beauty, power, grace, you have it all. You will make me the perfect Queen."

I started. His Queen? This guy was even more delusional than I thought. Plastering a smile on my face, I moved out from the curtains and toward him. Taking his outstretched hands, I allowed him to pull me closer. He raised my hands to his lips, staring directly into my eyes, no doubt trying to further his hold on my mind.

"And now, to take care of business." I tensed as he turned toward Tristan and the Elders. "It seems to me that some of you have overstayed your position. I think it is time you stepped down…permanently." Raising his hands, they crackled with energy. I could feel the hot pulse of his spell and knew it was deadly. With Elder Avner controlling all of them physically, the Elders and Tristan were like sitting ducks, staring wide-eyed but unable to do anything. Larkin smiled wickedly as he threw the spell in their direction.

I screamed, and without thought for myself, jumped in front of it. The spell hit me square in the chest, throwing me back against the dais. The whole room seemed to shake with the impact. Gasping as I collapsed to the floor, I felt the magic crawling across my skin.

I vaguely heard shouts and lots of movement around me, but it all faded into the background as it took every bit of my concentration to keep Larkin's spell from killing me. I lay there shivering and panting, certain I would die, when I unexpectedly felt…nothing. I was oddly standing over my body, looking down at myself. I didn't think I was dead, as I could see the breath moving in and out of my body as I lay on the floor. I just wasn't in it anymore. I realized I must be incorporeal. Just like Iridia could do, my soul had left my body.

Looking around, I saw Tristan's forces fighting Larkin's. The ballroom had erupted into complete pandemonium. I watched as

Tristan jumped from the dais and gathered me into his arms. I saw him chanting and his eyes glow, so I knew he was trying to use his healing magic. I heard an almost animalistic growl and turned to see Keane running toward Tristan, bellowing my name. Suddenly, I was terrified of what would happen to him if I were to die.

I tried everything I could think of to get back into my body, but nothing seemed to work. Frustrated, I looked around as I struggled to come up with a solution. That's when I saw him... Larkin. He was lying on the floor not far from my body. No one seemed to be paying him any attention. As his eyes opened, he shook his head as if to clear it before slowly regaining his feet. I yelled a warning to Tristan and Keane, but of course neither of them could see or hear me. Larkin looked around in confusion and disbelief at the chaos around him before his eyes landed on my inert body. His features contorted in anger.

As he started to move toward me, I put myself between him and my body. Raising my hands, I pulled on the magic within me. Thankfully, I seemed to have it even in my spirit form. I quickly put up a protective bubble around Tristan, Keane, and myself. Larkin crashed into it and fell back. Pulling his gaze from my body, he looked up and down and raised his hands to feel the shield. He let out a roar of rage, which was quickly drowned out in the battle going on around us. Pounding his fists against my barrier, he cursed me up and down.

"Damn you, Carolina. You will pay for this treachery! I will make you beg and grovel before me. I will torture you until you cede. I will have control of you and the clans. There is nowhere you can go, no one you love who will be safe from me until I have what I want."

At his threats, a deep, burning anger ignited in my belly. I stepped through the barrier to stand before him, even though I knew he couldn't see me. Frustrated, I thought about how Iridia could make herself corporeal to some people in this state. It was like the spell I used for ghosts. Thinking along those lines, I closed my eyes and placed my hand on Larkin's chest, matching my energy vibrations to his. As I did, he suddenly stared down at me in disbelief.

"You!"

Time unexpectedly stopped, and it was just the two of us able to move amid the chaos. He looked around before glancing between my body and spirit. A dawning understanding moved over his face, one I didn't understand.

"By the gods…"

I didn't let him finish. "You will never have me, do you understand? I am no one's to own or control."

I felt his charm magic start flowing around us, and he reached a hand toward me. "You are simply magnificent, Carolina. More powerful than even I imagined. How did I not see it before? The blood flowing through your veins… Together, we can rule the clans—no, the world. No one will be able to withstand our power."

I pulled my arm from his grip and sneered at him. "You can drop the charm crap. It doesn't work on me. You are nothing, Larkin. Nothing but a measly little manipulator. A leach trying to use the strength of others to further yourself. Hiding behind those whose skills outmatch yours so no one knows what a weakling you really are."

His placating expression dropped, and anger contorted his face again. "I am not weak. I am more powerful than anyone gives me credit for." Without warning, he grasped my wrist, twisting it. I felt a wash of magic flow through me. I cried out and fell to my knees as it gripped me tightly, snuffing out the connection to my magic. "I will have control of the clans, and you *will* help me." He looked down at me maliciously.

I couldn't believe it. He had trapped my magic within me. I couldn't touch it. I was at his mercy. How had he done it? I'd thought that was Warlock magic.

"That's right, you're not the only one who can wield ley line magic. Turns out my great-great-grandfather was a Warlock, so it runs in my blood. And though diluted, I can tap into it for a few spells."

With the loss of the connection to my magic, time snapped back into existence, and the bubble I had set up around Tristan and Keane dissolved, leaving them exposed. I watched helplessly as Larkin started drawing together a spell I knew was meant to kill.

"You may have thwarted my attempt to kill the Elders, but I will take care of Tristan, and your protector. And you will sit here and watch, knowing you are the weak one. Helpless to do anything without your precious magic."

My heart rate accelerated. There had to be something I could do. There was no way I could just sit here and watch as he killed two of the most important men in my life. I cursed the fact that I didn't have my weapons on me.

As he started to let go of my wrist, no doubt to finish his spell, I acted on instinct. I had been depending so much on my magic lately that I had almost forgotten the other skills I'd learned and perfected. Grabbing his wrist, I pulled him forward to distract him from his spell, then used my other hand to push hard against his chest while grabbing his leg and pulling it out from under him. As he lost his footing and fell back, I gripped his wrist again and used his body weight to pull me along with him until I straddled his chest, my knees landing on his arms, pinning them to the floor.

I used one of my hands to push his jaw forward, while I laid the other on his Adam's apple and pressed. He immediately started choking and tried to dislodge me. I let up pressure on his throat just a bit but tightened my thighs around his chest to compress his lungs. He gasped for air, and I shoved my face into his.

"You are wrong, Larkin. I am not weak without my magic. I lived without it for most of my life. It doesn't define who I am or what I can do."

"You will never survive in the Fae world without it, and until I give it back to you, you will be helpless against me and those like me." He let out a choking laugh. "I hold control over you. You are mine. Even if you stop me now, I will be back, and I will kill everyone you have ever cared about or loved."

His words seemed to kindle something deep inside me, and I felt a trembling of the trapped golden ball at my center. Rage started burning through every part of my being. I would not be controlled. I would not be manipulated. I would not allow anyone I loved to be hurt by him again.

Closing my eyes, I reached deep within. I tore at the bindings holding my magic until they suddenly seemed to crack and finally exploded apart.

Larkin stiffened beneath me. "It can't be. No one can break that kind of spell."

I took in a deep breath as the magic flowed through me once more before opening my eyes and staring down harshly at Larkin. Drawing on my magic, I took all the powers I had been blessed with, all the different types of magic flowing within my veins, and manipulated them into something completely new. I no longer drew on one or the other like before. They all coalesced into one stream, flowing through me, my anger making it burn brighter and hotter within me. My hair started to float, and my skin glowed. Larkin's eyes opened wide, and true fear danced in their depths.

I looked around me and, putting my hand out, consciously stopped time. When everything had ground to a halt, I looked back down at Larkin, my voice seeming to come from someone else when I spoke. I punctuated each word. "Now. You. Are. Mine."

As I let go of Larkin's chin, my hand turned incorporeal, falling into a ghostly mist. I looked at it briefly before plunging it into Larkin's chest. He screamed. Reaching in, I grabbed the magic that pooled at his center. I held it in my hand, toying with it and him. He whimpered, his face now a mask of pain and fear. I looked directly into his eyes, and he knew in that moment what I planned to do, however impossible it seemed.

"No..."

I smiled malevolently and yanked my hand out. He screamed again as I ripped his magic from him. I sat there holding it in my hand, looking down at him and relishing the moment before I put it to my lips and swallowed it. I felt it moving through my body until it reached my center. Then, it melded with the golden ball of *my* magic. I took a deep breath and let it out slowly as I felt Larkin's powers becoming mine.

I stood and looked down at him in disgust, knowing there was nothing he could do now. He sat up, gulping in big breaths of air, grasping at his chest. He seemed to be searching inside himself, becoming more and more frantic.

"It's gone, all of it. You took it. My Wolf, my charm, everything." He shook his head in denial. "No, it's impossible."

I reached down and picked him up by his shirt front as if he weighed nothing. "Oh, it's possible. You have no idea who I am or what I am truly capable of." I laughed a bit maniacally, feeling high on the power flowing within me. I threw Larkin across the floor. He landed in a heap at the bottom of the stairs before trying to scramble up them to escape, but I was across the room in seconds.

I picked him up and threw him across the floor again, this time into one of the platforms in a darkened corner. It splintered where he hit his head on it, and blood oozed from the wound. As he tried to stand, I put my foot on his chest to hold him down.

"I should kill you for everything you've done." I raised my hand, a glowing red mass within it.

Larkin abruptly stopped struggling and looked up at me through half-closed eyes, laughter bubbling up. "Oh, Carolina, we are so much alike, you and I."

I paused and looked angrily at him. "I am nothing like you!"

"Aren't you? Look at you. Riding high on power, even ready to kill with it to get what you want."

I stared at him in shock before I took a stilted step back, the spell dying in my hands, my eyes widening as I looked down at myself in horror. What was I doing? I had let my anger take control of me and the magic. I hadn't been thinking of anything but destroying Larkin, using the very power I had stolen from him.

Trying to capitalize on my inner struggle, he adopted a cajoling tone. "You could just let me go. You've stolen my power from me, what harm could I be now? I promise I won't tell anyone about your special skills. It will be our little secret. No one needs to know."

I looked at him sharply. "Why would anyone care about my skills?"

He smirked. "The power to take everything, all the power from any Fae you want to? That is a very dangerous skill for someone to possess. I would think the Elders would want to lock you up and keep you under wraps if they knew. No more freedom like you are used to, always under watch. Or perhaps they would consider it too risky to leave you alive. Yes, I think you would be considered quite a dangerous Fae, indeed."

I stared at him, dismay dawning. He was right. If anyone learned of my ability, they would never just let me walk around unchecked. I would be considered a possible threat to everyone, or a weapon for someone to use. I didn't want to be locked away forever or killed. I looked down at Larkin. He watched me speculatively. I couldn't just let him go. He had to be held accountable for what he'd done, both past and present. But if I turned him over to the Elders, there is no doubt they would discover what I had done to him.

He seemed to sense my weakening resolve. "If you let me go, I promise to disappear. You will never hear from me again. No one will ever need know your secrets, you have my word."

I stared down at him, unsure what to do. Suddenly, I felt a presence over my shoulder.

"Perhaps I can be of some assistance?"

I whirled around in surprise. "Sebastian."

Larkin tried to take advantage of the distraction and dove to the side, trying to skirt away, but Sebastian merely plucked him off the floor and set him back in front of us. Without a word or gesture, a set of gold ropes appeared and tied themselves around Larkin's wrists and ankles.

"Oh, Sebastian. I...I've done something I shouldn't have. Something that shouldn't be possible."

"Hush. No need to go into it. I am well aware of your powers."

"You...you are?"

Sebastian nodded. "Of course. I have been watching over you for a long time."

"But..."

He shook his head. "No buts, Blue. It is who you are. You need to learn to accept that."

"But the Elders, the clans..."

"Do not need to know. When the time is right, it will all be revealed. Until then, those who know will continue to protect you and the knowledge from those that would seek to use it and you." We both looked down at Larkin.

"What about him?"

"I will take care of our mutual friend here. I have a few associates who have been looking for him for quite some time." Larkin's eyes widened in fear, causing Sebastian to smile down at him. "In the meantime, you need to reconnect with your body, Blue. They can't heal you without your spirit in there."

I looked down at myself, confused. "Heal me? But there is nothing wrong with me."

"Hmm, while your spirit may seem unaffected from the death spell that hit you earlier, it is slowly killing your body. As your body dies, so will your power, and so will you."

"But I don't know how to get back in. I tried everything I could think of. Do you?"

Sebastian shook his head. "It is only something the gods or those of their direct birth line know how to do, and it is a well-kept secret among them."

"The gods? Wait, what are you saying? That I am part of some god's birth line?"

"I knew it. I just knew it!"

Sebastian turned to glare at Larkin. With a flick of his wrist, a gag appeared and tied itself around Larkin's mouth. Satisfied, Sebastian turned back to me. "Of course. Haven't you figured that out by now?"

I looked at him in confusion. "How could I be of some god's direct birth line? My mother was Iridia, and Kieran believes my father was Aiden."

Sebastian shook his head. "Aiden isn't your father, Blue."

"But who?"

"What have you always felt drawn to in your life and can't seem to go long without? What soothes your soul, no matter what is going on?"

My eyes widened. "The ocean. Are you telling me…?"

He gave me a lopsided grin.

"Poseidon? Poseidon is my father?" Sebastian nodded, a smile spreading across his face. "So that's why Poseidon sent you to look after me. Why Triton was so eager to help me. But why keep it a secret?"

"Because you are extremely rare, even for a child of the gods."

"I don't understand. Aren't I just like Iridia?"

As he shook his head, a sudden bout of vertigo overtook me, causing me to reach out and grab on to him. He looked at me with deepening concern. "Blue, we don't have time to discuss this right now. If you don't reunite with your body, you will die."

I looked over to where my body lay. I could feel the life waning from it. I took a few steps forward before looking back helplessly, but Sebastian was nowhere to be seen, nor was Larkin. I hoped that would be the last I ever saw of Larkin, but I had a feeling not everything was done where he was concerned. An intense pain shuddered through my body, dropping me to my knees, and the world suddenly came back to life.

I crawled over to where Tristan and Keane were working together, using both of their powers to try to heal me. I tried to match my energy signature to theirs so I could make myself visible like I had with Larkin, but it wasn't working. I didn't know what to do. I laid my hand on Keane's shoulder, causing him to jump and look around in confusion. I jerked my hand back in surprise. He could feel me! Curious, I laid a hand on Tristan's shoulder, but he didn't even flinch. I thought about that. It had to be my connection to Keane. Supposedly, our bond was through our souls. Maybe this was how I could get back.

I still couldn't seem to talk to him, even telepathically, but since I could sense his emotions, I hoped he could feel mine. Praying it worked, I poured the emotions I wanted him to identify into our connection. After a brief look of shock passed over his face, I watched as he closed his eyes and concentrated. It took less than a heartbeat until I felt it. He knew what needed to be done. He opened his now dark red eyes with a new determination and leaned over my prone body, his fangs out.

Tristan looked at him in horror. "What the hell, Keane? You're going to feed on her now?" Tristan tried to push Keane back, but he held firm.

"Trust me, Tristan. I'm not sure what happened, but I need to be connected to her as closely as I can."

Tristan growled in frustration but backed off. Keane lay down next to me and closed his eyes, pulling on his Vaimpír powers before carefully sinking his teeth into my neck. I felt the pull, even in my incorporeal state. Lying down weirdly over myself, I prayed I had just enough magic left to bring my fangs out, as it was a small spell. Thankfully, after a second, I felt them drop, but it left me with nothing. I could barely hold my head up.

Reaching up with the last fragment of my strength, I bit Keane. I felt him start as the feeling of it jolted through him, even though my body hadn't physically moved. Magic danced back and forth between our souls, moving faster and faster and seeming to erase the separate lines. I felt the moment it all clicked into place, the soulbond complete. His to mine, and mine to his. We were one.

Almost instantly, I was back in my body, and the excruciating pain it was experiencing. That must have been what had driven me out in the first place. I gasped in a large breath, and Keane pulled back immediately.

"Blue, can you hear me?"

I nodded weakly.

Tristan pushed Keane away and finished the spell he had been conjuring to heal me. I immediately felt relief. It was like a cooling wave passing over and through me.

"Better?" He looked down at me, concern etching his face.

I gave a grateful sigh. "Thank you."

"No, thank you. If you hadn't jumped in front of that spell, I would be dead. How you survived is a miracle."

"I guess we're even, then." I smiled tiredly.

He gave me a crooked grin. "I don't know about being even. There was that time after you were poisoned..."

I smacked him lightly on the chest. "Sure, now you bring that up. Okay, so maybe I still owe you one."

Tristan chuckled but then turned serious. "Blue, when I tried to heal you at first, it was like you were here but weren't. My magic couldn't tether to you."

"I..."

Keane interrupted. "I think Blue's had enough excitement for one night. We'll talk later...with less of an audience."

Tristan nodded, looking conflicted as he helped me to stand from the floor. Almost as soon as I got to my feet, I felt myself falling backward, not having the strength to hold myself up. Keane quickly reached over and scooped me up into his arms.

Tristan's expression turned harsh as he watched me. "I will kill Larkin myself when we find him, very slowly."

I looked at Tristan a bit guiltily. "Tristan, about Larkin..."

His expression softened. "Hush. Let me worry about Larkin. We are going to find him, and we will make him pay for what he has done. I believe that all the clans will be open to joining to take him down now. There is nowhere he can go that we won't find him."

After a brief hesitation, he leaned over and kissed me on the forehead. "Go, get some rest." Then he turned and walked back up the steps to where the Elders were crowded in a circle, conversing about something.

I took a breath to call Tristan back and tell him about Larkin when Keane leaned down and took my lips in a searing kiss. I hesitated, but then kissed him back, my fingers threading themselves into his hair. As I did, I felt the tug of our connection. Suddenly, Keane's emotions were mine. I felt the panic and fear he had felt when he saw me take the spell, the overwhelming pain he felt when they couldn't seem to revive me and my body started to die, his shock when he realized that the reason they couldn't heal me was because my soul wasn't in my body, and finally the desperation and relief he currently tried to hide.

I pulled back and stared into his eyes, realization dawning. "You know, don't you?"

"Know what?"

"What I am. Who my father is?"

Keane looked at me for a moment and then nodded.

"How long have you known?"

"I had an inkling after the Sebastian incident, but it was confirmed with what you just did."

"What I just did?" I was suddenly afraid. There was nothing I could hide from him, he knew exactly what had just gone down with Larkin. He could see in my mind what I could do.

"Blue, you have to know I would never reveal your secrets."

"But what I can do…"

"Shhh. It doesn't matter to me. We'll talk about it later if you really feel the need to, but not here."

I looked around at the chaos. The room was in shambles. People were everywhere, looking worse for wear, some appearing confused as if wondering how they had gotten here. It appeared as if Larkin's supporters had been subdued and were gathered together at the far end of the room, currently surrounded by Tristan's guards. I didn't see a few faces I expected to, and that concerned me.

"What happened to Celeste and Elder Avner?"

He shook his head. "They escaped in the ensuing mayhem created by your spell."

I looked at him confused. "What spell?"

"As Larkin's killing blow struck you, a gold light erupted from you and infused everything in the room. Those who were under Larkin's or Elder Avner's enchantments were instantly released. Whatever you did freed them."

"I don't get it. I didn't consciously do anything. I don't even remember feeling it."

Keane glanced briefly to where the Elders were. "That's not all it did."

"What do you mean?"

As soon as I asked the question, the Elders parted to reveal Riona. While that in itself wouldn't be unusual, as she had been around them for months, what *was* unusual was they were now talking to her, touching her. Her eyes sparkled with excitement, and she beamed with happiness. Seeing me looking at her, she ran up to where Keane held me.

"Oh, Blue. Thank you. Thank you so much!"

"For what?" I was a bit shocked that she was talking *to* me, not just in my head.

"For making it so everyone can see and hear me. I am no longer just a shadow passing by who someone senses might be a ghost. I'm corporeal again."

I was even more confused about this supposed spell I had created now. What had I done? Keane, sensing my unease, nodded regally to Riona and executed a slight bow, turning and moving across the room with me in his arms. As he mounted the steps, I heard Elder Demirtas call for quiet from the dais. The people all turned toward him to listen. Keane continued up the steps.

"I know it has been a very harrowing night, but before you disperse, we would like to make an important announcement. In light of recent events, we are calling an end to the Trials."

I snorted into Keane's shoulder. "Big surprise. Maybe if they'd listened to me weeks ago…"

Keane just laughed and tucked me tighter into his embrace. "Shush."

"We do, however, have a solution in the matter of the Queen."

My ears perked up at that. They were going to make the decision themselves? This would be interesting. Keane stopped at the top of the stairs and turned so we could hear the announcement.

"Your former Queen, the late Riona, has returned to us in spirit." Riona moved to his side, and I heard gasps and whispers start moving through the crowd. Huh, so they all could see her. "Not only that, but she is a corporeal spirit." He took her hand and raised it for all to see. "The Council of Elders has deemed that Riona will resume her place as Queen of the Moon Tree Clan to rule until such a time that she is unable." The crowd cheered and applauded.

"Well, what do you know…?"

Keane looked down at me and raised his brows. "Disappointed?"

I looked from Riona's beaming expression to Tristan's smiling face. He was now standing at her side, holding her hand. "No, not really. It's a fitting solution for now."

"For now?"

"You know as well as I do that corporeal ghosts usually lose their sanity over time. I wonder how long she will last." I watched as Riona stood regally before her people, nodding and acknowledging everyone.

"Kind of bittersweet, isn't it?"

I turned my head toward the new voice. It was Cedric. "Why do you say that?"

"Having been through everything you have in the past few months, only to have the Queen show back up and take it all away."

"Actually, it's a relief."

Cedric turned surprised eyes toward me.

"Contrary to what everyone believes, I didn't want to be Queen. My sole purpose in those Trials was to stay alive while keeping Celeste and Tatiana from taking the throne."

"But you and Tristan..."

I shook my head with a small smile, then turned my gaze back down to the scene below us. "Fate can be funny sometimes, can't it?" I was, of course, thinking about who his parents were. Glancing at him, I considered telling him but then decided against it. I didn't think now was the right time.

Cedric nodded. "You do have to wonder why it throws certain people in your path when it does. Sometimes, you think they mean one thing, but in reality, they are there for an entirely different purpose." He looked at me with a strange expression I couldn't quite interpret, much like the ones he used to wear. After a moment, he leaned over and gave me a kiss on the cheek, then stepped away and looked up at Keane. "Take care of her, okay?"

At Keane's nod, Cedric turned and walked away, disappearing into the shadows from whence he had first appeared.

I stared after him for a moment before sighing. "I don't know about you, but I'm ready to get out of here. How about taking me home?"

Keane glanced at me. "Are you sure? A lot still needs to be worked out here."

As I looked out over the assemblage below, Tristan's gaze suddenly caught mine and held. We stared at each other, just as we had that very first time outside of the Dock Street Theatre, and I knew things were definitely far from settled here. As that strange green glowing started in the back of his eyes, I dropped his gaze. I wasn't sure, but I had a feeling I now knew what it meant, and I was far from ready to deal with it.

Dropping my head to Keane's chest, I closed my eyes. "What would you say to a midnight swim in the ocean? No suits."

Keane seemed about to say something, but then he just shook his head and grinned. Turning, he walked out of the ballroom with me in his arms, closing the doors softly behind us.

Want to know what happens next?

Be on the lookout for Book 2 in the Blue Series...

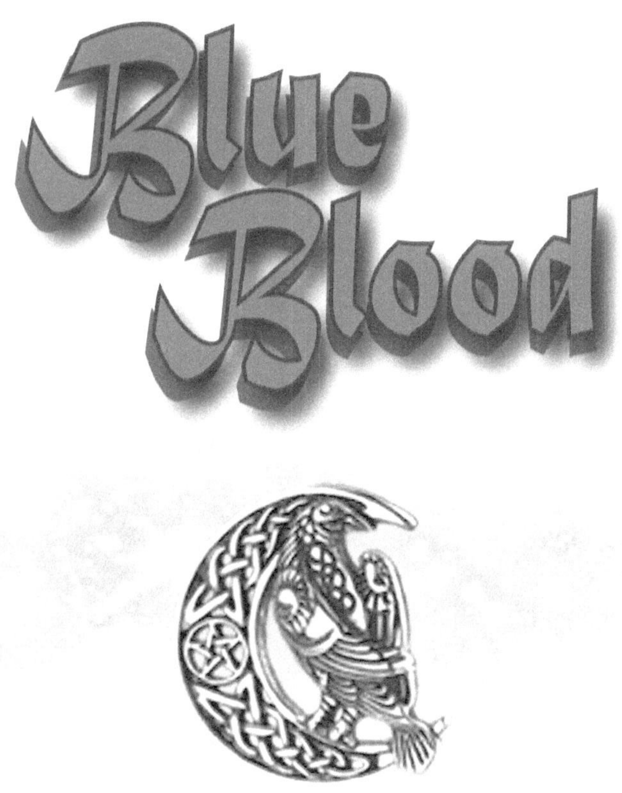

Ethereal Mutation Productions, LLC

# Acknowledgments

W ow. Where to start? There are so many people that I need to acknowledge who have been instrumental in getting this book ready to face the world.

First and foremost—and most important—my husband Derek, without whom this never would have happened. Carolina Blue was merely a creative outlet sitting on my computer collecting proverbial dust until he decided one day that he wanted to read it. Surprised but pleased, I recorded an audiobook version just for him, and when he was done—he was in awe. I remember him saying he couldn't believe I had created that in my head, LOL. From that moment forward, he did nothing but encourage and support me in so many ways, including helping me write the second book of the series—I think he's as attached to the characters as I am. He has been my cheerleader, content editor, promotor, sounding board, support system... Honestly my everything, and I couldn't have done it without him.

Next, I have to thank my mentor and friend, Liz Berry. Even though she didn't know me from anyone at the start, she took the time to sit and talk with me—and answer my extensive questions—about my goals and what publishing a book would entail. She even set me up with my amazing editor, for which I will be forever grateful. I am so glad that fate brought us together.

And speaking of editors, I couldn't leave out the lovely, Chelle Olson. She took me on even when she was so bogged down with work that I wasn't sure how she managed to get through it all. While I love to write, punctuation is my sworn enemy—which is probably pretty evident here since I didn't have her edit the acknowledgments, LOL. I just can't seem to figure out where all those blasted commas need to go. Chelle bravely waded through my mess of run-on sentences and bad punctuation to polish my book to a shine. Her invaluable skills, along with her extensive humor, truly made the editing experience a joy. <3

To my Beta readers, thank you from the bottom of my heart. Your feedback and creative criticisms were essential in taking a good story and making it a great one. The boost to my confidence you always managed to provide didn't hurt either. I appreciate all of you and hope you're ready to take on book 2.

To our son, our friends and family, my work family, my husband's Golden Oak family, my Curv Live family, and everyone else in between—you know who you are. Thank you for all of the love, support, and encouragement. Even taking the time to ask me how my book was going made a difference.

And finally, to my followers on Facebook, TikTok, and Instagram, it may seem like a small part to play but all of your comments and interactions on my "Trying to visualize Book Expressions while Writing..." series were one of the things that helped to keep me sane when things got intense. Your love and support, not only of my videos but also of my upcoming book, was nothing short of amazing. Thank you!

# About the Author

Heather Bartleson lives in sunny Florida with her husband and son. When not writing, you can be sure to find her on some beach searching for shells or sitting with a good book in hand—especially if it's by the clear waters of the Gulf Coast. A voracious reader since childhood, Heather has consumed everything from the classics to the smuttiest of smut and has loved every bit of it. It's not unheard of for her to polish off several books in a day when the mood strikes. In addition to reading and writing, she also enjoys creating art in all its forms.

If you haven't already, make sure to check out her series on social media, "Trying to Visualize Book Expressions while Writing..."

www.facebook.com/heatherbartleson_author
Instagram @heatherbartleson_author
TikTok @heatherbartleson_author

* 9 7 9 8 9 8 9 8 3 3 5 1 1 *